RAPTUS

Other works by the same author:

novels:

The Red Army

The Cannibal

Red-Hot Poker

Desarts of Vast Eternity (with Grosse Fuge)

novella:

Houses That Are Homes

Film-script:

Raptus (1992)

Stage-play:

Raptus (1993)

Radio plays:

Here Comes A Chopper

Raptus (1993)

RAPTUS

a novel about Beethoven
based on the source material

by

Susan Lund

Annotated, with introductory articles

MELSTAMPS (Cambs)

P.O. Box 4, Melbourn, Royston, Herts. SG8 6PQ, England.

1995

RAPTUS

the self-contained final part of a four-volume novel about Beethoven based on the source material; originally titled: The Lover, The Child, The Litigant, The Father.

Annotated, with introductory articles.

Copyright © 1995 Susan Lund

A CIP catalogue record for this book is available from the British Library

ISBN 0 9525676 0 1

First published 1995 by MELSTAMPS (Cambs)
PO Box 4, Melbourn, Royston, Herts., SG8 6PQ, England.

Printed by Pardy & Sons (Printers) Ltd.,
Parkside, Ringwood, Hampshire, BH24 3SF, England.

An earlier, shorter version of 'Beethoven: a True "Fleshly Father"?' was originally published in 2 parts in *The Beethoven Newsletter*/San Jose State University, Spring & Summer 1988. Copyright © 1988 by Susan Lund.
All rights reserved.

A shorter version of 'If One Has Only One Son' appeared in *The Beethoven Newsletter*, Spring 1991. Copyright © 1991 by Susan Lund.
All rights reserved.

To my husband, Brian, with all my love

Author's Note

'Why a novel about Beethoven? If we want to know about the composer, we can read a biography.' But RAPTUS contains new research: a discovery which alters the perception of the man and of the composition of his music. Just as Beethoven cannot be isolated from the art which was his core, so the music cannot be divorced from the biography at its source. Scholars should not be expected to provide an insight into the position of art in an artist's life, and Beethoven was predominantly an artist.

Originally written as the final part of a four-volume novel, RAPTUS is nevertheless self-contained. The book consists of articles with their own notes, followed by the text of the novel, with its own annotations at the end. This does not attempt to be a full list of sources but is merely a list of the sources of quotations. The *Iliad* and *Odyssey* Greek texts are taken from the Macmillan edition. Translations from Greek, Latin and Portuguese are by Brian Crowther.

Rough translation of Beethoven's *Konversationshefte* volumes 1, 2 & 4 was by Hanne Yates. Polished translations of extracts from *Hefte* 6-10 of volume 1 were by Gudrun and Dr R.T. Llewellyn. All translations veer towards the colloquial rather than the pedantic in my final selection, for which I of course take full responsibility.

Thanks are due to those publishers who generously gave their permission for quotation of extracts, full details of which appear in the list of abbreviations and acknowledgements; to Goethe Museum & Deutsche Staatsbibliothek for their kind permission to quote from unpublished letters; to my friend Maynard Solomon for his great generosity in bringing these to my attention, besides his many other acts of support; to the helpful staff at Cambridge University Library; above all to my husband, Brian Crowther, to whom RAPTUS is dedicated.

Melbourn, 1995

Note on Monetary Values

1 paper florin = 1 florin W.W. = 60 kreuzer
(also known as gulden)

1 silver florin = 1 florin C.M. = 2.50 paper florins

1 gold ducat = 4.50 silver fl. = 11.25 paper florins

The florin W.W. referred to above was introduced after the bankruptcy of the Austrian state in 1811. One result of this was that Redemption bonds replaced bank notes at the rate of 1 for 5. In terms of Beethoven's income from his three patrons, the 4000 florins guaranteed in 1809 fell to approximately 1600 florins in 1811. However, the original value of his income was restored when by 1815 the payments became 3400 florins in Redemption bonds, the equivalent of 1360 florins C.M.

Conversion rates fluctuated widely. However, by 1820 standards, £1 was equivalent to 10 silver florins, 1 guinea to 10 fl. 30 kr. C.M., and $1 to 2 fl. 15 kr. C.M.

Beethoven: A True 'Fleshly Father'?

We owe to Maynard Solomon the identification of Antonie Brentano as Beethoven's 'Immortal Beloved'.[1] In a later article, 'Beethoven & His Nephew: A Reappraisal,' writing of the adoption by Beethoven of his nephew Karl in 1816, Solomon shows that Beethoven believed that he had become a father:

> 'The death of his brother presented Beethoven, perpetually thwarted in his attempts at "normal" object relations, with an opportunity of becoming the head of a family. So deep was Beethoven's desire to accomplish this, so great his need to find a mode of substitute creativity at this difficult moment of his musical evolution, that his perception of reality blurred, and he persuaded himself that he had become a father in fact. On 13th May 1816, he wrote to Countess Erdödy: "I now regard myself as his father."[2] "You will regard K. as your own child," he wrote in his *Tagebuch*: "Ignore all gossip, all pettiness for the sake of this holy cause."[3] In September 1816, he wrote to Kanka: "I am now the real physical father (*wirklicher leiblicher Vater*) of my deceased brother's child."[4] A few weeks later he wrote to Wegeler: "You are a husband and a father. So am I, but without a wife."[5][6]

Solomon attributes this to a delusion on Beethoven's part. I hope to show that Beethoven was a father, and that removing this from the realms of fantasy clarifies much else in Beethoven's life.

In the nature of things, direct evidence for this is hardly likely to be forthcoming. That does not mean that the changes in Beethoven's own personal circumstances, the volume and nature of his work, significant changes in his relationships, and certain aberrations in the survival or non-survival of source material, coupled with the evidence which has survived, do not, taken together, constitute a formidable body of evidence.

Let us look at the evidence which has survived.

Antonie Brentano, born 28th May 1780 as Johanna Antonie Josefa Edle von Birkenstock, was the only daughter of the Viennese statesman and art-collector Johann Melchior Edler von Birkenstock.[7] Her mother had died when she was a child; she had been educated by Ursuline nuns.[8] A scholarly man, Birkenstock must have viewed her as a great responsibility which he was eager to get off his hands by establishing her in a secure marriage. He chose for this purpose Franz Dominicus Maria Josef Brentano, with whose father he had had business dealings going back some decades. At the age of seventeen, when she was already in love with someone else, her father told her, according to Antonie herself, that she was betrothed to Franz Brentano.[9] That this was a marriage of affection on Franz' part is evidenced by letters written during his courtship. In another sense, however, this was a marriage of convenience on his part also: his father died at this time; Franz, head of a family of half-brothers and sisters, a man of stable disposition, already in his thirties, cannot have been unaware of his need to select a wife to help him raise that family. Antonie complained that, even during their courtship, he put his work before her: 'For such an unimportant person as I am, he will not undertake a journey, and then he is now so occupied with business.'[10] The marriage took place on 23rd July 1798 at St. Stephen's Cathedral.

The couple moved straightaway to Frankfurt, where Antonie unhappily headed the household. Their first child, a girl born in July 1799, died suddenly in April the following year. Their four other children, a boy and three girls, born between 1801 and 1806, all survived.

The family moved to Antonie's beloved Vienna in 1809 shortly before her father's death. Here Franz, a merchant, set up a branch of his company while Antonie undertook the sale of part of her father's art collection. It was during this period that Antonie met Beethoven: in May 1810 she accompanied Franz' half-sister, Bettina, on her first visit to the composer. They apparently arrived when Beethoven was shaving.[11]

It was Bettina to whom Beethoven was first attracted, on the rebound from his rejection by Therese Malfatti. Evidently Antonie had to break the news to him the following year of Bettina's marriage to Achim von Arnim.[12]

This year provides the first evidence of Antonie's veneration for him: she tells Bettina's brother Clemens that she will place his cantata text 'in the holy hands of Beethoven.'[13]

Beethoven became a frequent visitor to the Birkenstock House.[14] He attended string quartet concerts there.[15] He visited regularly during the depression which Antonie suffered following the death of her father, when he would 'seat himself at a pianoforte in her anteroom and improvise; after he had finished "telling her everything and bringing comfort," in his language, he would go as he had come without taking notice of another person.'[16]

Antonie Brentano's children visited Beethoven with gifts of fruit and flowers:[17] as Solomon implies,[18] it may well have been she who pursued him; she may even have sent her children to him in an effort to continue the relationship when he perhaps wanted to end it.[19] Her choice of Beethoven reflects certain aspects of her father's character: Antonie was used to artistic men, not merchants.[20]

Solomon presents a variety of evidence to the effect that the marriage was not happy: 'It is fair to surmise that there were serious unresolved difficulties in their relationship, most clearly signalled by her desire to return to Vienna, her despondency and withdrawal, and, perhaps, by the fact that no further children were born to them between 1806 and 1813.'[21]

That the love affair was prospering in June is evidenced by Beethoven's gift to Antonie's daughter, Maxe, of his one-movement piano trio, WoO 39: the only child of a friend to be so honoured.[22] As Solomon says, this can be construed as a gift to her mother through her; a gift 'of the highest order,'[23] since Beethoven had given her the autograph of the piece, signed with a dedication to her.[24]

At the end of the month Beethoven travelled to Prague on the first stage of his journey to the Bohemian spas where he was to spend the summer. Antonie Brentano and Franz followed with, at least, their youngest child: Fanny, aged six.[25]

On the last day of his stay in Prague, Antonie Brentano visited Beethoven unexpectedly[26] and told him, according to Solomon, that she wanted to live with him in Vienna.[27] By my reckoning, she told him that she was pregnant.

Antonie Brentano was one month pregnant at the time of her meeting in Prague with Beethoven. Since she had already had five children, it seems reasonable to assume that she knew she was pregnant. I find it *inconceivable* that Beethoven would have considered setting up home with a woman he knew to be already pregnant by another man: the conclusion one has to reach if one follows Maynard Solomon.

I cannot accept Solomon's initial premise that Beethoven had an inbuilt reluctance to marry.[28] 'No one can be rejected so consistently without having in some way contributed to the process,' he writes.[29] This blanket assessment overlooks the fact that, on at least two previous occasions that we know of, Beethoven was right to follow his instincts in pursuing aristocratic women: in 1801 Giulietta Guicciardi told Beethoven she loved him;[30] several years later, Josephine Deym accepted his advances to the extent that her family called the liaison 'dangerous';[31] Therese Brunsvik later lamented that her sister had not married him.[32] In 1817, Beethoven wrote in his *Tagebuch*, 'Sensual gratification without a spiritual union is and remains bestial, afterwards one has no trace of noble feeling but rather remorse.'[33] In his identification of Beethoven's relationship with Antonie Brentano as non-sexual,[34] Solomon does not explain with whom if not the Immortal Beloved Beethoven had the 'sensual gratification with spiritual union' needed to write this entry. A certain strength in Beethoven's reaction to brother Johann's cuckolding in 1823 suggests that this is not the response of a man who himself has known only platonic love.[35] If Antonie Brentano did pursue Beethoven, it would seem impossible for the relationship not to have been of a sexual nature. If Antonie Brentano's pregnancy had been by her husband, it is hardly possible for a man who had suffered rejection as Beethoven had at the hands of Giulietta and Josephine not to have been devastated by betrayal, let alone writing four years later of her loyalty.[36] If a *Tagebuch* entry of

13th May 1813[37] as Solomon suggests refers to the Immortal Beloved, it
would hardly be possible for Beethoven to be writing of 'foregoing a great
deed,' if by this he meant attaching himself to Antonie Brentano, had she
just given birth to Franz' child.

Solomon assumes Beethoven's virginity during the composer's early
years in Vienna.[38] To me, Beethoven's request to his old friend Nikolaus
Simrock in Bonn to fashion one of his daughters 'to be my bride. For if I
have to live in Bonn as a bachelor, I will certainly not stay there for
long,'[39] speaks of a man who has discovered sexual experience in Vienna
and knows himself incapable of returning alone to the more constrained
confines of Bonn. 'Do be on your guard against the whole tribe of bad
women,'[40] Solomon quotes Beethoven's admonition to his brother
Johann, assuring us that 'We may assume that he, too, was on his
guard.'[41] To me again, Beethoven is as likely to have been involved with
the 'bad women' and himself had bad experiences.

I think that Beethoven did not want his sexuality noticed, which is not
the same thing as not being sexual.

Beethoven was not a Brahms: 'Unfortunately I never married and am,
thank God, still a bachelor.'[42]

He may have been free to marry her, but she was not free to marry him:
she was already married and she had four children. Given that she had
been orphaned of her own mother at the age of seven, it may have been
easier for Antonie Brentano to envisage leaving her children than for
Beethoven to face taking her from them.

The text of the Immortal Beloved letter[43] reflects his ambivalence.

Beethoven's letter to the Immortal Beloved is the only time that we
know of when he ever addressed a woman as 'du' and signed himself
'Ludwig.'

The letter ends with an outpouring of love to his Immortal Beloved and
the reassertion of 'our purpose to live together'. The facsimile shows that
Beethoven finished the letter, signed 'L' with a flourish, and then, as an
afterthought, added a new message in the margin. The last word of this,
unß in the German, is generally taken as an abbreviation of *unsere*: 'ours'
(the Sterbas' translator gives 'us'). Either way, 'Ever thine, ever mine,
ever ours' now takes on a new meaning.

That Beethoven had had a shock is evident from his letters of this
period. Solomon[44] has shown that Beethoven had been due to meet
Varnhagen on his last evening in Prague, until the unexpected arrival of
Antonie. Apologizing later for his failure, he writes, 'I was sorry, dear
V(arnhagen), not to have been able to spend the last evening in Prague
with you, and I found that shocking (*unanständig*), but a circumstance
which I could not foresee prevented me from doing so.' In this letter he
bemoans living 'alone – alone! alone!' concluding with the admonition,
perhaps intended for himself, 'Demolish what is evil and keep yourself
above it.'[45] In a letter a few days later to 'Emilie', a little girl who had sent

him a present, he praised family life, adding that he was 'staying on in Teplitz for four more weeks.'[46] On the 24th, to Breitkopf & Härtel, he wrote of himself to his publisher as a 'poor Austrian musical bungler – povero musico! (and yet not in the manner-': Miss Anderson postulates the following deleted phrase as being 'of a castrato.'[47]

Beethoven discarded his initial plan to stay in Teplitz 'for four more weeks,' on about the 25th[48] departing abruptly for Karlsbad where he stayed in 'adjoining quarters' to the Brentanos.[49] He moved on with the Brentanos to Franzensbad, allegedly on his doctor's orders – hardly credible, unless Staudenheim was travelling round with his patient: this was the height of the holiday season, in fashionable spas.

What more likely than that Beethoven would flee to his Beloved at this stage in their relationship? The evidence points to his visit's being unexpected – perhaps he even took over part of their rooms? He left Teplitz so quickly that he forgot his passport.[50] Goethe believed that Beethoven was returning to Teplitz almost immediately because he twice (the second time on August 2nd) asked his wife Christiane to give Beethoven a letter to bring back with him.[51] We have no evidence of what happened between Beethoven, Franz and Antonie; any scenes may have been mitigated by the presence of the couple's young daughter, Fanny. In a letter from Franzensbad to Breitkopf & Härtel, Beethoven wrote that he was 'weary of many other unavoidable incidents and startling events.'[52]

On September 8th he returned, alone, to Karlsbad, whence he returned to Teplitz and from there to Linz to try to prevent the marriage of his brother Johann. As Solomon suggests, he may have stayed at Linz until the Brentanos had returned permanently to Frankfurt.[53]

'Our journey depends upon Toni's recovery,' Franz Brentano wrote to his half-brother Clemens from Vienna on October 6th.[54] From Solomon's quote it could be deduced that, four months into the pregnancy, Franz Brentano chose not to admit that his wife was pregnant: the state of the marriage if this is true can be imagined.

It is not known what Beethoven was doing between his visit to Linz and the very end of 1812: there are no letters. It is believed to have been at about this time, on his return to Vienna, that he began his *Tagebuch*. The first entry in this reads in part:

'You must not be a *human being, not for yourself, but only for others*: for you there is no longer any happiness except within yourself, in your art. O God! give me strength to conquer myself, nothing at all must fetter me to life. – In this manner with A everything goes to ruin.'[55]

In letters of this time to the Archduke Rudolph, Beethoven complains of suffering a mental breakdown:

'Since Sunday I have been ailing, although mentally, it is true, more than physically.'[56]

and again in January 1813:

> 'As for my health, it is pretty much the same, the more so as moral factors are affecting it and these apparently are not very speedily removed; the more so as I must now look to myself alone for help . . .'[57]

On February 25th he signed himself to Zmeskall, 'Ludwig van Beethoven miserabilis.'[58]

On March 8th, 1813, Antonie Brentano's last child, Karl Josef, was born.[59]

Part 2

Beethoven's depression in 1813 has for long been attributed to his financial plight, caused by the effect of devaluation on his annuity. In fact, during February, Beethoven signed receipts for 2 cheques, for £121.18.5d and £73.2.6d respectively, from George Thomson of Edinburgh in payment for several of his Scottish songs.[60]

At the time of Karl Josef's birth, Beethoven's brother Caspar Carl was thought to be dying of tuberculosis. Caspar Carl's will making Beethoven sole guardian of his six year old son, Karl, was made out on 12th April 1813. Beethoven later claimed to have given 10,000 florins in Viennese currency to his brother between the time of the start of his illness in 1813 and his death in 1815.[61] On October 22nd 1813 Beethoven stood surety for a 1,500 florin loan from the publisher Steiner to Caspar Carl's wife, Johanna.[62] According to Hotschevar's testimony during the court case at the end of 1818 regarding Karl's custody, the boy was said to have become 'an object of transaction between the two brothers.'[63]

An entry in Beethoven's *Tagebuch* of 13th May 1813 reads:

> 'To forego what could be a great deed and to stay like this. O how different from a shiftless life, which I often pictured to myself. O terrible circumstances, which do not suppress my longing for domesticity, but (prevent) its realisation. O God, God, look down upon the unhappy B., do not let it continue like this any longer.'[64]

On the 27th of May Beethoven wrote to the Archduke, ' . . . a number of unfortunate incidents occurring one after the other have really driven me into a state bordering on mental confusion.'[65] In that same summer he wrote to his friend Franz Brunsvik in Buda, ' . . . I have nothing to provide for save my own miserable person *(elendes Individuum)*.'[66]

'Not only did he not have a single good coat, but not a whole shirt,' related Frau Streicher to Schindler. 'I must hesitate to describe his condition exactly as it was.'[67] According to Solomon, it was during this summer that Beethoven attempted to kill himself by starving to death in the grounds of Countess Erdödy's palace.[68] In 1815, when the Countess tried to revive the friendship between them, Beethoven could not at first bring himself to visit her:[69] a further indication that something had happened. Beethoven called the Countess his Father Confessor.

In contrast to his prodigious productivity of the period up to autumn 1812, his composition now came to a halt. Beethoven wrote virtually nothing in 1813 until the *Battle* Symphony, Opus 91.

Beethoven wrote the orchestral version to commemorate Wellington's victory at Vittoria on June 21st, his purpose, with Mälzel, being to provide music for a concert for widows and orphans of the fallen.[70] At the time of its composition, however, Napoleon had proved victorious at the Battle of Hanau and was retreating through Frankfurt.[71] It is not difficult to imagine the anguish of a man who had an unclaimed son in Frankfurt.

There are no references to the Brentanos in Beethoven's correspondence at this time. A *Tagebuch* entry, 'Wrote to x about x,'[72] may conceivably apply.

The first reference to Antonie Brentano by name (or initial) in the *Tagebuch* occurs in 1814: 'I owe F.A.B. 2300 florins, once 1100 florins and 60 ducats.'[73]

In the summer of that year, the revision of his opera *Fidelio* seems to have revived at least his artistic spirit:

'There is much to be done on earth, do it soon!
'I must not continue my present everyday life; art demands this sacrifice too. – Rest and find diversion only in order to act all the more forcefully in art.'[74]

The following entry is also pertinent:

'For Fate gave Man the courage to endure to the end.'[75]

A letter to Beethoven from his long-absent friend Karl Amenda in spring 1815 prompted the reply: 'You live *happily*, you have *children* ... Unfortunately for my good or that of others ... I must live almost in estrangement from all persons whom I love or could love.'[76]

In November Caspar Carl died, after making a new will naming his wife, Johanna, co-guardian with Beethoven of their son, Karl. The parts of the will naming Johanna as co-guardian were defaced; the day before his death, Caspar Carl made out a codicil reinstating Johanna as co-guardian.[77] In the light of the will of April 1813, the apparent agitation of Caspar Carl for more money which led to the agreement with Steiner of October 1813,[78] Beethoven's quarrel with Caspar Carl before Karl and Johanna, later made up on the Ferdinand Bridge (which Thayer dates 1813 but which I believe was more likely to have occurred in 1815, given the surrounding evidence[79]), it does not seem to me fanciful to suggest that it was Beethoven himself who made the deletions in Caspar Carl's will.[80]

Beethoven was not a saint but there can be no doubt that he was a God-fearing man. The strength of purpose demanded to change his dying brother's will illustrates the depth of his need to stand acknowledged by the world as the father of a son.

References to guilt abound in Beethoven's writings. Note, for example, a *Tagebuch* entry of this time:

'Under the tiger's tooth I heard the sufferer pray:
Thanks to you, sublime one, I die in pain but free of guilt.'[81]

a Schiller entry of 1817:

'This one thing I feel and clearly perceive:
Life is not the sovereign good,
But the greatest evil is guilt.'[82]

and Cooper's comments on the setting of *Peccata* throughout the *Missa Solemnis*.[83]

Note also his adjurations to silence, addressed to himself throughout his *Tagebuch*: 'Learn to keep silent, O friend. Speech is like silver, but to be silent at the right moment is pure gold.'[84] (1813); 'Spare even the closest friend your secrets;/How can you ask fidelity of him, when you deny it to yourself?'[85] (1815); and '*Audi multa, loquere pauca.*'[86] (1817).

Contemporary with the central of the above entries is Beethoven's copying of the gloss on Hesiod:

'For vice walks many paths full of present sinful desires and thereby induces many to follow it. But virtue leads on to a steep path and cannot attract men as easily and swiftly, *especially if elsewhere there are those who call them to a sloping and pleasant road.*'[87]

By early February 1816 Beethoven had temporarily emerged victorious as the sole guardian of Karl. The copy of *Othello* found in Beethoven's *Nachlass* bore three question-marks at 'I had rather to adopt a child than get it.'

Having given his examples of Beethoven's calling himself a father, Maynard Solomon goes on to relate this to a fantasy marriage with Johanna.[88] In fact in 1816 there is much evidence of a renewal of Beethoven's interest in Antonie.

We have no evidence of a response from Antonie to Beethoven's letter of November 1815[89] but response one can assume that there was in the light of the following. It can hardly be supposed that a woman Beethoven called, along with her husband, his 'best friends in the world'[90] could have ignored the wry suicidal plea: 'for his (Caspar Carl's) life is very precious to him, though indeed I would gladly relinquish mine!!' The reference to Antonie's 'devotion' in a *Tagebuch* entry of circa autumn 1816[91] also indicates that a warm concerned response had been forthcoming during the intervening months. Beethoven wrote to Antonie in February 1816 enclosing a copperplate engraving of himself.[92] On March 4th he wrote to Franz introducing him to the winedealer, Neberich, who was to act as a courier later for letters from Frankfurt.[93] In April, Antonie Brentano was writing to a friend of her father's 'that the consecration of art is beautiful, "but more beautiful is the art of love, having been taught by nature . . . the most beautiful is the mutual interchange of happiness between two people."'[94] Beethoven was then writing *An die ferne Geliebte*.[95]

It was during what appears to have been a low point in this year that Beethoven adjured himself to 'Regard K as your own child.' The entry immediately following reads: 'In any event the sign has been accepted.'[96]

There is clearly here an atonement factor. We have already seen Beethoven referring to his adopted nephew as 'this holy cause.'[97] 'I know of no more sacred duty than that of supervising the education and training of a child,' Beethoven was to tell the *Magistrat*.[98] Beethoven's needs here are very complex: guilt, a debt to God and those he felt he had wronged (Karl Josef, Antonie, Franz and, as Maynard Solomon suggests, Johanna, whose son he *needed* to appropriate, but whose sufferings occasioned by himself instigated another source of guilt).[99]

There is besides Beethoven's need to reproduce his line in music: to found a Bach-like dynasty. In 1819 he wrote to his attorney of his desire '*by means of my nephew* to establish a fresh memorial to my name.'[100]

The scenario is no less involved than Solomon envisages it, though as I read the facts it runs along different lines.

'Unfortunately I have no wife,' Beethoven wrote to Ries in the summer of 1816. 'I have found *only one*, whom no doubt I shall *never possess*.'[101] A few days before calling himself 'a true fleshly father' he had wished his publisher Steiner 'the penis of a stallion.'[102] It is probable that he had heard from the Brentanos.[103] His letter of September 29th to Antonie refers to recent news of them: that Franz had become a Senator 'and instead of becoming older is becoming younger and younger.'[104] In this letter too he refers to himself as a father. This letter was also the introduction to Brentano of Simrock. Also despatched through Peter Joseph Simrock was the letter of the same date to Wegeler in which Beethoven referred to himself as a husband and father, but without a wife. During this month too occurred the famous scene at Baden when Beethoven told Giannatasio, in the half-hearing of his curious daughters, about his five-year old romance.[105]

This summer seems to have been one of Beethoven's happier spells, despite Karl's hernia operation: the letter to Dr Bihler[106] telling him of 'excellent health' is written in Beethoven's granite fist, and he had resumed his piano improvisations.[107]

By circa November he was writing in his *Tagebuch*, in an entry generally thought to refer to the Immortal Beloved:

'With regard to T there is nothing else but to leave it to God, never to go there where one could do wrong out of weakness; only leave this totally to Him alone, the all-knowing God!'[108]

From a November letter it can be seen that Giannatasio had told Beethoven that Karl was lazy.[109] Beethoven confronted Karl with this. The boy, close to the anniversary of his father's death, may have given his grief as the cause of his laziness, since Beethoven writes that he is taking the boy to visit his father's grave. It may have been this reminder of his duties to his adopted nephew which led to Beethoven's second *Tagebuch* entry of this period concerning Antonie, in which he appears to counsel renunciation:

> 'Nevertheless be as good as possible towards T; her devotion deserves never to be forgotten, although unfortunately advantageous consequences could never accrue to you.'[110]

Nevertheless Beethoven did talk of leaving the country in December. According to Fanny's diary, he was ill and distraught.[111] It will be recalled that Beethoven was tied to Vienna by the terms of his annuity.[112] He was, however, allowed to travel on business 'for the furtherance of his art.' Beethoven had thought of travelling to England at least as early as 1812.[113] By 1815 this had become a definite proposition, after the letters through Häring to George Smart.[114] By 1817 a proposal was on the table.[115] This journey was discussed periodically throughout the remainder of his life, but was never to materialize. Solomon writes in relation to Beethoven's talk in his last years of a journey to Bonn that this 'might possibly reunite him with the Brentanos,'[116] but this applies equally to any of these mooted journeys to England. Thoughts of Beethoven's travel plans did however recur in the summer of 1817.

As we have seen, Beethoven had sent the Bonn publisher's son Simrock to Frankfurt with the letter of 29th September to Antonie. Peter Joseph Simrock wrote to Beethoven on October 23rd; this letter Beethoven claimed never to have seen.[117] It is possible that Beethoven did see this letter and that it contained the first hints that all was not well with Karl Josef.

Any such fears seem to have subsided or to have been negated by Franz, to whom according to a letter of early 1817 Beethoven had sent some music.[118] This letter is an incredible missive from one man to another if read at face value: 'I myself would like you to believe that frequently I have prayed to Heaven for long preservation of your life so that for many years you may be usefully active for your family as its esteemed head.' Solomon quotes this at face value; but see the conversation book entry of February 1823 where Beethoven writes of an earlier rival in love, 'He was my enemy, and for this reason I was as good to him as possible.'[119] It takes no stretch of the imagination to assume that Beethoven was guilt-filled at wishing this particular 'head of a family' dead.[120]

As I reconstruct the story, it was in April 1817 that Beethoven learned of Karl Josef's illness. Hearing the news, presumably from Franz, one can only suppose that Beethoven sought to discuss this with his own doctor. In a letter of June 19th to Countess Erdödy,[121] Beethoven dates the incident of his break with Malfatti virtually to the day, since by April 15th he was taking powders prescribed by his new doctor. In this letter, Beethoven states that Malfatti had 'powerful secondary motives where I was concerned.' In 1810, Beethoven had proposed to Malfatti's niece.

Solomon describes Karl Josef's illness thus:

'At an early age (Karl Josef) was stricken with partial paralysis of the legs. More seriously, in his fourth year he showed signs of severe mental retardation coupled with epileptiform seizures and violent behaviour which required that he be constantly watched and restrained. During the last fifteen years of his life (he died in 1850) he was perpetually under the care of three attendants.'[122]

Beethoven himself was violent at the time of his discovery of Karl Josef's illness, biting his pupil Hirsch in the shoulder.[123]

The lost letters to Frankfurt begin to be noted in the *Tagebuch* at this time.[124] Beethoven appears to have written frantically, at times every few days.[125] As Solomon says, the entries relating to Frankfurt are surrounded by 'several of his most intimate and profound confessional utterances.'[126]

He thought of visiting a spa near Frankfurt that summer.[127] According to Thayer's reading, he adjured himself to 'make plans and be consoled for the sake of T.'[128] His anxiety state is evident from his numerous letters to Frau Streicher, repetitious with worries about his laundry[129] and somewhat vulgar punning on her name.[130] This year he even punned upon his own name.[131]

His letters this year are full of guilt and misery. On December 27th he wrote to Frau Streicher, 'I rely on your love of human nature which moves your inner spirit to do good. I can't do that, I can't meet you on the same terms. Unfortunately I realized this a long time ago. . . . "each one of us *errs, though always in a different way.*" . . . As soon as you return from Klosterneuburg, please be *very good to me!*'[132] In an unsigned letter to Zmeskall, he wrote, '*In the predicament in which I am now placed,* I need *indulgence* in all directions. For I am a poor, unhappy man.'[133] On the 21st of August he wrote to Zmeskall, 'I often despair and would like to die.'[134] It is interesting to note that this is only two days after Beethoven's injunction to Schnyder von Wartensee, 'Continue to raise yourself higher and higher into the divine realm of art. For there is no more undisturbed, more unalloyed or purer pleasure than that which comes from such an experience.'[135] After almost a year bereft of composing, it was not until circa November that Beethoven began to work, first on several short fugal pieces, including the string quintet Opus 137,[136] later on the *Hammerklavier*, Opus 106. The latter was dedicated to the Archduke Rudolph for whom, according to Beethoven, it had always been intended.[137] Indeed, the first movement opens with a pianistic fanfare to which Beethoven had originally added the words 'Vivat, vivat Rudolphus.' It is a striking coincidence that, like Karl Josef, the Archduke Rudolph suffered from epilepsy.

As Solomon says, these years saw a deepening of Beethoven's religious faith.[138] His *Tagebuch* entries for this year show that, whatever the date when Beethoven learned of the Archduke's appointment to the Archbishopric of Olmütz, by the first half of 1818 Beethoven was primed to begin work on the *Missa Solemnis*.[139]

The diary came abruptly to an end when Beethoven stood in danger of losing his adopted son. By autumn 1818 Johanna, evidently supported by her distant relative, Hotschevar, began to contest Beethoven's custody through the courts. The court case of December 1818 was followed by that of the 11th of January: the papers for this are missing. Since Hotschevar's testimony[140] dates from the first of these, it is possible that the question of the defaced will was raised at the January court appearance. Suspicion is heightened since someone has been really thorough and destroyed what appear to be the corresponding pages which dealt with this incident in Beethoven's draft memorandum.[141] (The actual memorandum is also missing).

As a result of this court case, Beethoven was deprived of Karl.[142]

However, he still had control of the boy's education. In February Beethoven turned to Antonie Brentano, soliciting her help in getting Karl placed under the tuition of Sailer, her religious adviser, at Landshut. It is intriguing to find Beethoven when writing of this claiming that he still had some relatives at Landshut.[143] No relatives of Beethoven are known to exist in Landshut. However, when discussing education with his friends a month or so later, the names of *Antonie's* relatives, Clemens and Christian Brentano, are mentioned.[144]

Frau Brentano complied with his request in a letter which bears witness to her surviving devotion to Beethoven, whom she describes as even greater as a man than as an artist.[145] Her letter confirms that she also wrote directly to Beethoven.

The attempt to have Karl educated at Landshut failed when the *Obervormundschaft* or guardianship authority objected to Karl's being granted a passport. Contact between Beethoven and the Brentanos was however continued in that year through Stieler, whom Franz Brentano commissioned to paint Beethoven's portrait for his wife. The conversation books show that Beethoven gave Stieler several sittings. Secrecy seems to have been a factor.[146] There was even talk of a life-size portrait of Beethoven.[147] In a conversation book of late 1819, a striking entry in the hand of Beethoven's friend Oliva reads, 'Because you always talk about the woman, the husband will recognize as your child amongst his children the one who possesses musical talent.'[148] An entry in Beethoven's hand a month later reads, in the context of taking a child from its father, 'And that I was and am.'[149]

Since June 1819 Karl had been a boarder in the educational institute of

Joseph Blöchlinger. Blöchlinger's son in his memoires tells us that Beethoven had given Karl over to his father 'with the stipulation that the young lad's mother was never to visit or see her son.'[150] Franz had presumably forbidden Beethoven to make contact with his son: is not Beethoven here doing to a mother exactly what was being done to him as a father?

At the time when Beethoven was fighting his last, successful, court battle to win Karl, Franz became active as his agent with the Bonn publisher Simrock, first for the piano and flute variations, Opus 107, later in the protracted, frustrated, and, to him, expensive negotiations over the *Missa Solemnis*.[151]

In 1820 we hear too of a 'quarrel with the Brentano woman,'[152] possibly occasioned by a letter brought to Beethoven from Frankfurt by Neberich.[153] It has been postulated that the 'Brentano woman' was Antonie's daughter, Maxe,[154] although the childhood teasing of a nine year old by Beethoven when she was with him seems unlikely to have continued after an absence of eight years, when the girl was seventeen. However, it is the case that Beethoven at this time began work on Opus 109 which he was later to dedicate to Maxe.[155] I follow Köhler-Herre in believing that this quarrel was with Antonie Brentano, possibly over his continued failure to visit in spite of his summer plans of 1817 and frequent discussion of a trip to England. Antonie Brentano may have felt that Beethoven should see his son;[156] there may also have been authorizations for medical treatment which Franz Brentano too would have wished to discuss with Beethoven.[157] By the time of the dedication to Maxe,[158] Antonie had taken Karl Josef to the phrenologist, Gall, in Paris.[159]

The year 1821 had been taken up with the composition of Opus 110 and Opus 111, both of which were intended for Antonie Brentano.[160] The most striking example of Beethoven's close involvement with Antonie at this time comes in a letter in his own hand to her husband, in which he refers to her as 'Your excellent, one and only glorious Toni.'[161] The context of this is also striking: Beethoven has just wished Brentano joy 'as pater familias in your children.'

During 1822 letters continued to pass between Beethoven and Franz regarding the sale of the Mass, on which Franz had by now advanced Beethoven money.[162] In 1823 Beethoven completed his *Diabelli* Variations (begun at the time of Antonie's help with Sailer) and dedicated the work to Antonie. He had thus dedicated or intended to dedicate each of his four last major piano works to Antonie Brentano or her daughter. It will be recalled that Beethoven had played for Antonie in Vienna to comfort her during her illness. There may be another reason why Beethoven was composing for the piano at this time:

'Karl's room was directly above his mother's, so that his fits and paroxysms caused her unceasing anguish and sleeplessness. The sole means by which she could temporarily tame his behaviour was through a repetition of Beethoven's treatment of her depression in Vienna: she would play the piano for Karl, and "the playing soothed the sufferer so that he would lean his head upon her shoulder." But this would last only for the briefest time, after which "he would spring up and rave so wildly that she herself was forced to flee.'"[163]

It is usually said that Franz Brentano had sent Beethoven a dunning letter regarding the money Beethoven owed him over the sale of the Mass.[164] In fact, Beethoven in his reply thanks Franz for his 'friendly communication.' This is the one occasion in the extant[165] correspondence in which Beethoven refers to Karl Josef specifically:

> 'You said in your letter that your little boy's health is improving. I am extremely glad about this. I hope that your wife too is well and also all your children and brothers and sisters. For all your family are always very dear to me.'[166]

The specific exclusion of the 'little boy' from the other Brentano children is striking, especially when it is recalled that Karl Josef was the only one whom Beethoven had never met.

We have no knowledge of any contact between Beethoven and the Brentanos after this year.[167]

Part 3

Thereafter the aging composer, suffering progressively from the after-effects of jaundice, seems to have turned his gaze upon other women: the *Kapellmeister's* wife in 1823: 'Sideways on she has a magnificent bottom';[168] Sontag and Unger in 1822-4, his soprano and alto in the *Choral* and *Missa Solemnis*, known variously as 'the two beauties' and 'the girls';[169] and, in 1825, 'the Cibbini', who was said to have resembled 'a bacchante' during the first performance of Opus 132. The publisher Moritz Schlesinger questioned Beethoven as to whether he had wanted to marry her. Their talk extended to Schlesinger's telling Beethoven that he would be the first to whom any new bride of his own was introduced:[170] shades of his relationships with his friends' wives, Frau Peters and Frau Janitschek, in 1820.[171]

His fifty-fifth birthday found Beethoven writing execrable verses to some unknown charmer.[172] On the anniversary of this one year later, Beethoven was being taught multiplication by Karl.

The nature of his son's condition raises the question of Beethoven's alleged V.D. Evidence for this is not forthcoming until 1819.[173] This illness is now thought to have been of the gonorrhoea type rather than syphilis.[174]

In any event we have here a reason for Beethoven's repression of nephew Karl's sexuality: not only did he not want the boy to repeat his own mistakes, was there not also an element of seeing the boy as younger than he was?[175] The animosity between the two men at one stage resulted in Karl's attempting to throttle his uncle[176] – as Beethoven had earlier threatened his nephew when Karl had still been a boy.[177] Indeed there were periods when Beethoven's frantic dependence upon his adopted son was said to have verged on the psychotic in terms of its wild veering between love and hatred: Karl had failed to follow him in music, failed to identify him fully as his father – was not Beethoven dissatisfied with 'the sign' because nephew Karl was no more able to realize his hopes of Karl Josef than was Karl Josef himself?

In 1825, at a time of illness, of trauma with Karl – and the composition of some of his greatest music – Beethoven wrote of his misery to Bernard: 'That awful fourth floor, O God, *without a wife* . . .'[178] In the midst of a stream of letters to Karl from Baden hailing him 'Dear Son!' and signed 'Your loving father,' 'Your faithful father,' is one concluding with 'Unfortunately your father – or, better still, not your father.'[179] A letter of June the following year is signed 'Your real and true father,'[180] to which Beethoven adds, 'Do come – do not permit my poor heart *to bleed any longer.*' Karl was at this time telling people, 'My uncle! I can do with him what I want: some flattery and friendly gestures make things all right right away,' and calling him 'the old fool.'[181] Karl's suicide attempt caused Beethoven to be described as 'cast down as a father who has lost his much-loved son.'[182]

From Fanny we learn that on his deathbed Beethoven grew agitated at the thought of women visitors.[183] This cannot have applied to all women, however: according to Ferdinand Hiller, Beethoven 'begged of Hummel to bring his wife to see him' on March 13th and, three days before his death, was grateful for the ministrations of Frau Hummel who mopped his brow.[184]

Beethoven insisted on being seen by Malfatti (alone according to Schindler).[185] By my hypothesis, Beethoven had told Malfatti of Karl Josef a decade earlier, at their last meeting. It is possible that Beethoven could have returned any letters from Antonie through him.

We have no evidence that Beethoven told anyone else of Karl Josef during his lifetime other than that which points to his having confided in his *Beichtvater*, Countess Erdödy, in whose garden according to Röckel he had tried to starve to death. If Beethoven did confide elsewhere it seems more likely that this was in a close friend such as Zmeskall or Holz, who were both also drinking companions, rather than in his brother Johann, the immorality of whose wife and daughter he was wont to bandy. At the start of his last illness, Beethoven sent Holz a canon to the words, 'We all err, but each one errs in a different way.'[186] Oliva's conversation book entry of 1819[187] suggests that Beethoven did talk of someone; Wolf, Stieler and Neberich, who all had Frankfurt connections, seemed to treat 'Frankfurt' as a joke involving Beethoven: it is not impossible that this joke had sexual innuendoes. 'Three cheers for Madame Brentano!' Wolf exclaimed;[188] Frau Janitschek served him 'a dish from Frankfurt.'[189] It seems inconceivable that Beethoven did not, when drunk, drop hints or make references in the course of his conversation as he did in his letters: the fact that both boys were called Karl and that Beethoven called his nephew 'my son' may well have led to their not being picked up. Karl himself wrote his name 'Carl', after his father; Beethoven almost invariably wrote 'Karl'. To Beethoven in the drafting of his last will, a 'natural heir' was 'the same thing' as a 'legitimate' one.[190]

We have one reason to suspect that conversation took place about Karl Josef as Beethoven's son at the time of Beethoven's death, perhaps during the heated exchanges between Johann, Breuning, Schindler and Holz during the search for Beethoven's bank shares.[191] Of all the people to whom Johann could have written after his brother's death describing his last days, we know only that he wrote to Antonie Brentano.[192]

There had been much misdating of the Brentano evidence prior to the researches of MacArdle and Solomon, a lot of it suggesting that the Brentanos had stayed in Vienna until 1814, thus taking the heat off the events of 1812 and 1813. If my theory is correct, Franz Brentano himself had a vested interest in altering what passed down to posterity and later, through Schindler, the opportunity of doing so.

Franz Brentano objected to Bettina's 'advertising their intimate relationships with famous personages.'[193] Bettina too now has a motive for falsifying letters from Beethoven, at the time of the second of which, according to her, he was in Teplitz with her rather than, as was the case, in Franzensbad with Antonie.[194] Bettina had been inimical towards Antonie when the young wife, a mere six years her senior, had acquired the position of her putative step-mother. Later, when she was herself a mother, her attitude to her sister-in-law changed and she wrote that 'Tonie, through this child, has changed from a scheming, mocking woman into an angel of sorrow.'[195]

Clemens too suffered a change of attitude, from over-adoration to something close to hatred and resentment: 'He told Franz things concerning Toni for which Franz was entitled to throw him out of the house.'[196] Clemens was in Vienna in 1813 and is known to have met Beethoven – and hero-worshipped him. Clemens stayed in the Birkenstock House – Antonie's house, inherited from her father: the house at which Beethoven had visited regularly and played to Antonie. It is conceivable that Beethoven, a few months after Karl Josef's birth, pumped Clemens for news of Antonie and the child and that Clemens only realized the significance of this several years later, perhaps after other hints of Beethoven as the father had reached his ears.

It is my belief that Thayer found out about Karl Josef and that this was the cause of the 'headaches' which led him perpetually to postpone the remainder of his biography once he had reached the year 1817.[197] The Sterbas speculate that Thayer could no longer bring himself to work on his Beethoven biography because he was appalled by Beethoven's behaviour regarding Karl.[198] The Sterbas do not tell us why this should have happened when Thayer reached 1817, when Karl was settled at Giannatasio's school and relations were fairly quiet between Beethoven and Johanna. Certainly there were no court cases at this time and Beethoven's reactions to Johanna during the argument of August that year[199] are far milder than the vilifications heaped upon her in 1816, when he called her a prostitute.[200]

'But it must not be forgotten that Beethoven, on his death-bed ... expressed "his honest desire that whatever might some day be said of him should adhere strictly to the truth in every respect, regardless of whether or not it might give pain to this or the other person or affect his own person."'[201] Thayer places this statement by Schindler in 1817. Schindler too I believe found out, but only after Beethoven's death: the defacement of Beethoven's papers was undertaken by Schindler,[202] who from 1833 visited or periodically resided in or near Frankfurt, the home of Antonie and Franz.

As Krehbiel writes, Schindler's conversation book forgeries amount to 'mutilations, interlineations and defacements ... for the purpose of bolstering up mistaken statements.'[203] Stadlen makes the point that, besides trying to convince the world that he had known Beethoven several years earlier than had been the case, many of the forgeries relate to 'private vendettas such as Schindler engaged in' (e.g. against Ries, Johann and Holz); while others, inspired by 'Schindler's own devotion and boundless admiration ... exaggerate out of all proportion his standing with the composer and the quality of their relationship.'[204] But there are also cases known where entire pages or sections were removed for the purpose of protecting Beethoven's reputation, such as those covering the apparently bawdy party with the Danish musician Friedrich Kuhlau on September 2nd 1825,[205] and sections leading to Karl's suicide attempt.[206] It is not impossible that other such sections (or entire books?) were destroyed – not merely by Schindler? Of this latter we would today have no evidence. Two points can be made in this connection. That Schindler was not averse to making a living out of his contact with Beethoven is shown by his ultimate sale to the Berlin library of the conversation books: books which he is now believed to have stolen.[207] Franz' own desire for suppression is borne out by his injunction, above, to Bettina, plus the evidence of the lost letters to Frankfurt itemized in Beethoven's *Tagebuch*, which must be set in the context of the Brentanos' knowing the worth of Beethoven and retaining *some* letters.

Writing of Beethoven's debt to the Brentanos, Schindler says:

'The beginnings of the matter take us back to 1813, the year in which fate seemed to have knotted itself around our hero's head so tightly that he was never able to completely free himself. It was from the master himself that I learned of this debt but I was ignorant of its origins, and, *like so many other incidents of that unhappy year whose roots lay deep within his complex nature, they did not become clear to me until my protracted stay in Frankfurt.*'[208]

Both Schindler and Thayer attempted a cover-up by pointing to another candidate as the Immortal beloved: in Schindler's case, Giulietta Guicciardi, based on Beethoven's talk with him about her in 1823;[209] in Thayer's, Therese Brunsvik.

'Something snapped' in Thayer, writes Sonneck.[210] Nothing snapped in Thayer; but something had snapped in Beethoven. Let us now consider the change in Beethoven's music. The *Battle* is an occasional piece; Opus 90 is old-style Beethoven.[211] From then on there is a change in his music: the importance of the fugue, starting with the piano sonata Opus 101 and the 'cello sonatas Opus 102.[212] Virtually every major work thereafter contains either or both variation form or fugal treatment, the latter culminating in the great piano fugue of Opus 106 and the *Große Fuge* itself, Opus 133.[213]

It has long been said – and felt by his listeners – that Beethoven's late quartets are the nearest approach to words in music.[214] I should like to have put fresh thought into the meaning behind the musical words. Listen afresh also to the '*et incarnatus est*' of the *Missa Solemnis*.[215] Compare the whole of this setting of the Mass with that in C, which Beethoven was busy finalizing with his publisher at the time when he learned of Karl Josef's conception. The difference in approach is the measure of the change that had taken place in the man.

Beethoven did not 'always distinguish clearly what had actually happened and what had been merely imagined,' wrote Grillparzer, but Grillparzer did not know Beethoven until 1823 and this was written in 1844, and in self-justification of Beethoven's failure to set his opera *Melusine*.[216] It is possible to construct a case whereby many of Beethoven's supposed fantasies are explicable by other means.[217] The willing acceptance by some scholars of the Sterbas' view of Beethoven points up the fact that there is generally felt to be a hiatus in what is known of Beethoven: this much-discussed 'gap' between the man and his music; although, as Solomon writes, the Sterbas' interpretation is 'one which would force us to believe that the masterpieces of Beethoven's last years were composed by a cruel and unethical human being.'[218] I hope to have set Beethoven researchers devising a new scenario for several old, accepted but not necessarily proven Beethoven clichés. There is no longer a need to resort to the Sterbas' allegations of sadism to make sense of Beethoven's actions. Beethoven was a father: by putting this piece into the jigsaw, much else falls into place.

If One Has Only One Son . . .
— *the contrast between a letter by Beethoven and one by Franz Brentano*

Do we have evidence that Franz Brentano did not regard himself as the father of his wife Antonie's youngest child?

I can demonstrate that such evidence has come down to us.

To begin with, we now know from a primary source that Antonie Brentano was ill in Prague. In a letter of 15th July 1812 from Karlsbad, Franz Brentano tells his half-brother, Clemens, that he had sought but failed to find him in Prague.[1] This can only refer to the Brentanos' brief stop-off there on July 3rd-4th. After a reply from Clemens on October 1st, Franz takes up this topic in his answer of 6th October, from Vienna:[2]

> I was sorry not to see you in Prague, your presence would have cheered me up considerably. I had need of this because *my Toni was also very ill there*. (italics mine).

Further on in the same letter, Franz writes:

> In 4 or 5 weeks time, *as soon as Toni is completely well*, we shall return home again (i.e. to Frankfurt.) (italics mine.)

Antonie Brentano was by this time some 4 months pregnant. It is notable that nowhere in this letter does Franz Brentano tell his half-brother that his wife is pregnant, even though he goes on to refer to her health again:

> If my impending return journey was not determined by the restoration of my wife's health (which I hope is not far off), I would invite you here where you could stay with us. However, I feel a powerful urge to return home and my restless wanderings have lasted too long already.

What he does say instead is startling. Writing of his son Georg's education, he says:

> *If one has only one son* one must be twice as careful at least to attempt the best for him. (italics mine)

He concludes the letter by saying:

> *My children are growing up and make me feel old.* (italics mine).

To my mind these are not the words of a man who knows himself about to become a father again in five months time: a man, moreover, of almost 47, whose youngest child is already six and who, by his own admission, is and has for some time been unwell:

> I have been already unwell for a lengthy time, being unable to bear this climate.

It is scarcely possible that Franz did not know the nature of Antonie's 'illness': the father of 5 himself, he had grown up in a house where his father, in the course of three marriages, had produced a dozen surviving children. The symptoms of pregnancy were hardly unknown to him. It does not seem feasible that he did not know that his own wife was four months pregnant. The reference to her being better 'in 4 or 5 weeks' may indeed have been based on the pattern of her earlier pregnancies.

He knows she is pregnant, *but he is not admitting it*. Why? Why is this man of close on 47, by his own admission ill, down-in-the-mouth, not boasting to his brother, 'Hey, guess what, the old stud's done it again!' He was, after all, married to her: there is no earthly reason why he should not have boasted about his forthcoming fatherhood *had this been the case*.

How, one wonders, did Franz finally admit Antonie's pregnancy to Clemens at the end of the day? Was he perhaps hoping that the pregnancy would not go full-term and that his wife would miscarry? If present, this sensation can have been only partial, since he had witnessed and doubtless shared her grief on the death of their own first child, the poignant memories of which come through in Antonie's letter to Clemens of as late as January 9th, 1812:

> You wrote to me on the death of my first child. I still stood at the desolate cradle with bleeding heart; I lowered my eyes to the grave but you did not let me succumb. You wrote to me in such a way that I shall remember it in eternity.[3]

So is it then that Franz knows that his wife is pregnant but is not sure whether he is the father? In other words, has he himself been sleeping with Antonie at the same time as Beethoven's involvement with her?

A woman having an affair puts off her husband. Deceit of this nature would go doubly against Antonie's Catholicism. Franz' illness speaks against it. Further references to Franz' own illness appear in his letter to Clemens of 15th July, 1812.

> I need to take the waters here (i.e. Karlsbad) because of the ill-health I have been suffering and I shall spend some time here and in Eger (Franzensbad), returning by way of Prague.[4]

References to Franz' illness appear as early as January 1812, in the previously-quoted letter from Antonie Brentano to Clemens:

Franz sends his greetings. For several weeks he succumbed to a kind of hypochondria which frightened me but now things are better and soon he'll be quite well again I hope.[5]

Most conclusive of all is the letter itself. Franz writes like a man *who knows that he has had his last child*. 'If one has only one son,' he writes. This is not the statement of a man whose wife might be about to present him with another in five months time. *He* does not believe that he is about to become a father.

Equally this is not a man who is trying to convince himself that he is the father. There is nothing here of a man who feels that he *may* be about to have another son. This is a man who feels the years closing in on him and circumstances closing in on him.

This would also explain the emphasis on Georg's education. He is having to concentrate on Georg as his heir. May it not be Franz' over-concentration – perhaps over-indulgence – on Georg which leads to the boy's troubles in the 1820s? Is not Franz' over-indulgence of Georg's ill-behaviour towards him in 1830 a vivid illustration of this?[6]

If Franz really was giving up his house and everything to an eleven year old boy, he was virtually abdicating his masculinity, his headship of the family, to his son and heir while he himself was still alive. In fact this seems to have been an over-reaction at the time of the letter on Franz' part: we do not hear of the Brentanos moving into a new mansion until 1820.[7]

One other point comes through very strongly. 'My Toni' and 'my wife' are as firmly in evidence here as 'my future child' is absent – i.e. Franz is staking his claim to Toni; as to *any* prospect of future fatherhood, he has drawn a line.

Contrast this with the outpouring of emotion in Beethoven's Immortal Beloved letter.[8]

Here a diversion is perhaps necessary. Discussion of this letter has been hampered by the fact that certain scholars down the years (and very many recent ones) have taken the view that this is a negative letter. I do not believe that this position can be supported by the actual text. In the first part – July 6, in the morning – he tells her that 'We shall surely see each other soon.' He tells her that his thoughts – presumably worries – about his own life would disappear 'If our hearts were always close together.' He calls her 'my true, my only treasure, my all as I am yours.' He ends by affirming that 'The gods must send us the rest, what for us must and shall be.' Given the vagaries of Beethoven's letter-writing technique, this is pretty positive stuff. What makes it doubly so is the apparently forgotten fact that this is a letter written by a man of forty-one who had just endured one or possibly two nights in succession with very little sleep, followed by another in which he had apparently been troubled by 'thoughts . . . touching my own life.' On the night of July 4th he is known to have been enduring a 'fearful journey,' which he graphically describes. It can hardly be thought that he enjoyed much if any sleep on that post-coach. The Sterbas and Solomon may apply psycho-analytical interpretations to this aspect of the letter;[9] the fact remains that Beethoven was here describing actual events on an actual journey that he had endured, long before Freud was around to make him think of writing circumspectly, and doing so, moreover, not for the scholars of posterity but for the eyes of one concerned, loving woman.

But on the night of July 3rd he had also abandoned all thoughts of keeping his arranged meeting with Varnhagen,[10] presumably to attend to Toni (whose arrival at his rooms in Prague was thus obviously unexpected). One can hardly think that he enjoyed much sleep that night either, assuming that my suppositions are correct. Solomon indeed points out that the Immortal Beloved letter itself, taken literally, 'implies that they parted on July 4th.'[11]

Nothing very negative about the second part, written on the evening of Monday, July 6. He tells her that 'Wherever I am, you are with me.' He writes, for the first time, 'I will arrange it with you and me that I can live with you.' Nor can I see anything very ambiguous in the line, 'Much as you love me – I love you more.' He describes their love as 'a heavenly structure, as firm as the firmament.'

The third part is where the difficulty lies. Here two points I believe have been overlooked: the dramatic change in the handwriting which occurs in the middle of this third part – July 7, in the morning – and a clue that is contained within the letter itself. Beethoven begins 'still in bed' – he says so. However, coinciding with the dramatic change of handwriting (and mood) he reveals a newly-accquired piece of information: 'I have just learned that the post goes every day.' One of three things must have happened: someone came in and told Beethoven this; or, whilst writing this passionate letter, Beethoven was sharing his bed or room with someone who inexplicably had failed to give him this vital piece of information; or Beethoven got up, had coffee, perhaps breakfast, walked round the inn, and came upon the post-times notice yet again, whereupon either he noticed or someone pointed out to him the smaller-print note at the bottom to the effect that, to the Austrian Imperial dominions, the post 'leaves daily before noon.'[12]

The change in both the tone of the letter and the handwriting leads me to believe that the last of these is what occurred: this is Beethoven in a different mood from the first-thing-in-the-morning, bleary-eyed writer of the beginning of the third part. (Perhaps he had a hangover?) Anyway, I can't see very much that is negative here. In evidently fast, passionate, scrawling hand, he is again calling her 'Angel,' repeating his intention to live with her, telling her of his tearful yearnings for her, and assuring her of his fidelity. The 'farewell' seems to be taken out of context: he has just told her he wants to live with her; he has already written, in the first part, of their 'seeing each other soon.' He is scarcely bidding the woman goodbye for ever! This is surely a man pelting to catch the post.

Indeed it is known that Beethoven, apparently without room reservations and at the height of the holiday season, abandoned his stated plans to stay on in Teplitz and left, evidently in a hurry, forgetting his passport, to be with his Beloved in Karlsbad and to accompany her and her husband and child when they moved to Franzensbad. By the time Beethoven left, on the 8th of September, Antonie was already three months into her pregnancy. What sort of a man would this be who hung about knowing that he had been deceived in love – and this time at the bitterest level – and knowing that he could not be the father of her child? And who, moreover, went on writing of her devotion as late as 1816[13] and who wrote of her in glowing terms such as he used for no other woman as late as 1821?[14]

To revert to the letter itself: the first part begins, 'My angel, my all, my very self,' the second part of the letter starts, 'You are suffering, you, my dearest creature,' and the letter ends, 'ever thine, ever mine, ever ours' – any one of which can be taken as a reference to her newly-discovered pregnancy. Since Antonie is now known to have been ill in Prague, the 'suffering' can now be taken as being physical as well as emotional, supporting my belief that it may well have been sickness during the long journey from Vienna to Prague which confirmed Antonie in her suspicions that she was pregnant.

What did she do when she knew? She fled to see Beethoven. What did he do when he knew? He wrote her a letter on fire with emotion. *He* does not think he isn't the father. *He* doesn't need any convincing. He may wake up on the morning of July 7th like a bear with a sore head, wondering how the hell he is going to cope with it all: she is married, she already has four children, he has no money, he was going to go to England; this does not stop him, later on that same morning, repeating what he has already told her in the second part of the letter, that he too shares their 'purpose to live together.' What but his conviction of his beloved's pregnancy and the equal conviction that he was the father would have drawn this letter out of Beethoven: to a married woman whose family he was proposing to destroy? Surely not the unconsummated fantasy romance, untriggered by knowledge of the pregnancy, that is postulated by Maynard Solomon.[15]

And when he got the letter back – for I am convinced he sent it – he kept it for the remainder of his life and left it to be found. He called himself a father. *He wanted us to know.*

Maynard Solomon's implicit contention that Franz Brentano knew himself to be the father of his wife's last child does not stand up. I hope to have shown that the further possibility that Franz might have been the father, i.e. that Antonie Brentano had relations with Franz and Beethoven during the summer of 1812, can also not be drawn from the statements in his letter of October 6th 1812.

In this case, this letter is 'the smoking gun,' confirming that Beethoven was the father of Antonie Brentano's youngest child.

Notes to 'Fleshly Father'

1 Maynard Solomon, 'New Light on Beethoven's Letter to an Unknown Woman,' *Musical Quarterly* lviii (1972) pp. 572-87; *Beethoven* (New York: Schirmer/1977) Chapter 15. This identification has been generally accepted by Beethoven scholars: Lewis Lockwood in his review of Solomon's book (*19th Century Music* iii (1979-80) p. 78) calls it 'one of the most Holmesian pieces of document-interpretation I have seen in years.' Alan Tyson writes in *The New Grove Beethoven* (London: Macmillan/ 1983 p. 55) that Frau Brentano 'fulfils all the chronological and topographical requirements.' Rebuttal of Josephine Deym as Beethoven's Immortal Beloved is well documented in Solomon's article, 'Recherche de Josephine Deym,' *Beethoven News-letter* (San Jose) volume 2, no. 2. For refutation of the notion of Beethoven's sister-in-law Johanna as the Immortal Beloved, see Edward Rothstein, *New York Times*, January 1, 1995, pp. 31 & 34; and Joseph Kerman's piece in *New York Newsday*, December 19, 1994.

2 Emily Anderson, editor and translator, *The Letters of Beethoven* (London: Macmillan/ 1961, 3 vols.) letter no. 633. (In the abbreviation used hereafter, the number refers to the letter not page unless otherwise specified.)

3 Maynard Solomon, 'Beethoven's *Tagebuch* of 1812-1818,' *Beethoven Studies 3*, edited by Alan Tyson (Cambridge/1982) pp. 193-288; *Tagebuch* entry no. 80. (In the abbreviation used hereafter, the number refers to the entry not page unless otherwise specified.)

4 Anderson 654.

5 Anderson 661.

6 'Beethoven & His nephew: A Reappraisal' in *Beethoven Studies 2*, edited by Alan Tyson (Oxford/1977) p. 167.

7 Details of Beethoven's relationship with the Brentanos may be found in Donald W. MacArdle, 'The Brentano Family in its Relations with Beethoven,' *Music Review* xix (1958) pp. 6–19; Solomon's works listed in note 1; Solomon, 'Antonie Brentano & Beethoven,' *Music & Letters* lviii (1977) pp. 153-169; and pp. 166-189 of his *Beethoven Essays* (Harvard/1988).

I am indebted to Maynard Solomon for kindly letting me see an early draft of this chapter prior to its publication. I cannot stress too strongly, however, that the views expressed in this present paper are solely my own and not those of Maynard Solomon.

I should also stress here that, without his spade-work, this discussion could not be held at all.

8 It was for nuns of this order that Beethoven performed much of his charitable work after 1811 in freely providing the scores and parts of such works as the Oratorio *Christus am Ölberge*, Opus 85, to the extent of suggesting that their organisation premier his 7th Symphony (Anderson 369).

9 Solomon, 'Antonie Brentano & Beethoven' p. 154.

10 Quoted by Franz in a letter to Sophia Brentano of October 4th, 1797: Solomon, *Beethoven*, note 75 to Chapter 15.

11 MacArdle, 'Brentano Family in its Relations with Beethoven', p. 16.

12 Anderson 296.

13 Letter of 26th January 1811. See Solomon, 'Antonie Brentano & Beethoven' p. 161, n. 46. Beethoven did not set this cantata.

14 *Thayer's Life of Beethoven*, revised & edited by Elliot Forbes, (Princeton/1973) (hereafter Thayer-Forbes) p. 491 gives Bettina's vivid description of this house.

15 Quoted in Solomon, 'Antonie Brentano & Beethoven' p. 158 from A.W. Thayer, *Ludwig van Beethovens Leben*, ed. H. Deiters & H. Riemann, 5 vols. (Leipzig/1866-1917) (hereafter 'TDR') volume iii, p. 216.

16 Thayer-Forbes p. 492.

17 As note 15.

18 Solomon, *Beethoven* pp. 184-5.

19 Note, however, that the love-song *An die Geliebte*, WoO 140, was given to Antonie in December 1811; there are two versions, one for piano, the other for piano or guitar, Antonie's own instrument. Solomon, 'Antonie Brentano & Beethoven' p. 161.

20 Solomon, 'Antonie Brentano & Beethoven' p. 160: 'It is my assumption that she fled to Beethoven . . . to one who represented for her a higher form of existence, to one who embodied in his music the spiritual essence of her native city.'

21 'Antonie Brentano & Beethoven' p. 159.

22 Solomon, *Beethoven Essays* p. 182.

23 Solomon, 'Beethoven's Letter to an Unknown Woman' p. 584.

24 The title-page of the autograph is reproduced in Robert Bory's iconography *Ludwig van Beethoven* (London: Thames & Hudson/1966) p. 139. Note that the date has been altered to June 26th from June 2nd.

25 Solomon, 'Beethoven's Letter to an Unknown Woman' p. 576 item 3, confirms their arrival on July 3rd.

26 *ibid.* pp. 577-8, item 5.

27 Solomon, *Beethoven* pp. 184-5: 'Beethoven, it seems, was unprepared for this sudden turn of events.'

28 This view is not confined to Maynard Solomon. Solomon's quotation, 'Beethoven & His Nephew: A Reappraisal' p. 144, of Joseph Kerman, 'An die ferne Geliebte,' *Beethoven Studies 1* ed. Alan Tyson (New York: Norton/1973) p. 129, in a passage itself derived from Martin Cooper, *Beethoven: The Last Decade 1817-1827* (Oxford/1970) p. 13 & 32, shows how ubiquitous has grown the view of Beethoven's sexuality propagated by the Sterbas (Editha & Richard Sterba, trans. Willard R. Trask, *Beethoven & His Nephew* London: Dobson/1957). Tyson, *The New Grove* p. 140 agrees that 'it seems plain that he shrank from a total involvement with a woman.' Edward Larkin, in Cooper's Appendix A, pp. 461-2, writes that it is unrealistic to try to explain Beethoven's sexuality, but dismisses the notion that he was homosexual.

29 Solomon, *Beethoven* p. 184. Solomon's suggestion, on the same page, that Beethoven had 'lifelong inhibitions about taking his place as the head of a family' I find amazing, in the light of his 'fathering' while still a boy of his two younger brothers and the furious battle he later put up to win Karl. In any case, Solomon himself contradicts this: in the quotation at the start of this article, he writes of Beethoven's 'deep' desire to become 'the head of a family.'

30 Anderson 54.

31 Letter of Charlotte Brunsvik of December 19th, 1804 (Thayer-Forbes p. 359). Josephine's refusal to satisfy his 'sensuous love' caused him 'anger': Thayer-Forbes p. 379.

32 Thayer-Forbes p. 775: diary entry of July 12th, 1817.

33 *Tagebuch* 122.

34 'Antonie Brentano & Beethoven' p. 162 n. 51.

35 Anderson 1231, p. 1081 n. 4: ' . . . that former and still active whore, with whom her fellow miscreant slept no less than three times during your illness and who, moreover, has full control of your money, oh, abominable shame, is there no spark of manhood in you?!!!'

36 *Tagebuch* 107

37 *Tagebuch* 3.

38 *Beethoven* pp. 83-4. See also p. 41.

39 Anderson 12 of August 2nd (1794).

40 Anderson 16 of February 19th (1796).

41 *Beethoven* p. 84.

42 Solomon himself writes of ' . . . his bachelorhood, to which he never became fully reconciled.' (*Beethoven* p. 81).

43 Anderson 373, Thayer-Forbes pp. 533-4, Solomon *Beethoven* pp. 159-60, Sterbas pp. 101-3 etc. The facsimile is published in Bory pp. 145-7. See '*One Son*' note 8.

44 *Beethoven* p. 164.

45 Anderson 374.

46 Anderson 376 of July 17th. He repeated this latter in Anderson 378 of the 19th.

47 Anderson 379 n. 2. Cf also the salutation of Anderson 651 to his publisher Steiner of September 4th, 1816, when his *Tagebuch* suggests a revival of his feelings for Antonie (*Tagebuch* 104, *Tagebuch* 107).

48 According to Goethe's diary: Solomon, 'Beethoven's Letter to an Unknown Woman' p. 579 n. 18.

49 Solomon, 'Beethoven's Letter to an Unknown Woman,' p. 580.

50 *ibid.* n. 18.

51 Thayer-Forbes 537.

52 Anderson 380 of August 9th.

53 'Antonie Brentano & Beethoven' p. 162.

54 *ibid.* note 50.

55 *Tagebuch* 1.

56 Anderson 394.

57 Anderson 402.

58 Anderson 406.

59 Solomon, 'Antonie Brentano & Beethoven' p. 162. Evidence that Antonie Brentano had been in Vienna in early June is forthcoming: she had been involved in the final auction of part of her father's art-collection. See Solomon, 'Beethoven's Letter to an Unknown Woman' p. 579 n. 17. Beethoven had tried to persuade the Archduke Rudolph to bid for some items at an earlier auction (Anderson 316).

Part 2

60 Donald W. MacArdle & Ludwig Misch, translators & annotators, *New Beethoven Letters* (Norman, Oklahoma: University of Oklahoma Press/1957), letters 117 of 4th February and 119 of 27th February.

61 Anderson 572. The voluntary nature of this giving did not prevent Beethoven from pleading poverty on account of his 'great generosity.' See Anderson 411 to Varena. In Anderson 412 to Pasqualati he claims to have 'not a farthing left.' Höfel reports that in restaurants he left without paying, claiming that his brother would settle the bill, 'which Carl Caspar did.' (Thayer-Forbes p. 590)

62 Thayer-Forbes p. 551. The composition of Opus 90 and Opus 101 was tied in with the repayment terms for this loan. See also Thayer-Forbes p. 616. Beethoven's debts to Steiner detailed on p. 767 indicate that interest on this loan was still outstanding as late as 1820; see also Anderson 1257 p. 1102 n. 2.

63 TDR, vol. iv, p. 544. It is interesting in this connection to note that Beethoven owed Franz Brentano large sums which were never fully repaid: see Solomon, 'Antonie Brentano & Beethoven,' pp. 165-7 for a summary of these debts and their partial repayment. That is not to imply that this, if there is a connection, was pre-meditated on Beethoven's part: the 'unsolicited cheque' (should be of 1813-14: see *Tagebuch* 33) seems to have been just that (Anderson 659), perhaps sparked by Beethoven's meeting with Clemens Brentano that summer. See note 73.

64 *Tagebuch* 3.

65 Anderson 426.

66 Anderson 427.

67 Thayer-Forbes p. 554.

68 Solomon's date, derived from Röckel: *Beethoven* pp. 219-20. Schindler describes the incident (Anton Felix Schindler, edited by Donald W. MacArdle & translated by Constance Jolly, *Beethoven As I Knew Him* (London: Faber/1966) pp. 101-4), attributing it to 1803.

69 Anderson 532.

70 These performances took place on the 8th and 12th of December. Thayer-Forbes pp. 564-6.

71 Napoleon was in Frankfurt on November 2nd.

72 *Tagebuch* 15. Solomon, working from Gräffer's copy (the original is lost), comments that the missing names were probably not entered by Beethoven.

73 *Tagebuch* 33. F.A.B. = Franz & Antonie Brentano. Solomon suggests that 'this sum probably includes one of the loans that she told Nohl was given to Beethoven "when she learned of his condition through her doctor."' (*Beethoven Essays* p. 178.) See note 63 regarding this and future debts to Franz Brentano incurred when the latter acted as Beethoven's agent for the putative sale to Simrock of the *Missa Solemnis*.

74 *Tagebuch* 25.

75 *Tagebuch* 26. Romain Rolland, however, takes the suppressed words of *Tagebuch* 20 as a reference to suicide.

76 Thayer-Forbes pp. 617-8 (in Anderson as letter no. 541). Beethoven repeated similar sentiments to another visitor introduced to him the following year by Amenda, Dr Karl von Bursy (Thayer-Forbes 643-5).

77 Will and codicil can be found in Thayer-Forbes pp. 623-5.

78 See Beethoven's letter to Dr Joseph Reger of December 18th 1813, Anderson 441, in which he refers to Caspar Carl as 'My greatest enemy!' and reference to 'brother' in Anderson 427 to Franz Brunsvik.

79 As I reconstruct this, Beethoven's argument with his brother, 'You thief! Where are my notes!' (Thayer-Forbes pp. 551) relates to some or all of the works which Beethoven subsequently sold to Steiner in a deal in which Caspar Carl seems to have acted as agent, the first letter concerning which is dated February 1st 1815 (Thayer-Forbes p. 616). Anderson 528 and Anderson 531 of February 1815 refer to Caspar Carl's renewed ill-health. Hotschevar accused Caspar Carl of only loving his brother when he could get something out of him (TDR iv, 544).

80 Note Beethoven's later remarks about this, quoted variously in Thayer-Forbes p. 625, Anderson 1009 and MacArdle/Misch letter 286. The most likely date for this draft fragment by my reconstruction would seem to be soon after the court case of January 1819.

81 *Tagebuch* 55: Herder, 'Dank des Sterbenden'.

82 *Tagebuch* 118 (*Die Braut von Messina*, closing lines). This was presumably a frequent utterance by Beethoven since his friends Bernard and Peters comment on it in a conversation book entry of 1820: Karl-Heinz Köhler, Grita Herre, Dagmar Beck et al., editors, *Ludwig van Beethovens Konversationshefte* (Leipzig: Deutscher Verlag für Musik/1968 continuing, 9 volumes to date) vol. i, book 8, 49r and 50r (p. 297).

83 Cooper p. 269. See also p. 232, where Cooper writes that the *Gloria* 'reveals unmistakably how deeply Beethoven felt the need of mercy and forgiveness.'

84 *Tagebuch* 5: Herder, 'Das Schweigen'. Solomon's very full annotation gives details of the canon on this text, WoO 168 no. 1, given by Beethoven to Charles Neate on 24th January 1816, and a canon that he is said to have written on the same text for the Giannatasio family.

85 *Tagebuch* 59: Herder, 'Verschweigenheit'.

86 *Tagebuch* 115: 'Listen to much, but speak only a little.'

87 *Tagebuch* 68b: Hesiod, *Works & Days* lines 287-92; italics mine.

88 'Beethoven & His Nephew: A Reappraisal' pp. 167-8.

89 Anderson 570.

90 Schindler/MacArdle 259; see Anderson 1125.

91 *Tagebuch* 107. Here and in *Tagebuch* 104 it is generally agreed that 'T' = Toni (Antonie).

92 Anderson 607. This letter together with the engraving was sold to a private buyer at Sotheby's London sale of May 9th, 1985.

93 Anderson 619

94 Solomon, *Beethoven Essays*, p. 188. Letter of 21st April 1816 to Johann Isaak von Gerning.

95 Opus 98. Investigation has failed to establish that the verses were published elsewhere; it is possible that Beethoven commissioned them to his own specification. See Joseph Kerman, 'An die ferne Geliebte' p. 123.

96 *Tagebuch* 80 and *Tagebuch* 81.

97 *Tagebuch* 80. As Solomon points out (*Beethoven* p. 235), in bringing up Karl 'Beethoven believed that he was carrying out a sacred task', though if this were in substitution for the duty he felt he owed to Karl Josef then its source was scarcely 'of an unspecified nature.'

 98 Anderson appendix C, no. 14, of 7th January 1820, p. 1387.
 99 See, for example, *Tagebuch* 159, *Tagebuch* 160 and *Tagebuch* 164 for expressions of this.
100 Anderson 937 of c.1st February.
101 Anderson 632.
102 Anderson 651. Cf. deleted passage in Anderson 379 (note 47).
103 Anderson 924 is more probably dated summer of 1816, as Miss Anderson suggests.
104 Anderson 660; cf. also Anderson 758.
105 Fanny Giannatasio's diary of September 13th (writing of the 12th), reproduced in Thayer-Forbes pp. 646-7. On January 11th 1817 Nanni Giannatasio asked him about 'the ring he always wears.' (TDR iv, p. 539).
106 Anderson 646, autograph in the British Library, Stephan Zweig collection, which is certainly not of 1817 when Beethoven's health was wretched.
107 *Tagebuch* 102. Marie-Elisabeth Tellenbach's suggestion ('Beethoven & the Countess Josephine Brunswick, 1799-1821,' *Beethoven Newsletter* vol. 2, no. 3, pp. 46-7) that Beethoven was enjoying a resurgence of his romance of a decade earlier with Josephine Deym, whom she identifies as his Immortal Beloved, would seem to be contradicted by the page found by Fanny Giannatasio on which Beethoven had written, 'My heart runs over at the sight of lovely nature – although she is not here!' (Thayer-Forbes p. 646)
108 *Tagebuch* 104. See note 91. The reference to polyandry in *Tagebuch* 94f is also pertinent.
109 Anderson 672.
110 *Tagebuch* 107. See note 91.
111 Diary entry of December 5th, relating to the 3rd. TDR iv, p. 537.
112 Thayer-Forbes p. 457 gives the terms of this annuity. 'Conditions hold me here,' he had told Bursy during a splenetic outburst against Vienna in 1816 (Thayer-Forbes p. 644).
113 Thayer-Forbes pp. 531-2 refers to a planned trip with Oliva, pp. 563-4 to that with Mälzel. See also Solomon's annotation to *Tagebuch* 50.
114 Thayer-Forbes pp. 614-5. It will be noted that, even at this stage, Häring tells Smart that Beethoven's journey is unthinkable on account of the composer's growing deafness.
115 Thayer-Forbes pp. 674-5.
116 'Antonie Brentano & Beethoven' p. 162. See, for example, Anderson 1028 of 5th August 1820.
117 Anderson 759.
118 Anderson 758 (see note 104).
119 Köhler-Beck, vol. ii, book 22, 45v-46r (p. 366).
120 Solomon, 'Antonie Brentano & Beethoven' p. 169, also goes on to quote the postscript to this letter, 'all my best greetings to my beloved friend Toni and to your dear children,' as a dismissive afterthought without highlighting that Beethoven has in the body of the letter lamented the lack of the company of 'your wife and your dear children.'
121 Anderson 783.
122 'Antonie Brentano & Beethoven' p. 163.
123 Thayer-Forbes p. 664. As though, by imitating an act, to bring it into the realm of normality. (Note that this was done to a child. In a letter of 1815 to Countess Erdödy, Anderson 531, Beethoven claimed to love children.)
124 *Tagebuch* 123, *Tagebuch* 133, *Tagebuch* 139, *Tagebuch* 141. The date of the first of these letters, 'a few days' before 22nd April, coincides with the date of discovery as mid-April (see note 121).
125 In 1816 the death of the son of another 'beloved' woman friend, Countess Erdödy, had elicited only one letter (Anderson 634), albeit clumsy and heartfelt.
126 'Beethoven's Letter to an Unknown Woman' p. 582 n. 31. This was also the time when he told Nanni Giannatasio of his conversion to a belief in free love: TDR iv, p. 540.
127 *Tagebuch* 121

128 On p. 670 Thayer-Forbes gives this as '"C"' according to Jahn' (see also Solomon's notes to *Tagebuch* 120); on p. 686, however, Thayer remarks that this 'was probably T.' Note that Thayer tells the reader to connect Beethoven's desire to travel in 1817 to 'T'.

129 See, for example, Anderson 810.

130 Anderson 789, Anderson 792.

131 Anderson 808.

132 Anderson 838.

133 Anderson 828.

134 Anderson 805. He refers to his death again in Anderson 877.

135 Anderson 803.

136 The suicidal song 'Resignation' WoO 149 was also written at this time.

137 Anderson 948 of 1819.

138 *Beethoven Studies 3*, p. 208. See, for example, *Tagebuch* 171.

139 *Tagebuch* 155a, *Tagebuch* 168.

140 TDR iv pp. 543-8.

141 Anderson appendix C no. 15 of February 18th 1820, p. 1392 (pp. 7 & 8 of Beethoven's draft). Whilst Anderson p. 1388 n. 2 states that there is 'no documentary evidence to show that this memorandum was submitted,' Köhler-Herre i, book 9, 21r (p. 330) shows that this was offered to Winter by Schlemmer (to whom Beethoven had presumably entrusted the copying), a point which Anderson 1010 of 6th March 1820 to Winter confirms. Solomon states that a copy was also given to Schmerling (*Beethoven* p. 249).

142 Thayer-Forbes p. 721: Fanny Giannatasio writes of Beethoven's deprivation.

143 Anderson 946 n. 1 (p. 811).

144 Köhler-Herre i, book 2, 35v (p. 53). Both these men, as well as Antonie's brother-in-law Savigny, had connections with Sailer at Landshut.

145 Her letter is quoted in part in Solomon's 'Antonie Brentano & Beethoven' (pp. 161-2), in full in *Beethoven Essays* pp. 178-180. Solomon's reference to her mention of his 'pure intentions' ('Antonie Brentano & Beethoven' p. 162 n. 51), which he evinces as a pointer to the relationship's being non-sexual, can equally well be taken the other way.

146 Köhler-Herre i, book 9, 36r (p. 338).

147 *ibid.* book 6, 31r (p. 196).

148 *ibid.* book 5, 10r (p. 149).

149 *ibid.* book 6, 24v (p. 193).

150 Frimmel, *Beethoven-Studien* (Munich & Leipzig/1905-6), ii, p. 114.

151 Anderson 1011 n. 5 (p. 880), Anderson 1012 (p. 882).

152 Köhler-Herre i, book 7, 53r (p. 253).

153 *ibid.* book 6, 49r & 49v (p. 205).

154 MacArdle, 'The Brentano Family in its Relations with Beethoven' pp. 11-12 n. 3.

155 Robert Winter, 'The Sources for Beethoven's *Missa Solemnis*,' *Beethoven Essays* edited by Lewis Lockwood & Phyllis Benjamin (Harvard/1984) pp. 237-8, dates the start of Opus 109 as prior to Schlesinger's letter of 11th April 1820 which, since it is lost, we can only assume may have requested new piano sonatas. At the same time, Beethoven 'resurrect(ed) the germinal symphony' whose completion might have taken him to England – and Frankfurt.

156 Solomon, 'Antonie Brentano & Beethoven' p. 163: 'I am begging for help,' she wrote to Savigny, 'I call for help to God and to people, and the feeling friend will understand my urgency and will not deny me what is in his power.' The date of this is 25th October, 1820.

157 There are 10 letters to the Simrocks this year; with the exception of Anderson 1038 of 28th November, the corresponding letters to Franz have not survived.

Beethoven was talking of a trip to Bonn in August (Anderson 1028 of the 5th) and November 1820 (Anderson 1037). This was repeated on March 14th the following year (Anderson 1051). That Simrock at least took Beethoven seriously is shown by his letter to Beethoven of 13th May 1822: 'We thought that we would see you here during the past summer as you had promised in your letter of March 19th, but this has not happened either.' (Thayer-Forbes p. 784).

158 Anderson 1062 of 6th December 1821.
159 Solomon, *Beethoven Essays* p. 187.
160 Anderson 1118 to Schindler. The London edition of Opus 111 appeared in April 1823
     with a dedication to Antonie Brentano: Alan Tyson, *The Authentic English Editions of
     Beethoven* (London/1963) p. 110. Perhaps significantly, the autograph of this work is
     signed 'Ludwig Ludwig'.
161 Thayer-Forbes p. 780; in Anderson as no. 1064: December 20th, 1821.
162 Thayer-Forbes pp. 784-7 provides a summary of the letters regarding Simrock/
     Brentano and the Mass this year. Beethoven was simultaneously attempting to sell his
     '*greatest* work' (Anderson 1079 of 5th June 1822 to C.F. Peters) to several other
     publishers.
163 Solomon, 'Antonie Brentano & Beethoven' pp. 163-4. Internal quotations taken from
     A. Niedermayer, *Frau Schöff: Johanna Antonia Brentano, ein Lebensbild*, (Frankfurt/1869)
     p. 12 (Solomon's note 56).
164 His debt to Brentano may be the reason why Beethoven had briefly considered
     dedicating Opus 120 to him: Köhler-Beck iii, book 27, 31r (p. 139). Ironically, it was
     presumably through the Brentanos that Beethoven sold one of his subscription copies
     of his Mass – that to the Cäcilia Society of Frankfurt.
165 Solomon himself says ('Antonie Brentano & Beethoven' p. 169) that many of
     Beethoven's letters to the Brentanos 'in view of their probable nature' have
     presumably been suppressed or destroyed.
166 Anderson 1226 of August 2nd, 1823.
167 A reference to Antonie Brentano in January 1826 (Köhler-Herre viii, book 102, 26r
     (p. 284)) by Mathias Artaria precedes a sketch for Opus 131.

Part 3

168 Köhler-Herre iv, book 38, 7r (p. 25).
169 See, for example, Anderson 1097 of 8th September 1822 to Beethoven's brother;
     Thayer-Forbes pp. 896-7; and Köhler-Herre v, book 53, 10v-13r (pp. 77-80).
170 A.W. Thayer *The Life of Ludwig van Beethoven*, Eng. trans. ed. Henry Edward
     Krehbiel, 3 vols. (New York/1921; reprinted London: Centaur/1960) vol iii, p. 205;
     Anderson 1433, which includes a canon.
171 Köhler-Herre i, book 6, 7v (p. 184) & 57r (p. 208) etc.
172 Thayer-Forbes p. 969.
173 Köhler-Herre i, book 2, 41r (p. 55) & n. 92. Larkin suggests that the book here
     referred to may have been bought for Karl: 'He could easily have been preparing
     himself to tell Karl what a young man should know.' (Cooper, p. 451 n. 1). However,
     since it specifically deals with ' . . . its effects and symptoms in the older person,' one
     can assume that this relates to Thayer's cryptic 'he did not always escape the common
     penalties of transgressing the laws of strict purity.' (Thayer-Forbes pp. 244-5). This
     reference to the consequences of non-celibacy, incidentally, could be an oblique hint
     at the paternity of Karl Josef.
174 See Larkin's medical appendix in Cooper, pp. 449-53; Solomon, *Beethoven* p. 262;
     T.G. Palferman, 'Beethoven – The Case Against Syphilis,' *Journal of the Royal College
     of Physicians of London*, vol. 26 no. 1, January 1992, pp. 112-114. Whatever the illness
     Beethoven may have suffered in 1819, he lived on – and worked – until 1827; Antonie
     Brentano lived until 1869.
175 Thayer writes that: 'Beethoven never seems to have realized that Karl had outgrown
     the period when he could be treated as a child . . .' (Thayer-Forbes p. 882).
176 Thayer-Forbes p. 993.
177 *ibid.* p. 709.
178 Anderson 1387 of June 10th.
179 Anderson 1379 of May 31st, 1825.
180 Thayer-Forbes p. 994. Anderson 1489 translates this as 'Your sincere and loving
     father.'
181 Thayer-Forbes pp. 994-5.
182 *ibid.* p. 1000.

183 J-G Prod'homme, *Beethoven Raconté par Ceux qui L'Ont Vu* (Paris/1927) p. 91: 'Beethoven during this period was very afraid of visits by women to the extent that, when he thought a woman was coming, he showed himself most anxious and became defensive.'

184 Thayer-Forbes pp. 1046-7. It is possible that Antonie sent Beethoven one or two books which appeared in his *Nachlass*. It is more likely, however, that these books, by Sailer, were bought by Beethoven in 1819 when he was contemplating sending Karl to Landshut: Köhler-Herre i, book 2, 97r-v (p. 77).

185 Thayer-Forbes pp. 1031-2.

186 Anderson 1541. Cf Anderson 838 of December 1817 to Frau Streicher.

187 See note 148.

188 Köhler-Herre i, book 9, 35v (p. 338). In the context she seems to have sent him, through Neberich, a sausage!

189 *ibid.* book 6, 67r (p. 213).

190 Thayer-Forbes p. 1047.

191 ibid. pp. 1051-2. In the light of the rest of the evidence that a cover-up took place, it is significant that the miniature of Antonie found at this time was for long held to be that of the Countess Erdödy. See Solomon, 'Beethoven's Letter to an Unknown Woman' pp. 585-7 and n. 39.

192 Thayer-Forbes p. 1051 n. 61; Solomon *Beethoven* p. 183 points out that this was sent to Antonie.

193 Solomon, 'Antonie Brentano & Beethoven' p. 169 n. 80.

194 Thayer-Krehbiel ii, p. 227.

195 Bettina to von Arnim, 20th March 1822: Solomon, 'Antonie Brentano & Beethoven' p. 164.

196 *ibid.*: Bettina to von Arnim, 31st August 1824. A later letter, from Arnim to her, repeats the same impression. It is interesting to note that it was in 1817 that Clemens' religious attitude abruptly changed and he became an ardent Catholic: MacArdle, 'The Brentano Family in its Relations with Beethoven' p. 14.

197 Solomon, 'Beethoven's Letter to an Unknown Woman' p. 584: '"Toni" Brentano, in all probability, was the woman whose family Thayer attempted to shield from harmful publicity.'

198 *Beethoven & His Nephew* pp. 16-17.

199 Anderson 800.

200 Anderson 611.

201 Thayer-Forbes p. 664.

202 Peter Stadlen, 'Schindler's Beethoven Forgeries', *Musical Times* 1977 pp. 549-52 and 'Schindler and the Conversation Books', *Soundings*, no. 7 (June 1978) pp. 2-18; Dagmar Beck & Grita Herre, 'Anton Schindlers fingierte Eintragungen in den Konversationsheften,' *Zu Beethoven*, ed. Harry Goldschmidt (Berlin: Verlag Neue Musik/1979) pp. 11-89.

203 Thayer-Krehbiel iii, p. 281.

204 'Schindler & the Conversation Books,' p. 17.

205 Thayer-Forbes p. 958.

206 *ibid.* p. 996.

207 Stadlen, 'Schindler's Beethoven Forgeries' p. 550: 'There is evidence that, after the composer's death, the guardian of Beethoven's nephew planned to take Schindler to court for removing a great many scores, sketchbooks and documents (which must have included the conversation books) from the officially sealed flat.'

208 Schindler/MacArdle p. 259, italics mine. It should not be forgotten that Antonie Brentano herself was alive to quash any rumours until 1869: Schindler pre-deceased her, having published three editions of his biography.

209 Köhler-Beck ii, book 22, 44r-48r (pp. 365-7).

210 O.G. Sonneck, *The Riddle of the Immortal Beloved* (New York/1927) p. 21.

211 Kerman *The New Grove* pp. 121-2 includes Opus 90 among those works in which 'a new feature is the intimacy and delicacy.' Opus 90 it will be recalled was the first work written by Beethoven for Steiner under the terms of the loan to Johanna of October 1813, by which according to Hotschevar Caspar Carl bartered his son. See notes 62 and 63.

212 According to Georg Schünemann his penmanship changed with Opus 102; (*Musiker-Handschriften von Bach bis Schumann*, Berlin/1936 pp. 74-5); this became even more marked with Opus 111 (Cooper, p. 129).

213 This, of course, was the true finale of Opus 130, described at the time of its composition as Beethoven's *Leibquartett* (Thayer-Forbes p. 974).

214 Kerman, *The New Grove* p. 122 writes of the *beklemmt* passage of the Opus 130 *Cavatina*, 'Here instrumental music seems painfully to strive for articulate communication.'

215 Cooper writes of this *mezza voce*, solo flute passage: 'The delicate detail and exquisitely apt atmosphere of this whole passage can hardly be matched anywhere else in Beethoven's music.' (p. 245), and again on p. 247: 'for the Incarnation he humbles even his art, which seems to stammer the language of an earlier age in an access of tenderness. It is almost as though he were contemplating a separate mystery when the tenor soloist's tentative "et" and the horn's major third carry the music from (Dorian) D minor into the full light of D major, and the word "homo" is passed with delighted wonderment backwards and forwards between soloist and chorus.'

216 Grillparzer, 'Erinnerungen an Beethoven, 1844-45,' *Rheinische Musik und Theater-Zeitung*, 13 (1912): 508, 524. See also Donald W. MacArdle, 'Beethoven & Grillparzer,' *Music & Letters* xi (1959) pp. 52-4. His friends may, of course, have been covering up for him. There is also a sense in which this is a blanket excuse for Beethoven's less than honourable dealing with publishers: Beethoven's treatment of Franz in the Simrock affair regarding the sale of the Mass may well have been Beethoven's way of retaliation.

217 Beethoven was aware of his own inadequacy and lack of honourable dealing. According to Streicher, he said of himself, 'Everything I do apart from music is badly done and is stupid.' (Letter to C.F. Peters of 5th March 1825: see Anderson 1324 n. 2.)

218 *Beethoven* p. 252.

Notes to 'One Son'

1 The unpublished correspondence which follows is quoted, with permission, from Freies Deutsches Hochstift (Goethe Museum) Frankfurt. Transcription and translation by Gudrun and Dr R.T. Llewellyn. The spelling and capitalization are those of the original manuscripts. I am grateful to Maynard Solomon for bringing these letters to my attention.

'Bei meiner Durchreise durch Prag gaben wir uns alle mühe dich aufzufinden, u. sanden mehrmals einen Lohn Bedienten, in deine wohnung, zu einem Kupferstecher, u. zu andern Leuten wo man dich vermuthete, du warst aber nicht aufzufinden, u. wahrscheinlich wurde dir nicht ausgerichtet, daß wir den andern Tag vor 6 Uhr Frühe abreiseten, es thut uns leid daß wir dich verfehlt haben.'

'On passing through Prague we made every effort to find you and we sent a hired servant repeatedly to your flat, to an engraver and to other people where it was thought you may have been. You were, however, not to be found and probably not informed that we were leaving the next day before 6 o'clock in the morning. We are sorry we missed you.'

This letter then goes on to ask Clemens' advice regarding the education of Franz' son, Georg. See Maynard Solomon, *Beethoven Essays* p. 187. The fact that Franz' first paragraph in his letter of 6th October takes up this point indicates that Clemens' letter of October 1st was in direct reply to this letter of July 12 and that no other correspondence had intervened. Clemens' letter of 1st October is not known.

2   Wienden 6 8ᵇᵉʳ 1812
Lieber Clemens!
Ich erhielt dein Schreiben vom 1 O. es freut mich daß es mit deiner Gesundheit beßer geht, mit geduld kann man in der Welt das Ende von jedem übel erleben: es that mir leid dich in Prag nicht zu treffen, deine gegenwart hätte mich sehr aufgeheitert, ich bedurfte es, weil meine Toni auch daselbst noch sehr leidend war; ich danke dir herz-

lich für deinen freundlich Rath in ansehung der Erziehung meines Sohnes, du hast in allem Recht.
. . .

in 4 oder 5 wochen sobald Toni ganz wohl ist ziehen wir wieder nach Haußé, ich überlaße Georg das ganze Haußé, u. wohne in einem andern, ruhig und isoliert vonden übrigen dortigen bewohnern, u. da wird es mit der Erziehung schon gehen wie ich hoffe, wenn man nur einen Sohn hat, dann ist man doppelt aufmerksam, das beste wenigstens zu versuchen, u. ich bin schon eine geraume zeit nicht ganzwohl, u. kanndieses Clima nicht wohl vertragen, ich hoffe aber am Rhein wieder meine alte Gesundheit zu erlangen.
. . .

Wenn nicht meine nahe Rück reise auf die hoffentlich nahe Herstellung der Gesundheit meiner Frau berechnet würde, so würde ich dich zu uns einladen, wo du bei uns wohnen könntest, mich treibt es aber gewaltig nach Haußé, u. mein irrendes unruhiges leben dauert schon zu lange.
. . .

du gehest nach Berlin, grüse mir da alles hehrzlich wie ich immer fühlte, aber gelegenheitlich sage auch Bettina unter 4 augen, daß sie in Töplitz über mich u. Toni ja viel liebevoller vor fremden hätte sprechen sollen − unser ganzes Leben war Liebe und wohlwollen gegen sie, u. wird es auch bleiben − aber ich bitte dich, nur unter vier Augen.
Meine Kinder werden gros, u. machen mich alt, doch bleibt meine liebe zu all meinen geschwistern stets jugendlich, denn Franz bleibt sich ewig gleich

Vienna, 6th October 1812

Dear Clemens!

I received your letter of O(ctober) the 1st. I'm pleased that your health is improving. Patience eventually sees the end of every trouble in this world. I was sorry not to see you in Prague, your presence would have cheered me up considerably. I had need of this because my Toni was also very ill there; I thank you cordially for your friendly advice as regards the education of my son, you are completely right.
(Next few lines concern his son's education, about which Franz had asked advice in his letter of July 15th.)
. . . in 4 or 5 weeks time, as soon as Toni is completely well, we shall return home again, I am letting Georg have the whole house and shall live in another one, peaceful and isolated from the other inhabitants there and his education will proceed as I hope. If one has only one son one must be twice as careful at least to attempt the best for him and I have been already unwell for a lengthy time, being unable to bear this climate. I hope to regain my former state of health once I am back in the Rhineland.
(Next paragraphs deal with art and manuscripts)
If my impending return journey was not determined by the restoration of my wife's health (which I hope is not far off), I would invite you here where you could stay with us. However, I feel a powerful urge to return home and my restless wanderings have lasted too long already.
(Next paragraph: dealings about money)
You are going to Berlin. Greet everybody there cordially as was my wont, but when the occasion offers itself tell Bettina privately that she should have spoken much more lovingly in Teplitz about Toni and me in front of strangers − our entire life has consisted of love for and benevolence towards her and will remain so − but I entreat you to tell her only in private.
My children are growing up and make me feel old but my love for all my brothers and sisters remains young, for Franz never changes.

Extracts from this letter, differing significantly in translation in the first paragraph, appear in Maynard Solomon, 'Antonie Brentano & Beethoven' p. 162; *Beethoven* p. 183; and *Beethoven Essays* pp. 177-8.

3 'Du hast mir bey dem Tod meines ersten Kindes geschrieben, noch stand ich blutend an der öden Wiege, ins Grab senkte sich mein Blick, du ließest mich nicht versinken, so

schriebst du, daß ich es dir ewig gedenken werde.' This letter is interesting also in that the preceding sentence reads: 'Lasse nicht das Gute sinken was durch geistige Mittheilung leuchtet und wärmt.' 'Don't let the radiant and warming good things die away that spiritual communication provides.' Given the date at which this was written, and its association of 'radiant and warming good things' with the spiritual, and in the context that she was here writing about children (her own four, Bettina's child due in May, and her own dead first child), this may be taken as some indication that Antonie Brentano was at this time ready to have another child.

Further quotations from this letter occur in Solomon, 'Antonie Brentano & Beethoven' p. 160; *Beethoven* p. 180; and *Beethoven Essays* p. 174.

4 Ich brauche die hiesigen Bronnen für meine Gesundheit die gelitten hatte, u. werde noch einige Zeit hier u. in Eger bleiben, dann über dorten zurückreisen.

5 Franz grüßt dich, eine Art von Hipochondrie in die er seit mehreren Wochen verfiel machte mich bange, es geht aber besser, und bald hoffe ich, ganz gut.

6 Bettina von Arnim to Achim von Arnim, letter of 1 September 1830, from Rödelheim, in *Achim und Bettina in ihren Briefen – Briefwechsel Achim von Arnim und Bettina Brentano*, ed. Werner Vordtriede, (Frankfurt: Insel/1961) vol. 2 p. 895: 'Georg, her bad egg of a son, is so impudent as to make his own father an object of ridicule in public. Thus he recently invited several of his dissolute young friends to witness how he would go up to his father in company and tweak his nose without the father taking it amiss – something he actually carried out. He tells the whole town the man is crazy or simple-minded and provides the proof of it.'

7 *ibid*. Arnim to Bettina from Winkel, 8 November 1820, vol.1 p. 244. A Beethoven letter of 1820 (Anderson 1011 of 9th March) suggests that he is giving a new Frankfurt address to Simrock. The new mansion was at 22 Neue Mainzerstraße.

8   July 6, in the morning
My angel, my all, my very self, only a few words today, and those but in pencil – yours – Only tomorrow will my lodgings be definitely settled – what a worthless waste of time on such things! – Why this deep sorrow when necessity speaks? Can our love endure except through sacrifices – through not craving everything? Can you change the fact that you are not wholly mine and I am not wholly yours? – O God, look into fair nature and calm your heart over that which must be – Love demands all and rightly so – *so it is for me with you and for you with me*. If only you do not forget that I must live *for myself and for you*. – Were we wholly united, you would feel this pain as little as I. – My journey was terrible – I only reached here at four o'clock yesterday morning. Being short of horses the mail-coach chose another route, but what an awful one! At the stage before the last they warned me against travelling at night and put me in fear of a forest, but that only provoked me to go on – and I was wrong. The coach must needs break down on the dreadful road, a bottomless unsurfaced country road! Without four such postillions as I had I should have remained stuck on the road. Esterhazy had the same fortune with eight horses on the other usual road here as I had with four. – Yet in part I had some pleasure from it, as I always do if I come through some trouble. Now for a swift change to internal things from external! We shall surely see each other very soon; also today I cannot communicate to you the thoughts I have had concerning my life during these few days – Were our hearts always close together, I should have none of these. My heart is full of many things to say to you. – Ah! There are moments when I find that speech is nothing at all. – Cheer up – remain my faithful only treasure, my all as I am yours. The rest the gods must send, what for us must, and shall be –
                                                    Your faithful Ludwig.

                                                    Evening, Monday 6 July
You are suffering, you, my dearest creature – I have just learned that letters must be posted early in the morning on Mondays – and Thursdays – the only days when the mail-coach goes from here to K. You are suffering – Ah! Wherever I am, you are with me; with me and with you I talk, contrive that I can live with you! What a life!!! Thus!!! Without you – pursued hither and thither by the goodness of mankind, which I wish to deserve just as little as I do deserve it. Humility of man towards man – it pains me – and when I consider myself in relation to the universe, what I am and what is He

– whom one calls the Greatest! And yet – herein lies the divine in man – I weep when I think that you will probably receive the first news of me only on Saturday – However much you love me – I love you still more – Yet do not ever conceal yourself from me – Good night! As one taking the cure, I must go to bed. Ah God! – So near! So far! Is not our love a true structure of Heaven? And as firm as the firmament of Heaven –

Good morning, on July 7

Though still in bed, my thoughts press on to you, my immortal beloved, now and then with joy, and then again anxiously, waiting on fate to learn whether it will hear us. I can live only wholly with you or not at all. Yes, I have resolved to wander far far away until I can fly into your arms and call myself altogether at home with you and send my soul enwrapped by you into the realm of spirits. Yes, unfortunately it must be. You will be the more easy as you come to know my faithfulness to you. No other can ever possess my heart – never! – never! O God, why should the object of such love have to leave? And so my life in Vienna is now a wretched life – Your love brings me at once to the happiest and unhappiest condition. At my age I need steadiness and uniformity in my life – can this be so with our relationship?

– Angel, I have just heard that the post goes every day – so I must close so that you may receive the letter straightaway. Be calm! Only through calm contemplation of our existence can we attain our purpose to live together – Be calm – love me! Today – yesterday – what tearful yearning for you – you – you – my life – my all! Farewell! O go on loving me – never misjudge the most faithful heart of your beloved

L

Ever thine
Ever mine
Ever ours.

9 Editha & Richard Sterba, *Beethoven & His Nephew* p. 104; *Beethoven* p. 187.
10 Anderson 374.
11 *Beethoven* p. 168
12 *ibid.* p. 166.
13 *Tagebuch* 107.
14 Thayer-Forbes p. 780; Anderson 1064.
15 ' . . . it is improbable that Beethoven would continue to revere a married woman following a sexual experience, whereas an unconsummated affair would lead to a sublimated idealization of the beloved.' 'Antonie Brentano & Beethoven' p. 162 n. 51; 'Oddly enough, however, by a circuitous route thickly paved with discretion and resignation, they ultimately arrived at an ideal Romantic love, an infinite yearning for an eternally postponed union, each moment of which was its own fulfillment.' *Beethoven Essays*, p. 184; 'I think it is prudent to regard the Immortal Beloved letter as having been written without knowledge of Antonie Brentano's pregnancy.' *ibid.* p. 183.

RAPTUS

Ich weiß, ich bin ein Künstler.

I know I am an artist.

Ludwig van Beethoven

Chapter 1

... and, from the way she had touched the deaf man on the arm and turned him round to acknowledge the riotous applause that had greeted his *scherzo*, Karl knew that he had slept with her.

... Young enough to be his daughter! *My* age! How *could* she!

He didn't even like her now, after that 'vomitative' business when they'd been rehearsing the 9th, and her holding up rehearsals with her toothache.

But *he*, that *old man*, had *had her*. She, his own age, wouldn't even look at *him*!

Karl glared at the top of Unger's head as she wrote in the book while Beethoven read as she wrote and Sontag, the sedate one, went on quietly eating.

They dined in the Prater: his thank-you meal he had said for the contribution they'd made to his concert.

Since his jaundice three years ago, the broad leonine nose had become more pointy; Karl sometimes thought of him as rat-nose. ... This dirty old man, who grew sick, his skin in winter often the colour of cow-hide, half-blind last year as well as deaf, with bloated belly inside a truss and eyes rolled upwards exposing the yellowed whites; this more than ugly, *revolting* man with his disgusting habits: spitting into his *hand*, examining the mucus for blood: this fat yellow rat with its expanding body and shrinking head; and these talented beautiful girls of his own age cast not a glance at *him* but threw themselves, kissing and loving, all over *this*!

And he not even with the sense to see it was *for what they could get out of him*! Careers on the line! Sing one *part* by *Beethoven* and they were *made*. Famous for ever. Blast the man! Damn the yellow rat! And damn them too, for not looking at *him*! And curse even *Niemetz* for saying, 'Well what would you have him do? You'd be the first to call him, if he didn't look at girls.'

The contralto had visited him in Baden with Sontag, the soprano, in September 1822. They had wanted to kiss his hands; laughing, he had embraced each one in turn, offering her his mouth. 'One of them was all right, she was kissing him but it was just ordinary. The other one was really kissing him, pressing herself ... I mean, he is my *uncle*, I was *sixteen!*' Sitting in that room, bursting out of his skin for her. *She* had been high as a kite as well. Playing along with B all afternoon, going and sitting next to him; not even *pretending* to be shocked, *laughing*, when he had told them, 'If you'd come in here one at a time you'd have got more than you bargained for!'

He had had to write to his uncle Johann, at B's dictation, telling him of the incident. The filthy bastard had made him write, 'I offered them my mouth to kiss,' cackling helplessly, 'Add, add: "This is the shortest piece of news we can give you"'! He had topped it all by signing himself, 'guardian of my little rascal who is a minor'!

There had been more jokes about Unger a few months later when Bernard had told B he was a rival and what's more they both had another rival, a youth of 24. Bernard had given her a present so *rat* had sent her one. Schindler had brought back the message that B's acclaim and affection meant more to her than all the 24 year olds in Vienna. . . . The *rat*, at the time his tailor was taking him to court for unpaid bills, preening before them in new trousers, Mr Shitting simpering, 'O the cut is just right, the colour is very fashionable!' . . . The singer sending messages, 'She is always alone, no one's visiting her.' His uncle's bawled laugh, 'Well *I'll* visit!' He had bought a new body-belt to pull his fat belly in for her. S had called him 'an unrepentant sinner.'

The two girls had pursued him mercilessly, particularly Unger: inviting him for carriage rides, nagging him to write an opera for her. 'You ought to marry – perhaps you'd become more diligent!' Telling him that she was a virgin. Virgin! *That* one! ' . . . until I decide otherwise.' He had nothing against Sontag. It could even be argued that Sontag was better looking. But Sontag was younger, Sontag was more demure, Sontag was shorter and Sontag lived with her mother in Mödling. Unger might claim virginity but Schindler had got her bang to rights when he'd called her 'a devil of a girl!'

When Beethoven had finally won control of him from his mother in 1820, the old man had seemed to be losing his grip: debts, ill-health, jaundice, rheumatism. Since then he had finished the Mass, the Symphony, the piano sonatas . . . was being asked for quartets . . . the day after the concert, he had been at work on some bagatelles. Karl felt resentment as he recalled how B could twist them all round his finger about that concert: threatening to give the new works in Berlin. They had all come running. They all crawled to him. He had but to snap his fingers.

He was not an excessively fleshy man but one was aware of the flesh on him: the way he put his hand up to rub his eye, his old brow heavily wrinkling. His hand was often to his face, to the side of his head, for still as an old man he seemed to search for his lost hearing. Decker had made a sketch of him after the concert. The pain of his life showed through the eyes. Karl despite himself thought this.

B used to cut off the top hair himself, just to stop it falling into his eyes. The back hair at such times grew long and, though there was no bald patch but only a thinning, at the temples the hair was noticeably receding. Usually he shaved for portraits or was shown by the painter as having done so, so that the most striking previous example, by Wald-müller, for whom he sat for 5 minutes, showed him with his back hair as long as a woman's, a shaved chin, and a face the outer rim of which was the sole feature to have been drawn from the life.

It was after his jaundice of 1821 that he had got fat and floppy and worn a body-belt which he never could get to fit him. It had been over his requests to Lind to fit him for this that he had been threatened with being taken to court and had had to sell a bank-share to pay his debts. Karl had complained that he had even tried to get him to see to the adjustments he needed to his underpants.

Used to seeing B with his clothing unbrushed, his hair dishevelled, never attended by brush or comb and rarely by scissors, seldom it seemed washed save for the water that he poured over it to cool himself down after composition, Karl had been astonished by the transformation as he stood on the stage before his orchestra: dark tail-coat and trousers, knee-length hose, his hair cut and combed . . . The old bastard had even tried to get the medal from the King of France over his collar. It weighed half a pound in gold! 'It pulls my collar down . . .' When the Royal Academy of Music of Sweden had elected him to foreign membership, B had had this published in the papers, despite wryly claiming to pay no heed to such distinctions.

. . . He only had to play the piano and the silly bitches went weak at the knees. Karl was again torn, for he himself had been moved to extremity by his uncle's playing. He had once heard his uncle's booming laugh, spurning her, 'None of that with this one! As far as I'm concerned, this Mass is being played for *my son.*'

Why do I need a Mass? he had thought irately. As far as he knew, his uncle still held the same attitude towards religion that had led to such trouble when he'd been in Father Fröhlich's class in Mödling in 1818. 'Priests! *Parsons!*' Unger had not been able to resist letting Sontag know that she had seen him. 'Isn't it nice – he says as far as he's concerned this Mass is being given for his son.' 'Do you like his son?' 'That boy of his fancies himself. Well he's not really his, is he?'

. . . Sitting with it up to his ears, the girls ignoring him . . . That night, *hearing* his uncle: the horror of finding his own grunts, thrusts, threshing *tying-in.*

And then there had been that incident when the yellow rat had accused him of 'making an indecent gesture' against him. He had always been a prude. . . . Randy as hell, hard as a crow-bar, no *money* – to get a girl, to take her for cakes and coffee – and *he*, the yellow rat, had thrown himself at him in 'the fond embrace' – that was suitable for a 2 year old, not a grown *man!* – and, finding him not a two year old but a grown man, had thrust him away in disgust, complaining that he had made an 'indecent gesture.' The bastard had brought it upon himself! When you throw yourself upon something that's as hard as a stone priapus . . .

Had he only dreamed or did it really happen that, while he had been playing the piano and Sontag had been singing, his uncle had pulled Unger onto his dirty, fat old knee and resumed fondling?

Several rehearsals of the solo singers had taken place at his rooms. Unger had called him to his face 'a tyrant over all the vocal organs.' Still he had refused to change a note. 'Well then,' she had exclaimed to Sontag, 'we shall just have to go on torturing ourselves in the name of God.'

At the final rehearsal on May 6th, they had all been shocked at how overtly B had been moved by the performance of the *Kyrie*. . . . What on earth had he meant, 'This Mass is being played for my son'? . . . This man who grabs you out of the blue and shakes you and throttles you, sometimes . . . No, he wasn't really rat-face. Only when he was ill, and he wasn't ill now. He was in his element. For weeks he had been praised. When happy his nose was broad, his whole face filled out.

Unger was teasing him, writing in his small book, 'What line have you set twice?'

'Set twice?'

'. . . in both your Opera and this new one?'

'*Fidelio*?'

'And the Symphony?'

'I don't know. What line have I?'

'*Wer ein holdes Weib errungen*!'

Beethoven laughed. 'So I did!'

He had made sketches during the 8th Symphony which he had used later for the *Namensfeier* Overture, into which he had once thought of setting portions of Schiller's *Ode*. *Ode to Freedom* as he remembered it: *Beggers become princes' brothers*; *All men become brothers* was a later version. In 1812 he had been owed money by those slovenly Princes – Lobkowitz, Kinsky. Only the Archduke had brought his annuity up to the new money standard, paying in silver from the time of the devaluation. Kinsky had died from a fall from his horse in November 1812; Lobkowitz had gone bankrupt in 1813; he had had to drag both *noble* families through the courts.

Karl had begun talking to the girls about his beloved Schiller, so he wrote for his uncle. They were going on about *Alle Menschen*, Unger even apparently threatening to sing it if that waiter didn't look lively. Beethoven had turned from the book, his mind full of 1812, when he had been writing the 8th, with A, in Franzensbad. *Alle Menschen werden Brüder*! It was the line before that that they overlooked, he thought dryly. He had, without realizing, altered Schiller's *streng* to *frech*, so that instead of 'what custom sternly separated' he had set

Your magic re-unites
What custom impudently separated.

There were other parallels they hadn't spotted: the treatment of the *Ihr stürtz nieder, Millionen?* of the Symphony and the *Praeludium* of the Mass, where the congregation kneels during the consecration ... blast them, they hadn't played the *Sanctus*. Blast the censor. ... Checking copies of the Mass: 'From the heart – may it go to the heart,' he had written on the top of the *Kyrie*. He had begun the *Kyrie* when he had heard from Toni ... she had written to Sailer ... The tenderness in the women's 'Amens' at the end of the *Credo*. 'Prayer for inner and outer peace,' he had written on the score of the *Agnus Dei*.

... One of the great days of his life: coming up with that solo fiddle for the *Sanctus*. After jotting the idea he'd been preparing his coffee, singing a spontaneously made-up song:

My first coffee of the day
I'm making it good and strong
I like it a lot that way
I hope that it don't go wrong

bending down for his cup, creasing up at the merry idiocy of what he was singing. If you don't fall on your knees with tears in your eyes during the *Sanctus Benedictus* then they're not playing it or you're not listening. ... *Sanctus, Sanctus*. And sing it with awe, you bastards. He had stood on that stage fully alive in the music, thinking of Karl as well as his God, praying of one to the other; Falstaff with all his weight and paunch leading the fiddles, the instrument lost in this welter of flesh, seeming too small for the man, though he played as lustily as his namesake boozed, wenched and feasted.

There had been furore before the concert, because he had wanted Falstaff as the leader. Furore before that, when he had approached Count Brühl about putting on a concert in Berlin, whereupon his Viennese friends had co-signed a long eulogistic letter begging that the new works be premiered in their city. In it they had bemoaned 'that shallowness is abusing the name and insignia of art, and unworthy dalliance with sacred things is beclouding and dissipating appreciation of the pure and eternally beautiful.' He had taken this to be a reference to the brain-storming of Vienna by Rossini.

'Do not delay longer to lead us back to those departed days when the song of Polyhymnia moved powerfully and delighted the initiates of art and the hearts of the multitude! Need we tell you with what regret your retirement from public life has filled us? ... the *one man* whom all of us are compelled to acknowledge as foremost among living men in his domain ...'

They had all signed it: Prince Lichnowsky, Artaria, Diabelli, Castelli, Carl Czerny, Count Moritz Lichnowsky, Steiner, Streicher, his old friend Zmeskall, the first he had told about Karl Josef ... others who were less friends: Abbé Stadler, who revered above all others Mozart; Anton Halm, of whose playing of the Choral Fantasia he had remarked that 'Not every

stalk has ears of corn!' . . . Theatre directors like Palffy; Dietrichstein, who
had tried to get him the post of Imperial Royal *Kapellmeister*; his banker
friend, Fries, whose payments from George Thomson in 1813 of nearly
£200 had led him to believe that he had enough money to go to Frankfurt
and *marry her*. . . . Giving the £200 to his sick brother: showering ducats
over the bed. That had led to the business of the will, his getting Karl . . . *I
don't believe this*! *You* bought *each other's sons*!

They had published the letter, and people said he himself had been
behind it. His anger had doubled since that was the sort of thing that he
never had done, would never do – would never *think* of doing.

He had never had a concert that was more difficult to arrange. Should
it be in the *Theater-an-der-Wien*, whose director, Palffy, had been one of the
signatories of his letter and who was prepared to let him have the theatre
for 1,200 fl W.W. for lease of the house, the entire orchestra, and the opera
company? But he had never trusted Palffy since his concert at the time of
the Congress, when only the intervention of the Czarina had stopped
Palffy snatching back all his profits. Besides, at his theatre Seyfried was
Kapellmeister and Clement leader, whilst Beethoven wanted Umlauf, with
whom he had co-conducted before, and the leader's post he had promised
to his fat friend Schuppanzigh, whom he called *Falstaff*. Falstaff had led
Razumovsky's quartet until 1815; for several years until 1823 he had been
in Russia; he had returned fatter than ever but full of enthusiasm for the
developments he had heard of in new bows. Schindler had meanwhile
begun negotiations with Duport for the *Kärnthnerthor* Theatre. Here there
were no such problems about *Kapellmeister* or leader, but disagreements
had sprung up about the ticket prices, solo singers and the number of
rehearsals.

Advisers piled on him from all sides: Schindler, Lichnowsky, Falstaff;
brother Johann and nephew Karl. All his friends became involved:
'Piringer has said he will undertake the appointment of the instrument-
alists. Sonnleithner the chorus. Falstaff the orchestra. Blahetka the
announcements. So everything is looked after. You can give 2 concerts.'

. . . That dastardly business when Lichnowsky, Schindler and Falstaff
had 'accidently' dropped in at the same time and tricked him into signing
his affirmation to a list of points . . . He had seen through their ruse and
had dashed off 3 letters: 'I despise treachery. Visit me no more. There will
be no concert.'

All that talk about 'receipts would be 4000 fl . . . profit of 2000 fl for first
concert, 3000 fl for second.' And here he was, all that time and effort,
penniless! Bad as the Mass! They had promised him then he could earn
some grand sum – *peanuts*, after the copying!

Why do I let myself listen to these silly sods and their bad advice!
Ignorant! Treacherous! Land me in it! *My* money down the drain! *My*
precious time!

Everyone telling him that the concert must take place in Lent were he to make money. Clement had objected to standing down for Falstaff and his orchestra had sided with him. To-ing and fro-ing between *four* theatres, until the final decision to hold the concert at the *Kärnthnerthor*, Duport's theatre. The theatre manager had even had to apply to the Minister of Police to raise the ticket prices, and even then permission had been refused. He had thought that he had been getting this theatre for 400 fl, but now his terms were 1000 fl, chorus and orchestra and lighting included, option of 1 or 2 repeat performances on the same terms within 8-10 days. The copying alone was costing him 800 fl. At times 10 copyists worked in his rooms. Haslinger had wanted him to go in for engraving; after a flaming row he had agreed to let him lithograph the chorus parts. The orchestra was being augmented by amateurs from the *Gesellschaft – Fiends* of music. 24 violins, 10 violas, 12 contrabasses and 'cellos; the number of wind instruments doubled.

The censor had objected to church works being sung in a theatre. He had had to write to the censor, saying that only 3 sections of the Mass were to be performed and calling them '3 hymns'. They had already been copied. The costs had mounted. He had written to Schindler, 'I feel cooked, stewed and roasted. What is to be the outcome if ticket prices are not to be raised? What will be left for me after such heavy expenses?'

Beggers shall be princes' brothers! *Composers* shall be *beggers'* brothers, more like! His own plea to the censor to allow three parts of the Mass had been unsuccessful; Count Lichnowsky had had to appeal to Count Sedlnitzky, Chief of Police. By the time they had equivocated over subscription sales of the boxes and stalls, and whether to settle for Forti, who could handle the Symphony but not the Mass, or Preisinger, ideal for the Mass but no good for the Symphony, he had found himself in a position where, under Duport, he was limited to 5 or 6 choral rehearsals, with only 2 for the orchestra! And all the time Lent had been passing, the costs had been mounting, and everyone tried to pull to himself his own share of self-aggrandisement.

He had ended up with gross receipts of 2200 fl W.W. of which only 420 fl remained after the cost of administration and copying, with some minor expenses still outstanding. When he had accused the management and Schindler of swindling him, they had tried to tell him that the two theatre cashiers' receipts tallied and that Karl himself had been in charge of the box office! Schindler had told him the day after the concert, 'After yesterday you must now clearly see that you are trampling on your own interests by remaining here. I have no words to express my feelings at the wrong which you are doing to yourself.' In other words, *travel* so as to *make money*. That was what I set out to do in the first place!

They had had a meal, here in *zum wilden Mann*, two days after the concert, and it had ended up in another great row: he accusing Schindler and Duport; Falstaff sticking up for Schindler; the fiddler Böhm or one of them saying, 'I don't know why you ever give him responsibility.' Karl had told him Johann had said he was just waiting till after the concert to get rid of Schindler. He himself had told Karl last year not to gossip about S. 'He is sufficiently punished by being what he is.'

Beethoven had later written that he did not accuse Schindler of any wrongdoing but thought that he might be dangerous. 'Stopped-up sluices may overflow quickly ... I fear lest some great misfortune should some day happen to me through you.' He said he would rather reward his services with the odd present than have him eat with him. 'If you don't see a cheery face you mouth, "Bad weather again today." ... I love my independence too much.' ... Given up A, to be lumbered with *Schindler*!

In the midst of abusing Schindler, he sent him off on a fresh errand to Duport. Duport, who knew nothing of music but only of dancing, had again refused to allow the singers to perform in the *Landstächer Saal*, which he could have had already for the second concert. Duport, that *ballerina*, who had had the nerve to offer him the *small hall*! And he and that *Mr Shitting* had been in cahoots, trying to swindle ... Johann had estimated that with the proceeds from the concert he could repay his debt to Steiner 'and still have 2000 fl W.W. left over for the summer.' And now they were wanting him to give *another* concert! This time including *Rossini*!

He looked down to read what was being thrust before him. Karl had apparently been detailing for the girls the discrepancies between Schiller's Ode and his uncle's version. 'For instance,' he wrote, 'that you did not set the last strophe.' In 1812, when he had been thinking of setting this when he was with Toni, he had still been using the first version of Schiller's poem.

> Rescue from tyrants' bonds,
> Generosity even to the scoundrel,
> Hope on the deathbed,
> Mercy on the gallows!

'I've written an opera about that,' he told them and, when Unger protested that she hadn't seen much mercy to Pizzaro in *Fidelio*, stopped her with, 'So you two girls want to sing about tumbrils?'

He had planned to set Schiller when he was a boy in Bonn, he had wanted to start his 9th Symphony in 1812. A fugue which had found its way into the *scherzo* had occurred to him in 1815, when he had been writing Linke's 'cello sonatas. ... Telling Countess Erdödy, Linke's employer ... He tried to put such thoughts out of his mind.

He had thought up the fugue theme again two years later, when he had written the short fugue for string quintet. 1817, Karl Josef's illness ... He had even made sketches for the first movement then. He had had plans for vocal parts in the finale of a symphony while drafting thoughts on an *Adagio Cantique* when he had been composing the *Hammerklavier* piano sonata. The slow movement of that: writing to his own navel, composing for himself alone. He recalled telling A of the *Eroica*, 'Sometimes a work of art has to save a life.'

. . . And in the middle of last year in the middle of the symphony he had written down a *melodie* in D-minor which he had called *Finale instrumental*. He startled them by abruptly announcing, 'I'm still in two minds about that whole choral finale.'

The girls looked at him as though he'd said he was going to kill his granny. He tapped Unger's nose, glaring, not without amusement, 'There's times when a man wishes he could still write for castrati!'

He had sunk into gloom again after announcing, 'What can you do in a country where on the stage even the word *liberty* is forbidden!' Unger was remembering that poor deaf sweetie trying to conduct, bobbing down behind the podium so they could not see him at *piano*, jumping up with his arms raised at *fortissimo*. All the orchestra, choir and soloists had been told to ignore him and follow the direction of Umlauf.

. . . Haslinger had told her that he'd even signed himself once *Mi contra Fa* – the Devil in music! He had refused to alter a note, not even the B-flat entry for the sopranos in the *Credo, et vitam* fugue. 'You can sing it,' he'd told them. 'You'll sing it.' She had been agitating to get him to give a concert for longer than anyone. 'Who says they won't like it? They'll love it! O, *obstinate one!*' The force in his music was overwhelming. Not only force: anger, *objection*. That was what she had meant when she had told him, 'When one is *once* possessed by the devil, then one can be content.'

Unger was teasing Beethoven. Karl was annoyed. Look at the old bloke, laughing and eating, chatting up two birds who were young enough to be his *granddaughters*. If they knew some of the things that were going on when B was writing his 'brotherhood' symphony! . . . Turning up at Blöchlinger's, wanting to collect him, as though he had been in kindergarten, wanting to walk arm in arm or to hold hands. Other students had laughed. I'm a grown man! He remembered complaining to Niemetz, 'He will never let you *show* love to him. He always grabs first. He never waits.' . . . Turning up at Blöchlinger's in that tall, broad-brimmed hat, in winter a black 'spenser' worn over his frock-coat. The other boys had laughed at B's clothes, particularly the way his bushy hair stuck out from beneath that broad-brimmed hat. He could still recall his uncle, standing in a recess by the classroom window, the vein in his temple pulsating, 'My name is known all over Europe; don't you *dare* besmirch my name!'

He had left Blöchlinger's in August last year and moved in with his uncle, then spending his summer at Baden. He was stone-deaf. Everything had to be written down. He went round with a small *Konversationsheft* in one pocket, a small sketchbook in another. At home he kept a slate for visitors. When he worked his conversation book was often left outside his room so that people could leave messages. He left these books lying around. Karl could always read what was going on.

He had written reams when he had first moved in with his uncle, but Beethoven did not seem to be grateful and Karl had found that he often *spoke* to no single human being all day. At times it had seemed to him that his uncle had craved to be back in his old isolation. The man would go whole days without food, partly because of his disordered stomach, forgetting that he, Karl, needed to eat. B would give him lists of errands for the following day, trips to Hertzendorf from Baden, but would not even wake him up – so long as *he* was up and at his desk, working, no thought that anyone else wanted time for breakfast or even to use the bathroom. And as for the sexual thing – no time let alone privacy if he woke up with an erection.

B had been deaf for so long and was now so profoundly deaf that he could not always articulate. Friends of long standing had kept up with the change, but this, coupled with the strong Rhenish accent which he had never lost and his sarcastic adoption over the years of the Viennese dialect, made him the most difficult man for his servants to understand. Before he had reached his seventeenth birthday, Karl had been helping his uncle to get the household under some sort of control.

B was always suspicious when he saw laughter, like the time Karl had gone to the privy but, unable to stand the stench of the perfume the girl used to scent the room, had covered his nose with his hanky declaiming, 'I'd sooner have the stink of the privy than this!' Seeing them both laughing, B had assumed that they were laughing at him.

The very first day he'd been with B, after he'd left Blöchlinger's, just before his seventeenth birthday, there had been a fight in which B had shouted, 'One more word out of you and you'll go to your mother.' At that Karl had exploded: 'One more word: *YOU GO TO MOTHER!*' Karl had been shocked out of his skin: that very first morning, B had been going on about the importance of honesty and feeling; the young man had wholeheartedly agreed; at first he had believed that he was being blamed for not showing greater joy at leaving Blöchlinger's and all his friends. He had *told* him his stay at Blöchlinger's had been 'a sad time,' during which only Niemetz had befriended him.

Beethoven let his suspicions fester; he never gave any indication of his anger before the row and, only when Karl had thought the altercation over, Beethoven's anger had burst out in full force. It was that day he had realized that, every time that he went into town, let alone spent a night in town, B believed that he was seeing prostitutes.

The following month he had invited his friend Niemetz to visit them in Baden. The boy was poor but good-hearted. B had hated him. 'This is not the friend for you!' Karl had stood up for his friend. 'I love him as I should love a brother if I had one.' B had become obsessed by the thought that he took up with older women. B had even suspected Niemetz of having designs on the housekeeper – old Frau Schnaps, who was fifteen years older than B!

In good mood Karl addressed his uncle as Bester! To N he was not above calling him Bestie. 'This boy is not the friend for you.' 'He is poor. The poor are not to be dispised.' 'No, the poor are not to be dispised, but just because a man is poor does not always mean that he is worthy.' He had been narked that Niemetz was there at all when, as per usual, he had had no time for visitors and wanted to get on with his bloody symphony.

... B and his other uncle and his uncle's friends and this that or the other co-guardian, all with their own separate notions for him: be a doctor, like me; don't stop there, young man: be a surgeon – that last from *Staudenheim*, who, as he had told B, 'Did not cure my father.' ... Follow your father into business ... your uncle into music ... your other uncle into apothecary.

He had tried to save his uncle money by persuading him to travel or at least let *him* travel in a public coach for 1 fl. instead of always hiring a private coach between Baden and Vienna for about 10 fl.

B's housekeeping was bad and far too costly; he chopped and changed servants far too often; many were dense; one maid had got pregnant; several cheated him; those who were honest grew indignant when B accused them of cheating. One of these girls had not wanted to empty the night chamber-pot because it stank; Karl had taken her severely to task.

B spent too much on drink for other people. He seemed to think that this was hospitality, though in fact he pressed some too earnestly to partake of more than they liked and they grew drunk or miserable. B asked his opinion of the soup then disagreed violently when he said that he thought that it tasted all right, apart from having too much water.

Funnily enough he didn't mind drinking – he had always done enough of it himself. Karl at first had been cautious. 'I would sooner see water in my glass than wine.' He had told him of a composer they had entertained. 'Eckschlager got so drunk when he dined with you that, when he met someone in the street who asked him about something, he took a paper from his pocket and wrote down the answer, thinking that he was still talking to you!' Then Karl himself had got drunk and had let him have it. That had taken pages to explain. He had had to call him 'My dearest Father! ... I promise you that I will never drink another drop of wine again ... What kind of a man would I be if I had the intention of hurting you? I won't drink any more wine, that's certain, because that was the cause of my breakdown and I didn't know where I was. Once again I beg you, forgive me!'

A day or so after that, when he had been running round doing errands for him all day, only to find that some ducats were less than full value and the restaurant cook couldn't make stuffing for just one chicken, Karl had exploded at his uncle's complaints. 'I don't know why you find fault with me every minute.'

His old uncle fell asleep after his meal, woke up with a start grumbling,

'Where is my conversation book?' as though, seeing him there, he wanted him to start straight away.

Nor was he entitled to any opinions. 'Only mediocre people can become rich,' he had written, 'because they rarely stop at any means to reach their goal.' B would often put him down. 'You're too young to know what's what.' 'Does the truth always have to have a white beard if it is to be believed?'

In November he had gone to University to read Philosophy and Philology under Stein. Karl regarded Stein as a pedant; Beethoven, who had called upon the Professor for backing at the time of his litigation with Karl's mother over his custody, viewed him as a worthy man. Karl grew annoyed by his uncle's rigid attitude. He had gone into details of his notions of classical and modern Greek pronunciation, and of Latin. Later he had gone into even greater philological detail, only to hear his uncle declaim that the man must be distinguished, he was a Professor at Vienna University.

'He could be far less in order to be a Professor at Vienna University!'

Karl had told his uncle, trying to make a joke of it, 'From Monday I am going to read Philosophy, so I beg you to honour me accordingly.' And what had happened? The man had accompanied him to the University and, in front of a fellow student, criticized Karl's study arrangements. Karl had seen the boy pull a face. 'He won't keep it to himself, and then it will be said that you are making me into a traitor and other such niceties. That's how Stein thinks.'

His uncle had complained that he did not see enough of him. He had told him that they would be dining together three times a week. His uncle had still had him running around dealing with the subscription copies of the Mass even between university studies.

The man would quibble about spending money even when it was that Psychology book by Feder that he really needed. Yet he recalled as a boy seeing his uncle dance a jig for joy when he had got from the Archduke's or Lobkowitz' library something pertinent to his studies of the Mass.

And yet the old fool wanted him to excel, liked best when he could show him off: like some trained dog he was expected to get on his hind legs and come up with some Greek riddle designed to impress.

Yet he was fast enough to pull down others. Once when he'd brought up Cherubini's name, telling his uncle with some amusement that that composer had grown mad when some other man's opera had been chosen in preference to his, B had just sniffed, 'Man isn't writing as much these days.' Karl had picked up the pencil and told him, 'Wait another 20 years: you won't be writing as fast any more either!'

Karl had told his uncle, 'Salieri has cut his throat, but he is still alive.' His uncle's main concern was whether the man's post was up for grabs. 'Your *great grandfather* was a *Kapellmeister*!'

He had got caught up in his uncle's financial problems. B still owed

Steiner money and the publisher had begun to cut Karl when they regularly passed in the street. Bernard had also been cool towards him at a concert. B had not yet set his oratorio. 'It's *me* that they cut,' he told Niemetz. 'Neither one of those stooges has the nerve to cut *him*.'

Even when he'd found his uncle a good new housekeeper, B had started off with suspicion before he had met her. 'She hasn't taken anything from us – if anything she's put in from her own money!' Karl had tried to reason with him. 'I think you really go too far with your mistrust.' They had even had one maid who went to bed fully dressed so as not to have to get dressed in the morning. One had taken to spitting 'Go to the devil!' in front of them, when she was to be sacked, that they had not left her in her previous post with a Countess. Karl had written of one maid, 'She was in bed; that was at 5.30. I thought she was ill but she said she was just lying down. I didn't like her from the start, because she talked very proudly; also she exposed her breast without covering it, on the contrary, she stretched herself up even more.'

. . . The evening when Schuppanzigh had visited. Karl had discovered that B called the fat man Falstaff and that B and the fat man used the third person singular form of address to each other. Falstaff had told him, 'It's short for Best*er*!' As they evening wore on and they all became more drunk, Karl had gleefully adopted this.

When the fat man had gone Karl had said, 'It's like Caesar: give me men about me who are *fat*!'

B, in his cups, had begun to grow rowdy. '*Taceas, amice*! Bester! You are waking people up!' He had done some more sums for him. B had grown maudlin, complaining of neglect, taking up Falstaff's talk which reminded him of failed ambitions: a Mass for the Emperor, a complete edition of his works. 'How has my life turned out? This isn't what I expected. Thought that I could write music . . .' 'Bester! You need nothing!' B had turned rheumy, drink-reddened eyes on him. 'What about you? Eh? How'll you turn out? Made mistakes there, have I?' 'O, you are sure to be satisfied with me!' B had nearly knocked over his glass and now picked it up, holding it at a tilt, gazing into its depths. 'Bester! You can hold your liquor! Drink up!' Karl had wanted to go to bed.

'What else has been happening today?'

'Bester! I have already related all the events that have happened.'

'Where are you off to?'

'To bed!'

'You haven't said your prayers. You haven't said goodnight to me.'

He was always expected to kiss him goodnight, unless he fell asleep first. Whenever he stayed awake long enough, they still knelt and said their prayers together. B's always ended, 'And God bless Karl. Bless Karl.'

Instead of that B had complained that his ears were hurting then asked him to write down how much they had spent that day. Downing his glass, B had apparently decided to go to bed since he glared at the figures, said his ears were playing him up, he would not be able to sleep, then rambling, 'You love me, son? I haven't failed you!' pulled him to him in a drunken embrace.

It had been up to his ears and B had got the full force of it.

Hurling him off, calling the girl in, declaiming suspicions which must have been festering for days: the keys to the money-box; misplaced handkerchiefs; refusing to get Lind to adjust his underpants.

The girl in tears, trembling; Beethoven livid; he abruptly dropping the 'ihr' and 'Bester.' 'Obscene little prat! You! Love me! *My son!*' Not even placated when he had written, 'I do love you, more than I would my own father, if he were still alive.'   ·

The old bastard never stopped worrying about immorality. You'd think he'd got it on the brain. If it wasn't 'Have you got a girlfriend?' with glaring eyes and accusatory tone, it was, 'Can this housekeeper be trusted? Is she going to turn up with her fancy man?'

They were forever on the lookout for somebody old and ugly. 'She is past those years; besides, rather ugly than pretty, nothing to fear there.' They had leapt out of the frying pan into the fire when they'd sacked Frau Schnaps. 'At least you could always console the old woman with a glass of wine.' The young ones were trollops who painted their faces and poured perfume over themselves; the old ones were coffee-and-prayer sisters. 'The one in our house is terribly made-up. It's no good relying on such people, who wash themselves with perfumed water, because usually they will stoop to anything to satisfy these needs.' He was always on the look-out for a widow with a pension.

Karl had hated what he'd found at the University: that smart-arsed Stein whom his uncle had so revered; discovering that there was to be no philosophy at all for the first year; having to go to confession; not officially allowed to go into a coffee-house. Some of these tutors couldn't even keep order. 'Go to Professor Stein, you could hear a mouse.'

For a while things had seemed calmer. They had both made an effort to cut down on their drinking. Beethoven was immersed in the Symphony. Karl had found the books he needed in the University's library.

He was so touchy about his deafness. He seemed to think that was the only thing people remembered in connection with his name. Karl had mentioned a doctor who had said in public he wanted to cure him. 'Is that all they think about! *Deafness!*' – smashing the by-now thick manuscript hard against his desk.

'People don't say anything except that they want an opera. Nobody ever mentions deafness. You will see when you give a concert.' He had been improvising a lot at that time, it seemed to flow out from the Symphony; not the Symphony's themes but an overflow from it. He had always said that, when he was creative, rather than conserve his resources he had more to spare. 'If you improvise at the concert as you are doing today, the success would be fantastic.'

That was when they had sacked the servant they'd thought was pregnant. B knew about her lover; Karl had even been joking about it. He had gone on to tell him about some prankster at the University who had put a ball filled with gunpowder on the floor during the lecture of their 70 year old History professor so that it went off with a bang when it was accidentally trodden on. In the midst of all this B had suddenly gone mad, accusing him of having a relationship with their ex-servant, of being the father of her child.

'Come on, prove you're innocent! Prove it! Prove it!'

'Of course I can't prove to you that I have no relationship with her at all; I can't prove either that it is the truth when I say that I have no idea where she is living; even if there is much in me which ought to be different, I don't believe I have given you cause through my behaviour to think something like that about me: all the more so since you know how we have already talked about this point and, thank God! agreed about it, too.'

'You are a dirty young scoundrel!'

'That is a silly reproach.'

Karl was jerked from his reverie by Unger's laughing. Apparently she'd started in about 'vomitative.' The cruel little cow! Karl shot to feeling protective towards his uncle, who now looked downcast.

There had been a problem with the bass, in that the Mass was scored for bass but the Symphony required a baritone. Preisinger had been chosen above Forti. Beethoven had even changed the concluding passage of the recitative, because Preisinger could not sing the high F-sharp. Preisinger was the only one for whom he had re-written any part. Even after he'd re-written it, he couldn't sing it. '*Maestro*, it is outside my range.'

Beethoven had been present at that rehearsal. He had had half a mind to stand up and sing it himself. Can't write for singers, forsooth! 'Don't tell *me* what singers can do! I'm *descended* from professional singers!' His grandfather had been a bass, his father a tenor. He had set this for his own baritone. But the singer who stood before him was a bass: Preisinger, whose deep bass was just what he needed for the *Agnus Dei*.

He had told Umlauf to have him sing it again. He had seen the orchestra strike up, the string players raise their fiddles, the bass inhale and start to sing, and suddenly they had all stopped and they were *laughing*.

He was thunderstruck. They were howling. This was where he, not Schiller, had written the text. If they weren't laughing at his music, they were laughing at him for writing such silly words. He had turned from the howling mob in rage, in pain, in unspeakable agony. God had never before hit him here. God had blocked his ears, taken his wife and kid, made his son a retarded cripple. All the fighting of years caught up with him. God, now You've got them laughing at my *music*. So devastated was he that by the time Schindler caught up with him he had confused the

Mass with the Symphony, convinced that they had been jeering at his Mass.

Schindler had tried to tell him, grabbing someone's score and writing on the back, 'It's Unger! She's such a silly young thing! He'd made such an awful noise before, this time when he opened his mouth Unger shouted out, "From *Vomitative!*"'

Karl wanted to hit her. Fancy reminding him of that! He's made your damn name! You're eating his food! You deserve to stay singing fucking *Rossini!*

They had sacked Preisinger. It was too late to go back to Forti. Instead the nasal Seipelt had sung the part. Umlauf had made the sign of the cross over the orchestra as he walked onto the stage. . . . The visual impact of that concert, with everyone wondering, what the hell is he going to do with that lot, and when? B's old friend Zmeskall, crippled with gout, had been there in his sedan chair. The Giannatasio family, at whose school he had boarded when B had first taken him from his mother, had also been there. Above all, despite previous rumours to the contrary, the Imperial box had been occupied. The applause for B had been greater than that for the Imperial family, with cries of *Vivat!* and the Police Commissioner shouting, 'Order!' People had been fighting to get in at the box office.

Uncle Johann it had been who had pointed the finger at Schindler over the cash receipts. He had heard Uncle Johann saying, 'We want to get rid of Schindler before the second concert.' Schindler had once written down for B, 'Karl wants to write an opera under the title of Uncle Johann and the uncle will pay him 30,000 fl. It will *modify* poor Uncle Johann, it will make him infirm.' Johann let himself be walked all over by his wife, she shat on him, he let her do it: lovers in the house during his illness, brazen as you like, in his own home. Niemetz had put to him, 'Well who would you rather be with: the one who actually wrote the stuff or the fool who went round afterwards telling perfect strangers, "I am B's *brother!*"'

Everyone went on about the Symphony, but Karl had been overawed by the Mass. . . . The opening of the *Agnus Dei*, even with the new bass . . . The ending of the *Agnus Dei*, Pacem Pacem. Pacem. Pacem. It had been a *prayer*. . . . What had he meant, 'This Mass is being played for my son'?

He remembered Fröhlich, that vicar in Mödling in 1818. B had taken him out of Giannatasio's and had had him living with him and during that summer had put him in that village school to be taught by the priest. He'd been thrown out for blabbing in class and being disrespectful. And who had he learnt that disrespect from? He had only parroted his uncle. 'Priests! *Parsons!*' B hated all the rigmarole of the church, he'd always mocked it. How had such a man come to write a Mass like *that!* . . . A Mass that had had Karl, as he had sat there listening, wanting to break out of the confines of the hall, of the city, of the universe, to break out of being Karl, to enter a state that took him into . . . He had resented feeling like that even as he was swept up by the emotion. And O, it wasn't sentiment, no mood of the moment, he could still remember it, lived with it vividly, he thought he never would forget that Mass.

Bugger the Symphony. The Symphony was all right. But that Mass . . .

And here he sat at table with the two girls who had sung it and the man who had written it, all of them now in a rather vile mood.

People said his uncle knew so little of Catholicism that he had even talked of setting the *Graduale* and the *Offertorium*, which no composer ever set. Such a Christian was the old buffer that he had come close to being blackmailed by Pulai, a converted Jew and one of Karl's teachers, who had overheard him saying, 'Christ was nothing but a crucified Jew.'

Karl had been very fond of his uncle before the concert, taking charge of the box-office, telling him of the sale of the tickets, calling him 'Most beloved Uncle!' and signing himself 'Your son Carl.' B had once said to him, 'I know you're not my son – of my flesh. But a father has also to bring up a child.'

. . . 'Give the Viennese enough drums and cymbals for them to think that their own silly heads are being bashed together!' The old bastard had not forgotten the lessons he'd learnt from the *Battle*, but this time he'd turned it into art.

He had never expected to find himself thinking, 'Bugger the Symphony.' He himself had urged B to set Schiller, and to get more Schiller into his library. But the *Ode to Joy* he had apparently first thought of setting long ago, when he had been his age, in Bonn. He had selected the verses, written the introduction. 'Not setting the drinking verses, Ludwig?' Johann had asked. 'No, I'm not having it as a drinking song. I want to say something else here.'

The choral finale had worked in that concert. It had made sense in terms of that hall: with soloists and choir and large orchestra already arrayed for the Mass. Whether it worked all right for the Symphony in terms of just the Symphony they still discussed. The girls of course thought that it was marvellous. More work for them. '*Tochter aus Elysium.*'

The girl who had sung *Pacem Pacem* so as to bring tears to his eyes giggled and helped herself to another cherry.

. . . The Symphony that creeps up out of nothing, emerging out of silence as though the silence were its beginning. Never mind the *Ode to joy*, you can hear the man enjoying himself in his *scherzos* – like a dancing bear in this movement. At the earlier rehearsals the drum-beats had been played from *forte* to increasingly *diminuendo* until B had found out what they were doing and stood before the drummer yelling, '*That, that, that, that* and *then* that!' beating his clenched fist hard into the inside of his clenched elbow.

The *andante* he had always loved and had told his uncle so as soon as he had written it. Its beauty was unsentimental, its poignancy not too overt. A toughness to its beauty which answered a need for that which was stern, rigid and truthful in his 17 year old heart. That night when he'd embraced his uncle he had felt that his uncle was right in what he wanted him to be and that he too shared his uncle's ideals.

There was so much in that last movement before you got to the vocal gymnastics that would drag the *Phaeacian* Viennese from their ices and little sausages. That 'cello recitative: one of the most beautiful pieces of music ever written and everything that the *andante* was not: which pulled at the heart-strings so mercilessly and so successfully that no wonder the old bastard got away with it: they were all shocked into submission long before the poor old bass who should be a baritone opened his mouth.

And there was his bloody uncle bellyaching on about whether the choral finale worked or should he have stuck to an instrumental? Of course it works, you fucking cunt. I've got a quarter of your blood and I could never do a thing like that. He had snapped to Niemetz, 'Of course I'm jealous!'

Chapter 2

On Sunday the 23rd, getting dressed to go out to Beethoven's second concert, as he searched in a drawer for his best cravat Schindler came across Beethoven's recent letter to him.

'. . . I have on the whole a certain fear of you, lest some day through your action a great misfortune may befall me . . . in the Prater I was convinced that you had hurt me very deeply . . . rather repay your services with a small gift than *have you at my table* . . . your presence irritates me . . . your vulgar outlook . . .

'. . . As for friendship, in your case that is difficult. In no circumstances would I care to entrust my welfare to you . . . you never reflect but act quite arbitrarily. I have found you out once already, and so have *other people* . . . The purity of my character does not permit me to reward your kindness to me with friendship . . .'

He consoled himself with thoughts of Beethoven's inconsistency. Look at the way he had dealt with Johanna. Fighting her for years for the boy's custody and then, when he had won in the summer of 1820 and she had given birth to her bastard later that year, he had changed and begun helping her! The boy himself had spoken out against his mother. Beethoven had taken no notice, paid for her medicines. This year he had even sent her New Year greetings.

. . . Beethoven would send him round soup which he said tasted dreadful so as to have his opinion confirmed. It was never wise to disagree with Beethoven about the soup. The old housekeeper was getting on; Beethoven said she could neither see nor smell nor taste. 'Frau Schnaps' he had called her, or 'The swift-sailing frigate,' given that it took her all day to relay messages between Beethoven in Hetzendorf and him in Vienna.

. . . Back and forth all last summer, with messages about his town lodgings. Schindler had been staying there, in the *Kothgasse*, next door to Johann at his brother-in-law, the baker's, but Beethoven as ever would not let him handle it: that is to say, he dealt with this as he dealt with everything, putting the execution of the task into Schindler's hands whilst himself firmly holding onto the reins. No wonder his carts all fell over and they all landed on their necks! This time he had been full of complaints about the continuous brutality of the landlord, who he had feared would enter his rooms in his absence, who had given him notice before he was entitled to do so, who had failed to give him a receipt for rent because of some dispute over an unpaid bill for lighting. There had been other disputes: about the storm windows, about the chimney without a stove-flue. Beethoven had directed him to go straight to the police, laying the whole on the authorities: 'I cannot comprehend how it is possible that *so shameful a chimney, ruinous to human health, can be tolerated by the government.*'

He had demanded he go to the police about the landlord; he had demanded he go to the police about Johann's wife, Therese. Beethoven's chosen method of dealing with anything was to go to the police. Or, rather, send *him* to them!

Schindler was director of the orchestra of the *Josephstadt Theater*, praised for his unusually strong tone. In the last few years he had taken over as Beethoven's errand-boy and *dogsbody*, following the departure of Oliva to Russia at the end of 1820. He had first studied law, occasionally visiting Beethoven with documents when he had worked at the office of Beethoven's attorney, Bach. Now at twenty-eight he had given up law, reverting to his first love, music. Last summer, Beethoven had constantly complained that he was late, forgetting that he had to rush from the theatre to Hetzendorf after the morning rehearsals, then hurry the four miles back to give the evening performance. 'Mr High-flyer who never arrives, Mr Rock-bottom who cannot be fathomed,' he had called him.

Beethoven had worn his hair so long that summer that it had flowed like a woman's over his stout shoulders: pure white, from a distance. He also rarely shaved. One visitor seeing him for the first time had exclaimed, 'He looks like King Lear!'

... Why, he himself had drawn Beethoven's attention to Therese's carryings on with her lover while Johann had languished in his bed. *He* had been at Hetzendorf at the time. That daughter of hers was no better. He had written Beethoven a letter about it. 'They deserve to be shut up, the old one in prison, the young one in a house of correction ... He might have died a hundred times without the one in the Prater or at Nussdorf, the other at the baker's, deigning to give him a look. ... He often wept over the conduct of his family and once gave way completely to his grief and begged me to let you know how he is being treated so that you might come and give the two the beating they deserve ... It is most unnatural and more than barbarous if that woman, while her husband is lying ill, introduces her lover into his room, prinks herself like a sleigh horse in his presence and then goes driving with him, leaving the sick husband languishing at home. She did this very often. Your brother himself called my attention to it, and is a fool for tolerating it so long.'

Beethoven himself was not above calling Johann 'that diplomat ... that schemer!' once threatening to have come up with something 'that will hit that fellow like a pistol shot.' There had been bad blood between the brothers after Beethoven had given Johann some of his compositions in lieu of debt repayment. Johann had made moves to sell these at what Beethoven had thought inflated prices. Beethoven accused his brother of making money out of him. '*Bruder Kain!*' On top of that there had been that business of Beethoven's trying to persuade him to cut Therese and *Bastard* out of his will in favour of Karl. When Beethoven read of Johann's complaints of his wife's infidelities during his illness, he had gone barging in like a bull in a china shop, 'I told you! I told you! What brothers I have! What a pair of brothers! Not *one* whore in the family but two! *Three*! With the *Bastard*! They *both* marry prostitutes!'; Johann's retaliating, 'I only married her because you drove me to it! Going to see the *Bishop*! Expulsion to *Vienna*! Of *course* I married the damn bitch – to spite *you*!'; Beethoven's letter: 'During your illness she slept with her fellow miscreant *three times*! O abominable shame! Is there no spark of manhood in you!' – culminating in Therese's standing behind her door with an upraised poker, waiting for Beethoven. *He* had nearly copped that. 'Don't hit *me*! I'm *Schindler*!'

Despite his bad eyes, his brother's illness, the immorality of *Fat little dangler* and *Bastard*, and the extra responsibility of Karl's being about to leave Blöchlinger's and often being with him, even bringing that poor specimen of humanity, Niemetz, who he said was a long-time friend from school, Beethoven had been occupied almost to obsession with work on the *Symphony for England*.

It had been left to him, Schindler, to deal with the consequent mess-up in Beethoven's domestic affairs. He went walking and came back without his hat; arrived back home so late that his food was inedible. 'The weather is bad,' he had written in June. 'But even if I am alone, I am never *lonely*.' He had stayed with Baron Pronay in Hetzendorf until the grovelling bows of the Baron had led him to flee to Baden. He, Schindler, had had to supervise the finding of rooms; then of course there had been even more trouble over the two *wretched* servants, whose *beautiful* food had *ruined my belly*. And all the time the man had filled fat notebook after fat notebook with what was to become his Ninth Symphony.

. . . The way Beethoven just casually writes, 'Be here at 5 in the morning to help me move' – when he is in Hetzendorf, I in Vienna! One and a half hour's walk even for a Beethoven! In the end they had got him into the same house where he had stayed in 1821, because the landlord had been able to sell the window-shutters on which Beethoven had scribbled.

He had acted as the man's servant, secretary, amanuensis, taken pension payments to Johanna; he had even done the man's shopping! He didn't blame Beethoven so much, he blamed his brother. . . . Not to mention all the work he had put in over arrangements for the concerts! – The time, the place, the price of seats, the choir and the orchestra – without me there would have been no concert!

. . . 'I have on the whole a certain fear of you, lest some day through your action a great misfortune may befall me.' Calling him a stopped-up sluice which may suddenly overflow! 'That day in the Prater I was convinced that you had hurt me very deeply. . . . If you see me looking not very cheerful you mouth, "Nasty day again, isn't it?"' . . . that to have him constantly near him 'would upset my whole existence.' For all that it had begun as a letter of apology, in typical Beethoven fashion he had reverted to saying, 'I have found you out once already, and so have *other people.*'

... He had sent him soup to taste; at Hetzendorf, saved dinner for him ...

No credit for any of his efforts. He was not above writing disparagingly of him to other people, even to Grillparzer: 'If you want to come, please come alone. This importunate appendix of a Schindler, as you must have noticed in Hetzendorf, has long been extremely objectionable to me – *Otium est vitium –*'

O you might want to scupper me but, by God, you need me! Always a dogsbody to put the blame on! Oliva, then me! Look at that business about the Mass and Diabelli. The contract had been as good as signed, according to the publisher; it was *he*, Schindler, that Diabelli had threatened to haul into court!

... Having him taste his soup, snapping at his response, 'Your opinion is of no consequence! It is a *bad soup!*' He could be most sarcastic. 'O very wise one! I kiss the hem of your coat!' It was never done to disagree with Beethoven about the soup.

Beethoven thought nothing of calling him 'vile,' 'contemptible,' 'wretch,' 'arch-scoundrel,' blaming him for everything that went wrong, as he had done with Ries over the non-dedication of Opus 120 to Ries' wife.

But he did this with everyone ... servants ... brother ... was happy to blame everyone save himself and Karl.

Beethoven had promised him 50 fl. W.W. for his efforts over the sale of the subscription copies of the Mass when the 50 ducats from the Czar finally arrived. Beethoven had mentioned it in several letters, asking him to be patient. He never received his 50 florins.

... Johann was the culprit, of course, he knew that. He had visited that man three or four times a day throughout his illness, entertained him by the hour! That wife of his waiting behind the door with a poker! Beethoven when he received that letter had fled to Johann, bent upon making a scene. Schindler had lured him away on the pretext that Johann wanted to sleep, for Therese as he had written down afterwards 'began to rage terribly, then went away, but immediately afterwards the nurse rushed into the room and told me that the mistress was standing in the hall with a poker, to welcome you with it! I was terrified and didn't know what to do except keep you away on the pretext that Johann wanted to sleep.' And then he had gone back to tell her Beethoven had left and Therese had damn near brought it down on *him*! No, mate, if she had got you with that, without me there really would have been no Ninth Symphony!

Beethoven had been getting bored by his stay at Hetzendorf. Apart from his bad eyes, his troubles with his family, he was also weighed down by the Baron's grovelling. The Baron had shown Beethoven with pride round his gardens, but Beethoven hated formalized nature, claiming that garden air made him ill.

The Baron with his botanical parklands had turned out to be in love with a Baroness who was already married. According to Karl she spoke in Viennese dialect and sounded like 'our kitchen maid.' She turned out to be a fat, slouching woman. The boy called her *Fatlump*, like Therese.

Schindler had visited Beethoven at Hetzendorf. The maid had been tearful at having been reprimanded by the old woman. Apparently this had begun with the girl's dragging the tables across the floor instead of lifting them.

When Beethoven learned that she had been instructed to be careful about this, and to be quiet in setting the china since the Baron was sleeping in the room beneath, Beethoven thought to repay the Baron's obsequies by lifting and banging down the table, his anger increasing with each violent thrust.

And after this, he stormed, he, Schindler, had crawled, just because he had tried to placate the situation: the terrified girl, in fear for her job, their disturbed host: it had been *midnight*!

He had tried to defend himself, saying that he detested reverence of man for man as much as Beethoven did, 'I have always shown it, that Count or Prince never make me bow or scrape on account of their position.'

'Ha! You! You were born with your belly to the ground!'

'Put me to the test . . . you will be convinced that I'm not as weak as you think!'

'I don't know which is least the man: you or my brother!'

'You really often judge me too harshly, only a little patience, I beg you, for, if I really fail, I don't fail as much as many others, and, if I stumble, I fall right on the ground.'

They had left the next morning, on foot, to Vienna.

In the next list he had made, Beethoven had written, 'Base slave! Miserable fox-pelt!' Three days after his move to Baden, Beethoven had been calling him to Karl 'that contemptible object,' and, three days later, to Johann, he was 'that low-minded, contemptible fellow.' Karl evidently took up his uncle's complaints. A day or so later, Schindler had come across, in Karl's hand, in the conversation book, 'The main reason was your brother, because Schindler has no will of his own, he is everyone's slave; it was Johann who ordered him, because he fears that you might spend too much in Baden.'

It had seemed Beethoven could not forgive him after that. He had spurned him for months, calling him names, calling him in only rarely when he wanted something doing.

He had called him in fast enough when it had come to the concert:

Schindler run here, Schindler run there, write this, arrange that, flap your wings and fly for me, Schindler.

'That man is a poodle,' Johann had said.

'At least I am a man,' Schindler had said when he'd heard. '*I*'d never let myself be walked all over by *that trollop.*'

Johann had laughed, 'More normal to have a woman treat you like this! Schindler kow-tows to *my brother!*'

. . . *Papageno* he called him, vowing him to silence on threat of having his mouth padlocked, or *Samothracian Scoundrel*, meaning that, as an initiate into his musical plans, he had to keep quiet.

It didn't matter what you did; nothing was ever enough for him; he played off the one against the other – himself; Johann; blamed any who was to hand for his own mistakes; was quite capable of blaming both himself and Johann to some third party whom he had in turn earlier blamed.

Beethoven was equally capable of hailing him 'Most excellent fellow!'

He could be sarcy, too. 'O, very wise one! I kiss the hem of your coat!' – though this may have been after he had been persistent in trying to get a reference for a young musician. He had forgotten that Beethoven hated child prodigies. Apparently this was normal though – he had put Liszt through the mill, as he himself had first been doubted by Mozart. He was always afraid of being the object of envy and persecution. He didn't care how much he put your back up in the way he conveyed this to you. 'Don't say anything more than is necessary,' he had written, 'for people will only get annoyed with you,' and, on another occasion, 'When you write to me, just write in exactly the same way as I write to you, that is, without giving me a title, without addressing me, without signing your name. *Vita brevis, ars longa.* And you need not use figures of speech, but just say precisely what is necessary.' Schindler had sometimes signed himself *Papageno*, signifying that his lips were sealed on Beethoven's business.

. . . Blaming him for the fact that the *Diabelli Variations* had not been dedicated to Ries' wife but instead to that Brentano woman. He left letters lying around in the process of writing them; Schindler had read that he'd called him to Ries 'an arch-scoundrel – a bigger wretch I never knew on God's earth.'

. . . *Papageno* . . . *Samothracian* . . . *Lumpenkerl* . . . *Hauptlumpenkerl* . . . *Papageno* – and also *Mr. Shitting.*

. . . Issuing him with *hattisherifs* – apparently a Turkish government edict made irrevocable by a Sultan's mark. . . . Beethoven's letters to Falstaff, Lichnowsky and him, 'I despise treachery. There will be no concert.' – but that was not given with a *hattisherif* – he, Falstaff and Lichnowsky had ignored it.

During Beethoven's explosion at *zum wilden Mann* he had come up with a new term of abuse, in front of others, friends, fellow-musicians.

'This new title should be a punishment for me, or how is it to be interpreted according to the body of law?'

Beethoven had not deigned to answer him.

Schindler pulled on his coat, took his hat and stick and locked the door. As late as the 19th of May they had still been discussing in which venue to hold the second concert. Unger had said, 'In the *Redoutensalle* it is better in any case for, in the first instance, you will certainly get 1200 florins, and secondly the music sounds better. Thirdly, you have no anxieties. Fourth, and that's my opinion!'

Karl had told Beethoven, 'They're feuding again.'

Schindler wrote down that he had said to Unger, 'Your singing teacher was there. Secondly, he has composed a very beautiful poem to you which will soon be printed. Thirdly, he has a thorough understanding of music . . .'

Unger had been all over Beethoven. 'I am studying *Iphigenia* and I should like to study *Fidelio* too and you would make me boundlessly happy if you would lend me the piano part. Will do you it?!!!! Yes?!!'

Schindler had told him, 'She wants to be quite the man!'

Beethoven had laughed. 'Unlike some men in my family, *I* wear the trousers!'

Unger had gone prancing on, laughing delightedly at their good reviews, flirting with him as usual, even throwing him a salute as they punned about standing up to sing and standing to attention. It had been left to him, Schindler, to persist with the business. 'Give me your firm decision now, so that we know what to do.'

Now here they all were, gathering in the *Redoutensalle*, settling into their seats for the second concert.

Chapter 3

Still in his conductor's costume – tail-coat, knee breeches, silk hose and buckled shoes – the voluble short stumpy man arrested attention. His voice, huge and imprecise because of his deafness, sounded across the streets outside the theatre. Orchestral players, some with instruments, several each with a 'cello and one with a double-bass, were leaving the hall, as were the singers, and a surprising number still of the audience. Concert-goers seemed more numerous out here than they had in the auditorium.

Karl had warned Beethoven to be quiet in his own interest. Beethoven had made a lunge at him. People were all around, leaving the concert. Groups were stopping and staring.

Karl began to run. Beethoven ran after him, still shouting abuse at him. Schindler had run ahead of Beethoven, catching up with Karl. 'I know how you feel. Your uncle's been calling me too. I think he's finished with me. He blames me for the concert.'

The weather was vile. Howling wind blew lashing rain against them. They stopped and stood, panting, by the *Karlskirche*. Schindler was clutching his side. 'Tell him I'm not to blame for the concert. I don't know what went wrong, or why. He'll say I chose the wrong hall or time, but we all thought it was best ... Umlauf ... Unger. And he blames me that there is that tax to pay. I didn't know there was a tax. I've only just heard about it. Schuppanzigh tells me you always have to pay a fifth, or a third, to the authorities, when you put on a concert for your own benefit. I tried to get it down, as low as I could, as soon as I knew. I talked to Duport.'

Karl said, 'He knows there's a tax. He should have done. It's not the first benefit concert he's given. He must have paid it before.' The boy recalled having heard his uncle abuse Palffy over deductions at one of his concerts during the Congress. 'The Czarina intervened then. He didn't pay it. He never thinks he ought to pay taxes. Or interest.'

The fifty-three year old caught up with the two younger men, force spent by his long run though still shouting, 'Karl! Karl!' Schindler told Karl, who had turned to approach his uncle, 'He'll forgive you but he'll never forgive me.' As Karl returned to Beethoven, Schindler called after him, 'Don't let him accuse you of conspiring with me.'

'He's a creep,' Johann said, several days after the concert. He had come to give his brother sound business advice. 'Any man with balls would have buggered off then, after you'd chowed him out in public; not hung around

26

till after your second concert. Like a little dog: yap yap yap. Will he take me back?'

Beethoven and Karl laughed, though Karl knew that that was nothing to what Beethoven had said of Johann. Karl himself had called Johann, writing a poem about his dyeing his hair; saying he set himself up as an information bureau; accusing him of washing in an old pan that the dog had eaten out of and of never cleaning his teeth since he was too mean to buy a glass.

Karl had once laughed with his uncle that Schindler and Johann were both men of arrestingly comical appearance, Schindler tall and gaunt with a nasal voice and windmill gestures.

Beethoven's brother dressed like a dandy: rather, he tried to, but it didn't work. Tall beside Ludwig though not an outstandingly tall man, he was outlandishly angular and crooked. His elbows stuck out. His large, long nose was bent. His mouth was crooked. His squint was so pronounced that he appeared to have a glass eye. His hands were broad but the fingers were thin, thin and bony: that was why he could never get gloves to fit. Ludwig had always called him 'sausage fingers.' The ends of his loose gloves stuck out or flapped over the tips of his fingers: a fact which everybody noticed about him and which even his nephew had commented on. Ludwig was the only one who did not laugh at this aspect of his brother. 'When he was born you could see through his fingers.'

Ludwig laughed harder than anyone else at the man's lack of music. '*This* is the unmusicalest Beethoven of them all!' He had once asked him about it. 'How can you be? Father was a court tenor. Grandfather sang bass at court, and *he* became the Electoral *Kapellmeister*. Karl plays well; Caspar Carl came to Vienna thinking he would make a career out of music. You don't even *look* like us! Bugger me, I think you're a *foundling!*'

Beethoven was no copper-plate himself but, as he'd told Toni, 'Beside him I look like a Greek god!'

. . . Brother *Johann*. An *apothecary*. *He* made *his* money selling medical supplies to the *French* during the Napoleonic wars. The *French*! But that was typical of Johann. Only married his wife and took on her bastard after *he* had gone to the Bishop of Linz and complained of her immorality. . . . Tried to take Karl off him, too, he remembered, during that court fiasco of 1819 . . .

In the days when he had owed 3,000 florins to Steiner, another 1,000 to Artaria, Beethoven had finally borrowed from his brother. Seeing him again after so long an absence, Beethoven had registered anew what an angular and crooked man his brother was. 'My husband doesn't look like you at all except for his eyes,' Therese had told him. Beethoven's friends ridiculed Johann to his face. 'Everyone thinks him a fool.'

'Peace, let there be peace between us,' he had told him then. 'I have nothing against your wife.' He had tried to make it up with Therese, even sending a sample of linen for her feminine opinion.

Steiner had been pushing him into a corner, wanting works for the 3,000 florins he still owed while outrageously claiming that he owed them interest. 'As a tradesman you are always a good counsellor,' Beethoven had told Johann. Johann had taken over the organization of some of Beethoven's business affairs, just as their late brother, Caspar Carl, had done. ... Frantically bringing up-to-date old scores so that he might sell them and make some money: *Opferlied, Gratulationsmenuett* and *Der Kuss*. He had given Johann, instead of money owed, several of these works: the Overture *Die Weihe des Hauses*, 3 songs, some bagatelles ... By February 1823 he had been accusing him to Ries of having bought works from him simply to make money out of them, and of having offered the Overture to Boosey in London 'without asking me' when he had already promised it to the Philharmonic Society who had commissioned the 9th. At about the same time he had paid Johann back: 'I have given my *brother Kain* his 200 florins today.'

His finances had come to a head early in 1823. He had needed his pants widening and a new body-belt from Lind. Instead the tailor had presented him with unpaid bills, threatening him with legal action. Beethoven had referred the tailor to his brother. Johann had let the matter slide. Next thing he knew, he was being threatened with being hauled off to court – over a *tailor's bill!* – and he had had to sell one of his 8 bank shares. He had put these bank shares aside for Karl, as a sacred trust, the boy's inheritance. *I'll see he's provided for in my will.*

After that he had written to Schindler that Johann's behaviour was 'quite typical of him.' He had once warned Diabelli, 'In all matters which concern me you must trust neither my worthy brother nor Schindler. *Each is true to his type, but in a different way.*'

Schindler had once come to him telling him that Johann had been determined to tell him not to write any more operas, the opera was finished. Then Johann himself had advised him that 'An opera would be best, you could sell it 5 or 6 times.'

Schindler had told him at the end of last year, 'We have reason to be happy about *Fratello*: he rarely lets the woman drive out, usually eats outside his home, and says that, at the first chance he has to get proof of his suspicions, he will have her interned. He can't get divorced because according to our laws he would have to give her half his capital, but he is exerting his domestic authority more and more.' Karl had told him, 'Your brother has been enlightened by these latest events. He says during his illness he really got to know her, and now he is treating her like a proper patriarch: when he buys something nice, she is not having any of it, he eats it with us instead, like those oysters yesterday. At home they have their food; *he* is out all day and only goes home to eat and sleep.' The boy had gone on to say, 'He enjoys most of all that she is getting old now so nobody turns his head when she passes, so all she can do is behave herself.'

Beethoven had still angled for a divorce.

'I suppose there were some special contracts which he regrets now, but they can't be changed.'

'Tell him I want her out of this family.'

'It won't take long now but, when she does end it, she'll only end it with a complete separation. He is absolutely convinced.'

'Why has he put up with it!'

'Up to now he probably still found her to have some charm; all this is finished, because she is growing old.'

'The sooner she goes the better.'

'He isn't half as mean any more, I have already noticed that. But he's far more crude.'

At the end of last year Johann had started taking them for rides in his carriage.

They saw him off in his carriage now. Johann was driving himself today.

He drove down the street and turned the corner, out of sight of them, feeling that he had done his duty by his brother. He was not the easiest man to get on with and they had not always seen eye to eye.

He called Therese *Fatlump*, Amalie *Bastard* or *Bankert*, had even written a canon, *Fettlümmerl, Bankert haben triumphiert*.

'*Alle Menschen werden Brüder* doesn't include his own, apparently,' Johann had told Therese bitterly when he had first heard that Beethoven was setting this.

'Comes from never having won *eine liebe Frau*,' Therese had replied dismissively, picking up her parasol to go out.

'He only loves mankind in theory, not when it comes a-knocking at his door.'

He himself had not mastered music. Never been interested. What a palaver, though, his two growing brothers had made of that. 'Sausage fingers!' Ludwig had teased him and, the tease become torment, egged on by Ludwig, Caspar Carl had taunted, '*Cloth ears!*'

Why did it matter so much? It was only *music*. He had never felt the slightest interest. Neither of *them* had made any money anyway: Caspar Carl going to Ludwig for cash, and now Ludwig coming to *him*.

Johann had not arrived in Vienna until December 1795. In the spring of that year he had worked as a trainee pharmacist in Bonn at a French military hospital during the French occupation. By 1808 he had bought his own apothecary shop at Linz. I worked! To make something of that business! Selling the iron gratings from the windows, the tin pots from the shelves, to keep the place going, until the arrival of Napoleon's armies had secured the basis of his fortune: having dealt with the French in Bonn, he now secured contracts to furnish their medical supplies. All Beethoven ever stormed was that the contract was with 'the enemy!' and that in the spring of 1814 someone had sought to bring a charge that his medicaments were not of the standard quality. 'You'll ruin my name!' All he ever thought of. No thought of brotherly support.

And what had happened when he had got to Linz and got settled? He had let part of the house to a doctor and his wife. The doctor's wife's sister had visited. This was Therese. In those days she had not been bad looking, never beautiful but a fine figure of a woman. He had got to know her, she had become his housekeeper, though everyone knew what was going on. No one minded. Then along comes Beethoven, storming in on him after not having seen him for years, full of hate, full of fury. Summer of 1812, fresh from the Bohemian spas. A right Turk he had been, seething fire and brimstone: 'I will not have you living with that whore!' Storming to the authorities, the Bishop. The result was they issued Therese with a banning order: expulsion to Vienna if she remained in the town. He had done what any man would. He had put his foot down. He had married her. The row when he announced this intention had been even worse. Therese had a five year old daughter. 'Is that your child? She's not your child! She must be *free* for the *father* to marry her!' That had ended in blows. He had won that fight. Ha! Won the fight! He had never *wanted* to marry the cow, but what else would any man do, faced with an ultimatum like this, from his brother? Playing God, in my house, the big I-am.

. . . He just wished that turd Schindler hadn't been there to overhear their row about that last summer.

In August 1819 he had bought his estate at Gneixendorf, near Krems, 40 miles west of Vienna on the Danube. Here he spent his summers, staying in winter with his brother-in-law, the baker Obermeyer, in Vienna. He'd had to work for what he'd got. His brother had always patronized, put him down. 'Land-owner' he'd signed himself in one New Year's greeting. His brother had written back signing himself 'Brain-owner.'

Beethoven flew into a rage at New Year or name-day cards. 'Social tomfoolery and two-faced deception. Giving should come from the heart, not be a duty!' He hated having cards, gifts, expected of him; likewise he hated bitterly getting a present in return: 'Giving should be spontanous! *Duty* giving!'

He was never consistent, though, even in this: he grew angry enough if Karl should forget his name-day. This year he had even sent Johanna a New Year card, or she had sent him one and he had acknowledged it, granting her Karl's half of her pension and assuring her of their best wishes at all times. Even trying to get him, 'my pig-headed brother,' to contribute to her welfare. This after years of roundly abusing her, calling her a prostitute, a *Rabenmutter*.

Beethoven was adamant that he not become Karl's guardian in the event of his death; he had even stipulated this in his will. He always was sensitive about that boy – thought he had been going to 'steal' him in 1819, accused him of 'plotting' with Johanna – though in truth there had been then no legal guardian, no established authority in charge of the boy.

He was always calling him: 'pig-headed brother,' 'brainless land-owner.' 'You've got good sense – in your pants!' – this when he had been urging him to call and give advice about the sale of the Mass! He had hardly uttered a word to him for a decade after he'd left them at Linz, seeking him out only in 1822 and then, as he'd suspected, only because he had wanted to borrow money. At that time he had not finished the Mass, he had started but by no means finished the *Diabelli Variations*. The sole products of the last few years which he had finished and could sell had been those 3 piano sonatas and the re-hashing of minor earlier pieces, some of them dating back to as far as Bonn.

He had come to him after the return of ill-health, when he had complained of being at the mercy of strangers. They had seemed to get on quite well. Johann had given good business advice on Beethoven's letter to the Leipzig publisher, Peters, and sounded out Steiner and Artaria about the Mass, to both of whom Beethoven still owed money. Beethoven had still been hoping to sell his collected works and buy a house, both projects dear to him over several years. Beethoven had come up with an astonishing document about that. ' . . . so many greedy brain-pickers and lovers of that noble dish . . . all kinds of preserves, ragouts and fricassees are made from it . . . the author would be glad to have as many groschen as are sometimes disbursed for his work . . . the *human brain* cannot be sold either like coffee beans or like cheese which, as everybody knows, has first to be produced from *milk*, *urine* and so forth –

'The human brain is not a saleable commodity –

'A revised edition of my works should be announced, seeing that so many inaccurate and forged editions of my work are wandering about – anarchy! (Between ourselves, although we are convinced republicans, yet there is something to be said for the oligarchical aristocracy) . . .'

He was right, of course: why should those others make profit from his work? Especially those pirated editions . . .

Rossini, then in Vienna, had asked after Beethoven, and had been roundly mocked by Karl in the vulgar dialect 'Says he' song. Johann himself had met Rossini. 'Rossini became rich from his operas, I think you, too, should write more operas.' Rossini had even talked of buying a house for Beethoven. 'I'll get 10,000 florins C.M. for my collected works, and buy my own house!'

Even Therese had seemed to get on with him at this time, finding a housekeeper for him who 'will be happy to have a good place where she can spend the rest of her life contentedly;' telling him that 'an English doctor prescribes a different sort of wild game daily for melancholy.'

Things had progressed in jolly mood, Beethoven hailing him, 'Best little brother! Most high and mighty property owner!' asking him for a loan that he might go to Baden, promising that, that winter, he and 'my little son' would eat him out of house and home. He had told him of his problems with Steiner then later grown fearful lest Johann had had a row with the publisher.

After that he had started flaying about in all directions, offering the Mass left right and centre in an attempt to get money, fleeing like a scalded cat when all the publishers naturally took him up. Yet he himself had been boasting of how publishers were scrambling for his works. '*What an unhappy yet happy man am I!*'

He had written to him in great relief after finding him not in Krems but still in Vienna. 'Most excellent little brother! Owner of all the islands in the Danube near Krems! Director of the entire Austrian pharmacy!' but with this he had, as he recalled, sent some music: old and new copies of the same overture, pianoforte arrangements of this and that, a detailed list of music to be offered to Steiner, at what rates – of all of which, as a non-musician, he had known nothing. With these he was meant to negotiate on Beethoven's behalf – and did *he* want him to sell the Mass to Simrock, or would he lose in the transaction from the money he'd already lent!

When Beethoven had moved in next door to the baker's, he had hated the rooms, calling them 'evil,' abusing him for refusing to hear anything on the topic.

He had still gone on trying to help him, answering business letters like that from Pacini, an Italian publisher in Paris who'd wanted 'quartets or quintets' even before that Russian 'cellist, Prince Galitzin.

Beethoven had given him a few smaller works in lieu of repayment of a loan. The minute he began to try to sell them, Beethoven was on his back, writing to people like Ries in London, 'My brother *bought them* from me in order to traffic in them. O Frater!' – This of the Overture *The Consecration of the House* which he had apparently promised to the Philharmonic Society of London to keep them sweet over their delayed symphony.

Johann had felt bitter: advancing Beethoven cash on these works, only to be blamed by Beethoven for his own double-dealing. He had had this trouble with Ludwig before. In 1807 he had loaned Ludwig 1500 florins; by the time he was seeking to close his deal for the apothecary shop in Linz later that year, Beethoven had been bellyaching about him to Gleichenstein, coupling him with Caspar in having 'a spirit of revenge against me!' – even though he had been able to lay hands on the sum by the sale of some works and thus had been quite able to pay him back the money.

He had done his best to be brotherly: offered Beethoven a house on his estate; this year he'd even offered him one rent-free. And yet he was quite capable of writing to him, 'Your brains are in your breeches.'

He accused anybody of scheming against him – as if anyone had the time or the inclination! ... And then there had been that business with Lind. He had called him for messing up things with the tailor, who had been asked to use him as an agent – as was everyone at that time: about the Mass, about the subscription copies. Johann had considered Lind's bill excessive. Lind had apparently gone back to Beethoven direct with threats of legal action.

... Beethoven had come to him, eager for his business help, when he had already promised the Mass to at least two publishers, Simrock and Peters. He had put into his hands specifically several minor works, only to find Beethoven slagging him off about these to Ries in London. Ries had been Beethoven's pupil, their families had known each other since Bonn. He had borrowed 200 florins then kicked up a stink about repayment. He was never above accusing him to other people, who took his side, so that he'd heard that Count Moritz Lichnowsky had slagged him off: 'You ought to stop him doing business or carrying on correspondence without your signature. Perhaps he's already closed a contract in your name.'

He'd only given him a few trifling works! The way that old bugger went on you'd think he had given him the *Missa Solemnis*!

That bastard had even gone to *Bach*, discussing *his* business with a *lawyer*! Trying to get him to cut out Therese and leave all his money to Karl. 'A legal contract is valid within a marriage but one quarter of the assets goes to the legitimate heirs, that is, the next of kin. If he's made a legal contract he can't change it. But if he's made a will he can alter it radically.' He'd read it himself, in the conversation book, later!

No wonder Therese waited for him with a poker! Beethoven called her 'Fat little dangler,' referring to her pendulous breasts. He had once overheard one of them saying, 'No doubt that accounts for Johann's perpetual leer!'

... 'You couldn't even give me a kid!'

'Give you a kid! Give you a kid! How could I give you a kid! You're never here!'

'I was here long enough! In the early days! You and that brother of yours! You're just the same! Useless!'

Beethoven had tried to get him to leave Therese and come and stay with him during his illness. 'You see how right I was to withhold you from these, etc. Come to me and stay with us. I need nothing from you. How bad if you had to entrust your spirit under such hands.

'If you want to come, come alone, for I won't see her.'

He had tried to persuade him to live with him and Karl. 'What could be better than to live with a highly educated young man?' Johann had thought at the time that this could reflect Beethoven's own fears at being about to have Karl leave Blöchlinger's and live with him. Then again, he had reflected, this could be Beethoven reverting to the father role of his youth, when their mother had died and their own father had been too drunk half the time and too broken to care for them. Here was Beethoven still assuming that same sort of authority.

Mind you he had been ill then: as low and alone as Beethoven had been when he had come to him. He had had Karl tell his uncle, 'The brother is now really to be pitied; quite alone, under these beasts, badly nursed. He looks like death.' That brat Schindler had gloated, 'He's worthy of pity!' though in his weakened state even Schindler had been used to urge Beethoven to come to him when Amalie had reluctantly nursed him, grumbling, her face turned away.

Johann thought Karl quite balanced for one so young, mature and steadfast, not least in the way he stood up to his uncle. He was not without his studious, philosophical side, urging Beethoven to put more Schiller into his library, once telling his uncle, before he had reached the age of 17, 'There is no untroubled happiness.' Of course he was arrogant too, talking dismissively of Blöchlinger and his wife before he'd left their school, telling his uncle that one of his teachers 'said himself I was the only one of his pupils who gives him hope.' But since then he had gone on to the university. In this last year Karl had grown up apace.

When he had recovered enough to travel to Gneixendorf Beethoven had written to him there. 'You will not be entirely neglected, whatever those two *canailles*, that loutish fat woman and her bastard, may do to you ... For, however little you may deserve it so far as I am concerned, yet I shall never forget that you are my brother; and in due course a good spirit will imbue your heart and soul – a good spirit which will separate you from those two *canailles*, that former and still active whore, with whom her fellow miscreant slept no less than three times during your illness and who, moreover, has full control of your money. O, abominable shame, is there no spark of manhood in you?!!! ... Am I to become so degraded as to mix in such low company? ... I hover over you unseen and influence you through others so that the scum of the earth may not strangle you.'

Therese had got hold of it and crossed out all the abusive references to herself and her daughter. What a letter for a man to receive from his brother! And this when he was writing his brotherhood symphony! *Alle Menschen werden Brüder*! Aye, all excepting his own!

... Standing behind the door with a poker to clonk him, nearly clonking Schindler! Johann laughed. He had forgiven his wife, to his brother's chagrin. Therese had relinquished her marriage contract. She had no claims to his money now. But he kept her with him.

'More scandal to divorce than to keeping things the way they are,' he had told his brother.

Chapter 4

June-July

Beethoven still smarted at the failure of his concert, even as he tried to get into the country and to get on with his string quartet.

He had been granted 500 florins C.M. from Duport, but then there was the tax, and the expenses. As it was, he felt reluctant to accept it, having learned that Duport would get nothing.

Worse than the finances was the failure of his concert – his Symphony, his Mass. They had only played one part of the Mass, the *Kyrie*, substituting instead an old Terzet, *Tremati, empi, tremate*, which to his fury had been described as new, and filling in with that *Rossini* aria, *Di tanti palpiti*, from *Tancredi*! The wife of the Archduke Karl had been there. Now he would be a laughing-stock at court!

Rossini arias at *his* concert! Karl had told him afterwards, 'Everyone was indignant about the aria. Stadler had a little group round him who amused themselves over it. People take exception to the fact that your compositions have been placed in the same category as Rossini's and so have been desecrated.' Someone said David had sung it 'mediocrely;' only since had he learnt that the idiot had transposed it several tones higher and sung it throughout in a mock falsetto. No wonder Stadler's group had tittered!

The whole concert had been a fiasco. They could hardly wait to get out after the Ninth. He had forgotten to send Haslinger tickets; people had sneered at the Terzet, 'Heard that in 1814!' A laudatory poem about him, twenty stanzas long, by some Italian, had been distributed in the hall. After a fiasco like that! People must think he was mad!

He had not even wanted to put on a second concert. He had warned them, 'The Viennese! One concert only! Novelty is all!' His 9th and his Mass: already *passé*. Five years' sodding work down the drain. . . . Putting off the start of that second concert until a quarter to one, to see if the hall filled. Standing in the wings with Schindler. 'Umlauf and Falstaff say they are going to start without you.' Now he had heard that Duport was 800 florins out of pocket.

'The brother says Schindler was responsible for the concert not being on the Friday, since he made the proposition to Duport that it would be better held in the *Redoutensaal*.' Karl had told him Johann had said that Schindler had gone to Duport out of revenge for his onslaught. Duport had seized the opportunity with both hands for, with a Sunday lunch time concert, he'd been left with an evening free for further lucrative bookings.

'Duport himself is sorry now that he didn't have the concert put on in the theatre.' There, orchestra and choir came with the booking. 'He has to pay for everything now.' There had even been some trouble with the copying of the parts of the Terzet, which Schindler had been in charge of. . . . Gläser, the copyist he'd chowed out for his bad work on the 9th. 'Everything comes from Schindler, who put him up to it . . .'

He'd been right in what he had written to the boy last year. 'His evil character, addicted to intriguing, demands that he be treated seriously.' Beethoven was fully aware of the aggression that lay behind Schindler's sycophancy: that kow-towing that mocked even as it grovelled. Meant to befriend, meant to explain the world to him in his deaf state, Schindler could come up with such beauties as, 'The talk is about the landlady who forbids the residents to laugh when Your Grace takes a summer stroll in the garden.' . . . Calling him 'Your Grace!' 'Go to the devil with your "Gracious Sir!"' he had exploded at a copyist. '*Only God can be called gracious!*' . . . Grovelling like a wet prick at that Baron Pronay's place last year, that filthy, immoral Baron with his fat lardy bit of fluff . . . He had been terrified then, last year, when he had got conjunctivitis. Bach had gone blind, Handel had gone blind; and now it seemed that, as well as being deaf, Beethoven would go blind. And now he had lost the only reliable person – the only one anyway he could always rely on to *be there*. He was deaf, for God's sake! He never knew what was going on. It had taken him weeks to understand what had happened at the concert! No one ever saw things from his point of view – no one ever seemed to understand this.

Anyway he had not gone blind. He was still here, composing. At least Johann was letting him have some money . . .

Johann was urging him to sell the Mass. Of course he could make money from his finished works. His problem had been, especially with the Mass and the Symphony, that their creation had taken so long that he had had no money flowing in; he had had to borrow; and then, when the bills fell due, he had had to borrow again. The further complication with the Mass had been that, once he had embarked upon the course of selling subscription copies to princes, he wanted to treat these sovereigns as fairly as normal patrons by withholding publication for a year. Diabelli had wanted the Mass for publication by July 1st last year; Beethoven had objected on the grounds that he would be defrauding the sovereigns who had applied for subscription copies at fifty ducats apiece. It had ended with Beethoven raging about his honour. 'You cannot publish that Mass within a year!' In the event it was taking that long to despatch all of the subscription copies. Beethoven was still trying to find an honest reliable publisher who would publish on his terms.

Besides subscribing to the Mass, the Russian 'cellist Prince Galitzin had had it performed in St Petersburg, in full, before those castrated concerts in Vienna. He had also commissioned three quartets. Beethoven was working on the first. On the death of Teyber in late 1822 he had applied for the post of Imperial and Royal Chamber Music Composer, to be told that the post was not going to be filled. Won't give me the post of Royal Chamber Music Composer! I'll show them who's the only man in Vienna to be Royal and Imperial Chamber Music Composer – God Almighty I will!

He had planned to write a quartet since late spring 1822, before he had mentioned it to Peters, Pacini, months before he had heard from Galitzin. When he had heard from Toni about Karl Josef's treatment with Gall . . .

Galitzin had now commissioned three. What's more he would let him publish them at once. The man was a dream of a patron. He had written to him late last year, 'I am really impatient to have a new quartet by you; nevertheless I beg you not to mind and to be guided only by your inclination and inspiration, for no one knows better than I that you cannot command genius, rather that it should be left alone, and we know that you are not the sort of person to sacrifice artistic for personal interest . . .' Beethoven wondered: what sort of person is that? . . . No, no, it's not like that *at all*: what else would I rather be doing? . . . Holidays? . . . But holidays are for *work*. Love affairs? Too old. He sat and could think of no 'interest' that could come within a million miles of 'interest' in composition; he sat and was highly amused.

'. . . *and I wanted to kick her in the teeth*: you *don't have a hard life at all!*' He thought of Antonie's hard life and sighed.

The first performance of the Mass, for the benefit of musicians' widows, had taken place in St Petersburg on April 7th. Galitzin had told him, 'The effect of this music on the public cannot be described and I doubt if I exaggerate when I say that for my part I have never heard anything so sublime; I don't even except the masterpieces of Mozart which with their eternal beauties have not created for me the same sensations that you have given me, Monsieur, by the *Kyrie* and *Gloria* of your Mass. The masterly harmony and the moving melody of the *Benedictus* transport the heart to a plane that is really blissful. This whole work in fact is a treasure of beauties; it can be said that your genius has anticipated the centuries and that there are not listeners perhaps enlightened enough to experience all the beauty of this music; but it is posterity that will pay homage and will bless your memory much better than your contemporaries can.'

In a letter to him last month Beethoven had talked of dedicating the Mass to the Czar. What he was after of course was a present. A *cash* gift! He recalled the Congress: the long-delayed gift from Alexander for the dedication of those fiddle sonatas – though that had been brought about by the Czarina. The Czarina's own present to him for her Polonaise: '10 ducats per minute!' Zmeskall had exclaimed. 'A *right* royal rate of pay!' He had told Galitzin of the medal of half a pound in gold from the King of France *pour encourager les autres*, and, what the hell, about the Italian verses.

He had had Bernard publicize news of this medal in the *Wiener Zeitung* which he edited. 'His Majesty did not just want to *fob me off* by paying for his copy . . . shows that he is a generous King and a man of refined feeling.' He had forgotten Bernard's harsh words about the Bourbons. In 1820, when it had looked as though the family would die out with the murder of the Duke de Berry, Bernard had gloated, saying it was a pity they could not bring back Napoleon. Not that he hadn't shared his views on that. 'Napoleon – once I couldn't stand the man. These days I think quite differently.'

Bernard had been his friend for a decade. He it was who had advised him to place Karl in Giannatasio's. For a time they had met almost daily, when Bernard's friend Peters had become Karl's co-guardian . . . 1819, 1820, the time of the court battles over Karl's custody. The younger man had since married; these days it seemed they rarely saw each other.

In 1815 the *Gesellschaft der Musikfreunde* had approached Beethoven to write them an oratorio. In June 1819 they had paid an advance of 400 florins W.W. for this work. Bernard had been chosen to write the text. After much delay, caused by Bernard's being 'too busy' with work for his paper and Beethoven's losing parts Bernard said he had already given him, by October last year a text had finally been produced. *Der Sieg des Kreuzes.* The Victory of the Cross. Beethoven had never wanted to set it. They had collaborated before, but that had been on rousing patriotic silly things for the Congress: *Ihr wiesen Gründer*, and some other piece which the censor had banned. He had offered the Society, to offset its advance, proceeds from the second concert – this had been in January, before anyone could have anticipated what a fiasco that second concert would be. The Society had assessed this offer but decided that the expenses would be too great and had turned it down. After that meeting they had written asking him pretty firmly 'to inform the Society categorically whether you will set to music the poem delivered by Herr Bernard and at what time we may hope to receive this work to which every friend of music and admirer of your great talent has been looking forward for so long with keen expectation.' He had replied that he had *not* chosen Bernard to write the text and that 'a great many passages must be altered. . . . I would rather set Homer, Klopstock, Schiller. If they offer difficulties to be overcome, *these immortal poets* at least are worthy of it.' He had told them he had not asked for the advance. He wished he had never received their 400 florins. The very thought of that damned oratorio depressed him.

It wasn't, as he had thought it would be, at all about Christ on the cross, but some airy fairy notion of some woman seeing an apparition and hearing voices and later being condemned to martyrdom by her husband. It was full of stuff about augurs, allegorical figures representing Hate and Discord. He wanted none of these, though he was prepared to accept the Christian equivalents: Faith, Hope and Charity. Bernard when he learned of this had declaimed, 'You've made nonsense of it!' He had offered the damn thing back, but people still pressurized him to set it.

Why do people keep giving me *fairy stories* to write! he had thought furiously. Grillparzer had done the same. For years his brother, his friends, had been urging, 'Write a new opera! You will make money!' Count Moritz Lichnowsky had sought to bring him together with Grillparzer so that they might write an opera – *Macbeth*, he had thought, or *Romeo & Juliet*. Instead of these, or *The Odyssey*, which each had separately thought of setting, the man had come up with *Melusine*. *Melusine*! A fucking *fairy-story*!

The man had failed to spot his irony. 'Wonderful. Wonderful. Only I don't know what to do with the hunters' chorus. Weber used 4 horns, therefore I must have 8: where will this end?'

Grillparzer had asked him once if he had any prospect of wife and children. He had laughed out loud. 'No, my Leonore left me in my dungeon.' . . . 'You really do think she's going to come to you, but your dungeon is of your own making . . .' What else was it that Zmeskall had said? 'That woman is going to spend the rest of her life wondering if you'll turn up on her doorstep.' 'Why should she wonder that?' 'You did it once.'

Yes. I did it once.

Walking that day with his sketchbook among the mountains, he saw in the distance an upright, slender woman. He remembered once saying to Zmeskall, 'She's got such a slender body I feel like a hulk beside her. At the same time, she makes me enjoy being the hulk I am.'

. . . Poor Zmeskall, with gout, in his sedan chair. He can't enjoy a romp on the mountains. Poor bastard can't even play his 'cello. His mind reeled in dread at the thought of being unable to play his instrument, being unable to walk.

He hated his celebrity. What use was that to a working artist!

'Oo look, there's Beethoven!'

'Dun't 'e look funny?'

'Sh!'

'S'a'righ'. 'E can't 'ear you. 'E's deaf.'

He had witnessed this or something like it many times.

He wanted to stay in the country, getting on with his string quartet, yet fretted about Karl who had stayed in Vienna to prepare for his exams at the University.

In Vienna he lived in the *Landstraße*, corner of *Bockgaße* and *Ungargaße* . . . the *Landstraße* suburb, where Toni had her house. The house was still standing. He rarely stood and gazed at it these days. Karl had remained in the city with Enk, a studious young man who had just reached his majority. Beethoven trusted the 24 year old to keep an eye on Karl. The two young men studied Latin and Greek and read the ancients together.

On one of his visits, in late June, he learned that Karl expected to fail his exams and wanted to quit the University. The boy feared the mockery of sitting the first year again.

'So what do you want to do?'

The boy hesitated before writing. 'In that case do you give me a free choice?'

He had finally dragged it out of him: *soldier*!

'In whose company did you come up with that one? You don't know any soldiers! O, I see! That friend of yours! Niemetz! I pay all this money to have him educated with the sons of Counts and noblemen, to give him a start in life that I never had, and what does he do? Comes home with the poorest boy in the whole school. *Niemetz*! Not just poverty! Poverty of *spirit*!'

The boy was still writing! ' ... the art of fortification ...' Beethoven lowered his face beside the boy's, leering,

'Wide-thundering Zeus strips half the good of a man

Upon the day when he becomes a *slave*!'

Karl saw his uncle stride to the piano.

Beethoven, his face suffused with malice, began playing *fortissimo* from Figaro's aria to Cherubino, accompanying his vicious baritone,

'*Non più andrai, farfallone amoroso ...*

Tra guerrieri, poffar bacco!'

He took especial pleasure in 'Lots of honour, little money,' began repeating, 'Little money,' began varying it.

For the rest of the evening, whenever he encountered his nephew, he confronted him with a gleam in his eye, rubbing his fingers across his palm, leering, '*Poco contante ... poco contante ...*'

When Karl was undressing for bed, he heard his uncle singing, the viciousness hard-formed now, 'You'll dance to my tune!'

Beethoven seethed still, alone again in the country. Lack of interest in his studies! Cutting lectures! Telling him he wanted to be a soldier! ... Willisen, Varnhagen, those soldiers he had known, at that time, at those spas ... His chosen young librettist who was to set *Odysseus' Return*, killed in battle in August 1813, his letter still in his pocket, now stained with blood ... His heart cried out once in fear and rage: I didn't raise you for *that*! ... not that, my boy, not that. I've *been* under fire − so have you, he remembered: in Caspar Carl's cellar, pressing those cushions to his ears, crouched down on the floor, keening, going mad at the slaughtering of his ears. Karl had toddled up to him and, in a lull in the fighting, Beethoven had sat on a chair and lifted the boy onto his knee. ... Gazing down at the 2 or 3 year old, his soft childhood hair, the incredible smoothness of his cheek. The boy had always been bright − alert − intelligent: why did he want to do this! *Soldier*!

Art of fortification! He remembered the days when he and Zmeskall had called prostitutes 'fortresses'.

A soldier! The lowest of the low! A base *slave*, like Schindler! A man

with no will of his own, who takes orders, *submits*! Why, he recalled the
boy's telling him himself, of some boy who'd left Blöchlinger's to become a
cadet in the cavalry, 'They get very hard punishment. The young ones are
hit with rods, the older ones with sticks, and the eldest are whipped.'
When he had objected Karl had told him, 'But they're often very wild.
One beat the Major over the head with a gun, he was immediately
arrested . . .' . . . That boy had himself defied his own mother to join – was
that where he'd got it from? Defiance!

Karl as a soldier . . . He remembered his fears that the six month old
Karl Josef when grown would have to serve as a soldier and be killed in
war, when Napoleon had won the Battle of Hanau and his troops had
marched through Frankfurt . . . His *Battle* Symphony had first been
performed for the benefit of Austrian and Bavarian soldiers wounded at
Hanau . . .

And there was so much good in the boy. He had shown concern for
Wunderl, the copyist helping Frau Schlemmer after her husband's death.
He had tried to get him to see an eye specialist during his illness. He had
been contemptuous of an eye-specialist who had refused to treat a patient
because he lacked money. Once after the monstrances had been stolen
from a church nearby Karl had asked him about religion. 'But I don't
understand why He said He was God . . . But it's written clearly: I am the
Son of God; whosoever doesn't believe in me does not believe in my
Father.' He had asked his opinion of life after death. 'So it's uncertain
whether the bad are punished after death and the good rewarded, because
here the bad ones are often well off and the good ones poor. It's said that
nature itself punishes: that may be so, so long as one has an active
conscience; if not then the baddy has no punishment. But with the good
person it is not so. He is often badly off; shouldn't there be retribution on
the other side?' Beethoven had told him that the worst thing that a man
could do was to judge another man. 'But the good person? How is he
compensated?' Beethoven had told him that there were many religions.
What mattered was believing in God and living your life as a God-fearing
man. . . . Soldier! My kid a soldier! *Mine!*

At the time when Karl was having to go to church regularly in order to
be seen as fit to take up his place at the the University, the boy had
remarked of the Pope, 'I find it extremely humiliating that all Christen-
dom – among them many people of different views from His Holiness –
have to kiss this man's slipper, and that the honouring of God and the
honouring of the Pope is only differentiated by the words "to pray" and
"to adore."'

But the boy had disagreed on Napoleon, telling a story of a commander
of several of his regiments 'who came over to our side with several
companies. He excused his treachery against Napoleon by saying he
couldn't stand his atrocities any more. Napoleon had, in fact, immediately after the battle, surrounded by heavily wounded and crying soldiers,

calmly eaten his dinner, and when asked how he could enjoy it amongst all those dead and wounded who had fallen for his sake replied, "I don't care for the dogs."'

Beethoven dismissed Karl's dissension. The boy was a child.

Karl had told his uncle, 'If I could have been a person from the olden days I would have been Hannibal. *He* is my favourite. Also Ulysses. Rather than Achilles. – But he had a good heart, so it seems from his domestic circumstances.'

His preferred Homer was in Vienna, but Beethoven picked up now and read *The Iliad*. ... Odysseus, when Agamemnon has upbraided him for being the first to sit down at a banquet and now not preparing for battle: 'The wily Odysseus glared at him and said, "Son of Atreus, what speech is this that slipped from your lips? How can you say that we hold back from battle when the Achaeans stir up harsh war? If that is what troubles you, you shall see, as you wished, the father of Telemachus get to grips with the front rank of the horse-training Trojans."' ... Of Strife: ' ... increasing the groans of dying men.' ... Of Simoisius: 'He did not give back to his parents the cost of rearing him for his life was cut off short when he was slain by the spear of great-hearted Aias.' He did not warm to this book as to his beloved *Odyssey*, though re-reading now he admitted that this description of death, as a wainwright's felling of a young poplar, was very beautiful.

... He had once kissed Karl goodbye then sat by the window watching him leave then dreamed that Karl in his shirtsleeves sitting beside him became Karl Josef, a little boy in his nightshirt.

And the little boy put his little arms round his neck and kissed his father's bristly face.

On the 3rd of July Johann helped him reply to publishers about the Mass. Dealings with publishers about the Mass went back to the start of the decade. Simrock was to have had it at first, until Oliva had pointed out that the Bonn publisher's offer, in louis d'or, had been less than he thought he was getting once the sum was converted into gold ducats. ... He had taken the sum offered by Simrock from Brentano in Frankfurt, who had acted as his agent ...

Peters of Leipzig had also deposited money. Beethoven had offered him smaller works. He recalled Peters' reaction to the bagatelles he had sent. ' ... Unworthy of you.' *That* had arrived the day he had presented the Archduke with his copy of the Mass: down on one knee, begging forgiveness for the lateness, both men grinning at each other yet not unmoved. ... Well *Peters* wasn't getting it, what's more *he* could wait for his money!

Viennese publishers had wanted it – Artaria, he thought, had been in there with them somewhere. But he had borrowed from Artaria and did not want him to deduct from the fee what he still owed. ... Diabelli, with his dishonour ... Steiner wanted to publish everything he wrote but, apart from the man's dunning letters, and charging him *interest*, he still had not published overtures that he had had for years. At one time, when Steiner had even threatened him with legal action over the money owed, Beethoven had thought of bringing a counter-charge. He was now paying Steiner his money: no Mass for *him*!

The two Schlesingers, of Paris and Berlin, had wanted it. They had published his last three piano sonatas, but not well, there had been too many mistakes. Probst, also of Leipzig, might have heard bad reports of him from Peters: he wanted the works deposited with a firm of Viennese bankers first.

The most recent petitioners on the scene were Schotts of Mainz, near Frankfurt. The wheel had come full circle. Johann had said to him, 'You really must dispose of the Mass soon. And the Symphony. They're both finished now – it's silly to be short of money when you can sell them.' He too was finding the business tedious: all those many letters over so many years. He wanted to find a firm who would take both Mass and Symphony, at good rates, good honourable people with whom it would be a pleasure to deal, who would bring out excellent editions and go on being his publishers. He did not want to be grovelled to but he was buggered if he was going to be doubted.

There were further complications: the Mass, having been offered by subscription at 50 ducats, mainly to Sovereigns, 10 copies in all, though one had gone to the Frankfurt *Cäcilia* Society, ought not to be published too soon, lest subscribers feel cheated; likewise the Symphony, commissioned by the Philharmonic Society of London, remained their property for one year. He wanted to place both, for deferred publication, but he wanted the money now.

He had headed off Probst with offers of minor works – those rejected by Peters, since given to Johann – for which he now asked that a hundred ducats be deposited with Probst's Viennese agent. To Schott he got down to the nitty-gritty: Mass, Symphony, the quartet upon which he had just been working, answering their letter of May 27th.

They had written in March in a spirit of friendship, enclosing a copy of their review, *Cäcilia*, asking if he could become its Viennese editor, mentioning a fellow composer, Rummel, who wished to call on him for advice. Beethoven had met him the day before the second concert. This *Kapellmeister* from Wiesbaden, who composed for wind instruments and also arranged symphonic works for the piano, had turned out to be a decent fellow.

He had offered them the Mass for 1000 florins C.M., the Symphony for 600, payment to be made by drafts of 600 florins for the first month, 500 for the second, and 500 for the fourth, starting from the present. They also wanted the quartet, for 50 ducats, which he now promised them 'within 6 weeks.'

He had told Grillparzer he had finished his opera, Bernard he had finished his oratorio. He had had the notion of writing another mass, for the Emperor, perhaps another mass after that, the second symphony he still planned for England; then he could satisfy all those publishers; but to write just that one Mass had taken him years. When the work flowed, as now, with the quartet, it was all so *easy*: as though he could compose ten works at once! He was constantly astonished by the time it all took . . . if only one could *wish* one's works onto paper, out of the head!

Beethoven moved from Penzing to Baden on the advice of his doctor, who told him to bathe 40 times and to drink the spring water. Through his lawyer, Bach, he had found splendid rooms in the hermitage of the Gutenbrunn Castle. The Archduke he had heard was coming to Baden this month.

Rudolph had been in Olmütz in May and had consequently missed both concerts; he had never heard the Mass which had been composed for his own inauguration. The Archduke's brother, Ferdinand of Tuscany, had died on the 18th of June. He had been one of the subscribers to the Mass. In July last year, assessing his debts at 2,300 florins C.M., Beethoven had also applied to the Archduke to draw a subscription out of his brother, the King of Saxony.

'The Archduke will make you happy once he receives the Mass,' his friends had told him. He had envisaged an increase in his annuity, a cash gift, a position as the Archduke's *Kapellmeister*. He had talked of a journey to London to make money in 1820; rather than take the hint, the Archduke had wished him *bon voyage*.

Rumours had spread: that he had been made *Kapellmeister*; that his pension had been increased by incredible sums. He had to waste valuable time quashing such rumours and quelling intrigues. His favourite Fidelio, Milder-Hauptman, visiting Vienna from Berlin, had told him that it was thought that he received 4000 florins C.M. pension from Rudolph.

Archduke Rudolph, the youngest son of Emperor Leopold II and half-brother of Emperor Franz, had first studied music under Tayber, the Imperial Chamber Music *Kapellmeister* whose job Beethoven had tried to fill. Almost two decades younger than Beethoven, the Archduke had become his pupil when in his mid-teens. Beethoven had first heard him play in the salons of Lobkowitz. In those days Beethoven had thought nothing of twisting his fingers. When Rudolph had reminded him of his place, Beethoven had told him, 'God has made many princes but only one Beethoven.' These days Rudolph said, 'I love the man. He's the most genuine creature I've ever had near me.' Beethoven had written the piano part of the Triple Concerto for him as early as 1804. 'Challenge the boy. He can play it.'

By 1809 the King of Westphalia, Bonaparte's brother, had offered Beethoven the post of his Chief *Kapellmeister*. To persuade Beethoven to stay in Vienna, the Archduke Rudolph, Prince Kinsky and Prince Lobkowitz had pledged Beethoven an annuity which in those days had stood at 4000 florins. Since then there had been various vicissitudes: the bankruptcy of Lobkowitz; the death of Kinsky, in 1812, from a fall from his horse. Beethoven had had to threaten to take both noble families to court. This and the devaluation of the currency in 1811 had cast him into poverty for a period. Now the annuity stood at 1,360 florins in silver. He had bought his bank shares from the lump sums for arrears of annuity and gifts from the Congress.

The Archduke had travelled to Prague to try to bring about a resolution of the Kinsky affair. The Archduke had enthusiastically introduced Beethoven to nobles and monarchs at the Congress, glorying in his teacher's success. Beethoven had sought the Archduke's help in 1819 when he had petitioned the Archduke Ludwig for help in his battle to win back his nephew and get a passport to send him out of the country. When his name was being slandered by Johanna, the Archduke had agreed to bear testimony on his behalf.

In 1819 Rudolph had been created Cardinal Archbishop of Olmütz. The *Missa Solemnis* had been promised to him by Beethoven for his solemnization. The official ceremony had taken place on March 9th, 1820. Beethoven had presented the Mass to him on 19th March, 1823.

To the Archduke's declaration that Beethoven was 'one of my most precious possessions,' Beethoven had responded by likening himself to Blondel. 'If there is no Richard for me in this world, God will be my Richard.' The Archduke's letter had been an act of kindness and reassurance, coming as it did only weeks after his inauguration at which Beethoven's Mass should have been performed. Later that year, the Archduke had stood surety for a 750 florin C.M. loan from Artaria. In the summer of 1822 Beethoven had told Johann, 'The Cardinal Archduke is here and I go to him twice a week. I have no hope of generous treatment or money, I admit. But I am on such a good, familiar footing with him that it would hurt me deeply not to be pleasant to him. Besides, I do believe that his apparent niggardliness is not his fault.'

Both men were frequently ill: the Archduke with rheumatism of the hands and epilepsy, from which he suffered regular fits; Beethoven with his intestines, catarrh, chest colds and aching ears, more recently with rheumatism and jaundice. Their sympathy for each other at these times was sincere.

He had set themes for variation by the Archduke and had praised his efforts – for, besides the piano, the Archduke was the only pupil he had ever taught regularly in composition. 'Continue to practice, jotting down your ideas briefly at the piano. For this a little table beside the piano will be necessary. By this means not only is the creative fancy strengthened, but one also learns to grasp the remotest ideas. It is also necessary to write without the piano; and sometimes to develop a simple chorale melody with simple and again with varied figurations with counterpoint and again without. This will cause no headache to Y.I.H. but will rather give you great pleasure at finding yourself absorbed in the art. Gradually there comes the capacity to represent just what we wish and feel, an essential need in the case of men of noble mold.' The Archduke had been one of the 50 other composers who had contributed to Diabelli's variations. His had been a fugue. Beethoven had told the Archduke, of composition, 'There is nothing higher than to approach the Godhead more nearly than other mortals and by means of that contact to spread the rays of the Godhead through the human race.'

Of all his patrons, he had dedicated to Rudolph the greatest number of his greatest works: the piano sonata, Opus 106; Opus 111, though that one had been meant for Toni ... He had dedicated the song-cycle to Lobkowitz; the old Prince had died just before it had been published. Peters, the tutor of Lobkowitz' sons, was now Karl's co-guardian. All Lobkowitz had got recently had been a Cantata for the young Prince's 26th birthday. He couldn't remember that Kinsky had had anything since 1815, when the second *An die Hoffnung* had been sent to his widow, and the last dedication he could recall to Lichnowsky had been a canon to Count Moritz calling him a sheep!

In spring last year the Archduke's presence in Vienna had clashed with his trying to sort out his financial affairs, supervise the copying of the subscription copies of the Mass, and urgently despatch outstanding works. He had complained heatedly to Ries, his former pupil, in London, that these daily lessons of two and a half to three hours robbed him of time and left him not fit to think. He had even thought of fleeing to London to escape. 'Things have become too difficult. I am being shorn by the Cardinal more closely than I used to be. If I don't go to him, my absence is regarded as *lèse-majesté*.' He had set the Archduke a theme for variation and the man had been eager for his supervision at every stage. He had again been writing, 'I know only too well how eagerly some people are striving to prejudice Y.I.H. *against me*,' again dropping a hint about his impecunious circumstances. The only 'additional payment' he had received was that he now had to draw his pittance by means of a stamped form! He had even had to ask the Archduke's permission to publish the Mass and obtain a written testimonial to the effect that the Mass was finished and could be sold! He had begun writing him a canon, *Grossen Dank*. ... Nerving himself to tell the Archduke about the subscription copies, several months after he had begun the project ...

The subscription project! What a farce that had been! Only 10 copies in all, 500 ducats minus the cost of copying, which had been colossal; kowtowing like a Schindler to every damn court toady! He had rebuked one, some ill-mannered Hofrat, 'Do not call on me again!' only to learn that this fathead had been in the service of the Grand Duke of Darmstadt, to whom he had been selling a copy! He had gone on amending the Mass throughout the preparation of the subscription copies, after the presentation to the Archduke: adding trombones, wearing a hole in the very thick paper with his revisions for the timpani part of the *Agnus Dei*.

Last year Beethoven had urged the Archduke to recommend Drechsler as second court organist against the candidate put forward by Abbé Stadler, the fool who had laughed at his concert, though Drechsler had not got the post.

There were those, Beethoven knew, who disliked him for his lack of etiquette. He had even himself joked about it: 'At court and no courtier! Why, the possibilities are endless!' The Archduke himself had long since accepted his inability to conform, but others did not, and there were those, he felt, who hated him for this alone and who would happily intrigue against him.

Rudolph called him 'My most precious possession' yet nothing induced him to part with more money. And yet the original annuity agreement had read, 'only one who is as free from care as possible can devote himself to a single area of activity and create works of magnitude which are exalted and which ennoble art.' He had *accepted* the annuity on the understanding that the post of Imperial *Kapellmeister* would be his later! But Rudolph had not even made him his own *Kapellmeister*. Oliva had told him, 'You would have hated it in Olmütz – official dinners, surrounded by Cardinals . . .' 'Needn't have been Olmütz! I could have stayed here. All he wants from me is works! He's getting that, isn't he! Jesus Christ! I bust my guts!'

'O yes. Ideal words for the Cardinal's table. "Jesus Christ. I bust my guts."'

He was also bound by the terms of the annuity not to travel without the signatories' permission, which these days meant the Archduke. Their estates still paid up, but it was the Archduke he dealt with. The Archduke had never refused him permission to travel, when he had wanted to go to England – in 1818; again in 1820 – but he detested being in the position of having to ask and put his case. Beethoven had once called him dryly 'The only lord and master I have in this world.'

. . . Wanting to travel, in 1818, 1820, 1821 . . . wanting to go to her . . . Down on one knee, presenting the beautifully copied Mass to his epileptic Prince, his soul full of Karl Josef, happily that day, what he would do for him . . . Telling Galitzin to try to get the Czar's permission to dedicate the Mass . . . Rudolph had *asked* that the Mass be dedicated to him! . . . Writing the Mass, writing the *Hammerklavier*, for Rudolph, in 1817, when he had first known . . . he had thought Rudolph an epileptic, *like his son* . . . Even as he was thinking this he saw the unreality, besides the futility, of his bitterness, felt sickened at the thought of all those years of seeing his son in Rudolph: *Rudolph is an epileptic and I can teach him, he plays, he composes.* The recollection of his high manic brightness lacerated like a whip drenched in filth; he was also no longer delighted but bitter that the Mass had first been performed for musicians' widows: what right have *I – I* shall never have *a widow*, *I* was never *married to her* . . . And the Choral *let him who has not a loving wife creep away swiftly from our band* – the support he had got from her in writing that, the memory of *her* – Let him who has not a *mad son* whom he has *never seen* and never done a *hand's turn* to *help*, never even *gone to see*, to *try* . . . He could not bear his own self-hatred, though his thoughts would not free him: whom he was not even *entitled* to *create* . . . let him be *born* . . . left him to *other people* . . .

He stood on a rock, staring across the beautiful mountains of the *Helenenthal. Woman, behold thy son.*

On July the 13th he wrote to Steiner, enclosing two annuity receipts from Rudolph and Kinsky to be cashed against his outstanding debt. In April he had got £50 from the English for their Symphony. He would have to live off that and what was left of the money from Duport. After this he only owed Steiner 150 florins W.W. He warned Steiner that the 750 from the Archduke could only be drawn 'on a stamped sheet of paper. This is the only advantage I have gained from the elevation of my most eminent patron.' He had also given the Archduke's February payment to Steiner.

It had not always been so. He had deposited money with Steiner after the Congress: 4000 florins in silver from his arrears and from the little pouch-bags full of ducats that sovereigns distributed as if they were bags of sweets . . . In those days he had written to them in the language of Napoleon: Diabelli *Herr Diabolus*, Haslinger *The Little Adjutant*, Steiner *Lieutenant General* and he himself *Generalissimus*. '60 well-armed men' had been 60 ducats, his price for Opus 101. By that time he had already owed them 1300 florins, for he would not touch his capital.

He had used Steiner as his banker, having him change bills, cash drafts, and advance money against such debts as payment of Karl's surgeon after his hernia operation. Five years ago he had withdrawn his capital, investing in 8 shares of bank stock, though he had not paid back his debt. At the end of 1820 Steiner had sent him a dunning letter saying that he had paid Beethoven 8% on his investment and only charged him 6% on his loan. Beethoven had then assessed his debts to Steiner as being in the region of 2,500 florins. Arrangements had been made to pay this in two twice-yearly instalments, but Beethoven had not been able to pay. The payment of the first instalment, two years overdue, of 600 florins C.M., which Beethoven had again had to borrow, had ultimately led to the sale of his bank share.

By 1823 Steiner had been threatening to sue him for the balance, his debt to Brentano was still outstanding, and Lind his tailor was also threatening to sue. Johann had refused to loan money or stand as his guarantor. He remembered that time: the storms had been dreadful, the snow thick. He had had diarrhoea all year. Schindler had told him to drink less cold water, his apothecary brother had told him to take powdered rhubarb and avoid fish! And in this condition, in this weather, he had been expected to run hither and thither to check that *Johann* had dealt with his tailor and *Schindler* with the sale of his bank share! Just as he had been trying to sell, the turmoil in Spain had affected the price of his shares; he had had to sell one and pledge another in order to receive the required sum.

Bach had visited him that January when he had thought of bringing a counter-claim against Steiner for withholding from publication his three overtures. Karl had written that Bach had said he was glad he'd married because it meant that he didn't have to bother about housekeeping problems. 'An experience which Apollo hasn't had,' the lawyer had written. 'It's all right to be on your own if you can't be married. Marriage is the greatest bliss if one has found the right partner, but it's like being in hell with the devil himself if one has made the wrong choice.' That had been at the time when he had been making a fool of himself over Unger, when the re-introduction of Varnhagen into his life in connection with the sale of the Mass to Prince Radziwill had led him to recall that night in 1812 when he had been due to meet Varnhagen in Prague. Instead *she* had come to him. 'Ludwig, I'm having your baby.'

He had fretted a great deal about his debt to Brentano; he had even thought of dedicating the *Diabelli* Variations to him until he had learnt that the piano sonata in C had not been dedicated to Antonie by that bastard Schlesinger.

The sale of his bank share had realized 1,250 florins W.W. and he had still been in debt. It was then he had thought of selling the Mass by subscription. He had tried to sell one to the Weimar Court through Goethe. 'For now I am no longer alone,' he had written to Goethe, telling him of Karl. Goethe had known him in 1812 when he had been in the midst of his crisis: unable to be alone, unable to be with her. Goethe had visited him in Teplitz. Goethe had come from Karlsbad. Goethe had met *her* in Karlsbad, had even brought him a message from her. '*Franz* sends his love?' 'She says they both send their love.'

He had told Goethe and the courts that the Mass would not be published in the normal way 'for the present.' To Goethe's friend Zelter and the *Singakademie* of Berlin he had let them think that the Mass would not be published in the normal way at all. He had also sold a copy to the *Cäcilienverein* of Frankfurt on a similar understanding. He felt bad about all this, but what could he do: his debts were bad even after he had sold a bank share.

There had been no sale to the *Singakademie* through Zelter, nor one through Goethe from whom he had had no reply. They had paid between them 500 ducats, but he had had to oversee the production of 10 copies each fit for a king. His copyist had grown ill and died; Rampel, the man's replacement, was a presumptuous fool.

Haslinger was the reason why he still used Steiner's music shop in the little *Paternostergaße* as his *Poste Restante* address and still regularly visited there. Haslinger had been Steiner's partner since 1816. One of *Kapellmeister* Glöggl's singing-boys at Linz, Haslinger had learned diverse instruments and had studied composition. Beethoven had once roared at one of the young man's piano works. 'Asses' ears!' In 1821 Beethoven had written him a canon, 'Tobias dominus Haslinger O! O!'

For as long as he had been trying to sell the Mass, he had been trying to get a publisher to agree to bring out a collected edition of his works. Haslinger had begun to publish one, starting with the early piano sonata in E-flat, but this had not got beyond the second issue.

He had wanted to buy a house. He had thought that he could get 10,000 florins C.M. from an edition of his collected works, and buy a house of some sort. Johann had bought his estate in Krems in 1819, when he had been siding with Johanna, trying to cut *him* out of the guardianship. He himself had tried to buy a house in Mödling in 1819, tried again with the same house in 1820. He flinched as he recalled telling A about this, her hurt response, that he was putting his brother's child before his own, as though this cut out her and Karl Josef completely ...

In 1820 Haslinger had also begun having calligraphic copies made of Beethoven's works. He had sold these to the Archduke in 1823. Rudolph had paid 4000 florins C.M. for these. *Huh!* He'd have done better to have given this loot to his needy *Kapellmeister!*

With Frau Schnaps the other day, he had seen their ex-servant and her bastard. 'Dear girl, lovely child,' he had written dryly. He was still trying to arrange to see the father, and see that they were provided for. He could not see women and children suffer. He had made over her full pension to Johanna this year despite the objections of everyone, including Karl.

Frank's name had come up in the conversation a day or two ago and the boy had written, 'If they'd turned to Frank in my father's case! He himself has said he would have been saved.' Beethoven had registered with shock that the boy had still not come to terms with his father's death. Nor had he accepted him as his father.

Beethoven remembered: he had accused Johanna of poisoning her husband. He had had Bertolini carry out an autopsy. Nearly eight years after the event, Beethoven had shown the boy the unpleasant letter from his office sent to Caspar Carl less than a month before his death, implying that he was malingering and demanding his return to work. At this the boy had opened up about both his parents, writing about his mother, 'I remember her often telling me that, whenever she asked her father for money he said, "I won't give you any. But if you manage to get money from me without my noticing, then you can keep it." Naturally in this way she learnt to steal without punishment.'

The boy had turned against his mother in 1820 when, after fighting through the courts for custody of him, she had seemed to lose interest at the beginning of that year, involving herself in a liaison that had produced his illegitimate half-sister. Karl had not liked it when he had tried to help his mother in early 1823, when they had learned that she was ill, repeating Johann's accusations that the child was by Raicz, a Hungarian medical student who had lodged with them even when his father was alive, that Hofbauer didn't know this and believed the child was his; that helping her might encourage her even further in her wicked ways; that Bernard went running to her too; that she was always to be seen in the company of notorious whores.

Johann too had been bemused. ... This woman whom he had fought through all the courts of the land for custody of her son. It was even said he had defrauded the father's will to get the boy. In 1819 he had become so deranged and so obsessive that he, Johann, had had to step in, agreeing with Johanna to take over the guardianship or pay the boy's school fees if necessary. And yet at that very time, in the middle of the court battle, when he had not even been the guardian, Johann had since learnt that Beethoven had been writing to Bernard soliciting Steiner to make arrangements whereby Johanna's full pension could be made over to her.

Beethoven had opposed them all. He had made over to her that half of her pension which, according to their agreement of May 1817, she had been supposed to pay him for Karl's education. He had also taken over her outstanding debt to Steiner of 280 florins 25 kr. He had first borrowed money from Steiner on her behalf in 1813 when Caspar Carl, thinking he was dying, had made out his will granting him sole custody of Karl. ... The time his own Karl had been born ... '*I don't believe this*! *You* bought *each other's sons*!' O boy, boy, you don't know the half of it! ' ... Of course you did!' Zmeskall had stormed. 'You give your brother 1,500 florins, that bastard in Frankfurt gives you the same!'

His connection with Steiner began through Johanna: his need to get money quickly to give her. At the time of the will of 1813, Beethoven had helped them out then with £200 from George Thomson of Edinburgh for his Scottish songs: showering ducats about his brother on the bed. He had given his brother all his money, *so that he could not go to Frankfurt, so that he could not be tempted*. Later that year CC had approached him threatening to withdraw the will if further money was not forthcoming. It was then that he had entered into a deal with Steiner, standing surety for a loan to Johanna in return for two piano sonatas. ... The Brentanos had sent him money at the same time, he thought through Clemens. '*I don't believe this! You* bought *each other's sons*!' He had already owed Franz – was it 60 ducats – before he had left them at Franzensbad. Left them! Ha! Been *flung out*!

' ... Well why did you make that loan over to *her* if you knew she was not to be trusted!' Johanna had been had up for embezzlement; it had been on this ground that he had fought the court cases ...

... 1815, CC acting as agent, in a deal whereby he'd sold all his outstanding works to Steiner, including the 7th and 8th Symphonies, the *Battle* and *Fidelio*. CC had needed money at the time ...

And then his bastard of a brother on the day before his death had altered his will making Johanna co-guardian. Beethoven had got hold of this will and with his brother's quill, sitting beside his dying brother, deleted all parts that bore a reference to Johanna as co-guardian. And when he had left, Caspar Carl had made out a codicil reinstating Johanna. He had died before Beethoven could get hold of that.

It had come out in court that Beethoven had defaced his will, though it could not be proved. It had come out in court that Karl had been 'an object of transaction between the two brothers.' And then, *in the middle of the court cases*, Johanna had got pregnant. . . . Appealing to the Emperor with a belly on her out to here . . .

She had married Caspar Carl because she was pregnant: the wedding in May 1806, the boy born in September . . . Beethoven remembered: the forced marriage, the house arrest when in 1811 CC had brought a charge of embezzlement against her; the court cases of 1816, 1819, 1820; Johanna's dressing up as a sweep to try to see her son when Karl was at Giannatasio's; his calling her a whore, *The Queen of Night* . . .

They did not understand. He did not want to hurt her. He had had to have custody of Karl. When his brother had seemed to be dying in 1813, on the day he had learnt his own son had been born . . . O God, no one had any idea how he had fought then not to go to Frankfurt, to be with them, to stay with them . . . CC dying of tuberculosis, his wife and his son in poverty . . .

. . . They did not *understand*! No one *knew*! He had told no one, except Countess Erdödy, when he had tried to starve to death in her grounds, and Zmeskall, who had guessed anyway. Erdödy had long since left Vienna, had been had up herself on some charge of cruelty to her children: her son had died, her daughter been put into the care of nuns. Zmeskall had been crippled by gout since 1819, confined to his chair and his home. Neither of his brothers had ever known.

Karl himself, who had lied and cheated, stolen from him once, in those early days, run to her whenever he had been in trouble, now joined in the abuse which she inspired in Johann. Soon after their reunion in 1822, Beethoven had told his brother that he had 'shouldered a portion of the debts incurred by Karl's mother, for so long as Karl's prospects are not thereby endangered I am glad to be as kind to her as possible.' When last year Beethoven had learned that she was ill and could not pay for her medicines, Johann had said that Hofbauer had told him, 'She and her child have by now cost him 30,000 florins and he still gives her 40 florins per month.' Karl wrote down all Johann's accusations. 'Although she is my mother I have to confess that I believe that you should first make precise enquiries about her circumstances. For it could easily happen that with such a contribution she would be in a position to carry on her sordid way of life; and then it would be a question of supporting her vices rather than performing a good deed.' His bitterest thought seemed to be that his mother had been immoral when his father was still alive.

Johanna had sent them New Year greetings this year. Beethoven had responded with best wishes from himself and Karl. When Karl had seen this he had said, 'Not from me.' Beethoven had sat him down. . . . 1820, taking the boy to see his new half-sister: the babe in his arms, Karl slouching in the doorway, refusing to enter the room. In the street, clouting him, 'His own mother! No man calls his own mother a whore!' Reaching home to find scrawled on his slate, '*Whore!*'

By the end of July he had heard from Schotts who had offered to deal with him through his favourite bankers, Fries. He had dedicated the 7th to Fries. . . . Going to him to get money from George Thomson of Edinburgh when Karl Josef was born, longing to go to them, giving the money instead to CC. . . . They had promised to bring out excellent editions. Schotts struck him as music-lovers rather than just people out to pick his brains: they ran the *Cäcilia*; they had introduced him to Rummel, that *Kapellmeister* from Wiesbaden. . . . And now he was selling it to a publisher in Mainz, even nearer to them than Bonn . . . In 1821 Franz had advanced him the money from Simrock for the Mass. He had not sold to Simrock. He still owed Franz the money.

He had copied out and kept under glass on his writing desk three inscriptions from Schiller's essay *Die Sendung Moses*:

I AM THAT WHICH IS.

I AM ALL, WHAT IS, WHAT WAS, WHAT WILL BE.
NO MORTAL MAN HAS EVER LIFTED MY VEIL.

HE IS SOLELY OF HIMSELF, AND TO THIS ONLY ONE ALL THINGS OWE THEIR EXISTENCE.

He broke off from a good spell of work thinking, there are times in my life when for me to compose music is the easiest thing in the world. Easier than breathing, easier than shitting, easier than eating, easier than making love. And, when it was going well like this – O, everyone in the world, don't you wish you were me!

'Marriage is hard . . . you have to work at it,' he recalled as he swilled water over his hot face. O no, marriage isn't hard. Marriage is easy. You marry the right person and you don't have to work at it at all.

He towelled his face, neck and hands. Marriage isn't hard. Composing music isn't hard. Putting on concerts is hard. Bringing up kids is hard.

Chapter 5

August

The start of the month found him writing to his lawyer, Bach, concerning his will. As often when work was going well, he feared being cut short by death or illness. Of late this had taken the form of fearing that he would have a stroke like grandfather Ludwig, the Bonn *Kapellmeister*.

He left everything to Karl save his French piano, which was to go to Johann. The first 600 florins C.M. from Schotts he told his lawyer must be paid to the Brentanos.

In 1820 it had been agreed that he would see Simrock in Bonn and visit Frankfurt the following year, perhaps on his way to London. He had still had plans to do this by the early spring of 1821. Franz had advanced him Simrock's fee for the Mass so as to fund the journey.

Toni had grown increasingly desperate, begging for help from everyone for Karl Josef. By April the boy had been seen by various doctors and several treatments had been proposed. His regular doctor wanted to stick to the machines which they now felt hampered the necessary nourishment of his weak legs. Some ordered the boy to go sea-bathing. Some urged application of herbal poultices. Some advised them to do nothing at all. Walter in Bonn wanted to cauterize the eight year old boy in the loins.

Beethoven remembered: that church in Vienna where he had prayed daily in 1817, when he had first known, *Don't let them burn my child's loins!* Unkeening grief, sobless tears, praying before the icon of a child in whom he did not believe through a mother whom he could not deify, calling as intercessor Toni, that his doubt be made whole by her belief.

And now it was upon him: he had been asked by Franz to go to Frankfurt, to choose which of these treatments be deemed for his son; if necessary to give permission, as the natural father, for the burning of *his child's loins*.

All the years he had yearned: go to Frankfurt!

Asked! By Franz! To go to Frankfurt!

To give permission for the burning of his child's loins.

Advised by a doctor in *Bonn*.

He had fallen ill with jaundice.

He had been ill with jaundice all July, all August. In September his doctor had sent him to Baden. He had had to flee back to Vienna with diarrhoea.

In October Toni had taken Karl Josef to Gall in Paris.

How they had hoped! In December, sending Opus 109 to Maxe, when it had seemed as though all would be well, writing lyrically to the 19 year old of her 'excellent and gifted mother,' her father 'ever mindful of the welfare of his children,' of seeing them all in the *Landstrasse* as they had been when he had known them all, when he had lived within the bosom of that family he had so nearly destroyed.

Writing to Franz two weeks later, about the Mass, when it had seemed that all would be well, wishing him happiness in his children, sending through him warm greetings to 'your excellent, one and only, glorious Toni.'

14 times Gall had applied moxa, a woolly, light, inflammable material, burned against Karl Josef's loins.

Gall had held out great hope.

Toni had become an angel of grief.

Karl Josef still could not walk.

With the death of hope he had turned towards quartets, he had turned towards his brother, in need of help and comfort: the comfort and help of art, the comfort and help of some other human being. The depressed summer of 1822 when his hopes had been dashed, throwing caution to the winds in any attempt to get more money, quickly, for the Mass; spinning one yarn to Schlesinger, another to Brentano. On the 19th of May he had been writing to Brentano that he would keep faith with Simrock about the Mass even if it meant a loss, though at the start of that month he had written offering the Mass to Schlesinger. 'Such a kind, loveable and unselfish fellow,' he had called Franz to Schlesinger.

It seemed that he had been writing to Franz for years, 'Do not question my honesty . . . frequently I think of nothing but how your kind advance may soon be repaid . . . Please be patient . . . do not think that you have acted nobly towards an unworthy man.' In January 1823 he had tried to pay back the debt, until he found that this would have meant having to sell two bank shares. He had sent Franz instead 300 florins C.M.

A year ago he had had a warm letter from Franz telling him that Karl Josef was improving. He had replied asking for Franz' help in getting the *Missa Solemnis* to England, perhaps through the assistance of Franz' 23 year old son Georg, then in London. When Franz' reply had arrived one month later, he had been too terrified to open the letter, fearful lest the hitherto good news about Karl Josef now be replaced by bad.

All those years of looking at young boys in the street of roughly Karl Josef's age: does he look like this one? Or this one? I have a son, alive in this world, whom I have never seen, whom I would not recognize if I passed him in the street . . . I have a son, by a woman I have never seen since six months before his birth . . .

He had told Spohr last autumn, when he had had Karl living with him, how greatly he envied his peaceful family life. . . . Spohr, to whom he had gone night after night in 1813, detesting the man at times yet needing the comfort of his family, his wife who played the harp, their young children, when he had grieved in the first months of Karl Josef's life.

Karl had said at the time of Frau Blöchlinger's parents' golden wedding anniversary, 'They have been married almost as long as you have been in the world.' He had been writing the *adagio* of the *Choral* at the time.

He remembered the first time he had seen her, Bettina's open-faced vivacity contrasting with Toni's more solemn beauty. She was slender, gentle, pale and tall, elegant and aristocratic, with her long thin neck and erect stance. He had thought her cold when she had been, instead, unhappy. Her humour had not then been apparent. She had told him later, of that first visit, 'I did not want to come. Bettina dragged me there. I had heard that you were an ogre. I stopped being afraid of you before we met – when we overheard you and your servant.

'"Two women to see you."

'"Young?"

'"Yes."

'"Beautiful?"

'"Yes."

'"Married?"

'"One Frau, one Fräulein."

'"Hot water! Quick, man! I must shave!"'

Bettina had been all over him, dragging him out: on walks, to the Brentanos', where she was staying with her half-brother, Franz. By the time she had left Vienna at the end of that month, he had grown familiar with the whole family, visiting regularly, playing for them.

He thought she had rescued him from his misery after his rejection by Therese Malfatti. He had joined the Malfatti family circle through his friend Gleichenstein, who was engaged to Therese's sister. He had even wanted Gleichenstein to propose to Therese for him. How his friends must have laughed – there he was, writing off to Bonn for his birth certificate so that he could marry, involving all his friends in the project – Breuning, Wegeler – when all the time his doctor's niece and her parents and sister had seen him as nothing more than their own personal glorified music teacher!

That had happened in May 1810; that same month, Bettina had come to him. Less than a year later, there had been Toni, touching his hand sympathetically as she showed him Bettina's letter about her marriage to her old love, Arnim.

He had shaken her off. He hated her pity. He had not even seen her then: this married woman, wife of his friend, Franz, mother of four, a mere ten years younger than himself, older by far than girls he had hitherto courted. He had always seen himself marrying a Viennese aristocrat but this woman was too old, too queenly: God, she put other aristocrats in the shade, even if she was physically just his type, with legs that went on for ever, a slender waist and small round breasts. Razumovsky's quartet had started giving concerts round there, he'd even seen one of the men looking at her and wondered why. Yes, one who looked like that but younger, not flighty but vivacious, for God's sake, God, that one was cold: give me a bit of life! He remembered: he had even felt sorry for Franz, that warm friendly man, tied to that ice goddess.

And then a lot of things had happened at once. Franz' half-brother Clemens had sent him a cantata text he wanted setting, but instead of sending it through his half-brother he had sent it to her. He rejected the text but by this time he had learned of her accomplishments at the piano and at the guitar. He had first quickened to her beauty when she had had her long hair put up by her servant, the better to play the guitar, and he had caught sight of the nape of her slender neck.

. . . She had rushed to him after concerts, flinging her arms about his own neck – not, mark you, after his playing! O no! This brazen hussy had the nerve to run and so thank him after his *quartets*!

How she could talk! About his quartets! How she could listen: still, absorbed. If only I had a hall-full like her! he had thought once catching sight of her, in those early days.

She had started then coming to him for music – for her guitar! . . . Asking if he had her music, after one concert, Falstaff and the rest of the quartet all around, Franz with a face on him like thunder while he, an erection up to his eyeballs, had had to spin from her, making as though to look at music, bellowing, 'Ask *Schuppanzigh*!' Everyone knew at that, of course. He never called Falstaff anything but Falstaff. Yet he had never then laid hands on the woman outside her husband's sight.

He had borne it all year: going to Teplitz that summer, 1811, on doctor's orders, falling in with a group of new friends, screwing the arse off Varnhagen's fiancée, Rahel, who, although older, bore a passing look of her.

After the summer, back to Vienna. She had come to Vienna in 1809 to be with her father at his death, persuading her husband to stay on while she settled her father's estate. The imposing 40-room Birkenstock mansion, overlooking the grounds of Razumovsky's palace, was packed to the gills with the statesman's collection: paintings by Dürer, Holbein, Van Dyke, Raphael, Rembrandt; more copper-plate engravings and drawings than you could shake an elaborately-carved stick at; antique urns, Etruscan lamps; vases of marble; Chinese garments; coins; geological collections; sea insects; telescopes; precious documents; maps of antiquity. He had even got Rudolph to bid for something at one of her art auctions.

Her father's death had affected her badly. She stayed for whole days in her room. He had taken to going to play for her, in her antechamber, before going off to give Rudolph his lesson, after the by now obligatory session with one of the fortresses.

One day she came out to him while he was playing. . . . Talking about his *Razumovskys*, the bitch had been talking about his *Razumovskys*, in her

God-damn fucking *nightgown*! Afterwards he had always maintained that she had seduced him. 'You come to me . . . day after day . . . play your . . . fortepiano . . . in the anteroom . . . to my bed-chamber . . . and have the nerve . . . to say . . . that I seduced you!' she had told him, laughing, rocking him back and forth in Karlsbad.

'He let you play to her day after day in the anteroom to her bedchamber!' Zmeskall had bellowed. 'What the hell did the bastard *think* would happen! Betrayed a friend! I tell you, he *instigated* it! He was trying to get your kid out of her! It's just his bad luck he failed.'

He had tried to stop it. She had sent her beautiful daughters to him, with gifts of flowers and fruit. It had become a family joke: 'O, he never can resist Maxe!' Her nine-year old daughter announcing, 'When I'm grown up I'm going to marry Beethoven!' He had written a one-movement piano trio for her; they had planned to put it on, behind her parents' backs, as a surprise, with Falstaff and Linke accompanying her.

. . . Coming to him when he was writing the 7th, bawling her out. She had left, stayed away. His life empty, full, without her: missing her yet glad she wasn't there.

. . . Coming to him a fortnight later, when he had feared she might have typhoid. 'I wanted to have your baby and all I get is *food-poisoning*!' Walking back with her. 'Did you tell me you wanted to bear my child?' 'You've known that for ages . . .'

He had spent that night helpless with love for her. Then, the next day, that row about his silly remark when he had been teaching Maxe, 'O what am I going to do without you all when you're in Frankfurt!' He had forgotten he had said it. He had thought that she was taunting him. Fighting with her, when she had been ill. Yanking her head back. 'You ought to know that I couldn't go through this again! Not with *you*! A man can stand just so much!' Franz had sent her out with him to get some air, saying he had to work, though she had pestered to be taken not by him but by Franz.

'I spent all last night in a passion of tenderness for you!'

Feeling in his pockets, laughing, 'Pad and pencil, but no comb!'

'Toni, when you're better, do you want me to give you a child?'

. . . 'What a thing to tell a man when he can't do anything about it!' he had exclaimed a week later when they had started making love again.

Christ, I had forgotten how good it was with you, Toni, Toni, my own beauty. No, you never did taunt me. Easy. She had just come to him. Easy. All the years of struggle wiped out. This one, for ever. Easy. Easy. Christ, he had even worked with her, in the same room: gone round there once, when she had been ill, put his hat on to leave, sat working, on the 7th, still with his hat on. Franz had found them. 'But why is he composing in here?' Composing, in her bedroom, fully dressed, even down to his hat. 'You're the only man I can trust her with. And that, I suspect, is only because you are working. Still, I believe you about tonight.' Franz had bought her some earrings. 'Because she's my wife and I love her and she's been ill.' He had walked between them, one arm round Toni, one arm round Franz, promising them some fancy concert, his latest, still unpublished, quartet; deliriously happy, no conundrum at all, it would all be worked out; unconscionably in love with this woman whose husband had just bought her earrings in a renewed expression of his love; on their way downstairs to meet this couple's lovely children with whom he would play the piano and sing and laugh and play.

At the time of the third art auction, June 1812, just before their separate trips to the Bohemian spas, he had stood one night gazing up at her window: O God help me, I want to *marry* her!

They had not made any plans to meet that summer: he was to go to Teplitz, they to Karlsbad and Franzensbad. Both journeys coincided by way of Prague. He had set off a day or so before them. He had met Kinsky, to arrange an upgrading of his annuity payment following the devaluation of the Viennese currency. He had been about to leave the hotel to keep his appointment with Varnhagen, to discuss this business further, when Antonie had knocked on his door.

... 'I can't bear you to leave me!'

'I'm not leaving you!'

'You're going back to that girl – in Teplitz – from last year!'

'Her fiancé's here! She isn't going to be there!'

'I can't bear to lose you!'

... 'Would you marry me if you could?'

'I am married to you ...'

'O you will leave me. You will go back to him. God has never meant for me to be this happy!'

'Don't blaspheme!'

'I'm sorry ...'

'Ludwig, I'm having your baby.'

He had always known. He had known – from the time he was writing the 7th.

... 'You never even asked if it could be his!'

... Franz laughing, 'Never marry a beautiful woman, Beethoven! Marry an ugly one, that no one else wants! Especially not a beautiful woman who's ill all the time!'

Zmeskall: 'He didn't want *his*. He wanted *yours*! O, my son, Karl *Brentano*. The little *genius*! Do you think it would be the same if it had been Karl Schmidt or Karl Czerny or Karl Braun? He'd have flung her out of the house and the kid after her.'

She had been ill but they had stayed up all night, talking and making love. ... Exploding in passion, all the things he would do for her, what a great composer he would be now, now that he had her and the child to write for. Everything in his grasp. All easy.

Walking with her to her hotel through the flooding rain, his coat round

her head, his arm round her, he soaking wet and as merry as a lark, as
gleeful as a little kid, as deeply happy as if he were at one with God in
composition. Making her kiss him outside her hotel. Leaning on the wall
when she had gone in: O God, is this really me, am I still alive?

He had left the next day for Teplitz, she and Franz in their carriage to
Karlsbad. He could not then tell Franz: their 6 year old, Fanny, had been
with them.

He had endured a second night without sleep on that dreadful journey,
the post coach stuck in the mud of the flooded unmade-up roads. Telling
her about it, in that letter flooding with terror, flooding with love; calling
a woman *Du* for the first time unreservedly. 'My angel, my all, my very
self . . . I will see to it that you and I, that I can live with you . . . At my age
I need a steady, quiet life – can this be so in our connection?' Finding out
on the third day that the post went daily, rushing back to his room to
finish the letter. 'Be calm, only by calm consideration can we achieve our
purpose to live together . . . O continue to love me!' He had signed himself
'L' with a flourish and then, between flourish and margin, added, 'Ever
thine, ever mine, ever ours.'

. . . Seeing Goethe . . . wanting to be with her . . . eventually fleeing to
her . . . That first night, in her arms, at Karlsbad.

Wanting it to be known that she was his wife: his hand to her breast as
she bent to his ear in front of Franz after that concert he had given in aid
of the people of Baden who had lost their homes in that dreadful fire.

It had all come out in Franzensbad.

. . . Franz standing there, threatening him, with Fanny draped over his
shoulder. The child screaming. Seeing Toni later with a bruised face. She
must have been hysterical, he had had to slap her. My sweet, sweet Toni.
But you are *mine* now . . .

. . . Toni walking back from fetching bonbons for Fanny, her newly-
developing breasts wobbling, *I made her like that*, catching sight of him and
waving.

. . . Franz taunting him with Fanny sitting astride his neck . . .

. . . Asking Franz for an annulment. 'My father *told me* to marry you! I
was in love with someone else at the time! O yes! You knew! . . . Don't
accuse me of being disloyal when I never said I'd be loyal!'

. . . Giving him her father's ring on his name-day.

. . . 'You're a merchant's woman, a rich man's woman! I wish you knew
what living with me means! My God! I wish you had known!'

Leaving that church in Franzensbad with her:

'I want this child . . .'

'I know . . .'

'You don't know! *You* don't know, *he* doesn't know, you've *got* your
children and you *don't know*!'

. . . Franz leaving the baths with him: 'You two would be very happy if
I were dead.'

Horrified. Pretending not to hear.

Trying to do the right thing. Sending her to him. 'My children can grow up without a mother. I had to.'

Boxing his ears when she had found out what he had tried to do: 'Some men are pimps, but I've never heard of anyone who could do that to his *own child!*' He had lain there, taking it from her.

The next day Franz had given him the ultimatum.

He had heard scarcely any of it. 'I'll adopt him. Now. Before he is born. . . . I'll see he's provided for in my will.'

O you bastard you bastard you bastard you bastard *you bastard!*

. . . 'She's not a bastard. She's a love-child.'

Back in that church, praying for strength to leave her. 'It's a good job you're not a Lutheran. It would be very difficult were we not of the same faith.' God help me, if embracing Catholicism could win you for me then I probably should embrace Catholicism.

Praying for strength to leave her! He had prayed for some way to stay with her!

Seeing him return, Franz had sent Toni out to meet him.

'. . . Is it because I boxed your ears? I can't have shown you how much I love you! . . . She's yours! Don't give her away!'

Fanny had appeared, clutching her mother's skirts.

Turning from her, running, turning, 'Go to your dau . . . *to your daughter!*'

He had all my bags packed! I didn't realize!

Franz had had all his bags put into the carriage. Frantic about his music. '*Touch that* – again – and I shall *kill you!*' He had climbed aboard to make sure that everything was there and Franz had had his coachman drive off.

Finding among his music his letter to her, among his clothes his shirt which she had worn as a nightshirt.

He had gone to see his brother in Linz. When he got back to Vienna, they had gone.

He went to the locked drawer in his desk where he kept the letter, his bank share certificates, the miniature of her and the drawing of Karl Josef. He took out the miniature and the picture of his son.

O how they had prayed for this child to live, after the deaths they had known: his younger brother and his sisters; the death of her own eldest child.

He picked up the drawing of Karl Josef. Stieler had drawn this five years ago to try to persuade him to sit for him. Franz had commissioned a portrait of Beethoven for Toni. 'I've seen all her other . . . him I have never seen.' The painter from Fankfurt had drawn the boy as he had seen him some years earlier: a chubby young toddler with one hand to his mother's breast, Toni seated after the fashion of Raphael's *Madonna of the Chair* with Georg as the Baptist figure behind.

He recalled his joy when he had first seen this. He wasn't born funny! He's not . . . he wasn't . . . my God, that baby is a dream!

I gave her a normal baby.

. . . Laughing at his being called 'an unlicked bear.' Pulling his hand to her belly, 'Baby bear.'

O what a beauty you are! What beauties you both are! A part of him could not stop seeing them both like this: Toni young, her almond eyes saucy; Karl Josef as a toddler, about to start walking and jumping and laughing and singing and playing the piano.

For years he had determined that, irrespective of Franz, he would *teach him*.

. . . All those years of wanting to go to her, writing the song-cycle for her, wanting to give her another child. All those years of believing that, in Frankfurt, he had a normal child. *You have a son. Baptised Karl Josef. He and Antonie are well. Born yesterday, March 8th.* He still had this letter, found it, read it: dog-eared and torn, he must have carried it about in his pocket for months until he had shown it to Zmeskall. 'Now he's really told you he's yours: Josef, the patron saint of cuckolds!'

He had composed nothing in 1813 until the *Battle*. For over a year he had composed nothing until a few short fugal pieces before the *Hammerklavier* late in 1817. . . . Writing in that year to Zmeskall, asking him to find him a new servant: 'I would not mind if he were a bit hunchbacked, for then I should know the weak point at which to attack him.' . . . *Karl Josef cannot sit up quite straight . . . She* had written that.

He took up and read his marked piece in Sturm's *Reflections on the Works of God in Nature*: 'How unjustly do they act who . . . despise or treat with asperity those of their fellow creatures who have bodily defects . . . The perfections of the soul alone give man true merit and render him worthy of admiration . . . Have we not seen persons, distinguished by neither birth nor fortune, render the most important services to church and state? Crippled or deformed persons have often shown more magnanimity of soul than those who were favoured with the most beautiful and majestic form.'

. . . 1817, fighting God, abusing God, aware of being watched by God in his torment. He did not know how he had survived. And you, you poor bastard, how do you survive? Slumped in a chair . . . mentally retarded . . . epileptic. *I can't imagine you! I don't know you!*

My own flesh and blood. All those years when she had called upon him to help: go and see! Come to him, play to him! In 1819 she had told Maxe. Maxe had written, inviting him.

'Help! Help! I call to God and my fellow mortals, and anyone with sympathy for me understands the turmoil and stress and will not refuse me what is in his power.'

And what help have I given? Written *piano sonatas* for them! *Magnani-*

mity of soul! Toni was concerned for his soul, she wanted the boy to be aware, to choose, to know God, to know God and to praise Him.

... 'The boy loves piano music. When she plays, he rests his head against his mother's shoulder ...'

Toni had cried in 1821, 'How can one have any desire or strength at all if one has to drink daily, hourly, from such a cup of bitter sorrow?'

He had interrupted the Mass in March 1820 to compose Opus 109 for Maxe. After his jaundice he had interrupted the *Agnus Dei* to write Opus 110 for her. He had made sketches on BACH between those of the Mass and the start of Opus 110. He had finished Opus 110 by Christmas 1821 and Opus 111 three months later. He had then resumed work on the *Dona nobis pacem* and *Agnus Dei* of the Mass. He had then taken up work on the *Diabelli* Variations, begun in February 1819. And every one of these works had been meant for them.

She had grown bitter after his failure to visit. 'I know I mean nothing to you, but I did think that you would come for Maxe.' ... Opus 110 with its *Klagender Gesang*. ... February 1819, when she had written to Sailer for him, to try to get his nephew into the school run by her spiritual adviser in Landshut. ... She had accused him of putting another woman's child before his own.

She always forgave. There was nothing mean in Toni. But her burden was great and he did nothing to lift it, to share it, to participate in it.

... Toni of the slow movement of his Opus 74: 'It's like a man stroking a woman's hair, but women see it, men have to be told.' O God, it was so lovely, Toni! Why does it have to have this bitter end? He could hear her rebuking him: it isn't ended. He's alive. You're alive. Through God's great goodness anything may happen.

Chapter 6

August, Frankfurt

They had a family circle. He had not. He did not get on with his brother. He had fought his other brother's widow through the courts for custody of her son. Often during visits from his vast family of half-brothers and sisters – Bettina and her husband Arnim, Christian or Clemens – or as he watched his daughters at their work, sewing, baking or painting, or watched them with their mother put on some play for his name-day which he himself had performed decades ago for his own parents, Franz thought of the man's loneliness. He often recalled him piercingly when Maxe or Toni played the piano.

Arnim, in his first visit for a number of years, had seen the boy a year before his operations. Perhaps because he had sons of similar age, Arnim had been struck by him. Franz had seen him anew through this stranger's eyes. 'Only as old as that? But he's bigger than my eldest.' Side by side they had stood looking at the seven year old who could neither walk nor stand nor sit properly but who was constrained to half-lie 'Just in the way I have seen old people do who have been paralysed in the legs from a stroke,' Arnim had muttered. Seeing them across the room, the boy had started to talk. He had too long a tongue which he rolled around in his mouth. His speech was dull and broken and he raised his eyes at them in a strange way from below. After listening to him for a while, trying to understand and reply and listen for his answers, Arnim had observed, 'If you'd walked in in the middle of that you would take him for a simpleton, and yet he isn't.'

'Oh no. Before he became ill he was talking in French as well as German. He still brings out the odd French word or sentence sometimes.'

'It's as though it's just the impediment with his tongue that stops him from bringing out a clear, bright answer.'

'What is terrible is that he seems to have lost all the joy in learning that he used to have. For the first few years of his life he was so bright, so eager to learn, I thought he'd outstrip all my other children. He could *apply* himself to one thing – he never had a flighty mind, he could become really engrossed – and this in a three year old.'

Later, over a drink, Arnim had asked what was the cause of the boy's illness and Franz had repeated what they had been told. 'The doctors suspect water on the spinal cord. Walter wants to burn him.'

'Have you considered magnetism?'

'The doctors say that that would only work if there were some impediment in his development.'

'So what is the cause? Is it some disease?'

'They don't know. But it did come on suddenly. He was developing normally until he was three . . . getting on for four. He learnt to talk. As I say, he could speak two languages.'

'Could he walk?'

'Toni still tells people he can walk!'

'How about Toni?'

'O, it's broken her.'

Arnim had seemed surprised.

'She seems just the same . . .'

'O, she hides it. You can only tell when you see her alone. She had such hopes for this child . . . her youngest . . .' Arnim nodded. 'And, as I say, he always seemed so bright. It's ironical: he: retarded. He was streets ahead of the others, and they weren't exactly slouches. . . . Toni's great fear is that he will not have the capacity for spiritual development. You've no idea the grief that is to her. To save his soul . . . to develop his soul he must acquire the state of knowledge to be able to choose, to be able to know . . . Christian came round here once and tried to demonstrate that he may be his own source of happiness if he at least makes a good Christian! Fool! That is just the problem! Ended up by saying, "Well his soul may already be saved, if he is a divine innocent." He isn't that: there was too much knowledge before. It grieves me, God knows, that side of it, but it breaks his mother's heart. Christian with his sloppy talk just makes it worse.

'. . . We have got to decide. The boy is getting bigger every day. It's a physical burden: not just more weight for other people when they have to lift him, but more weight for him to bear. The boy should be given the chance to walk. But it's a horrible decision to have to take.'

'But what caused it?'

He himself could not remember: had it begun with the epilepsy? 'Toni says that it's an act of God.'

'Perhaps you should stimulate him more – get him out more.'

'He always has people round him. Yet you can't gainsay that he is stuck at the stage of development of a four year old.'

. . . But Arnim had seen the boy at a good time: no epilepsy, none of the violence. If he'd been born an idiot, it would have been better, from Toni's view. It would have been better. When a child is normal and grows normally for almost four years, you build up dreams, you invest your life, you will so much, for his life . . .

He had been right about Toni: at that time, she had not changed at all. She was still more beautiful than any other woman in his family. Often he had thought of this, when he thought of Beethoven's seeing her. Beethoven had been ill; he might have changed; he might have thought that she had changed; but one look, when he saw she hadn't . . .

Arnim had evidently told Bettina that, if Toni could give him some grasp of religion, this might be a consolation to him. That she could not was a grief seen only by himself. .... And along comes the boy's natural father like some knight in shining armour. 'From the heart. May it go to the heart.' Toni had been concerned that he save his immortal soul. There you are, boy. Save your immortal soul with *that*.

Others had said that she had aged after 1822 when she had endured grave disappointment after they had taken the boy to Gall. To him she was still his Toni. But the ease with which she held onto the controlled exterior had gone. She persisted for the sake of her daughters who were now of marriageable age, taking them into society, but all was now a great effort. She tried to be fair to the other children, but grief for Karl Josef ruled her life.

... Taking the boy to Paris with her, meeting Gall, giving authorization for any treatment needed as Beethoven's proxy.

And then coming home alone, to be met by Bettina's bright face. He had almost flung himself at her in his emotion: his joy to be back, his grief at what he had endured, his anxiety for Toni, on her own now, his anguish and his fears for Karl Josef. And then the next day a play and a party afterwards, at the house, laughter ringing, guilt at the joy of being without the constant looming presence of his sick son ...

The father deaf, the boy for the most part dumb, both raising their eyes and gazing at you in that strange way from below. Both taken for simpletons. Both twisting him round their little finger. In autumn last year, when his son Georg had gambled and lost 80,000 florins in that one year, when Beethoven had sent 300 florins C.M. instead of returning the full 900 for the Mass, above all when Bettina had quibbled about having Karl when they went to Berlin, preferring to palm him off on Savigny, he had stormed at his wife, 'You have brought Beethoven into this family and he has destroyed it!'

When he had said that she had flinched. He had wanted to bite his tongue off.

He still at nights cried out for her love.

If he walked through that door now, small, pock-marked and ugly, his fat belly held in with a truss, it would be as if there were no difference.

And that child bound them all together. The centre of all their lives. He had never seen him.

He wondered if he would ever come now, wondered it, dreaded it, thought it inevitable that he would.

The man's power was absolute. He could walk in here now and still ruin all their lives ... his, his daughters'.

He had been the most beautiful baby. 'You've got your little genius.'

'Can he write to me yet? Is he playing the piano?'

O God, boy, I grieve for you and you are not even mine. How must *he*?

He remembered when he had asked him to divorce her.

O God, the pain we have all been through together. . . . Like a great child himself. . . . Wanted that. O he wanted *that*! *Your excellent, one and only glorious Toni.* . . . Two middle-aged men with a crippled child between us and we'd still fight duels over the same woman.

He could not escape Beethoven's pain any more than Karl's, he felt both with his own.

And all the time he hid all this, being Franz, the devout businessman.

Sometimes he felt if the man came down he would embrace him for her sake. Sometimes he could not stand the tension. *Come on, man! Get it over with!*

I brought it about. I threw him out. A dozen years ago . . .

Well what was I supposed to do? He was taking my wife from me! From me and my children!

He could have hit Bettina. That had been what had triggered it: after her being there, so warm, virtually flinging himself into her arms when he got back from Gall in October 1821 and then, two years later, being snide about having Karl in her house.

He wondered how much Bettina knew. She had rationalized, 'It's not only him, it's his attendants, the house so full, perhaps Savigny could have him?'

He wondered if she had half-known then. The boy had begun to resemble Beethoven in some lights. He wondered how she felt – part-relieved not to be in Toni's shoes, part-jealous at not having meant more herself to Beethoven?

This year the resemblance he thought was greater. Clemens seemed to have worked it out. He had seen Beethoven not long after the boy's birth, in Vienna. Beethoven had pumped him for information then. 'Fascinated, Beethoven is, to know about your new child.' Now he was merciless towards Toni. Raising his face to heaven, 'God sees all!'

He remembered when Clemens had called him 'like a father – without you I would never have known what it meant to have a father.' He had brought them all up, his half-brothers and sisters. Beethoven had brought up his brothers when his father had turned to drink after the death of his mother.

Beethoven was always wishing him 'fatherly happiness in your children' . . . 'May the Lord long preserve *your dear ones for you.*'

After that business when Maxe had found out about him and her mother, he had heard her once screaming at Maxe, 'He's been deaf for years! He can't hear anything! People have to write to him in books! In *books*!' He had once overheard Toni say to Maxe, 'You pine for them, you know. You can't believe that that little boy is what this little boy's turned into. Your hopes don't die. Instead they seem to take on a life of their own.'

He wished he had someone to say to, it's a terrible thing to watch the woman you love grow old pining for another man. When some men sleep with their wives they dream they are making love to other women. When you've driven me to other women, I've dreamed that I was with you.

She had said to him after his outburst, 'Did you ever deep down know what was happening and want me to have his child?'

'. . . A part of me knows what you mean. A part of me is appalled by your very question.'

'At least I can't complain of lack of honesty in my men . . .'

'You've got nothing to complain of in your men. You've had love from two men such as few women have ever known . . .'

Often he watched her at parties, guiding the groups of cultured men amongst her artistic treasures, holding herself, as ever, very straight. One of the Grimm brothers had said of her, 'She has the bearing of a queen.' He had often dwelt upon the misery so glaringly reflected by that straight back. Not the fight itself but the failure in that one so had to fight: the straight back a symbol of the inability to slump into easy happiness; this ramrod straightness not in defiance of but at the behest of one's fate. *He* had it, too. Often Franz recalled the sight of the pair at Franzensbad; often reflected, how odd that two such ramrod creatures, noted for their upright posture, should have had a son like Karl.

Ja, Nie wird es zu hoch besungen
Retterin des Gatten sein.

Clemens' abuse had aroused deep griefs in Franz. *She had mine because she was married to me; she had his because she couldn't stop herself.*

Beethoven had refused for years to let his son be treated. He had written when they had first known, 'One doctor wants to burn his loins . . .' He had never replied. . . . The first year they had known of the illness, there had been some talk of Karl's taking a spa cure and Beethoven had said he would come down. He had got used by now to Beethoven's telling them he would visit and never coming. *She* hadn't. He had sent them piano sonatas instead. 'The boy loves music.' Last year he had sent that set of variations. One hour long. Dedicated to her.

When she had first had the variations played to her, she had started laughing in sheer delighted humour. 'It takes a genius to take another man's theme and absorb it into a variation he is already writing on another man's theme!' she had exclaimed of the variation on *Don Giovanni*. It had seemed to him then that it would be wicked to countermand her, her pleasure then had been so genuine; in fact, despite his misgivings, he had known heart-felt relief for her.

'I've had enough of you and him – and him!' he had exploded violently after several weeks of controlling a jealousy he had not known existed. 'If he dedicates anything else to you I'll kill him!' His anger expired as quickly as it had come, its place taken by warm magnanimous love, a feeling of well-being, of giving, outwardness to all. He felt that he had smashed her happiness: she had been so genuinely happy and, it now seemed to him, not for the reasons he had suspected but *musically*. He remembered their happiness *as a family* that night they had gathered to choose what to send as a present to Beethoven after his dedication to Maxe. He asked himself, why this hatred now? Nothing had happened. Nothing intrinsic in the situation had changed. Yet Karl had got worse; he had been duped by Beethoven, blackmailed by his son; and they had all got older. Sometimes in self-disgust he suspected: well was it not inherent in the situation that you would be duped by Beethoven?

She had wept with joy when she had received it, even more when she had looked it over and heard parts of it played. 'The old fox!' He could still see her face now, so high in joy she had been actually crying. 'The old fox! The sly old begger!' She had been almost speechless with joy, shaking her head, her soul laughing. The letter he had not seen, but that he suspected of being intimate: she held it to herself, her joy in that deeper and quieter. In terror at times he wondered, do you write to him?

They had had a family evening, two of the girls playing Beethoven's theme and variations for mandolin and piano. 'He was no older than Georg when he wrote this!' At the end she had exclaimed, 'That man twists music round his little finger!' Then she had begun to cry.

The mother prayed for a miracle and the father composed for one.

No, that was unfair. Antonie prayed for Karl to achieve a state whereby he might know God, and Beethoven was not a bad man, of course he wanted recovery, joy, for his son.

Perhaps even to have let them cry together as a family would have helped . . . He had visions of Beethoven's entering the room to see Karl Josef, enfolding the boy to his breast, holding out his arm to pull the mother to him.

Good God, the man gave up his *family*!

Toni thought that he had put his nephew entirely into Karl Josef's place: this was the healthy son he should have had, to bring up, to educate. Through him he fulfilled his duty. Through him he made his peace with God.

This was the woman's view. She could not see what he saw clearly: the man kept away through terror not only of what he might find but, even more, of what he might do.

Besides, the situation had existed before Karl Josef's illness: his brother had died, he had adopted the boy.

It was perhaps made worse by the fact that he had come to her for comfort, starting it up, and she had replied lovingly, in 1816, just before that fool, Simrock's son, had visited them straight from seeing him and then had written telling him, at their first suspicions, before he had had a chance to prepare him, 'Pity the little boy has his troubles.'

. . . Clemens, in his bath, singing,

Euch, edle Frau, allein,
Euch ziemt es, ganz ihn zu befein.

. . . Karl Josef on his rocking-horse, cracking his whip over the wooden steed. The boy had made a collection of whips; according to one coachman who had taken a shine to him, he had been pretty knowledgeable . . .

. . . Crying to Maxe after Toni had told her, 'There was a lot of joy to be had from that child and I had it, he didn't. . . . *I never did lay a finger on that child!*'

. . . Holding Karl after Beethoven's first letter to them, alone in the nursery when she had gone to a concert; realizing then that there would be a long gap before Georg or Maxe presented him with a grandchild, this would be the last babe he could hold like this for some years. Outside, Napoleon had been marching through the city. *I'll protect you, boy. You're in the right place.*

Most of his life he had looked like her. As a new baby, with one eye tight shut and the other tiredly open, he had looked like Beethoven; again with both eyes closed, mouth hanging down, he had looked like Beethoven after a drunken binge.

The boy thought *Beethoven* was the word for music. Beethoven's letters: *Does he yet play the piano?* In Frankfurt, at his good times, his son was crying out, whenever he wanted to be played to, 'More Beetho, Mummy! More Beetho! More Beetho!'

It had started with his biting Fanny. At about the same time, he had had his first fit. With age, Karl was getting worse. He was bigger now, he was aggressive. Sometimes he beat his mother black and blue.

Arnim had pointed out when the boy was no more than seven that he was big for his age – larger than his and Bettina's own son, who was ten months older. Karl Josef had inherited his father's head, big for his body and made bigger by the bushy crop of hair he was also inheriting. As Beethoven's own arms and shoulders were powerful from playing the piano, so Karl had developed a muscular torso, his arms and shoulders being his only means of hoisting himself about. It was necessary at times to lock the boy in a room lest he tear the house down. At these times, no one could control him. Beethoven had described him to Zmeskall as 'a little mad animal locked in a room.' He had not been, then, but he was now. The boy himself at times glared at them with his white-lipped deaf-man's eyes as though he hated them all for the burning.

His own elder brother, Anton, was simple-minded; that was why he had become the head of the family upon the death of their father. That was one reason why he had looked round at that time for a wife, found Toni. And now, of course, everyone had accepted Karl Josef as his because, after all, it runs in the family, look at Anton . . . He himself seemed to want to utter protest: Karl Josef had been bright, until he was four. . . . And what did they think it did to his own children's marriage prospects, all his girls, becoming of marriageable age: O, it runs in the family, watch out with *those* girls!

. . . Maxe, in 1819, Karl playing up at table: 'I'll never be able to marry! My child could be like Karl!' Her mother following her to her room and telling her, 'Karl is not your father's.'

The others did not know yet, he thought, but Maxe knew. Maxe writing to Beethoven, that December, when she was barely seventeen. Toni's anger with Beethoven that he did not come. 'He won't even visit when *Maxe* writes to him! He was supposed to be coming to see us! On his way to England!' His wife's wild-eyed face, tears of grief and anger. 'He should come and *play* to Karl!' Convinced that he could make him well.

He would share the piano stool with his mother – no easy task, given that his own legs were not self-supporting: leaning against her as she played, leaning his head on his mother. The music often seemed to soothe him. Sometimes he would twist his head round to try to watch her face, or, more easily, to observe her hands upon the keys. Sometimes he hit out at the keys with his own hands, and then he would topple over or fall against her and, tumbling, fall into an excess of rage. He lashed out at her sometimes, partly to regain his balance, partly from being locked in his wild fury of frustration. It was not infrequent to see her flee from there with a scratched hand or face.

'I have to keep doing it! What else can I do? He's my son! It's the only thing that ever makes him any better! It soothes him, at least for a moment . . . I have to keep doing it! It is *the only thing that I can do for him*!'

Although she shared their vivacity, Maximiliane, he felt, contained the most depth of all his daughters: perhaps because she had been the first daughter after the one they had lost, after less than a year of life. She had her mother's saucy eyes. He thought, with Beethoven, that all her children resembled her: all of them, including Karl.

At least that had been so. As the boy grew older, so he began to resemble his father. He was developing his father's chin. The chin was very distinctive, with its pronounced indentations to the left as well as, twistedly, in the middle. He had caught Bettina, once, looking at the boy thoughtfully.

His daughters were marvellous with him. Such good girls. The girls were all wonderful children: Maxe like him, some said, although renowned for her musical talent. 'O, isn't she like Toni!' Arnim had exclaimed of Josepha, their 'Fine'. 'She's like Toni, but she's got something of you – something Italian – Italian country girl.' There was something about her that was more domesticated than Toni, and yet she went into society with decorum. She was almost stringy, too thin, and yet there was an elegance about her. She was also wilful. Her mother said, 'That child does nothing for spiritual reasons!' Maxe, Arnim said, most resembled him, and yet he saw almost wholly her mother in her. She had Toni's elegance, grace in company, and some of her mother's inner strength. 'Maxe will marry well,' everyone thought. Fanny, his baby, eighteen now, seemed often sickly, but so good-hearted. Good-hearted they all were. And now Clemens had to come here and attack not only

Toni but all his daughters. 'Your brother is sick on account of *your* sins! You must pray hard, be good, so that he may get better!'

Clemens was here now, and so was Bettina. Bettina was horrified by his abuse of Toni. 'For what he says to you, you should throw him out of the house!'

'I wish you'd stop singing *Fidelio*,' Franz told Clemens.

'Why shouldn't I sing *Fidelio*? Reviewed it once. "Were I the leading singer and had been given no part in so glorious a work, I should join the chorus." Yessur.'

The once-hearty Clemens, who had himself been divorced and who had written the immensely successful *Des Knaben Wunderhorn* with his brother-in-law, Bettina's husband, Arnim, had in 1817 entered a monastery and had emerged a changed man with severe views of the world and a taut and pursed attitude to others. From being apathetic towards religion he was now a supporter of the Jesuits and Ultramontanists. He had left the monastery in Dülmen this year and was about to embark on his task of spreading Catholic propaganda in the Rhineland.

Clemens was saying now, as he towelled himself after his bath, 'When I met him in 1813, his first words to me were, "How is Toni?" and his second words to me were, "How is Karl?" Not a word about you! Not a dicky-bird about the rest of the family. Just: How is Toni? How is Karl? A bachelor of his age doesn't give a tinker's cuss about another man's wife and kids but, if they're his own, ah, that's a different story! I said to him then, "I'm surprised they didn't stay in Vienna, get you to be godfather." He said, "O, I couldn't be godfather. Wouldn't be right."'

Clemens was getting dressed. He pulled on his trousers. ' ... And I remember him after the Battle of Hanau. "I must write to them! O! I wonder if the boy's all right!" I remember that because he changed it to include Toni, something like, "O, I pray to God they're all all right!" Borrowed 50 ducats off me then. Perhaps he was thinking of coming to see you.'

Franz recalled Toni's anguish when Karl had had his first fit. He clung onto his silence lest he give himself away by anger. But Clemens talked openly downstairs as well. 'O don't think we don't know! We all know! Who is the father of *that* bastard! You only have to look at the bastard!

'O, how convenient! He thinks he can get away palming it on you because of Anton, mad brother Anton! Well Anton was born simple! *That* one wasn't! Calls it "An act of God." My God, she's right! Truest words that woman ever spoke! Caught in adultery! Aye, and punished!'

Franz had to shut him up, for the children; but Bettina had overheard.

'That's not right, what you say,' Bettina had rebuked her brother.

'O, I agree, it's not *right*, but it's the truth! Look at the bastard! That chin! Who else has a face like that? Who else? Eh?'

'A fine Christian you have turned out to be, Clemens. You ought to hear some of the things people say behind your back, brother. You spread pain and misery wherever you go. You've no right to say things like that about Toni.'

'Well I like that! You abused her most of all! Couldn't stand her! Went off to live with Kunigunde and Savigny, for two years, that's how much you couldn't stand her!'

'When we were growing up. It's changed now. All that she's been through . . . is still going through. Have a little sympathy for people. Don't try to hurt all the time.' She turned to her half-brother. 'As for you! I don't know why you let him say it! If he talked to Achim like that about me I trust my husband would throw him out of the house!'

'Well it wouldn't be true about you,' Clemens told her.

'It isn't true about Toni.'

Clemens laughed. 'A pair of women, sticking together! Just because you're both mothers! Aye, we never know who's fathered our kids, do we, Franz?'

Franz said quietly, 'I know who fathered that one.'

'O I know why you take her part!' Clemens was saying to Bettina. 'You're afraid that he,' pointing at Franz, 'is going to say to me, "Like most difficulties in this family, this one was initiated by Bettina."'

'What about you and Sophie Mereau!' Bettina lashed to Clemens. 'You made that woman get divorced to marry you! No one in this family jeered at you or said it was God's punishment when your first child died and when she died herself having your second! We all said it was dreadful. We all tried to support you!'

Clemens had adored Toni. He had dedicated to her effusively a copy of his work. Clemens had left the room. Bettina was saying, 'Clemens has never forgiven Beethoven for not setting his cantata on the death of Queen Luise of Prussia, especially when he'd set *Feuerfarb'* by Sophie. He's never forgiven himself for hero-worshipping Beethoven. You should not listen to him. He still loves Beethoven. He still loves Toni. That's what this is all about!'

Alone with her later, Bettina said to Toni, 'Don't let what Clemens says hurt you. He loved you too much . . . now he's turned against you. It's not hatred, it's love that he feels for you. . . . He has no right to say these things to you. . . . Franz himself says that Karl is his child.'

Antonie said angrily, 'I wish someone would think of Karl! He's alive, he's suffering. Why can't they expend this energy *helping him!*'

To Franz Bettina exclaimed later, 'My God! That man had a crush on Beethoven! Like a schoolgirl! He wrote *poems* about him! And I'll tell you what the real trouble is – he wanted to be immortalized by Beethoven, and Beethoven has never set him!'

. . . One day in the summer, in the first year of Karl's life, Toni had sat in the sunshine with her new baby, making to Bettina's eyes a vivid picture of new motherhood. She had asked confidentially, 'Are you glad it's a boy?' 'I'm glad for myself. For him I should have liked to have had a daughter.' Bettina had laughed, 'But Franz has *three* daughters!' That same year or perhaps later, she could not remember but Karl had been tiny, she had seen Antonie hoist him up, his little legs dangling, to way above her own head, 'O! What a father *you've* got!'

Clemens broke into her reverie. 'O I know what it would be like if *that one* had been normal. You'd be spouting it out to all and sundry, "Do you know, my sister-in-law has got this son . . ."'

By the end of the month Clemens had taken to saying that the boy was better and that this was all due to his prayers. Now he had a tailor round here, making him a cassock with capacious pockets since he 'had to carry eggs to the poor.' Being measured by the tailor, he made allegations to Franz about Georg. Franz watched the man grow gleeful with malice. 'In England, your eldest, is he?'

. . . Georg had pranced round in front of his father, pointing his fingers up from his own head. 'Cuckold! Cuckold! You come up to me: *Your mother is having another child.* I can remember it. I was twelve years old. Not: we're having another child. Not: you're going to have a brother. He's not your little bastard! Cuckold! Cuckold!' He had taken to threatening his father, promising what he would do to him for dissipating his inheritance on other people's mad bastard sons.

Georg was plagued with vile disease just as Toni's brother Hugo had been. Hugo's condition, Franz now supposed, was why Birkenstock had selected him to marry her out of the several suitors of whom he had suspected but not known: he had disowned his only son; suddenly he had been left with an heiress, a beautiful motherless daughter of seventeen who had been reared by nuns. She thought him unworldly; he was hardly that, given the way he had bickered over her dowry. Their two families had had business dealings going back several decades, father to father. The man had wanted to get her off his hands, quickly, before something happened to tarnish her reputation and he found himself without a daughter as well as without a son.

'Who's cuckolded you, eh? Who's screwed the arse off my aristocratic Mama and left you to bring up a little mad bastard, eh? The news is all round Europe! It will be, if you don't pay off my debts and give me the loot! Disown me? Why, I'm your only son! How much does it cost, all this round-the-clock attendance? Go dissipating *my* fortune on *that* bastard, would you! I'll spend my *own* fucking fortune *myself!*'

Franz thought again of Beethoven: two ageing men, brought grief with our grey hairs by our sons. He remembered writing to Clemens before Karl Josef had been born, saying he would give the whole house up to Georg and build a new one for the rest of them. What had he been thinking of? He must have been mad, then. Abdicate to an eleven year old! He had been mad, distraught with grief. But he had clung onto his family: Toni, Karl, Georg, Bettina, Clemens, he had clung onto them all.

He had re-built the estate in 1820, buying out eight smallholders, demolishing the old house, building at the front an English garden with a fountain and to the rear a garden that backed onto the Rhine. She slept in the room beneath Karl Josef. Her sleep was often disturbed. In her tiredness she became irritable. He had long had bitter thoughts about this, but what could he say?

Clemens had started up again. Franz was appalled lest Toni hear. He was terrified lest, even now, she should put the boy into a carriage and go to him.

. . . O no, how could she travel? Paradoxically, it was perhaps only her sick son that kept her with him.

He had seen what she had written in her prayer-book:

No matter how heavy the sorrows which I bear, I will adore Him. Though my wounds are burning, though the hour is dark and motionless, God has done this – and the child shall adore the Father.

Chapter 7

Vienna, May 1825

There the old fool had been, firing off seventeen and a half canons on learning of his safe return; and there *he* had been, getting to know all about women. He had got his leg over and felt quite the young buck. He was able now to stand up to his uncle. Put his foot down about the course of his own studies. Man of the world! I know as much about anything now as *he* does.

What's more, he was going to be a soldier, whatever his uncle said: a dashing young officer, who would pull all the birds.

And his uncle kept going on about the dreadful dragon's breath and poisonous dragons ... too late, uncle dear, too late! The dreadful poisonous dragons have already got me in their clutches! Ahhhgh! He acted this out for Niemetz and made his friend laugh.

Why seventeen and a half canon shots, when he had already been eighteen when that had happened, in October? The old man never could remember anyone's age. He had used the excuse of being at N's mother's. 'She has known me so long now.'

Beethoven had asked him, with glaring eyes, 'Have you ever spent the night away from home before?'

'When I was newly arrived in Vienna, I took lodgings with Frau Schnaps.'

Thereafter Beethoven had begun to suspect him of sleeping with older women.

To Stumpff, a visitor from England in the autumn, he had talked of sending him to England 'To make a man of him. You have heads on your shoulders, you English.' He thought highly of the British Constitution. 'A land where a man has the vote.'

Karl had had to move back to live with him after the summer, into new lodgings in the *Johannesgaße*. The scenes between himself and his uncle last winter had been such that their landlady had once thrown them out.

To try to rid his uncle of his rosy view of the University, he had told him of the dismissal of the Professor of Philosophy. 'The Dean of the faculty of Philosophy strode into the lecture hall and wanted to hold his lecture instead. No one would allow him to speak. At first everyone grumbled, finally there arose an outcry, "Vivat Rembold!" This was the Professor's name. This became so strong that the Dean had to retreat. The Kaiser heard of it at once and had several conscripted as soldiers.' Beethoven had just said, 'Shameful. You boys, given these chances. All you can do is make monkeys of yourselves.'

One row in December had started because Beethoven thought he had nicked his handkerchief. The servant had passed it to him by mistake. After that Beethoven had begun questioning his route between the University and home, presumably believing that he had stopped off to screw more old women.

'You're not home at the same time every day!'

'I leave when I have finished my assignment. Naturally that varies from day to day.'

'O, so now your uncle is a dunce for not knowing about such things! He never went to University! He has to ask!'

'I haven't said that you shouldn't ask about it.'

'That's not what I'm saying, you young scoundrel! You're snide, despising, come out with blarney!'

'I shall follow your wish and desist from it. It is sad that what passes for a sign of affection between other people should count for blarney between us.'

From Baden in September he had been telling the poet Nägeli that the Archduke 'is so talented that I am sorry not to be able to take as much interest in him as I used to,' in November he complained to Schotts of having to give the Archduke 'a lesson of two hours every day,' and by December he was writing that he had been making 'further attempts to shake off this yoke to a certain extent.' A fortnight later he had told them, 'He is fond of me and marks me out for his particular regard, but one cannot live off that. Although several people tell him that "whoever owns a lamp fills it with oil," he seems impervious to such arguments.'

Over Christmas they had joked about this. Johann had said, 'The Archduke should lick you.' Karl had laughed because he thought he had meant 'Lick your arse.'

Over Christmas he had been tarting up the works he had given to Johann. Schotts had offered 130 ducats for works for which Probst had offered but 100. Beethoven had commended Schotts to his brother as 'really genuine people, not vulgar businessmen.' Even Therese had visited them about the sale of these works. Karl had told his uncle, 'But he has always been in love with her. That is the basis of everything.' It didn't stop Johann still dyeing his hair. 'He gets 1,800 fl C.M. from the apothecary shop in Linz,' he had told Beethoven. 'He has two houses in Linz, and from a third he gets another 1,800 fl C.M. a year.'

... Pounding the piano like a madman when he had learnt that he did not want to stay on at the University and take the exams. 'What do you think I am? Made of money? Haven't you bled me dry? What more is it that you want out of me! God! God! God my witness! Have I not done my best? *Everything* for *this son*!'

He had had him sounded out by Peters, his co-guardian, and had

involved Stephan von Breuning, his childhood friend from Bonn. Karl
had endured many boring rigmaroles telling his uncle how hard he would
work, how he would keep up his Greek, how this time he would be
successful.

But he was free! To go to the Polytechnic Institute, follow his *father* into
a business career, above all to have his own lodgings in town.

He had moved into lodgings with Mathias Schlemmer, a Government
official, in the *Alleegasse*, close to the *Karlskirche*. The Polytechnic year
started in November and he had got a crammer to help him catch up,
especially in modern languages, of which he needed English, French and
Italian. He had also got a new co-guardian in the shape of Reisser, the
Vice-Director of the Polytechnic. He had not minded his co-guardian,
Peters, who had once written out for him in Greek

> When wine I drink deep
> My cares fall asleep

but Johann had selected Reisser, saying he would be a buffer between him
and Beethoven. 'I know you're a man. He doesn't understand. He still
thinks of you as a child. I've had my troubles, God knows, with Amalie
and her mother, but at least I have seen a child growing up: I know that
one day you look at the child in your family and that's it, they're grown.'

Johann had told him, at the Candlemas ball, that he suspected Therese
of being in the throes of some love affair again.

'Therese draws the interest on half his wealth, that means half of his
property, half of the farm, the vineyard, etc.,' Karl had told Beethoven.
'He can't allow himself to be cut off, since he has to give her half of
everything. If he gets to the stage of catching her, his whole property
would be saved.'

He had thought of touching Johann for a sub but Johann's miserliness
was so extreme that he rarely got anything out of him. 'He told me
recently that he would at times gladly take an ice or some such thing in
the coffee-house but did not venture to do so out of pure economy. At
lunchtime he seems to eat only very sparingly, so that in the evening,
when it doesn't cost him anything, he can cram more in. Last year he'd
really gone so far that he himself said he wanted to break the habit of his
excessive economy. But now it's even worse.'

Niemetz had laughed, 'Perhaps you ought to help him out with
Therese!' He was sharing a room, which he did not like, but at least he
had his freedom. And Beethoven was in Baden!

In Baden, Beethoven was still not sufficiently recovered from a serious
illness to compose. Rellstab, who had seen him first in April, when his
illness was at its height, had been struck by the sickly yellow tinge to his
high complexion, the nose sharp in illness, the eyes, too, small and paler
than expected. Beethoven was altogether smaller than as depicted in his
portraits: shrunken, invalid, truly a vulnerable little old man. His by now

almost entirely grey hair, bushy and untidy, part smooth, part stiff, part frizzled, rose from his pink scalp. The poor man had seemed at death's door, yet spoke with intensity about the opera Rellstab had wished to provide for him. 'The subject must attract me. I must be able to set about it with love and interest. I could not compose *Figaro* or *Don Giovanni*. I feel an aversion for such subjects. They are too frivolous for me.'

Beethoven fretted about being unable to work. He had finished one quartet and started another at the turn of the year, when he had also given to Johann the new set of bagatelles instead of the earlier, offered to Peters, which had since been sold. He had also revised *Opferlied* and *Bundeslied* for him. They were both delighted with Schotts, though a Viennese publisher had advised him to have nothing to do with them. Rumours had begun to be spread about him, he thought by Steiner in Vienna and possibly also by Probst or Peters in Leipzig. He had warned Schotts. He had written to Peters, 'You have *wronged yourself and me*,' saying that he was still wronging him over the bagatelles.

He had used Johann as a stick to prise Probst off his back; his friend Streicher was dealing with Peters.

He had discovered that a 4-hand piano arrangement of Opus 124 was being distributed by a publisher in Berlin before the original score had appeared, thus also jeopardizing Schotts' sales of their own 4-hand version made by Czerny. This was one of the works he had passed to Johann – now his brother would think him guilty of double-dealing. The man had replied that the overture had been included in the sale of Opus 114 and that he was within his rights in publishing the 4-hand version. He had had to insert a notice in the *Wiener Zeitschrift für Kunst, Literatur, Theater und Mode*, warning the public of this bastard version.

Later in January he had heard an even worse rumour, from Schotts, that the Mass had already been engraved. Beethoven put this down to Stockhausen, who had been allowed by the French court to make a copy for his singing club, but the pirated edition which had appeared in Paris had turned out to be of the Mass in C, not the *Missa Solemnis*.

He had also warned Schotts that Schlesinger was not to be trusted. 'He filches where he can.' He was trying to nudge Schotts into bringing out an edition of his complete works, feeling safe now with but one good publisher. Haslinger it had been who had advised him to have nothing to do with Schotts. He had retaliated by producing his 'romantic biography of Tobias Haslinger,' pedantic, somewhat disrespectful, and full of puns. 'Steiner,' he had told Schotts, 'is an out-and-out miser and a rogue of a fellow; *Tobias* is inclined to be *weak* and *accommodating*, yet I *need* him for *several things*.' Haslinger was the one he had called on last year when he'd been in a fright over the disappearance of 'Our Benjamin.' He had also sent Schotts two canons for their journal, one on the Berlin writer Hoffman, the other on the Hamburg musician Schwenke. He was delighted with Schotts, calling them 'Frank and ingenuous, qualities I have not found in publishers.' He had even talked of a visit to them.

This last year, he had had Schindler, Neate, Galitzin, Stumpff, all encouraging him to travel. Charles Neate had written in December inviting him on behalf of the Philharmonic Society to visit London. He had been offered 300 guineas for conducting at least one of his works at each of the Society's concerts and composing a new symphony and concerto which would be performed during his visit. He was promised an additional 500 for a concert of his own, and 100 more for his new quartets. Rehearsals of the *Choral* had been set for January 17th; he had been asked to direct its London premiere.

He had no notion what 300 guineas were. Moscheles had once told him that his flat in central London, consisting of 2 rooms and sleeping area, cost two and a half guineas a week. Someone had told him that a guinea was worth 10 florin C.M. Streicher had told him that it would cost 4,000 florins C.M. for a trip to London.

He had replied on January 15th requesting a further 100 guineas since he would need to buy a carriage; he would also need to bring a companion. Neate had responded on February 1st, regretfully reporting that the directors declined to amend their offer.

Everyone urged him to make the trip. Karl reminded him that Neate had told him that he would be free of financial care for the rest of his life. Johann urged that the journey would be good for his health. Beethoven had expressed fears at travelling at his age. 'Haydn went to London when he was 50,' Karl had told him, 'and he was not as famous as you.' Falstaff too brusquely encouraged the trip, putting himself forward as companion; or he could take his friend's son, young Streicher. Frau Streicher had helped him set up a household when he had first got Karl; Streicher, the piano-manufacturer, who had recently involved himself in his dealings with Peters, was trying to spur on an edition of his complete works.

In the end he had written that he would make the visit later, perhaps that autumn. They seemed to think he could conjure new symphonies, concertos, out of thin air! Drop everything! Catch the next post-coach! At my age! *What about my quartets!*

His ex-pupil Ries, who had lived for over a decade in London, was now back in the Rhineland. He too had written inviting Beethoven to visit his estate at Godesberg, near Bonn. He had flirted long-distance for years with Ries' beautiful wife, once even thinking of dedicating the London edition of the *Diabelli* to her. He had almost told Ries of Antonie in 1816, just before the first hints about Karl Josef . . . Writing to Ries, who had been asked to organize a music festival at Aix-la-Chapelle and who wanted to perform his 9th Symphony, Beethoven had told him how greatly he envied him his estate at Godesberg. 'But it seems that my life is not to work out the way I had hoped.'

All those years of thinking, something will happen when I am 50. *Yes,*

something did happen when I was 50: my kid turned out to be an imbecile.
Something had happened when he was 50: the *Choral* finale had made him
famous. He was using the proposed instrumental finale in his new work.
Something had happened: he was writing string quartets.

Falstaff was by now such a size that, writing to let him know that he
could perform the quartet, Beethoven had joked about Shakespeare's
'levers' to hoist him up to him on his fourth floor. Sending the quartet the
parts, he had enclosed a humorous pledge that each would vie with his
fellows in excellence.

His first quartet for nigh on a decade and a half, and Falstaff had to foul
it up! They had had a heated row, Falstaff quivering in every chin, with
talk of 'stupid twaddle' and 'foul accusations,' he telling Falstaff that, if he
had known it was under-rehearsed, why had he gone ahead and played it!
In the end, it appeared, Johann had mis-informed him. 'Do you believe
everything your brother tells you? Just let him say that to my face!' What
did Johann know about music? Karl had told him last year, 'The brother
is trying to acquire culture. He goes to concerts, applauds loudly, shouts
"Bravo!" Everyone says that he shows himself up as a fool.'

Falstaff had advertised the quartet in two successive Sunday concerts
but instead had only played it once. Böhm had then come forward with
the request to play it. Falstaff had told him Böhm was incapable of
playing a quartet of his properly. He'd wanted his part back to study, so
that he could perform it again. 'The reason I didn't put it on again that
second Sunday was that I realized that we did not know it well enough.'
He said the quartet was no harder than the Second or Third *Razumovsky*.
'There are no technical difficulties in it. Only the originality makes it
difficult, which one can't grasp in the first instance.'

But it was not only Johann who had derided Falstaff. Karl had told
him, 'There were many interruptions. At first they didn't play well
together, then Schuppanzigh broke a string, which also caused a long
interruption because he hadn't a single spare to hand.' Linke, who had
been the 'cellist, had told Johann that throughout the first quartet they
had been too quiet, as though suspecting that the new quartet wouldn't
go well. 'I told you this before, but Herr Schuppanzigh derided me.'
Falstaff himself had come back with, 'I must deny that it is too hard for
me in places, only the *ensemble* is difficult.' Holz, his second fiddle, had
written of Falstaff's performance that 'it had not yet finished baking.'
Karl had told him he had heard that Böhm played quartets beautifully.
After Falstaff had made a dog's breakfast of his quartet on March 6th,
he'd had Böhm rehearse it under his own eyes before letting him give
three performances, two on the same night of March 23rd, and then
another for his own benefit. Joseph Mayseder had then performed it a
couple of times at Dembscher's house during April. Steiner had heard
Böhm in rehearsal and had promptly offered 60 ducats for the quartet.
Beethoven's estranged friend Breuning, an official at the war department,

had heard of it through his colleague, Dembscher, and had resumed their friendship after a decade.

The affair split musical Vienna. 'Böhm says Haslinger is on Schuppanzigh's side.' Karl had told him, 'He'll certainly get a dig from the canons!' Steiner had apparently said, 'Doesn't seem like the self-same quartet Schuppanzigh played.' Falstaff wanted another crack of the whip; Karl said that he shouldn't have it. Johann wrote, 'In everything there was a mood that exists in no other quartet. The interweaving is so rich that one is fully occupied just observing a single voice; we all wished we could hear the quartet four times.' There had been praise too for Mayseder. 'He *conducts* the other three, while Böhm leaves them to conduct themselves.' Galitzin too had received the quartet and he too had heard it performed several times.

He had told Schotts of Steiner's offer. 'People are saying that this new quartet is the greatest and most beautiful work which I have composed.' He had written to them on the 7th, 'In regard to the publication of my collected works I now have the papers in front of me and will soon be able to put the necessary conditions before you, provided *that you are still interested in this project.*'

The recent concerts had made him famous. A failed composer, visiting Vienna, had sought him out in Baden and, finding him alone in his illness, had entered his rooms, scrawling obscenities on his slate.

Beethoven pulled himself together wearily. Even his doctor, now he was dying, wanted some music from him 'in your own hand.' He dragged himself out on the 11th and wrote him a canon, *Doctor, close the door on death*, which he signed 'at Baden, in the *Helenenthal*, at the second Antons Brücke looking toward Siechenfeld.' Because of his illness, Johann had persuaded Frau Schnaps to come with him to Baden, but she was old, she could not cope . . . As he returned to his lodgings the cold mountain air made him shudder, he recalled what Streicher had told him. 'In England it is much warmer than here, and in April already green.' He needed the summer: to work, to recover, seeing that he always had catarrh, rheumatism, in the winter. During those dark months his flat reeked of *Opodeldok*, a camphorated soap liniment. And this summer he had been ill for a month with inflammation of the bowels.

'No wine, no coffee, nothing spicy or seasoned,' Braunhofer had ordered. 'Breakfast: chocolate, without vanilla, with milk or water. Midday: soup, after my prescription. For you, the soup must be without parsley, without barley. And when you're hungry, a couple of soft eggs. That apart, you can't eat anything.' . . . Telling him to have patience, not to fight nature by constantly taking pills. . . . Having to drink warm water, being forbidden to drink. Don't drink means don't compose, because don't drink means don't sleep, and if I can't sleep I can't compose, and if I can't drink I can't sleep! None of them seemed to realize! He had tinnitus, for God's sake. He didn't have silence! Silence would be easy! You try getting to sleep with roars, whines, high-pitched whistles, not in the ears, inside the head. You try! See how much you can sleep! Then see how much work you can get through the next day, Doctor!

People's stupidity exasperated him. They seemed to think he drank for the sake of drink! This pattern he'd worked out was to do with *composition*. With his afternoon meal he drank to wind down, he could give up that, but at night he drank to *sleep*. He knew just how much he could take, just how much it needed. He drank enough to get him to bed by ten, to sleep he thought always before 11. And then he waked at five and got himself going with cup after cup of strong black coffee, 60 a time, he counted out the beans. And then he began composing. Coffee and booze! Stop those! Why, man, you're stopping my *composition*! 'Work during the day so that you can sleep at night.' I can't work because I can't sleep! A man can't compose on *chocolate*! Well Haydn could but Haydn wasn't deaf, Haydn didn't have tinnitus! Treat the whole man! *This* man is a *composer*!

He had not drunk chocolate since the days when he had been Haydn's pupil, a twenty-two year old, when the old man, having failed to teach him fugue and failed to take him to England with him owing to the unpleasantness of the Bonn Elector, had criticized the third of his Opus 1 trios and, on being proved wrong, had called him 'Our young Mogul!'

'Just a few lines in your own hand.' He looked at his pesky little canon and laughed. Why, Doctor, this is all I can do on *your* treatment! He grieved for his postponed quartet, in his weak state he could have wept for it. There was Galitzin, wanting the next one within a couple of months so that he could take it with him into the country.

As usual the cold weather caused him physical ear-ache. His tinnitus was worse too during the day now. Tinnitus interfered with his getting down to work but, once he was immersed, the work blocked out the tinnitus. He was too weak to hold his pen, let alone get immersed! Instead Braunhofer had told him to take walks in dry weather, but he was to take no baths as long as the weather remained damp and the symptoms of his illness persisted. He had kept asking for medicine to cure his stomach and Braunhofer had told him, 'You are Brown the second!' The fatuous fool had persisted in saying, 'Your constitution will recover of its own accord. I want to see you better!'

. . . Head-flushes, like some menopausal woman . . . water and almond-milk . . . soft-eggs . . . a *kiddie's* diet! Later he had been allowed a little piece of beef, with vegetables. 'I give you my word you will be fundament-ally healed. I know nature and man's life. Just be patient for a few days.' That had been *two weeks* ago! This had been going on since *April the 18th*! He had wanted to see him without Johann, so that he could prescribe something 'that has to be got from a proper apothecary.' Yet Johann had nursed him, taking his pulse, making him take a powder for 'a good night's sleep.'

He seemed to have suffered a string of illnesses over these last few years: rheumatism, jaundice, diarrhoea, bad eyes, stomach disorders, catarrh, besides his usual run of colds and ear-aches. And now he was experiencing a recurrence of the nose-bleeds he had endured the previous winter. It was bitterly cold, he could hardly hold his pen to write letters, let alone compose; he could hardly walk. On the 13th he wrote to Braunhofer enclosing his canon and writing a skit on Dr Brown, the interventionist, who believed in stimulating the weakened constitution, and Dr Stoll, who believed in letting nature take its course. He wrote that he was still very weak, still belching, begging to be allowed white wine with water instead of the evil-smelling beer he had been prescribed. 'I spit up a good deal of blood, probably only from my windpipe. But often it streams from my nose.'

He had written that he craved strength to sit again at his writing-desk but, as he set out to walk to the post with this letter and one to Piringer, director of the *concerts spirituels*, he felt so weak he thought he must die.

'I see that Karl has got very pale,' he had written in his conversation book. 'The cool mountain air must be responsible for the bleeding.' There was no one here. There was no one to cook for him, yet he felt too weak to try to get a meal at the tavern.

He was scared by his recent massive nose-bleed. Supposing he climbed up those four flights and it happened again? He was terrified of bleeding to death, alone. Once he had even suffered a spurt of blood that looked as though it might be a haemorrhage from his cock. How ignominious! What would the history books say? 'Beethoven bled to death through his cock.'

He did not know himself. He seemed diminished. He felt thin and unheld. He seemed haggard and small. He needed a woman to run her hands over his unfamiliar bony frame. Good healing hands. Ever since he had been ill he had been banging himself. He was covered in bruises. He needed soothing and comfort. It was different now. He was old. He didn't know how he had stood the events of his past − 1813, losing Karl and Toni; 1817, Karl Josef's illness; 1821, the burnings − he was older now, he couldn't stand it now, he had to have something, he had to have comfort.

It was like being in a prison of misery. He was not free. Misery was a ball and chain at his ankles, a weight which lowered his shoulders and bowed his neck. His horizons were as restricted as prison walls.

There is a deep coldness that comes from being alone, a coldness neither food nor warmth can remedy, assuaged only by the presence of another human being. He remembered the shock of his cold sheets, cold bed, when Antonie had left . . . when he had left Antonie. He had been physically ill. He envisaged Antonie with him: soothing him, caring for him; above all taking the panic: someone concerned, sharing, being there. He envisaged their lives together as it would have have been, had it gone that way . . . the image as quickly fading, not into despair but a resignation that was almost impatient: it had not gone that way, his life was thus, he must cope.

He found stale bread and cheese, minded briefly of the old Polish woman with gat-teeth who had brought him black bread in his grief at Karl Josef: *tool of the living God.* He stood this by his bed with a glass of cold water. He found an old shirt, tore two strips, made wads and pushed these up his nose. He fetched from his study his sketchbook and pencil and, sighing heavily for breath, climbed into bed.

In his run-down state he was still aware of tinnitus even as he began to work, but this was better than lying in misery, the tinnitus wracking him in addition to his physical pain: piercing whistles and hums, that drumming sound, worst of all random incessant *specks* of sound that kept him awake. Years of hearing machines, ear-trumpets, acoustic enhancers fixed to his piano. Almond-oil, bread, horseradish: everything it was possible for a man to have applied to his ear he had had in his. People were still giving him tips for treatment for his deafness. Only three months ago Karl had been telling him, 'Two relatives of the housekeeper who had been deaf for some time were quite cured by the Priest at Saint Stephen's.'

The shock of it at first. Your whole head feels like a drum, every sound has an echo. Everything muffled so that you are not sure if the sounds emanate from your own head or are real. Having to ask someone else, 'Is that a dog barking?' Nigh on two decades ago. For long the doctors had associated it with his sick belly, now he put it down to that vile attack of typhoid. A humming and buzzing, most pronounced in the left ear. It had begun to be painful to hear a soprano or a high fiddle. Although he had still heard through it, that ear had begun to feel blocked and the humming had become a low-pitched whistle. As the sounds from the outside had lessened, those in his head had boundlessly increased in volume and persistency.

He never discussed it, except with doctors. The only friends with whom he had ever discussed it had both been doctors: Wegeler and Weissenbach, the latter himself deaf. Antonie had told him, 'Your manhood doesn't reside in your ears!' He remembered Johanna making an issue of it during the court cases. As a deaf man he could only be a co-guardian.

. . . 1797: nigh on *three* decades ago! He suddenly realized that he had been deaf for longer than he had been a hearing man. Now what he got if he turned off the composing and the booze was a cacophony and a torture: imagine an ill-tuned, unmusical band, picking up and playing any instrument at whim: now a dull drum-beat, here a chortling wind which did not attempt to disguise its demonic venom.

He loved his work. It was all he had left. It was all he had started with. Without his work he could not live. Do himself in in a minute. Ever so. Ever so. It had always been like this. Make me the richest man in the world, make me king or emperor, give me love and all the wives and children, make me God Almighty Himself and, if I could not work, *that to* life! . . . *For Beethoven can compose, thank God, though he can do nothing else in the world.* He remembered writing to Schotts last year, 'Apollo and the Muses are not yet going to let me be handed over to Death, for I still owe them so much; and before departing for the Elysian fields I must leave behind me *what the Eternal Spirit has infused into my soul and bids me complete.* It really seems to me as if I had scarcely written a single note of music.'

Dear God, don't let me die before I have written it all! He laughed weakly. All the times in my life I have wanted to die! O I want to live now. I want to work! Were he but able to get well enough to work, work would keep him alive. Once he was working he could ignore the pain.

When he managed to sleep and woke and it was daylight, he wept that he was alive for another day.

He remembered the time some admirer had sent him Tokay. It had been sent through kindness, in the hope that it would ease his stomach and sooth his digestion. He had passed it on, he thought to Schindler. Tokay reminded him of that time in Countess Erdödy's garden in Jedlersee when he had tried to die by starvation after the loss of Karl and Toni. For three days he had not eaten, and one night his last conscious wish had been for Tokay. He wished he had some Tokay now.

The weather was still bitterly cold and gloomy and he had run out of chocolate. He was alone, dependent on Frau Schnaps who spent half her time in Vienna and some Viennese joiner who was supposed to be coming to Baden and might bring his chocolate. With no one to cook for him he had dined at an inn and was suffering from diarrhoea. Frau Schnaps had said that she too was ill and had told him that she wanted to die in hospital. In her old age she didn't care how unreliable she was, or what lies she told. He had called her to Karl 'a wicked old woman,' though a day or so later he tried to get her to a doctor. He himself was getting thin and felt weak and isolated, bearing down heavily on Karl to whom he wrote every day, telling him that it was only right that a youth of nearly 19 should assist his benefactor, as he himself had fulfilled his duties to his parents; asking him to visit; adding his fears, 'If only I were certain that your Sundays away from me were well spent,' referring to his own great sacrifices, 'O where have I not been wounded, nay, cut to the heart!'

On Saturday the 21st he visited Vienna and met the boy, who talked about the large amount of work he had to undertake for his course at the Polytechnic Institute. He left him to get on with his geography while he had a word with Frau Schnaps. She told him that she thought the boy had seen his mother. He stormed to see Johann who blithely said, 'What if he has? No harm in that. She's his mother, after all. Reisser said she'd popped round for a chat.'

Karl endured a stormy meal with Beethoven in which the boy further revealed that Sonnleithner, who taught business and bill of exchange law, had always felt that he should be free to see his mother if he so chose. 'I'm not telling you what I think, I'm telling you what he said!'

'If you think it's above board, why are you meeting her in secret!'

'I didn't say I'd seen her, I said people said I could!'

Beethoven grew fierce when his proprietorial rights were attacked: one whiff of someone else's mild approbation for Johanna and he was back fighting the court cases, vivid in the fear that he would lose Karl. He had travelled back to Baden alone and now sat writing to Karl, although the boy was due to visit in a few hours. He felt betrayed. Sonnleithner was a member of the *Gesellschaft*, his brother had written the first libretto for *Leonore*. Breuning had written the second. Breuning himself had been against his getting Karl in 1815 – was *he* in on it? All that time spent scribbling away about the Polytechnic, and not a word about it from the boy! And what about Johann! Why, he'd even wanted to borrow his French piano for his daughter, that *prostitute* of his, and he'd let him have it! Was Johann giving him money? He had only got 215 florins C.M. instead of 225 for the first quartet from Galitzin. He had been expecting 50 ducats. Johann had dealt with Galitzin's agent, Henikstein. Had Johann filched from him? Had Johann given Karl his money? Was Karl getting money from his mother? And, if they had been giving him money, what would a boy of that age be *spending it on?*

'Am I to experience once more the most horrible ingratitude? . . . Am I to mix myself up again in these vulgarities?' Someone the other day had tried to convey what he only now realized was, 'He's a grown man! You don't tell adults what to do.' If he's a grown man I've brought him up. So be it. I've done my job.

His last letter to Karl he had signed 'Your faithful,' too worn down by it all to have the heart to add 'father.' He now angrily wrote, 'For God's sake, if the pact oppresses you – I hand you over to Divine Providence. I have done my job and upon this I can appear before the Mightiest of all Judges.'

. . . Grown man! He's a boy! With his studies! Why, the boy is still at school!

Karl arrived with Frau Schnaps but Beethoven had had so little sleep that he slept after lunch and they talked desultorily, touching only briefly on Sonnleithner and Reisser until the boy left by the evening coach.

One day in late May he woke swollen with lust. He was tossing and threshing as if he were Karl's age. Any woman on the receiving end of that would definitely have been having a good time, he thought through his moans. He wished there were a woman, as the thrusts became harder. He looked on with satisfaction as the seed trickled over his fingers. *No blood.*

He did a bit of work and later, as he had known he would have to, he went back to bed.

This time he had to stop in the middle to write the notes that throbbed through his head. Still thrusting as he took up pad and pencil, he recalled saying to Zmeskall, 'Some of them you might as well write with your cock.'

This stop and start sex caused him physical pain, though what he was sketching was good. He had been terrified that, if he lost his sexuality, he would never work again.

Later, when he had got up and was in his study, he concentrated fully on the slow movement of Galitzin's second which had occurred to him this morning in bed – the hymn of thanksgiving of an invalid to God, upon feeling new strength. 'Notes will help us in our need,' he had told his doctor in his canon, and indeed they did . . .

It was almost worth being ill to experience the positive rush of wellbeing and good health that came upon recovery. He had been ill, he had begun to feel well, he had had a day of feeling eager to work and eating well and that night, standing his candle down beside his bed, he had suddenly felt, *I don't feel afraid any more.*

He was falling in love with it, yearned for nothing more than to spend time with it, craved for no society but only to be left alone to indulge his huge hot calm beautiful controlled huge growing hot calm passionate love for *this*. It wasn't there, but it was all there. He wanted to laugh out loud. The *conception* had occurred and it would grow, in him and through him, already he could see it, whole; unborn, *it exists.*

How lucky is the artist – that he is allowed to fall in love time after time after time!

He lay on his belly, lifting his feet in the air; setting up a pattering with his feet; tapping his pencil against his finger-nails and chuckling.

He composed until he felt his head was bursting out of his skull.

Yes, this is me. He had stopped composing like a stuffed prune and was composing like . . . like Beethoven! All the reins were falling back into his hands. He had done the first, done the second, before his illness, this was the third: the second a Viennese street song, the first with its B-A-C-H related opening. The finale he had, from the *Choral*; he laughed as he recalled how Unger's face fell. Never mind, old girl, she fits in right, here. O he wanted to embrace every string quartet in the world: every unwritten note, absorb them into him, give them out, one almighty splurge: *there*!

In 1818 he had planned a 'symphony in the ancient modes' which would employ a chorus. Well, he had never written that, but he had produced a 'symphony with a chorus'! *This* fellow was in the *Lydian* mode: the 'remedy for fatigue of the soul, and also that of the body.' He remembered his previous modal work: the *Dorian* for the *Incarnatus* of the *Missa Solemnis.*

It was as though he had been granted a new life: a brilliant new life, life seen through the fresh eyes of another person. Yet this new person contained within him the the victory of his own recent brush with death. What he had felt when Karl had become ill: the sharp-focused revelation – wanting a boy, wanting a girl, wanting the child to be a composer, when all that matters is that the child is alive and well.

Work! Work! Work! A new day granted! A new life – the rest of his life – to *work*!

Chapter 8

Early June

Running around, getting Beethoven his chocolate. Two letters in a row he had written about that. It was running around after Beethoven, sorting out his servants, taking down his letters and seeing to things like the subscription copies of the Mass, that had led him to fail at the University in the first place! Yet that didn't stop him begrudging the cost of the crammer. 'Do you realize that that, along with your board at Schlemmer's, is costing me 2,000 florins a year!'

He was again unshaven for long periods and his hair was touching his shoulders. Now that he'd lost weight he looked like a mountain goat. He could be boorish at times in the way he craved praise. As if he hadn't already got half the world down on its knees in praise of him! There was no one he wanted less to be with than his uncle; yet that bastard held the purse-strings: if he was ever to get a kreuzer to call his own, he had to suck up to the old billy.

Yet when they did meet it was nothing but feuding. Where's my small change? Have you got a girlfriend? Have you been seeing your mother? Yeah, of course I see Mama: only because Niemetz is round there; also because I can touch her for dough. *Mother!* Good Lord, man, I am eighteen: why should you think I want to be with Mother any more than I want to be with you! *Women* are what I need!

Beethoven had written at the end of May letting him know that he planned to spend the weekend in Vienna and asking him to make an appointment for him with Bach and to check that Johann's room in which he planned to stay was clean and aired. He had refused to let him go to the theatre. Karl had again been borrowing behind his back, this time from Reisser.

Spoilt as you are it would not do you any harm to cultivate *at last simplicity and truth.* For my heart has suffered too much from your deceitful behaviour to me; and it is hard to forget it. Even if I were to pull the whole burden like a yoked ox and without murmuring, yet your behaviour, if it is directed in this way against others, can never endear you to those who will love you – God is my witness that my sole dream is to get away completely from you and from that wretched brother and horrible family who have been thrust upon me. May God grant my wishes. For I *can* no longer trust *you* -

Unfortunately your father
or, better still, not your father.

89

On Saturday the 4th he visited Bach for details of how to apply for a form from the *Magistrat* for converting his bank shares into Rothschild lottery tickets. He told Bach how the Professors at the Polytechnic were allowing Johanna free access to Karl, in spite of the police prohibition against her seeing him.

'You're being badly dealt with,' the lawyer agreed.

'Not one of them lifted a finger to help me when I was ill . . .'

'Disgusting!'

'. . . my brother, and these Professors, who call themselves friends of mine! They say that the police prohibition only applied when he was at Blöchlinger's . . .'

'Professors can be loud oafs.'

Elated, he set off to see Braunhofer, to whom he had written of his recovery, 'Our heart and soul are inclined to overflow and might therefore cause you, Sir, some inconvenience. Hence we are observing a reverent silence.' The doctor was out. He left him another canon.

On Sunday it turned out that the boy had probably been to the theatre after all since he did not have a receipt for his rent. What's more he was asking straight out for more money. Beethoven wrote in French so that Frau Schnaps should not read, 'You get your florin and if you need anything else you must say and you must produce a note regarding the lodging.'

Once more he returned to Baden in a state of fury. The hours I spend, trying to budget, which bills can I pay, which can stay outstanding, and *that kid*, not satisfied with borrowing 5 florins from Reisser that must be paid back out of *my* pocket, bellyaches when I give him a florin, 'O is that all! I can't live on that!'

He was famous for the lists that he made; all his friends laughed; one year he had even got a summer residence after Schindler had promised that he would have shutters because, the year before, in abstraction, he'd apparently written all over the shutters and the landlord had found that he could sell them! Not notes! Hardly any sketches! Not music! Just *money*! O, his friends found it funny, the lists that he made. It isn't funny to *me*! I have to live somehow! And you, Master Karl, not satisfied with the way I provide for you. 'O. Is that all? One florin? Can't I have more?'

Reading his Bible, he came across:

Whoso keepeth the law is a wise son: but he that is a companion of riotous men shameth his father.

The Jews had been granted permission by the Emperor to build a large Synagogue and early in the year they had come to him requesting a choral work for which a large fee was involved. Rothschild himself was a party. He was to be paid *piece-rates*!

He had laughed when he'd heard: and to think I called publishers Jews! He had used it as a generic term for every publisher from Simrock onwards, after that trouble with ducats and louis d'or. When Probst's Viennese agent had turned up to collect Johann's works only to find he had sold them to Schotts, he had written, 'It is a misunderstanding: Probst a Jew!' Johann was dealing with these negotiations. Karl had said of him then, 'He's a Jew himself.'

He had started reading his Old Testament. Something from Genesis. Jacob's ladder. Yes, this was good stuff. A man with balls could set this. No *fairies* here! *And he was afraid, and said, How dreadful is this place! this is none other but the house of God, and this is the gate of heaven.*

Seven years Jacob served Laban as a shepherd
The father of Rachel, the mountain beauty
But it wasn't for the father that he served
But for her
For she alone
Was the prize he sought.

And when the Lord saw that Leah was hated, he opened her womb; but Rachel was barren.

Yes, that sounds like the Lord to me.

He wrung his hands in mock agony, revelling in the prospect of riches well-deserved. O Ludwig, Ludwig, one minute you compose a Mass, the next you compose for these heathens! What is to become of us all! 'The Jews of Vienna, and then those of Berlin, Frankfurt, Hamburg, etc., will raise a great outcry,' Karl had told him. 'Then they'll cry: "He's written for our people!"'

He wondered if Toni would feel the Mass diminished if he wrote this. He had long detested sectarianism. Putting one religion before another! '*One God! We all pray to! One God!*' Yelling at her, 'There's no need for any of it – Mary, Jesus; let alone priests. Of course God can forgive sins, raise the dead! Of course He can! . . . You don't need anything between you and God! You start qualifying God, He stops being God!'

Yelling at her once about Catholicism: 'I am made in God's image! God isn't made in my image!'

. . . 'You stand there, made in God's image, and call yourself an ugly little turd.'

He had never been much of a one for the Gentle Jesus. O there's a God, all right, but He's got balls.

He remembered Peters or someone saying to him, 'You will become glorified even if you don't believe. Your music is religion. You will arise with me from the dead – because you must. You will conduct the choir and I shall pray. Religion remains the same, only men are changeable.' Yet Peters said he was not a Christian. 'I want to become a *Redemptorist* if my wife dies. What do you think of that? I must lock myself up in order to be good.'

... Time of the last court cases, Peters and his friend Janitschek frequently offering him their wives. He had turned up at Frau P's door once with a sketch of a stallion left with him by Bernard. She had taken him in.

That discussion with Peters had depressed him. He could not believe in the Trinity yet it shocked him not to do so, for he wanted to acknowledge the Holy Ghost. Yet he could not accept Christ. He could not see the need. And he certainly could not accept priests, with their confessional: the authority of one man over another, the self-imposed authority. He believed in God and God through man, and the 'rising from the dead' he dismissed because he could not believe in, after death, being dead: the spirit lives on. What could be worse than the resurrection of the body? How could anyone want that? How could anyone take that as part of their religion, yet alone crave for, absorb it? Yet he'd envied her her Catholicism, once. The certainty of the genuflecting Catholic as he steps into his pew to pray. ... My son is being brought up a Catholic, and a strict one ...

He looked down at the words under glass on his desk. 'No, music is not my intermediary.' Music was given to him by a God already in contact with him. Music is my state of grace.

When I cannot compose, I have offended God.

... Falstaff, when he had been writing the Choral: '*Weber* speaks as God wishes, *Beethoven* speaks as Beethoven wishes.' Karl had enlarged, 'Weber wrote under his portrait, "As God wills it." Some wit added, "Other composers write as they like, but Weber writes as God likes, and Rossini writes as the Viennese like."' ... Some Englishman who'd wanted his compositions, reputedly saying, 'One God, one Beethoven.' Karl or someone had once told him, 'Spend one year in England and you'd have so much that you could buy ten country houses. ... Your path would be strewn with gold. ... You would be in danger of dying from embraces.'

He recalled telling Stumpff, his visitor from England, last year, on the *Helenenthal*, 'My spirit rises beyond these constellations so many millions of miles away to the primal source from which all creation flows and from which new creation shall flow eternally. ... Yes, it must come from above, that which strikes the heart, otherwise it is nothing but notes, body without spirit. What is body without spirit?'

He had said when someone had talked of reincarnation, 'Doesn't apply to me. If there is reincarnation, every man's last incarnation is as a creative artist.' At work on his quartet, he thought, perhaps there's just a heaven for creative artists. All other people must keep returning until they reach this last apotheosis.

... Antonie at Karlsbad: 'Do you really think that you will stop composing if you're not good?'

Walking alone in a quiet country lane, he saw in the distance a man walking with his dog. Drawing nearer he saw that it was not a dog but his toddler, of the age he always imagined Karl Josef.

... During his illness as he had tossed, feverish, with gastritis and a burning headache: *Has that money been paid?* he had wondered. The first 600 florins C.M. from Schotts to Franz ...

Good God! That man in Frankfurt is rearing my kid! Let me have some respect! 'I'll bring him up. I'll see he's provided for in my will.' My kid being brought up like a lord, *at another man's expense* – the least I can do is put *some* money by for the kid that *I* am rearing as my own!

And what happens? He spends it all! Bleeding it away, florin by florin. Having to run to Bach to see if his bank shares would do better as Rothschild lottery tickets. He had half let the boy believe that he had gone to Bach to change his will. And what had been the outcome? Indolence, greed, and mouthfuls of abuse.

... A couple coming towards him with two dogs. At first he thought that another dog sat on the man's shoulder, and then he saw that it was a two year old, his legs one either side of his father's neck. The woman beamed at the man, the man at her, the child leaned down to join in the hilarity; the dogs bounded, one hanging onto the man's hand; and the whole scene one of such vitality that he felt at once enchanted and stabbed with loss.

... The dream in which Franz had said to him, 'Prometheus was a thief. And so are you.'

... Exodus: the Lord's wrath on those who hurt the widow or fatherless child ... *the first-born of thy sons shalt thou give unto me.*

... The long-forgotten dream of attending his son's wedding. He had forgotten he had ever yearned for that. Yet the anticipation had sustained him for several years, during that bleak loneliness when he had had neither her and Karl Josef nor Karl.

There were more people now at Baden. No one else seemed alone. He sat down at a tavern table. He had such a bad cold that, in Maxe's phrase, 'Everything tasted of nose.' There had been some happiness in the Brentano household. Maxe had got engaged. Looking up from his meal he saw at the next table a man who reminded him of Giannatasio. The man was with someone who must be his grown-up daughter. Unlike Giannatasio's, his daughter was beautiful.

He went to bed that night recalling his long-forgotten wish for a daughter: to be himself with his grown-up daughter. 'Daughters love their fathers more.' Throughout his illness he had wished that he had had a daughter – someone to care for him – even old Johann had Amalie! He remembered sending Opus 109 to Maxe, packing the dedication copy for her: my beloved Maxe, the nearest I shall ever come to having a daughter – and I wish you were, O I wish you were. He had sat down to that task filled with sudden delight, remembering what he had once told Zmeskall,

'I'd like to have had a woman to cover with diamonds – be a rich man, and make rich presents to Toni and see her wearing them – and do the same with a daughter.' This was the nearest he'd ever get to giving a diamond to a young woman he had known in her girlhood who was deeply dear to him. . . . Walking in the *Landstrasse*, remembering teaching Maxe; the one-movement piano trio he had given her; their fight on the grass when he had been teaching her to play it, after she had poured ice-cold water over him. . . .'When I grow up I'm going to marry Beethoven!' . . . 'O God, I wish I had fathered that child!' . . . Turning the gold ring on his finger, saying to Fanny Giannatasio, 'I promised a little girl I would marry her when she grew up. This ring is her grandfather's.'

The way the girl had looked at the man, her father, as though he were the only one in the world, *the one*, special, a look she would not even give to her husband: a special love, a blood intimacy, choiceless, compelling; replete with beauty, power and grace.

He would never have that. O what joy to have it. He had changed and now threw back the covers and now thrust his legs down into the bed. Stupid little legs, stout and hairy – what beauty in you? – this still-flopping belly. Toni's face, close to his, smiling eagerly, 'She will love you. She will give you a *nickname!*'

He sometimes called himself *Ben* to Karl's *Benjamin*.

He had seen one family at Baden, the father obviously very close to his youngest daughter. In fact he had carried her often on his shoulders, as Franz had done with Fanny. Only later did he realize that the girl was crippled and later still learn that she was a love-child, not his, someone had said, but his dead sister's. Seeing them once again, the child perched on the man's shoulders, the thought shot through his mind, *For the sins of the fathers shall be visited upon the children.*

Packing the dedication copy, he had felt suddenly very near to her, almost as though she stood there before him and he could embrace her. He had made up the parcel confident, contented, *lovely Maxe, may it please you.* The nicest part of being a composer: dedicating a good work to someone you care for. 'When I'm grown up I'm going to marry Beethoven!' He had found himself laughing jubilantly. Pouring cold water over me! Maxe, Maxe, *play it to him!* Tears streaming down his face.

He had made great variations out of a cobbler's patch and of the great golden theme in his life, Antonie and all her variations, he had made a cobbler's patch. Gazing back, all those years, wondering how he had endured all the pain he was still enduring; all those songs filled with yearning: *An die Hoffnung, Die laute Klage, An die Geliebte, An die ferne Geliebte*, and suicide: *Resignation*. Opus 110, meant for her. Opus 111, meant for her, he had signed, on the autograph, *Ludwig Ludwig*.

Going to places they had been together – walking in woods, sitting in cafes – hoping that there she might be. Alone with an unwanted drink in a cafe where he was not known, subjected to the exclusive merriment and talk of couples, of friendly groups, of families with children.

Whenever he had entered his room she had kissed him or called out to him from the door, 'Hello my love!' Once he had entered his room, she had been there, she had called to him and come to him.

He entered his room these days recalling this, at times almost in expectation, at others in piercing grief. The weakness he felt after his illness had cast him back all those years, he felt naked and vulnerable as a new-born. He felt exhausted before the top of the four flights, his legs weary, aching, a deepening depression overtaking him as he reached the top so that he stumbled into his room in tears of grief and fell on his knees by the bed crying, 'O my Toni girl, my Toni girl, my Toni, Toni!'

He recalled saucy Unger, 'You ought to marry – you might work harder.' . . . In 1816 I got Karl and in 1816 Karl Josef became ill . . .

What sort of a bastard have I been to you, Toni?

No one else seemed to be feeling the cold as he did. These happy families. He had got to know, to nod to, a tall, scraggy man with a fat wife, both verging on the warted, gat-toothed side of homely, yet possessors of a stunningly exquisite god-like child whose every curve and limb jolted the onlooker with its unutterable beauty. The man perhaps shared the onlooker's shock at his own progeny, for, although Beethoven could not hear, the child seemed to be spoilt: he had often seen man and toddler in the lane together, the infant playing up his begetter, screaming with all his might down the whole length of the lane.

One day he came upon a most frightful scene. Walking down the narrow lane, he was laid hands on and dragged aside to escape the path of a speeding carriage. He had not begun to recover himself when he saw the carriage in the distance and, close by, the man leaning against his house, clenching his hands, banging his head in despair. At first he thought the carriage had clipped the so-angelic child until he saw the boy himself run out, his father catch him by the arm, upbraiding him once more, 'He nearly killed you! I *told* you never to run out! He nearly killed you! O God! O God!' – banging his head yet again, the boy watching his father perplexedly until the man again turned to him, 'It would have been *your fault!*' The boy ran into his garden.

The staggered man still clung to the wall. Beethoven invited him to the inn for a brandy but the man courteously but gratefully refused.

Beethoven himself went to the inn. His legs were shaking. How is a man supposed to forget that he's got a sick child whom he has never seen? 'Don't talk about him,' Franz had begun telling him. Don't talk about him! He's my son! He is my son! I've never seen him! Don't talk about him, don't think about him! For years, I never have told a living soul! No one knows! My nephew doesn't know! My own *brother* knows nothing!

Ill like that, and what have I ever done for him, never a visit from his father! . . . save write piano sonatas, 'The boy likes music . . .' and have three-fifths of a Mass played for him. Never a visit! I am his *father*!

He remembered when he had thought Franz would die first; he would go to Frankfurt and lay claim to A and his son . . .

O God, I could still go there and see him. He's still my child. I could see him.

At times he actively wanted to see the boy: me with my deaf ears and you with your deafened brain: a kindred soul.

He, who loved walking, had yearned for this throughout his illness, the timidity with which he had approached his first long walk soon turning to joy. Everything about walking he loved: the freedom; the sensation of his own firm stout briskly-moving limbs; the unexpected sights that one encountered; the beauties of nature; the swift flow or stab or slow dawning of musical thought. He could not bear to think of his child being unable to walk.

Someone had told him that there had been a performance of the *Choral* in Frankfurt on April 1st and that its review had been unlaudatory. 'It seems to us that the great master's genius was not present at its conception, and that in a purely formal quest for new tonal combinations it has lost its way.' The last time he had been in Vienna, he had encountered again a bad review of Opus 111. 'The devices that the composer has seen fit to employ for the development of his beautiful material are so artificial that we find them quite unworthy of his great genius . . . a miniature brush for a whole altar-piece . . .' Some other idiot had reviewed it as though it had been his own death-bed elegy. No, you fool. Not death but love. He recalled his letter to Franz of December 1821, when he had been starting this. When she had been with Karl Josef in France, taking him to Gall for treatment, addressing her through her husband: *Your excellent, one and only, glorious Toni.*

He had wanted to be with her then, to consummate their love afresh, to show her that, despite the sickness of their child, their love had been good, healthy love and he would do it all again.

He had had rheumatism that year. And then he had had jaundice. And that autumn, when he had been composing those two piano sonatas for her, he had gone for a walk along the canal and, his head full of them and his compositions, got lost. Peering through windows to orientate himself, in his hatless state, his old coat blowing open, he had been arrested as a tramp.

Returning from his walk, he wondered how Ries' performance of the *Choral* had gone. Besides the Symphony, of which he had not managed to send copies of all the parts, he had sent Ries several other works, including the *Kyrie* and *Gloria* of the Mass. He remembered writing to Ries, 'It seems my life is not to work out as I had hoped.' . . . The middle-aged couple, kissing in the street, seen from a carriage when he was being driven to conduct the first rehearsal of *Fidelio*. *I shall be like that with Toni. When I am fifty.*

He had unlocked his door and was climbing up his stairs.

May the gods grant you what your heart desires,
A husband and a home, and may they grant you also
That lucky harmony; for there is nothing greater or nobler
Than when a husband and wife who think as one
Keep house together . . .

He was losing weight yet his belly stuck out: the protruding abdomen he had had since jaundice, almost obscene on his now thin frame. His own big belly sometimes aroused him: he thought of Toni, carrying his Karl.

Later that night he went to his writing-desk. He felt groggy after his walk. Suddenly he felt very lonely. He had felt really cherished by Toni during the period of those big compositions. He had been giving; he had given what he could; at times he dreaded that he could give no more: though it was still coming, he was still working.

He laughed bitterly. It was the wrong daughter of Laban who had come back into his life! *O Rachel, ye daughter of Laban*! He opened and reread the Bible story: of how the half-brothers had sold Joseph as a slave to a merchant who was going to Egypt (as opposed to a merchant who was going to Frankfurt). And they dipped the coat of many colours into blood and went back and told their father that a wild beast must have devoured him.

He could not believe that Karl Josef was as he had been told. He expected the blood on the coat of many colours to be that of a wild beast and that he would end up with both Karl Josef and Karl Benjamin.

He had made a note to write to Reisser and Johann about his guardianship certificate. He had not heard from Karl. He had written to him on the 9th saying that arrangements had been made for him to visit Baden on Saturday by the 6 a.m. carriage. He could shave and change into fresh neckcloth and shirt in Baden. 'So if you will only work or study a little more before then, you will not lose any time. I am sorry to have to cause you this annoyance. . . . Even though I am cross with you, it is not without good cause; and indeed I should not like to have disbursed so much only to send *a vulgar man* into the world.' He had promised to greet frankness with understanding 'should the intrigues have already matured,' although by the next paragraph he was accusing him of neglect. The boy would not even enquire about new rooms for him! 'You know how I am living here, and in this cold weather. To be constantly alone makes me only weaker, and in fact I often feel faint. O don't hurt me any more. In any case Death with his scythe will not spare me for very much longer.'

Now on Friday the 10th he wrote to Bernard asking him to see Karl occasionally and supervise his reading. 'His manners are greatly deteriorating. His treatment of me is extremely offensive and is having a bad effect on my health.' He complained that Karl had now failed to answer three letters. 'Because I had to correct him on Sunday (and he absolutely refuses to be corrected) I had to face behaviour on his part such as I have only experienced from his deceased father, an uncouth fellow, on whom I nevertheless showered benefits.' He thought that Karl's 'monster of a mother' was probably in league with 'that gentleman, my brainless and heartless brother, who is always out to censure and to instruct me (as the sow does to Minerva in Demosthenes) because I refuse to have anything to do with his overfed whore and bastard and, still less, to live with people who are so very much my inferiors.'

In saying farewell to Stumpff, Beethoven had told him, 'That is my brother. Have nothing to do with him. He is not an honest man.' Johann had even taken Karl to a ball at Candlemas – no *wife*, just tickets for the two of them! In February the boy had told him that Therese was again involved in some love affair. What's more, in March he had learned that Johanna and Johann had been involved once in some business dealings – Johanna had set up a guarantor for him! No wonder they were collaborating now! And here he was, abused like a leper, yet still being expected to find the 6-800 florins that according to Johann Reisser had said it would cost him a year to provide for Karl's lodging, all found!

He had changed Karl's guardian from Peters to Reisser on Johann's account, since Peters was often out of Vienna. 'I thought this would be suitable for Karl. But I fear that there is trouble ahead, for I know nothing of Reisser, seeing that I have never met him. That much I have been able to extract from my ass of a brother, apart from his and Herr von R's anxiety that Karl should no longer be with me. How very clever of them! Yet I am still obliged to disburse the money.' He had once told Streicher, and Streicher had apparently repeated, to that Leipzig publisher, Peters, 'Everything I do apart from music is badly done and is stupid.' Aye, but my money's good enough, the money I earn sweating my life-blood!

. . . Streicher, that friend of Schiller, writing of him as though he were some fool, some fool who could do nothing but write music – after all the effort he had put into rearing that boy! . . . Reisser, Johann, interfering in *my* business! Who do these people think they are! . . . Reisser, some jumped-up academic, talks of *respect* for me, same as Sonnleithner. 'O, I'm an old friend!' Aye, when it suits him! *Reisser!* Well he'd got the certificate for him now, he'd get Bernard to show him! Bach had confirmed that this was 'a contract in perpetuity.' It has been as far as the Emperor, so you can't get out of it! *I'm* guardian! Bach had also said Johanna was 'still under police supervision!' By God, if *that kid* gets mixed up again with her in secret, if Johann or Reisser helps him do it, *by God* I shall bring the house down!

. . . All that talk a year or so ago, when he had decided to help her. *He* had not wanted that. 'Is it true that she slept with her lover while my dead father was in the house?' . . . Taking him to see his new-born half-sister: refusing to see her, yelling in the street, 'She's a whore! She's a whore!'

And now he was running *off to her*! He had not done that for years – not since he had been a real child. He had said he wanted nothing to do with her.

. . . Johann, one minute saying he'd finished with her, the next telling Karl he'd always loved her!

O you stupid bloody people! Is there no consistency in your life!

'I wrote to R from Baden only a few days ago, for I was *so* weak that I could hardly attend to anything; and how lovingly I was cared for, all that I shall tell you when we meet. That awful fourth floor, O God, *without a wife* . . .' I wish my son were healthy and I wish I had a daughter and I wish I could have spent my life with you. He had seen that same father out with his daughter, the girl unaware of his proud, love-filled glance. He recalled telling Antonie, 'A man should come home to a wife and several children.' She had promised him three . . .

People talk rubbish about marriage being hard. With Toni it wouldn't have been hard. It would have been like music: flowing, inevitable. It stops even being true that 'I love you'; becomes 'I am you'. The barriers dissolved. He had been there with Toni; recalled telling Zmeskall: *Joy in a woman's arms*. That had been when he had told him about Karl Josef . . .

People talk a load of rubbish about 'marriage is hard work – you have to work at it.' If you marry the right person in the first place, you don't have to work at it. Marriage is *easy*. She had simply fallen into his arms. Once in Karlsbad he had woken up singing love songs, just at the sheer delight of her being alive.

. . . 'Ludwig, I'm having your baby . . .'

He could still remember the radiance that had spread through him then. He hadn't been able to stop grinning.

. . . 'You'd grow old together and be insufferably smug.'

'I've always wanted to be smug with a woman.'

'I know you have.'

. . . To be an old man with an old wife of long duration, and to walk down the street with her, supporting her arm.

Chapter 9

Summer

He exclaimed as he saw a butterfly, the first of the summer after the bad spring. As it flew towards him it appeared the palest of pale blue; but as he inspected it on the grass where it had settled like a fallen blossom, the outside of the tiny wings bore striped markings of subtle yellow and grey.

Karl had no time to look at butterflies. Johann and Reisser were agreed. 'It's ridiculous that he won't let the boy go to the theatre!' 'It's too much that he tries to stop his mother seeing him!' Johann had nevertheless apparently written to Beethoven placating his fears. They had made up their row over the weekend and it was again all 'My dear son,' 'Son of my heart,' though he was still importuned to be thrifty by wearing old clothes indoors. He was still having to run around after him and being admonished to wake with aurora and hear all his moans about the servants. One wench Frau Schnaps had called 'a wild animal'; a new one had come, but she was not going to stay. 'Yesterday the dance began with the cooking ... I have talked to the old woman *like an old man* ... What I find most trying is to be alone at table. And really it is to be wondered at that I can compose here *even tolerably well*.' At least by late June it was hot and Beethoven had sent him money to bathe.

He had rebuked him for spending too much on blue cloth and a mirror. 'You are already a Viennese although I hope that you will not become a sport of Viennese currency. It does you no harm at your age to have to give a full account of the money you receive, since you do not reach your majority until you are 24 ... Do not make me recall incidents of long ago ... in the end you would only say as usual, "after all you are a very good guardian." If only you had some depth of character, you would always act quite differently.'

He had warned him not to be drawn into secret intrigues with Johann. 'Don't do anything secretly against me, against your most faithful father.' He had signed this 'Ben.'

In July he had him draft letters to Galitzin and Peters, fearful lest Galitzin thought him less hard up than he was. 'I have already experienced that these so-called great lords do not like to see *an artist*, who is already their *equal*, in affluent circumstances.' He hadn't read this in Galitzin's letter and thought that this must have been a mistranslation on Beethoven's part. To Peters he was to offer the new quartet.

And go to the tailor's for him, and the cobbler's. And the knife-seller. And Henikstein. He thought Johann had swindled him over Galitzin's roubles, though Galitzin had already said that he would re-imburse him for postage and handling charges, which Karl felt sure was all that this discrepancy amounted to.

This letter he had closed with 'Things will soon be over with your faithful father.'

On Tuesday the 12th Beethoven came to Vienna to visit Braunhofer. The doctor told him that the Baden sulphur baths only increased his agitation, he should restrict himself to the air-baths and a cleansing bath once a week, and even then he shouldn't soak for too long. 'You mustn't overdo anything. Besides a healthy diet, sleep is also necessary . . . Believe me, diet is the most important thing for your recovery . . . no irritants . . . avoidance of excessive medication . . . Only nutritious food gives energy to the body, drinks that make you flushed give you nothing at all. Your spirit is strong enough without the need of spirituous liquor!' About his hearing, nothing could be done.

Somewhat to his own surprise, Karl grew alarmed that Beethoven was ill again so soon. He wondered how serious it was. It was almost like a wake already. All the old beetles were crawling out of the woodwork. Even *Mr Shitting* had been round to see him – now there's a man with a nose for death and opportunity. But even Johann had seen him again and invited him to stay at the farm, despite what Beethoven said about Therese.

Despite his bad health he had finished another quartet. You had to hand it to him as a worker. Here was Johann, five years younger, going to relax on his estate; and here was Beethoven, producing works that gained him worldwide praise. Ries had written reporting the success of the *Choral*, enclosing 40 louis d'or as a fee; telling Beethoven that this work alone would have made him immortal. 'Whither yet will you lead us?'

Driving back to Baden from Vienna on the 9th, Beethoven had met Holz and Linke and two other musicians. Holz had driven back with him and dined with him. To Beethoven's embarrassment there had been scarcely any food. On the day of Johann's visit he had found himself with no soup, no beef, not even an egg. He wrote to Karl of his troubles with his servants: *Santanas*, with her 'seething wrath and madness,' . . . *the old witch* . . . *the old goose* . . . 'All week I have had to suffer and endure my sufferings like a saint. Away with that beastly rabble. What a reproach it is to our civilization that we need the services of such people, that we have to have around us people whom we despise.' To him he added in French, 'To the devil with these great rascals of nephews – Be my son, my beloved son – Farewell – I kiss you – Your sincere father, as always.'

He wrote every day, contradicting himself, Karl thought, as usual: 'Remember to tell people how ill I am and how much I do need the money,' yet 'We must not let them know that we need money too much.' On the 15th Beethoven had opened his letter, 'Come soon! Come soon! Come soon!' and closed it with 'I am pressing my loving seal on your dear loyalty to and affection for me . . . As always your loving father who cares for you.' He was as capable of writing, when he found that he had 'lied to me again' over some petty matter like getting quills, 'Surely God will set me free, *Libera me Domine de illis* . . .'

. . . 'You are always being given too much money . . . a Viennese will always be a Viennese. I was glad when I could help my poor parents. What a difference compared with you. Thoughtless fellow.' Yet he was always writing, 'How depressed I am when I again feel so lonely among all these people!'

When he had finished the second quartet it had been, 'Follow your guide and father, follow him whose one thought is always for your moral welfare.' Galitzin had written again, a letter he had sent by hand through his compatriot, Thal, a prominent businessman who might in the future he thought prove useful to Karl. 'Success is crowning my efforts.' He could never let well alone, Karl thought, as he read, 'Be on your best behaviour with Thal.' As though I were some sort of schoolboy!

Adjuring him to take care of his health in this heat. 'Dear son, do keep your good health. Avoid everything that can enfeeble and impair your youthful strength.' Karl had told him of homoeopathic treatment for deafness. Schlemmer had been hard of hearing for ten years, he'd been going to a practitioner of homoeopathy who gave him a powder in unbelievably small tins and prescribed him a diet so strict that he didn't dare to eat any food that people usually ate. 'Everything has to be cooked specially for him.' 'What use is that to me, with this rabble! I can't even get ordinary food!' had been his retort.

On the 2nd of August he wrote still complaining about the cooking, 'the brazen impertinence of that veritable old witch.' Karl was surprised to see that he talked of calling on Johann's help. This letter ended with a threat, 'What unheard-of dissonance there would be if you were *false* to me, in the way that some people indeed declare that you really are.'

Johann had told Beethoven before leaving, 'In winter if it's all right with you I will take Karl into my place and there it shouldn't cost you anything.'

'What unfortunate circumstances, and to have such a brother!' Beethoven had been bemoaning to Karl. 'Alas! Alas!' *Pseudo-brother*, he called him, *Signor Fratello, Asinaccio* . . .

Johann had told him before leaving, 'It goes badly with the Greeks.' Aye, and it goes badly with your brother, Beethoven thought, writing to ask him to come at once, 'For I can't put up any longer with this old witch who 200 years ago would certainly have been burnt . . . The evil nature of this female monster is the chief reason why she finds it impossible to show the slightest sign of goodness.' He told him that Schindler had been sniffing round. 'But I should like to say like the Viennese *I kiss my hand* to *Mr Shitting* – True enough, you too are a rascal and a pseudo-brother – At the same time, if *I must have someone near me*, my brother still has the first claim.'

Johann ignored this. He had exerted himself enough just to get the old woman to stay with him. His brother could get through any number of housekeepers. He had only found her for him in the first place through his brother-in-law, the baker – her late son had once owned the house next door. He had said to him way back in February, 'The best thing would be to live together, because my legs are getting more wretched daily with all this traipsing back and forth.' He had told him he couldn't take on a second family. He wouldn't have that, wouldn't have anything to do with Therese or Amalie. No, I'm not leaving Gneixendorf just to please him. Let him stew in his own juice.

Throughout all this Beethoven kept composing. 'Have you the desire to write another quartet?' Holz had asked him. Beethoven had laughed, 'Why, man, I'm already on the third movement!'

Holz was becoming a friend. 'Wood of Christ,' he called him, 'Most excellent chip! . . . Why, no one doubts that *wood* is a neuter noun!' Less than a decade older than Karl, he had studied music in Linz with Glöggl, the *Kapellmeister* Beethoven had called on daily during his bleak time there in 1812. He had played in Böhm's quartet until Falstaff's return from Russia, when he had become *Mylord's* second fiddle. He gave music lessons and occasionally conducted, yet he was not a full-time musician, holding a post in the Chancellery. Personable, well-read and witty though he found him, Beethoven was above all grateful for the young man's ability to help him sort out his finances. Holz for his part declared, 'I am no flatterer, but I assure you that the mere thought of Beethovenian music makes me supremely glad to be alive.'

He had talked of having a word with Steiner to find out what he would pay for a new quartet. He had discussed choral and religious projects, asking about Bernard's oratorio, suggesting other librettists, bursting out with 'Goethe should produce a text!' He thought Beethoven should write the *Requiem* commissioned by the rich Viennese cloth-merchant Wolf-mayer well over a decade ago: ' . . . the Requiem which summons the devil from hell!'

Holz had also begun reporting Karl's movements. 'He was out again on Saturday evening. He often goes to the theatre.'

'Who told you that?'

'The people in the house.'

Holz thought it would be better if Karl went to the *Burgtheater* rather than the *Josephstadt*. Beethoven didn't want him gadding about at all. 'He has too much work to do. The boy has *failed once*! My brother is behind this! Johann has ignored my letter.'

'Falstaff has told him more than once that he's the greatest swine if ever he opens his mouth about your art . . .'

Holz had become his friend. He had given him his new quartet, to have it copied. And now he was terrified lest Holz had lost it. Holz had not turned up. 'He usually comes.' He told Karl, 'Between ourselves, he is *a hard drinker.*' Haslinger had begged him for the new quartet. He was dangling it before Schlesinger, Peters . . . 'I am in a mortal fright.' . . . A lifetime, when work went well, of living in constant fear of his lodgings catching fire, burning down, his work being lost . . . taking short walks, often, never to be far from it, hurrying back . . . 'For God's sake do make my mind easy about the quartet, for that would be a terrible loss. The ideas for it are only jotted down on small scraps of paper; and I shall never be able to compose the whole quartet again in the same way.' For years he had written out great solid chunks in his sketchbooks; these days he wrote scrips and scraps, getting the whole thing as soon as he could into some proper form of score. This was what he had let Holz take . . . the fourth, fifth and sixth movements, and all but the first thirteen bars of the third . . .

Both Karl and Holz jumped to respond to this. The quartet was safely with the copyist. Beethoven cuddled it when he got it back, stroking the manuscript with his cheek. O my beautiful *Heiliger Dankgesang*!

At the end of July he had received Schotts' letter of the 19th through Frau Streicher, though none of the others which they had mentioned. He had written on August 2nd with some corrections for the Mass, making fun of them for taking up Johann's suggestion that Gottfried Weber should undertake some of his proof-reading, a suggestion which the other composer had turned down as rudely as he himself would have done.

Now on August 13th he wrote to them demanding a retraction of their publication of his humorous biography of Tobias Haslinger, which they had used in addition to his canons. ' . . . a jest sent to you as a friend . . . never meant for publication.'

Part 1 – Tobias appears as the apprentice of the famous *Kapellmeister* Fux, who is firm in his saddle – and he is holding the ladder to the latter's *Gradus ad Parnassum*. Then, as he feels inclined to indulge in practical jokes, Tobias by rattling and shaking the ladder makes many a person who has already climbed rather high suddenly break his neck. He then says goodbye to this earth of ours but again comes to light in Albrechtsberger's time. Part 2. Fux's *Nota cambiata* which has now appeared is soon discussed with Albrechtsberger, the *appoggiaturas* are meticulously analysed, the art of creating musical skeletons is exhaustively dealt with. Tobias then envelops himself like a caterpillar, undergoes another evolution, and reappears in this world for the third time. Part 3. The scarcely grown wings now enable him to fly to the little *Paternostergaße* and he becomes the *Kapellmeister* of the little *Paternostergaße*. Having passed through the school of *appoggiaturas* all that he retains is the *bills of exchange*. Thus he firmly establishes the friend of his youth and finally becomes a member of several *learned* societies.

He had been horrified at first when he had found this in print. All those puns . . . *Wechselnote* for *appoggiatura*, *Wechsel* for bill of exchange . . . *geleert* for *gelehrt*, empty-headed instead of learned! But Schotts had been annoyed that Haslinger had urged him to avoid them and, even as he wrote 'It is disgraceful,' he laughed that Haslinger was getting his just deserts. 'It's better than finding oneself in the jaws of some monster,' he had told Holz and, to Karl, who had been much amused, he wrote, 'Our age needs powerful minds to castigate these petty, deceitful, miserable wretches of human hearts – however much my heart refuses to give pain to anyone . . . Be my dear son, my only son, and imitate my virtues but not my *faults*. But, since a man must have faults, do not have worse faults than I . . .'

Writing to Haslinger himself, he had not been able to resist repeating the pun he had made on *Schreyvogel*, his one-time publisher, this time at the expense of Piringer, whose wife was about to go into labour, 'Piringer will *growl*, he can't *yell*; he is in the same predicament, I fancy, as Schreyvogel, of whom someone said "he could neither yell nor rape!"'

He was in labour himself, with this lot: quartets coming at him from all sides . . . 'I shall compose something pleasant in your company,' he told Karl when he wrote on the 22nd, though he added, 'You cannot conceive how depressed and sad I felt yesterday after you had all gone. It is too bad to be left alone again with this evil rabble who will never be reformed.'

They had begun looking for a new housekeeper. Haslinger had forgiven him. Karl had told him he ought to set Homer. Holz said that he had always displayed the greatest gratitude to his parents. 'Unto us a child is born,' Beethoven had written in his conversation book when he had heard of the birth of Piringer's son.

Johann was back but, instead of helping, all he had done was to usurp Holz' allotted task of talking to Steiner. Karl had suggested that the new quartet be played for Haslinger. He wasn't having that. *No* publisher gets *my* works *on approval*! By the 24th he was writing to his 'Most excellent piece of mahogany!' that offers to Peters and Schlesinger were being held over while he awaited a reply from Artaria at Mannheim. 'On the other hand it is all the same to me which hellhound licks or gnaws away at my brain.' He consigned Peters to the same Auerbach's cellar as that Mephistopheles Rochlitz, whose publication had had the nerve *in 1821* to say *he* was *written out*!

Still concerned about his health, Beethoven had in mid-August noted a book on *The art of healing illnesses of the ear* and, a week later, another on the treatment of the types of indigestion 'which most men begin to experience between their 20th and 25th year.' On the same day as his letter to Holz, he wrote to Karl that his stomach was in a bad state and he had no doctor.

'Since yesterday I have eaten nothing but soup and a couple of eggs and have drunk only water; my tongue is quite yellow; and without bowel motions and tonics my stomach will never, never be cured, in spite of what that doctor may say.' Nevertheless he was cheerful, telling Karl that the new quartet too would have 6 movements; he expected to finish it within a fortnight. 'Be fond of me, my dear fellow, and remember that, when I pain you, I am not doing so to hurt you but in order to do you good *for the future* ... I embrace you with all my heart. Provided you are kind, good, hard-working and sincere, that is all I need for my happiness.'

He was looking forward to a letter from him for his name-day on the 25th. When it did not come he could have hit him. That bastard! ... Kind, good, hard-working and sincere! He had even dropped hints reminding him about it! He wrote in cold anger, 'Although this day deserves to be taken notice of as little by you as by me, yet I hoped to have at least *a letter from you* ...'

He had even apologised for the fact that he had to run about after him so much! Never once did that bastard ever remember his name-day! ... It had been on August the 25th, thirteen years ago, that Antonie had given him her father's ring ...

Chapter 10

Late August-September

It was his favourite time of year, between his name-day and his birthday, when he and art fell in love with each other and hurled themselves into each other's arms.

He was at work on Galitzin's third, the slow movement, his *Cavatina*.

... 'You are too coarse-grained to appreciate the little jewel that's fallen into your lap. "Eigh-up," you say, "There's a little jewel fallen into my lap here."' He laughed at the memory of laughing with his Toni.

She had said to him once, 'You have your way, your truth and your light – you are the luckiest man God ever made.'

This bloody thing, when he was in it, felt as permanent as death. He laughed: 'As permanent as death!' O God, the bloody calmness of it – all about me suffer – I have no right to such God-given calm.

Not for the first time, his thoughts surprised him; he thought of Karl but he *saw*, he did not *feel* – always, always, it was thus, *when he was working*! In work: as in love. Whether this was an abnegation or a utilization of his feelings he did not know but, *God knows*, it is always like this!

Later, as he sat back replete in the joy of composition, he thought of the joys that arose out of suffering in his life. Is it like this for everyone? My little Karl! His life looks terrible – unmitigated – O God let it only seem so to us from the outside, God let there be *something* out of life for him – not just his service to other people, serving a cause – O God bring *him joy*!

In contrast to the sobbing heartbreak of the music there were times, writing this, when he had never felt happier in his life. It was one of those times when we are all in the world, from the youngest new-born to the frailest old man; each one with his equal right to the world's joy and glory; and he too was in the world, of it, amongst it; deep in his soul: all *right, belonging*. He felt strong in his art, secure, God-given, God was in His heaven and Beethoven was at his writing-desk. He thought of other composers, ditherers, people who wanted him to set operas about *fairies*, oratorios about *Hate* and *Discord*, and idiots who pressurized him, 'O, set it, B!' ... You do not succumb to *any* pressure from *anybody, ever*. Succumbing to pressure is what kiddies do. It's not what adults do. It's not what *artists* do. You lot wouldn't recognize integrity if it stamped on your foot. He recalled what people said of him: can't make decisions. My *work*! It's all decisions! Can't make decisions! Me! Huh!

For days, perhaps weeks on end, he could work like this: waking at dawn, to his desk with his coffee, out on his walks, working on until well after midnight. People said to him, 'You must have an iron will.' It wasn't an iron will at all; it was no will: as natural as breathing, the easiest thing he had ever done in his life. Iron-will is when you're forcing yourself to do it and it doesn't go right. He had no iron-will, he was a man with no will. Nor was he indulgent: he was an instrument. With no more will than that fiddle whether it were to be played, and no more say than that fiddle whether it be well-tuned.

Absolutely incredible God-like ecstasy. Perfectly pure. Nothing wrong with it. . . . Because you make it yourself . . . make it with God . . . because it is the nearest you ever come to God . . . without God you do not make it.

What you realize is that God is *so good*!

Lost once in work, he came to to find his left foot paralysed with pins and needles, at once senseless and absurdly swollen it seemed to him as he stood, banging it against the chair. It's funny, this 'being an artist' – like having an extra limb that you haul about with you. You no more think of being without it than you envisage slicing off your hand or your leg or your nose.

Art: that which lifts the spirit, that which brings one closer to God. Ah, Phonus Bollonus. Art is just what happens when I start to write.

Roaming the *Helenenthal* mountains, stripped almost to his underpants, his clothing borne behind his shoulder, strung out on his stick. He was working on the *Cavatina*, embodying his thoughts of earlier in the summer, his sense of loss and grief and tragic resignation . . . the *beklemmt* passage where the leader wails, underpinned by the sobs of the other instruments. As when someone wrote to him of Z's crippled plight, he felt twinges, but the very act of composition lifted him out of the pain he had felt then. He recalled poor old Zmeskall, who had tried all the spas, trying to cure himself of gout by tepid water and vomiting; rendered unproductive for a long time, finally pensioned off by the Hungarian Chancellery in June.

Love needs its fruits. But there is more than one kind of love. And more than one fruit.

The movement began by being very beautiful, as though it were going to be a hymn or a love-song, and as it became a lullaby the music began to cry. A perfect amalgam of subjective grief within a framework of classical restraint. And did I set out to compose subjectivity held taut within a classical framework? You bet your sweet baby's socks I didn't.

He recalled telling A of composition, kneeling to pray so comically that she had laughed. I don't know how it started. I don't know where it comes from. I only know, now, as it is, I pray and it does. He had once thought of saying to one of these idiots, 'How do I write 'em? Well, you see, I have this little lamp . . .'

Beethoven was writing quartets and all the hell-hounds were gathering in Vienna just when Beethoven wanted to be left in peace to write his quartets! Only a week ago he had talked of giving the third quartet to

Artaria and the second to Peters, but here was Moritz Schlesinger from Paris offering 80 ducats for each. He had been working the other day, and Schlesinger had popped in to see him just as he had dragged himself away from composing to attend to business matters, a condition he compared to being dragged from the heights of Etna to the glaciers of Switzerland.

On the 2nd a party of about ten musicians, including Piringer, Haslinger and Holz, turned up to see him in Baden with their guest of honour, Kuhlau. Sixteen years Beethoven's junior, Kuhlau, a German by birth, had fled to Copenhagen in his youth to escape military service at the Napoleonic academy of Hamburg. There he had made his name as a composer and piano virtuoso.

Beethoven led his party of brigands into the beautiful *Helenenthal*, there to set them tasks in hill climbing to show them how well he himself excelled. They repaired to an inn, where throughout the meal champagne was ordered and drunk with gusto. The heated hikers then followed Beethoven to his lodgings where bottles of the local red, Vöslauer, were produced.

'Last year we had good Vöslauer here and we thought it would be the same today,' Haslinger grumbled. 'We'll get together at my place in Vienna one evening. *Then* we'll drink Vöslauer!'

Piringer was getting his leg pulled. 'He's hen-pecked!' Haslinger told Beethoven, 'Piringer didn't get up until seven – he was still lying abed when we were already sitting in the carriage . . .'

Piringer wrote, 'I am Pilate!'

Holz wrote, 'Haslinger has on the shortest waistcoat today . . .'

Piringer added, 'And the longest leg-coverings, vulgarly called trousers.'

Piringer, having heard of Beethoven's jest on Schreyvogel, insisted on punning upon the names of the others. Haslinger had become 'baked hare.' Haslinger wrote, 'He must walk to Vienna as punishment.' Someone else was being called 'blue trout.' 'Monsieur de Bois,' Piringer wrote, 'sandalwood.' Holz objected, 'Wood of Christ!' A few pages later, Piringer was writing, 'Steiner throws stones at Haslinger. Fischer has trout to catch. Holz will be hooked tomorrow.' Holz wrote, 'I'll wait another five years and then marry the Director's daughter,' meaning Piringer's child of 1816 by his first marriage. His first wife had died when she had been born. 'Marry in the cloister or the dungeon,' Piringer told him. 'My daughter might have got gold, but not a man of wood!' This was followed by jokes about marital duties and drinking-men 'Who have no duties at all!' Holz came back with a reference to 'a fat wife' which had Beethoven laughing when he thought of Therese.

The pianist Würfel, old sober-sides, had descended like cold air upon this merry party. Instead of vulgar puns they ought to set their names to music, or at least their host and his leading guest should. Kuhlau wrote down the four-note motif Beethoven was to set and Würfel spelt out pedantically what he must do. Beethoven took up his pen and wrote a canon with B-A-C-H – B-flat, A, C, B-natural – as its opening motif, punning on Kuhlau's name: *Kühl, nicht lau*. Kuhlau laughed when he saw it, 'Cool, not luke-warm!'

Holz stayed behind when the others had left, having taken a room overnight in the spa. They talked of the party, they talked about music. 'Haydn said if he made a so-called grammatical blunder: Do you like it? "O yes!" Ah well, let's leave it!' Holz did not share Beethoven's high regard for Mozart. 'Apart from his genius as a musical artist, he was nothing. Handel had a dignity which Mozart never reached.'

Beethoven walked Holz back to his temporary Baden lodgings. He walked back alone feeling merry. He imagined Piringer getting it in the neck. 'Well of course he's been knocking it back – he hasn't got a bloody wife to answer to like you have!' He laughed, whooping for joy at his own joke. So much for doctors, telling *me* I'm finished! Look at me now! Fit as a fiddle! Kuhlau was a funny sod, writing *his* operas about fairies, *elves*! Funny-looking git, with his one eye. But then, there was old Ries, with his deformity – didn't stop him landing a noted beauty as bride. What funny things women were, that they could overlook physical deformity. But then, he had got Antonie, hadn't he? He had thought of her during their bawdiness, telling jokes of his own, laughing mightily, but, beneath it all, feeling warm, aglow: yes, Antonie does love me.

. . . Testing *me* to give them a canon on BACH, that sober toady Würfel writing down, 'That is the assignment, the resolution is . . .' BACH. That brook. 'This ocean.' 'Why is he dead?' He had been playing the 48 as a boy. Father had made him a present of the score. . . . The BACH-related opening of his last quartet . . . the desire to write a BACH-overture way back . . . with those piano sonatas for *her*.

He reeled back to his lodgings singing, 'Hantonie Ho Ant-huh-nie, Yho're the *Honly one* for me, Yho're the *honly one*!'

He awoke with a bad head, blank memory and a bad conscience. He sent Kuhlau his canon afresh through Holz, fearing that he might have written nonsense.

Schlesinger visited him the next day, wanting to publish his canon as well as the one from Kuhlau in reply. Beethoven had known Schlesinger since 1819 when the young man, then 21, had called on him at Mödling and sent him some veal after the dish had sold out at the inn. He and his father, who ran the Berlin firm, had since published his last three piano sonatas – so badly that Beethoven himself had helped Diabelli to bring out a pirated but correct edition of Opus 111. Now Schlesinger wanted to publish not only the two new quartets but one more in addition, as well as three quintets. He also wanted to hear the quartet which Schott had bought, his hope being to bring out his own full edition of Beethoven's trios, quartets and quintets.

He wanted to attend a rehearsal of the new work. Beethoven grew indignant, fearing that his artistry was being called into question, but Karl assured him that Schlesinger meant no insult, he merely wanted the pleasure of hearing the work.

Three days later, Schlesinger heard the work rehearsed in his rooms at *zum wilden Mann*. Beethoven had had doubts about letting Falstaff have the new quartet. 'Because of his fatness, Falstaff requires more time to master a work than previously,' he had written to Karl in the summer in a draft letter meant for Galitzin. Holz had re-assured him, 'I think you will find Mylord Falstaff will play this one well.'

Holz arrived on Thursday the 8th to tell him about the rehearsal. Wolfmayer had been there; at the *Heiliger Dankgesang* he had wept like a child. 'Tobias scratched his ear; he really regrets that Steiner didn't get this one.'

Reisser's absence for four weeks increased Beethoven's concern about Karl. He suspected that the boy was again skiving from his studies. 'Threaten Karl when you catch him in the act,' he had written to Holz. Now Holz told him, 'I was with Karl on Saturday to give him your note; it was evening, and I learned from the maid that he had gone out early in the morning and had not returned to eat. I have a plan to attach him more closely to me. I should like to win him over to my side; perhaps then I can get to know him and his way of life more easily. I have already lured him into going into a beer-house with me to find out if he drinks much, but this doesn't seem to be the case. Now I shall invite him to play billiards; then I'll see straight away if he has already been practising long.'

Beethoven grew fretful about where Karl went to play. Holz seemed surprised. 'What harm can come to him if he goes through the city from the *Alservorstadt?*'

'Women in doorways.'

'What?'

'Women in doorways!'

Holz grew flustered. 'What do other young people do about it?'

Beethoven expostulated, 'I bring him up, give him his education, give him a home! This is how the ungrateful toad repays me! *Billiards!*'

Holz tried to calm the situation, urging Beethoven to give Karl something from time to time 'for his efforts and the hardships he endures.'

'Where does he get the money to play billiards!'

'He's got the love of money from your brother.'

The following day Beethoven went to *zum wilden Mann*, Schlesinger's Viennese lodgings, where a larger room had been made available for the private performance of the new quartet. He was introduced to Sir George Smart, from England, who had conducted the *Choral* in London on March the 21st. A copy of the score was found for Smart. About a dozen other people were present, including Carl Czerny and Haslinger. Karl, Smart thought, possessed the Sicilian good looks of Count St Antonio, as did Böhm. Beethoven was pleased to see the young fiddler. After playing

Galitzin's first Böhm had asked him, 'Can you play this without setting your fiddle on fire?' Beethoven had laughed, mindful of saying to Falstaff's complaints of the *Rasumovskys*, 'Do you think I worry about your damn' fiddle when the muse is upon me!'

He had written Galitzin's second quartet with 6 movements but, perusing the autograph, he had realized that that slow movement had altered the balance. He had also realized that he needed something in his new quartet between the quirky yet lyrical third and the *Cavatina*. He had removed the *Alla danza tedesca* from the quartet in A and adapted it to fit into the new one. Galitzin's second now consisted of the first movement with its BACH-related opening; the second with its Viennese street-song, dreamed up years ago as some piano bagatelle; the slow movement with its *Heiliger Dankgesang*, and a march which led without a break into the movement originally planned for the *Choral* finale.

A had called him 'The most human of all composers.' Sometimes still when there was a vacant seat beside him he imagined turning to it and seeing her. Today however he was directing the performers. The quartet lasted for three-quarters of an hour and was played twice. At one point he took off his coat in the hot, crowded room, seized Holz' fiddle and played a staccato passage a quarter of a tone too flat.

Karl watched from the hall. Just before the start Beethoven had been heard remarking, 'You nearly didn't have a Beethoven just before I wrote that!' He was now in a better mood, deeply absorbed in his current work; this quartet now receiving its first performance already a part of his past; but at Wednesday's rehearsal the cloth-merchant Wolfmayer had been deeply moved. He had been found sobbing like a baby at the end of the slow movement. Some time later, when he sought words for the emotional turmoil he had undergone, he had told them, 'Mozart doesn't touch the depths that Beethoven touches. When you're happy or just all right Mozart provides you with beautiful music to listen to, but when you're low, depressed, or in grief, Beethoven is the one who has been there before and goes there with you.' Later still he had added, 'He's in there with you – you're with him – you're with him in his illness, his fear of death, and you *feel* the grateful surprise at the onset of recovery. – Return of strength! . . . but it's such a *gradual* return – dubious – not taken for granted. . . . But instead of being personal, taking you *to* him, into his troubles, he comes out to you and meets you in yours – it's this *joining*, it's incredible, he touches . . .' He had stopped, apparently made speechless by the universality he was discussing.

On the way out he had been heard to comment that Mozart was all high violins, sweeping, beautiful – 'O Mozart provides you with grand beauty!' He had laughed again, as though disbelieving that anyone could ever conceive of mentioning Mozart in the same breath as the man whom he surreptitiously clothed.

Despite Beethoven's own reverence for the composer, Holz was accustomed to saying, 'Mozart is not comparable with Beethoven. Beethoven is meat and Mozart gravy!' Wolfmayer had uttered, 'He comes at you with such power you can't withstand him!' They were into the finale now, the movement first conceived for the *Choral*. O how incredible it was! Karl had forgotten the sheer solid splendour of a string quartet in full flight – solid because these were no reedy fiddles but, like all great quartets, Falstaff and his sweating troop roared along like a string orchestra. But what a roar! That old bastard! You couldn't resist it! Once again Karl found himself swept along like the rest of the small, select, intense audience, fully at the mercy of the music, fully in love with its begetter. You old bastard! You've got us all in your power!

'A great string quartet flies . . .'

'You what?'

'It's so exciting . . . it grabs you and shakes you, you can't resist it . . .'

Beethoven too was sweating after his exertions in directing. He joined the players in calling for a pint of beer. Schlesinger'll damn well have to pay up after this! He was still pondering whether to take up some big work, the opera, the oratorio, just to get a lump of money. Schlesinger had told him, 'If you write quartets and quintets you'll get more money for your nephew than from all the great works.' Influenced by Beethoven's concern to get the most money he could out of his compositions for Karl, and Holz' determination that even the manuscript of the quartet be not given to him to publish from but saved as capital for the boy, Schlesinger now wrote for Beethoven, 'I said it depends on your nephew what you will write, and Falstaff said, no, it is up to him what Beethoven writes . . .'

Beethoven banged his chest and roared, 'It is up to *me* what Beethoven writes!'

The quartet was repeated on Sunday the 11th before a larger party which included Fräulein Eskeles and Frau Cibbini. Fräulein Eskeles' father, the Baron, had attended his second *Choral* concert the year before; to her mother, the Baroness Cäcilie, Beethoven had inscribed in her album a small piece for voice and piano from Goethe's *Göttliche*: '*Der edle Mensch sei hülfreich und gut.*' Beethoven had invested in bank shares in 1819 on the advice of Baron von Eskeles, director of the Viennese bank Amstein & Eskeles.

Abbé Stadler was also there. He too had been at that farcical second concert. Unlike Wolfmayer, Stadler believed that music ended with Mozart, grudgingly conceding that it perhaps began with Haydn. Beethoven was too new-fangled for his taste. 'I'm an old man and I'm set in my ways. I know a lot of you young blades think this Beethoven's marvellous but I'm too old now, I'll never change, never change!'

Schlesinger hosted dinner for Beethoven and Karl, Falstaff, Holz and the other two members of the quartet, Weiss and Linke; Carl Czerny, who had earlier joined Falstaff and Linke in a performance of Beethoven's piano trios Opus 70 and Opus 97; Sedlaczek, who played the flute, and Sir George Smart.

Beethoven was looking round. 'Where are the women?'

'Frau Cibbini really has left!' Falstaff laughed. 'She couldn't keep her eyes off you, eh? She's not bad!'

Beethoven had taken care with his appearance, partly to impress this young woman. There had been one good-looker even younger. 'Where is that other one? She'd do.'

'She's Count Wimpffen's bride,' Karl told him wearily. Here the old man was again, giving the glad eye to women half his age. Marie, Baroness von Eskeles, was twenty-four. Her wedding was in three weeks.

'O yes. What sort of quartets does he write, then?' Beethoven said, pulling his chair in disgustedly as his companions laughed.

The other day they'd been on about Unger, 'trilling in Naples.' Now Schlesinger was talking about getting a job for Karl, through Baroness Eskeles. 'I've told her your nephew wants to be a businessman.'

After the meal Smart drank Beethoven's health 'in the name of all English musicians.' Karl himself proposed a toast: 'To the quartet!' He had meant the music; some there took it to mean the players. After some talk with Smart and some larking about at the piano between Holz and Schlesinger, one singing, the other playing, 'Tobias, Tobias,' Schlesinger sat down with Beethoven to discuss Karl's future.

'I hope to contribute something to your nephew's good so that he soon may enter the Eskeles' counting-house.'

'How soon? He's still studying. I don't want him starting off at the bottom.'

'Fräulein Eskeles will soon look after that.'

'What's she like?'

'She has much understanding, a good heart, and much talent.'

'What's that fiancé of hers like?'

'I found out that he's a man of great family, apart from being a great lump.'

Beethoven laughed. 'Liked your new quartet, did you? Happy you bought it?' They were softening him up to play the piano, he saw through their ruse but he felt like playing. Holz was still murdering the instrument. 'Shift your arse. Let the dog see the rabbit.'

He was fingering the instrument.

'What shall I play?'

Smart answered at once. 'Upon that.'

An hour later, Karl was at the piano. Beethoven had played for twenty minutes, 'sometimes *fortissimo* but full of genius,' as Smart had noted. He had left the instrument in great agitation. The room had emptied and he had grown dismal, imbibed and fallen asleep.

When he awoke he was alone with his nephew. Karl was playing the piano. Beethoven called him over and put his arm round him. 'How're ye doin', boy? All right? Bringing you up all right, am I? Goin' te be a fine man, a' ye? Makin' a good job of it, eh?' Beethoven had his arm round him, squeezing him. 'Let's have a look at ye, eh? Fine lad, aren't ye, eh? A father can be proud of ye!'

Holz, who had stayed to have a drink with Sedlaczek, entered to try to quell their raised voices when Karl had shown Beethoven the house-keeper's bill and Beethoven had found that he had again borrowed from her.

'You were long ago forbidden to do this! Borrowing from that old hussy! Why do you do this!'

'Why!' Karl was laughing, enraged. 'He asks why!'

'I give you money!'

'You! Ha! *You* give me *less than enough* to keep a *flea* on! I couldn't even buy a beer for the quartet the other day!'

Holz too was furious. 'Keep your voice down! They're going mad out there! Threatening to have you both thrown out. He can't hear you but everyone else in the damn place can!'

'See!' Beethoven exclaimed to Holz. 'See his gratitude! Look at him, shouting in my face!'

'Get out of here, Karl,' Holz said, forcing the younger man towards the door.

'That's it! Go! Clear out! You! My son! You! Is *this* all I've got for a son!' Beethoven had come close, leering into Karl's face.

'Clear off! I don't need *you*! Go on! Clear out! Before I throttle you!' He was close again, leering, Holz holding the younger man away from the elder. '*Your* father! Huh! *Your* father! Leave off, Holz! Leave this little *whipper-snapper* in his *flumoxing finery* that *I* pay for!' Beethoven had hold of Karl's lapel. 'Won't help me! Won't visit me! Won't do his studies!' He flicked the lapel away disdainfully, half falling over.

'*Your* father!' he called, half-risen, one hand still on the floor, as Holz tried to jostle Karl through the door. '*Your* father! *Your* father! Your *true bodily* father!' He laughed disdainfully, half sitting half falling back into a large chair.

Holz felt Karl lose his resistance against him and got him out quickly.

'What does he mean?' The boy stood, white-faced, in the hall.

'He doesn't mean anything. He's drunk. You're both drunk.'

Karl shook his head. 'That's twice he's said that. He was talking. Muttering. In his sleep. He kept saying "Karl," but he wasn't calling me. It was too soft. He was muttering. He often does that. But that's not the first time he's said that. What does he mean? Does he mean he is my father? Has he told you, Holz? *Is* he my father?'

'Take no notice. He's drunk. Go home. Leave him to me.'

When Holz re-entered the room Beethoven was remonstrating loudly, 'I work my guts out, to write that quartet, damn near kill mesen, damn near die doing it, and today, when it's played, when I should be surrounded by friends to whom I have given pleasure, O no, that *kid* has to turn even *that* into a row!'

'You're driving that boy mad. He thinks you're telling him you are his father.'

Beethoven laughed in disparagement. 'Whoever else I am the father of, I'm not his.'

Holz had had to search round for something to write on, Schlesinger having kept the little book Beethoven had brought in from Baden. Karl himself produced another when Holz found him, sitting with Schlesinger.

Holz took the book, ignoring Schlesinger, saying to Karl, 'He's just told me it isn't true. So you can go home now.'

'I'm staying to have a drink with Schlesinger. You lot think I'm made of rubber – that things will just bounce off me. I loved my father ...'

'Don't wash your dirty linen in public,' Holz rebuked him, eyeing Schlesinger with dislike.

Karl was Schlesinger's advocate. Holz distrusted Schlesinger and warned Beethoven against placing too much reliance on the Parisian publisher. Schlesinger looked from one to the other in bewilderment. There had been Holz' comment over dinner, 'Two Karls against each other,' but he had thought then that that had occurred because Holz had appropriated Karl's toast to the quartet to mean the players.

Karl was glaring at Holz, his uncle's toady, Holz with his sly, catlike eyes, spying on him, reporting back, telling Beethoven things he had specifically asked him not to tell him. At their meeting with Schlesinger last Sunday, Holz had written to Beethoven, 'We want to bring you greetings for your name-day' – a dig at him for forgetting. It had been *his* nineteenth birthday – Sunday, September the 4th!

Schlesinger treated him like a man, would get him a job, just like his father. Anyway Beethoven had liked Schlesinger ever since he had called the Kaiser 'a dumb ox.'

Holz had returned to Beethoven with the book, calming him down with jokes about Sedlaczek, 'the false Tamino ... What do you think of our Englander? ... We don't need any Englander!'

Beethoven returned to the subject of Karl.

'You can't be angry with him, even when you're convinced of his frivolity,' Holz told him. He put the blame on the old housekeeper. 'If the new housekeeper comes everything will be better and Karl can stay with you. I know what it is to have got into bad company. It happened to me once, and I got out of the mire with difficulty. He's not without intelligence ...'

Beethoven grew interested. 'What was this bad company?'

'I should like you to get to know me first.' He went back to talking about Karl. 'The branch bent down by force easily springs back high.'

Beethoven wrote to Karl from Baden, angered by what he had learned on Sunday. 'I too do not want you to come to me on September 14th. It would be better for you to finish those studies – God has never foresaken me. No doubt someone will be found to close my eyes.' He said that there seemed to be a pre-conceived plan behind everything; he suspected Johann was behind it. 'I know that later on you too will not want to live with me; of course not, my manner of life is a bit too *pure*. . . . I would have managed for two years with the one frock-coat. Admittedly I have the bad habit of putting on a worn-out coat at home. But that gentleman Karl, faugh, the shame of it, and why should he do it? Well, because Herr L.v.B's money-bag is there solely for that purpose – You need not come this Sunday either, for owing to your behaviour there can never be true harmony and concord between us.'

There's Karl Josef, can't walk, and you spend your time playing *billiards*!

Few children indeed turn out like their fathers,
Most worse, few better than their fathers.

He recalled the scenes of Sunday, Holz' agitated scrawl on the back of some trodden-on napkin, 'You're driving that boy mad! He thinks you're telling him you are his father!' He resumed writing, 'He who, though he did not beget you, has certainly provided for you and, above all, has seen to the cultivation of your mind like a father, yes, even more than a father, most earnestly begs you to follow the only true path leading to all that is good and right.'

Before the end of the week Karl was again visiting Baden with tales of the quartet's success. 'Everyone was struck by your extemporizing, especially Sedlaczek who spoke of it with the greatest enthusiasm. Schlesinger takes it for particular good fortune that this happened while he was here. Frau Cibbini came close by me like a Baccante as the quartet was being played, it pleased her so much.'

Beethoven wanted to know how his studies were progressing. 'In October I must be really industrious, then it'll be all right.'

'What does your crammer say?'

'He's very satisfied with me. Fräulein Eskeles spoke about the beauties of the quartet and says she likes playing your music best. She would also like to tell her father that I've put the business in hand and she promised to get me a place in his company if I was inclined that way. Schlesinger also spoke to me on this subject and said that he could do a great deal in this because he was well-known in the company. Schlesinger also intimated that I would be very well looked after in a pecuniary way from the very beginning at Eskeles'.'

Karl was with him on the 16th when he entertained Smart, who had come to find out the tempi of the *Choral*. Smart was surprised to find a wooden ring for horsemanship outside Beethoven's Baden lodgings, until he reflected that it could not disturb the composer in his deafness. Indoors, Beethoven had four rooms, in one of which stood the Broadwood piano from England. On this out-of-tune instrument Beethoven gave him the tempi of several of his symphonies.

They went for a walk, Beethoven out in front, humming. Smart had told him that the London Philharmonic Society had started life on *8th March, 1813*! On days when he felt well Beethoven believed that he could easily make the trip to England. O that he could but set out this very day, whilst his illnesses were abated. Once the time came to make plans he would be ill again, it would be put off, it was ever so. He was tired of this particular circle of illness, hope, plans, illness. He felt that he knew that, even were he to make the trip to London and survive the long sea crossing, he would be ill again once he set foot in London, through panic and excitement. He wished he could fly there, as he still at times wished he could fly to Frankfurt: were travel to both places easier, he felt he would have visited each by now several times.

When they returned it was already two. The coach left for Vienna at four. Frau Schnaps bustled back and forth with the many copious dishes. Smart overheard Beethoven say, 'We will try how much the Englishman can drink,' but Smart was a two-bottles a day man, and those bottles of port; no Viennese reared on beer and wine could match him.

Frau Schnaps was still bringing in dishes when they got up to leave. Beethoven wrote Smart a canon, *Ars longa, vita brevis*. Smart made him a present of his diamond pin.

'I should think he did,' Karl told Schlesinger later. 'He cleared £1,000 from performances of the *Battle* Symphony alone. Don't tell him!'

In the following days Karl urged his uncle to take up Smart's offer of a trip to England. 'He said that in a short time you could make at least £1,000. And you'll find a thousand friends, who will do everything to help you. . . . You'll not leave London so quickly if we're once there. In two years you'd make at least 50,000 florins net. I am convinced that if you wanted to leave here, they would do everything to keep you.' Beethoven said that he was too busy to travel now. 'We'll wait till the year is out before going to England.'

'You can do better business with the publishers there than here,' Karl had told his uncle. Holz had gone so far as to call Schlesinger 'Judas, an out-and-out rogue.' Holz said that he meant to print the quartets in succession, so that the new one would not appear for two years. He advised Beethoven to 'make immediate publication a condition of sale . . . Threaten not to compose the quintets.'

Karl told his uncle that Schlesinger was buying the first quartet from Schotts. 'They are afraid that, if they don't give it to him, he will pirate it.' Karl too now agreed that Beethoven's manuscripts should be withheld. 'These really are capital.'

Holz was giving Schlesinger only an uncorrected score of the second quartet. 'Don't trust him, I beg you, and certainly don't promise him anything,' Holz had warned. 'You tend to see the good in everybody; if not for your own sake, do it for Karl.' Karl himself told his uncle, 'I've never known a publisher I've liked so much.'

On the 23rd Schlesinger introduced Karl to Eskeles. On their way out Schlesinger asked Karl, 'Do you really like the idea of going into an exchange office? I don't know why you don't become an art-dealer, not in Vienna certainly but somewhere abroad, especially in London.'

Karl bent double with merriment.

'What's the matter?'

'My uncle Johann suggested that once. Beethoven hit the roof!'

'Whyever not? If anybody else did it . . . but he's doing everything for you, he can't accuse you of trading on his name.'

'O, I know, I know, it makes perfect sense, he's always bellyaching about how much publishers make out of him, but there you are, that's his reaction!'

'Perhaps I could put something back.' Karl was hearing what he had hoped to hear. 'If your uncle would give his consent, and if you are not opposed, it would give me pleasure to take you to Paris. You would soon acquire all the requisite knowledge and thereafter you could set yourself up – a small sum is sufficient.'

Beethoven wanted something else for him: a professorship, it had seemed, when he had talked of the large sums earned by an accountant or the 1,500 fl C.M. made by quite a lowly clerk in Eskeles' who only spoke the German language. 'As long as you live I have no intention of dispensing with your guardianship,' Karl had had to tell him then. Now when he told his uncle that Schlesinger was worth over a million, Beethoven seemed to think that the publisher with all his wealth was trying to lure him. 'You can still bring me up,' he wrote.

Beethoven's objections were immense but undirected; one minute he was to be a businessman, but not a merchant, the next a scholar, but not a publisher.

'For someone else other things might be better, but with your name there is no doubt that I could do very well as a publisher.'

'In Paris? In London?'

'In London certainly.'

Beethoven was disgusted that Karl should even think of joining those 'pirates' and 'brain-eaters.' 'You'll be a filthy little merchant, yak yak yak,' Beethoven made to count money. 'You'll spend the rest of your life dealing with vile money-grabbers. Where will you ever meet decent people – artists – scholars . . .'

'A dealer *deals* with artists and scholars!'

Karl felt quite determined. 'Now I have for once taken this stand for myself, and now I do not see why only the other publishers should grow rich through you. You'll see how the English do this!' Karl was replete with a young man's hope, filled with the knowledge of his own power. Beethoven was acknowledged the best, and *he* would be the best, fulfilling himself and even giving back to his uncle. Reading in a notice of an edition of Albrechtsberger's collected works that he had been a teacher of Beethoven, Karl asked, 'Who was your first teacher?'

Beethoven was bullish. 'Nobody taught me. Not what I needed to know. Taught me rules. Didn't like it when I started to break 'em.'

'You have natural talent.'

Beethoven laughed, 'They didn't think so!'

Karl told his uncle, 'Cherubini was asked why he had not written quartets. He said, "If Beethoven had never written a quartet, I would write quartets; as it is, I cannot."'

The first quartet was played for Schlesinger on the 26th, Holz taking the leader's chair, Falstaff being absent. The second fiddle part was taken by Leon de Saint-Lubin, a member of the *Josephstadt Theater*. Afterwards Holz wrote a self-mocking canon to the words, 'Holz fiddles quartets the way they tread cabbage!'

Beethoven wrote a canon for Schlesinger, who was leaving Vienna. *Si non per portas, per muros*. Schlesinger had told Beethoven about his own unhappiness in love. 'Woman is like an angel on the outside, a devil within.' A few days ago, Schlesinger had asked him, 'Is it true that you once wanted to marry Cibbini?'

Beethoven had been amused. 'So, you've been gossiping about me!'

'Is it true?'

He had laughed. 'There's only one woman with whom I'd have walked into St. Stephen's! What about you? Met anyone yet? Don't forget: I want to meet her!'

'You shall be the first to whom I introduce my bride.'

Now Beethoven dedicated his canon, 'I wish you the most lovely bride.'

Chapter 11

Late September – mid-December
Große Fuge: tantôt libre, tantôt recherchée
Overtura

'Who's this woman you told Schlesinger you'd have walked into Saint Stephen's with?' Holz had asked him.

'Nosey lot of old buggers aren't you, all of a sudden?'

When his visitors had gone he returned to his old ways, spitting on the mirror thinking that it was the window, on the window thinking it to be open, so preoccupied with work that he did not know the difference. His sole commitment now was to the Archduke, now in Vienna and himself ill, with whom he had offered to 'spend time in a musical way.' The Archduke had been to a new brine-bath at Ischl, recommended for epileptics, and Beethoven was eager to learn his opinion of this new treatment.

In spring Karl had told Beethoven that the Archduke was paying the expenses of two young men at the Polytechnic Institute. Beethoven had just said, 'If he can afford to do that he ought to be paying me more.' Beethoven had told him that he wanted the money from Schlesinger in order to reimburse Peters. When Beethoven had had to pay for the court cases, so strapped for cash had he been that he had sent Peters an unfinished song. Karl had laughed then to Niemetz, 'There's Peters, thinking he's going to get the *Missa Solemnis*, and what he gets is a song without an end!' He had never seen his uncle so filled with a sense of failure as when he had come up to him and said, 'I'm sorry I had to sell one of your bank shares. . . . Let you down . . .'

. . . 'He's worth ten of you!' Holz had shouted at him after that second concert at *zum wilden Mann*. 'Just as I'm worth ten of that crook, Schlesinger! He's right: you are no judge of character.' With Schlesinger here, he had had a friend. Anything had seemed possible. He had almost reckoned, in Schlesinger's presence, on being able to persuade his uncle to let him give up studying straight away and take up a post in Schlesinger's office. He had seen himself now in Paris, next year in London, and these hopes had seemed realistic. Now he was back where he had always been, spied on by Holz, doubted by Beethoven, nagged by his tutor, studying like a schoolboy.

Recent patent of a steam (coffee) machine by means of a device which presses the aroma, liberated by hot steam, through blotting-paper with such force that not even an atom remains in the lixiviated coffee powder, whereby saving of coffee and speed is gained.

A man who is writing a great fugue deserves a new coffee-machine, Beethoven told himself; a man who is writing a great fugue deserves a peaceful, quiet life ... deserves to eat decent food. He had never seen himself so totally as the author of one work before. How could one even dream of creating a baby which would become so massive and whose birth would be so difficult as to be perhaps impossible? Yet the force was on him, the fugue was thrusting itself towards the world, the fugue had its own will to birth and he as usual was within that which he created: his creation was always like that, and yet he birthed the work, he did not birth himself. Albrechtsberger had taught him fugue, but this was a fugue of no type Albrechtsberger would have countenanced or even conceived of! 'There you have a Sonata which will have the pianists guessing in 50 years time!' he had announced buoyantly to Czerny of the *Hammerklavier*. The *Fuge* was in B-flat major, the same key as that of those other fugues, the *Hammerklavier* Finale and the *Et vitam venturi* of the *Missa Solemnis*.

   ... *Biting Albrechtberger's grandson, Hirsch, in the shoulder ... 1817, when he had learned of Karl Josef's illness ...*

Fuga

   Be fruitful and multiply, just like Bach. So what do I do? I *be* fruitful and multiply, and what do I get? A fine, healthy, beautiful little boy, to take after me, to *make music like me*, just like Bach. And what do You do? Take him from me and turn this beauty into a crippled, slavering ... that will never *play* the piano, let alone *compose*! O that's what You do. O yes. O You!

   Yet: love Me, obey Me, be faithful to Me, You command. Honour My word. Do good. *Write music for Me*!

   You made me so that the one thing I can do is write music for You!

   You made me so that the one thing that I cannot do is turn round to You and say, I'll stop writing music!

   You gave me – just enough – of what it was like – to be a man – to see – to convey – to others – *in my music*!

   The rest You took!

   Took it away!

   Gave me the pain – to put – into my music!

   And made me incapable of not writing music!

   O if I were a man I should defy You!

   I should stop doing *this* for *You*!

   You made me just enough of a *man* to be a *better-functioning music-making machine*!

   What is it *for*, God? *Why*?

   He could hear his baby's sobs now. The perfect, facetious, *artistic* sobs of the *Cavatina* rose to torment him now, to berate and mock him.

An aria without words!

A child without music!

That's what You gave to me!

To *me*!

And, fucking hell, when I tried to remedy it, when I tried to make my peace with You, didn't You just give me another!

One a soul that can't even walk, the other ignoring me to play *billiards*!

O thank You, Lord. Big deal.

B-A-C-H never knew how lucky *he* was! Son after son, to follow *him*!

And *I* without even the *balls* to *turn* on You and say: *that* to Your music!

Yes, everybody says, O he's all right, he's got his music. Doesn't matter that he's *deaf*. He's got his music. Doesn't matter that his *wife* belongs to another man. Doesn't matter that his *kid* is sick. He's got his music.

At least fucking *Faust* made a *pact* with the *devil*! *You* never gave *me* a *choice*!

Is-ra-e-li: one who takes on man and God – and wins! And wins! Aye, there's the rub! And *wins*!

All anybody ever tells me is that I'm doing it wrong! Except for the music! Ah, there I'm doing it *right*!

God of love!

O, I see Your game!

Sometimes I think that You have less love in You than I have in my little finger!

He recalled the old, gat-toothed woman.

He had written throughout his battles to win Karl. He had written throughout the court-cases. This year, save when too weak to hold a pen, he had written throughout his illnesses.

1813. 1817. For most of those two years, he had not composed.

When Toni had left he had written – O how he had written: great chunks of unfinished works, raw, unbidden, had flowed through him, he a mere conduit, a hand holding a pen, no brain attached. Unbidden, a flow, no desire, no thought. When Toni had left him? When he had left Toni. Those first few days, when he had been in Karlsbad again, briefly re-encountering Goethe. A trembling, raw man, naked in grief, unable to eat, suffering incessant diarrhoea. A wide-open conduit. He had seen even Goethe awed by this thing in him: an artist at the height of his art. There had been no artistry at all. God had composed and he had written down.

By the time he was in Teplitz he had not been working. He had been ill. Amalie Sebald had nursed him. Dear Amalie. A singer. Pupil of Zelter. Ordering the servants to make up his fire, bring him more blankets, as he had lain, trembling in grief, calling her Antonie.

At Johann's apothecary shop in Linz he had finished his Eighth Symphony. Johann had caught him one day, working, his miniature of Toni on his desk. 'Not bad-looking. Yes, I'd call her sister. You should marry her.'

Visiting the Cathedral *Kapellmeister* daily. His son following him like a shadow. Revered by the boy. Pitifully grateful for the boy's affection. Clumsy at one soirée. He had knocked over a table stacked with plates. The boy had come to him as he had sat, desolate, playing the piano. He had felt then as though the boy had saved his life. *3 equali for 4 trombones* he had written for the Cathedral *Kapellmeister*.

Ill again in Linz: the night of Johann's wedding, pacing the town, pulled back incessantly towards the coaching-inn: the next coach to Frankfurt, the next coach to Vienna, had the old coachman seen anything of the Brentano coach? Incoherent, confusing his words: Linz, Frankfurt, Vienna. The old coachman giving him brandy. 'Frankfurt, squire? The next coach?'

Squatting upon a low wall, knowing that he must go to her, wanting to pull his head off between his knees.

And when he had got back to Vienna, they had gone.

How had he ever finished that last movement of his last fiddle sonata for the Archduke to play with Rode? He must have given him something: they had played it at Christmas. He had revised it heavily later. Letter after letter to the Archduke, confessing that he was having a nervous breakdown.

Zmeskall had taken him to a fortress, fearing lest he was going to kill himself. And then he had become a conduit of a different sort, lust and fear flowing through him as he waited for news of his child's birth.

O, once he had known! Always a father! Never to be back on that other side of not knowing what it was to be a father. Flying, off the ground, wanting to rush round the streets of Vienna, still in his slippers. Dressing instead to go out through the storm to see his brother, Caspar Carl, the gusts hurling him back where he yearned to head: to the post-coach, to Frankfurt.

Back and forth like some beast in a cage, fighting the yearning flowing through him: to see him, to see her, to hold his child. Incapacitated by love.

Falling on his knees beside his nephew, burying his head into the six year old boy's shoulder, Johanna screaming into his ear, 'You're dripping all over him!'

At his brother's bedside: the breathing laboured, like a stricken sheep, 'Maw, maw.' O God, not today! *Please* don't let Caspar Carl die today! Back out into the storm. To see Zmeskall. Z had opened the door to some sort of stag-party. Voluble, at the piano:

'I have a son!
His name is Karl!
Karl Karl Karl Karl Karl Karl Karl!'

Zmeskall's stricken face. 'Has Toni just had your baby?'

Telling Z and the men that his brother was dying, that he was to have custody of his nephew.

Caspar Carl conscious the next day. 'O I don't think that's right. I always thought Johanna would bring him up . . .'

'She can't bring up a *son*! You said you were dying . . .'

'Have you got any money? Can you let us have some money now?'

Showering ducats about him on the bed, from George Thomson of Edinburgh for his Scottish songs, Caspar Carl laughing, 'For two hundred pounds sterling you can have Karl, Johanna and the house!'

He had made out the will granting him sole custody of Karl.

He had sunk his boats, burnt his bridges. No money now. Now he could only do right.

Anguish when he had realized what he had done. *O God, I've given up my son!*

Caspar Carl had not died. Coming to him for more money. Threatening to withdraw the will if he didn't get it. His loan to Johanna through Steiner, in return for two piano sonatas.

. . . Living in the grounds of Countess Erdödy's Jedlersee palace. Trying to starve to death. Being found, taken in, telling Countess Erdödy: the whole thing flooding out of him, her shock, her sympathy, her aghast face, though he had felt better for talking.

And after that, Frau Streicher taking him in hand at Baden, seeing to his wardrobe, ordering new shirts. By this time he wore always the shirt Toni had used as a night-shirt.

1813. That dreadful year. One song he had written, a bit of incidental music. That old crook, Mälzel, had saved him: music for his panharmonicon, which he had turned into a symphony. *Wellington's Victory at the Battle of Vittoria.* It had made him famous. Vienna loved him. Two unknown girls had given him free cherries!

Mälzel had made him ear-trumpets. He had been about to go to London with Mälzel. Instead Mälzel had stolen his *Battle.* . . . Zmeskall, yelling at him, 'You've been to *court* for your *music*! My God, *that* bastard has stolen your *child*!'

. . . Revising *Fidelio.* Travelling by carriage, to its rehearsal, seeing through the window that middle-aged couple, running to embrace each other: *I shall be like that with Toni. When I am 50.*

Success at the Congress. Fêted by princes. A favourite of the Czarina: tender-hearted, used to her deaf Czar. Favoured, in that maelstrom of debauchery, by girls of her court.

Pumping them about ear-trumpets only to find that the Czar of all the Russias was less well served by his doctors than he had been by that old crook Mälzel!

All that had come to a sharp end when the British had let Napoleon escape.

... Visiting the *Hofburg* daily, teaching the Archduke in his apartments: more chance of seeing Napoleon's son than his own ...

Caspar Carl's death, late 1815. Early 1816, granted custody of Karl over Johanna by the *Landrecht*, the court of the nobility, on the day when he had heard from Toni ...

Resurgence of his love for her in 1816. The song-cycle for her. Wanting to go to her. Wanting to give her another child.

And then, towards the end of that year, the first news of concern about Karl Josef, brought to him in a letter from Simrock's son.

Vowing then to go to England: desperate, sick, blurting his anger to the Giannatasios, vehemently blaming the Kaiser who had cast them all into poverty.

His fears of that time placated by Franz.

Franz had told him the truth in 1817.

Going to see his doctor, Malfatti, whose niece he had hoped to marry in 1810. 'O you won't help me, you won't help my son, all you can think of is: thank God we didn't let him into our family, thank God that child didn't come out of *her* belly!'

Telling Nanni Giannatasio it was a good thing he had never been fortunate enough to win any of the young women he had pursued in earlier days. 'Marriage restricts a woman's freedom.' Advocating free love.

Servantless, in Vienna, rooms thick with the reek of rancid milk, unemptied chamber-pot, stale coffee-grounds. Diarrhoea. Dehydration. He had thought he would die: by God's will, not by his own hand.

Day after day, into the church. Sobless tears streaming, unbidden. Kneeling before the statue of the woman for whom he saw no need, the child in her arms he could not deify; praying through her, through him, through Toni: without strength, without power, no more a man but supplicating soul. *Take everything. Take me. Take music. Demolish me but make my child whole.*

Day after day, into his kitchen, sobbing beneath his marble-topped table: howling, abusing God, clutching to him the conical loaf bought by the gat-toothed Polish woman. 'My son is baker. Take. Is free. Take.' Fat, frizzy-haired, gat-toothed woman: tool of the living God. *Prepare to meet thy baker*! The moral seems to be: you cannot kill yourself whilst nursing a conical loaf of black bread. More conscious of God's existence than of his own existence: this God who taunted him and mocked him, allowed him no pride, kept him alive by daily repeating this degrading scene. This God who watched yet made no move, who turned on him His full face but made no motion, throughout his prayers, ceaseless, remorseless: *punish me*! Not him! Not her! Even *I* tried not to hurt *children*!

The bread he left outside the church where it was removed by unseen poor of whom there were many after the bad harvest. Clambering over souls in rags, at times upon his very staircase.

Shopping for white bread, butter and cheese, rendered speechless by grief, his deaf muteness taken for imbecility.

O all those dreams: of seeing him, of going to his wedding; of being with him when he played the piano; of teaching him; of receiving this, his son's first composition, the same tremulous excitement flowing through both father and son.

Christmas Day concert, 1817. After he had conducted the Eighth, Seyfried had conducted his own revision of C.P.E. Bach's oratorio *The Israelites in the Wilderness*, prefaced by his own orchestration of the fugue on B-A-C-H and concluding with a double chorus, 'Holy, holy, holy.' . . . Seyfreid's immoral life, like his own with Toni . . . Bach's dynasty: *C.P.E. Bach* . . . the name of the oratorio, for was not he too in the wilderness . . . the fugue he had always wanted to set on B-A-C-H . . . his own work on Bach . . . the double-chorus: his own desire to set *Holy, holy, holy*!

Composing *nothing* for 13 months, from October 1816 until the following November. His work then had begun with fugue: short, mostly unfinished: a 2-minute fugue for string quintet.

Writing the *Hammerklavier* for the Archduke. Icy, introspective slow movement, like no other music he had written: cold, for himself; cold like himself. Unable to discuss his plight, unable to confess his sin to any save this cold-eyed God.

A *sin*, to make a *much-loved child*, that *You* have punished *in my stead*, a *sin*, to make a *child*, in greatest *love*?

If you want to know, I fucked the backside off her. And God has made us pay. As He always makes us pay. This God of love.

And we, helpless men, can do no more than go on living and pray for help to this God of love.

The God of love who is the God of music. The Creator of all good things. The giver of life to our children.

Meno mosso e moderato

Beethoven was planning to move to the *Schwarzspanierhaus* on the *Alservorstädter Glacis*, once the home of Spanish monks, now kept by a Countess. 'To the Countess come noisy, decrepit people who can't walk any more,' Karl had told his uncle. But Beethoven's childhood friend Breuning was to be a neighbour. Karl had already visited Breuning there.

The *Alservorstadt* suburb, where he had lived with his parents . . . the house that had been his home when his father had been alive. There his mother had kept peacocks; here now Karl saw a cockerel on their old lawn.

He went back the next time he was in the neighbourhood, this time to be greeted by a large white cat. The cat snuggled beneath his hand and he stroked the animal: the thickest fur he had ever encountered, a tail like a squirrel's, and the blue eyes that marked a deaf cat.

He had seen a deaf white cat just like this one when he had spent a day – at Baden? at Mödling? – with his uncle the first summer he had had him, in 1816. He had told Beethoven then how much he hated the country. Could this be the same cat? Surely not. Almost a decade ago.

A middle-aged woman came out of their old house and approached them.

'What's his name?'

'Caspar.'

Karl laughed. 'That was my father's name! We used to live here. When my father was alive.'

The motherly woman felt sorry for the young man who seemed not to have got over his father after all these years, inviting him into his old garden to see the rest of their menagerie: a couple of dogs, a duck that had narrowly survived an attack by one of them, several more cats, one a big tabby who was a good mouser, and, with a pen to himself, built low so that he could not raise his head and wake the neighbours on an early summer's dawn, the brightly-coloured cockerel.

In the sunshine the cockerel looked like a still-wet oil painting on stilts. Most striking were its long green-black tail feathers, glowing as though coated in oil and scintillating as it preened. The neck too seemed coated with thick oily substance, yellow merging to red, now rust, now bright orange.

The cockerel liked company; it would strut up to you; Karl had once caught it peering at him through a hedge. Yet the bird feigned indifference, its perky head cocking now this way, now that, avoiding your eye. When pleased by your attention, though, he would crow at you.

He was, Karl learned, not really a farm-yard cockerel but someone's pet. The bird had come from God knows where. He had flown to the top of a hay-cart and there slept. The cart had taken off with him. He had been found, a most mangy beast, flapping about in the middle of the road, pursued by barking dogs; the driver too laughingly chasing it, intent to wring its neck.

The man who now owned it had snatched it up from its pursuers and taken it into his courtyard. His neighbours had rowed when they had been woken. He had brought it out here to stay at his brother's.

Since his capture the bird had never fought, never mated. He had been nursed back from his mangy state. Totally unpecked and living on the lawn of a garden instead of the muck of a farmyard, he was immaculate, more like a peacock. The family had named him Percy.

Thereafter Karl called on the family often, stopping to admire the cockerel and to play with and to taunt the cat. The cat could well defend itself. The long fluffy hair grew even inside its ears. The tail was long and bushy, the legs, as it lay full length beside him on the grass, well covered with soft white fur, though at the pink pads, a bright clean pink – for the cat was often to be seen washing – the claw seemed to lack distinction. The eyes were an unreal pale blue in which even the veins showed, the perfectly-formed nose pink – he had never seen a cat with so leonine a face. He laughed to the cat, 'You're called Caspar! You should be called Ludwig!'

He had told Niemetz, 'Two blue eyes means that a cat is deaf.'

Niemetz had laughed. 'Why, what does one blue eye mean, then? That it's part-deaf?'

The cat would fight with any other, when a cat crossed the line of vision of its deep-set eyes; he had seen it weighing up a black whitepadded nearly-grown kitten, pale blue eyes eyeing deep green ones until the kitten, watching the slowly padding tail, darted off behind the shrubbery.

The cat was destructive, clumsy. The cat was stone deaf. He had tested it one day, calling to it full voice, '*Caspar!*' The cat did not turn.

Pale almost ethereal translucent grey-blue eyes which were very disturbing, as though the irises were very deep down in the eye itself. The cat looked blind, let alone deaf. The cat nuzzled his hand, pressing his head then his body along it, then finally its tail. After a while it began nuzzling his face. At times part of him with a rather sad passion wanted very much to own this cat.

Later on he found that it was a vicious cat. He'd turn on you for no reason. You could be stroking him, he'd be lapping it up, the next minute his claws were in you, this cat drew blood. Exclaiming and shaking the blood from his hand, Karl was minded of his uncle's comment on Weber's *Der Freischütz*: 'Caspar, the monster, stands out here like a house! Wherever the devil puts in his claws, they are felt!' 'A monster, with a voice like a house, you!' he yelled at the cat, which stood eyeing him from a few yards away. But Caspar was mute as well as deaf. The family had never heard him miaow. He did make one sound: a deep growl, from the chest, not from the throat.

He had not told his uncle of his trips to the *Alservorstadt*. B if he knew would accuse him of having ulterior motives towards the middle-aged woman and probably even towards the duck. Somebody had spied on him, though. In the middle of relating his talk with Schlesinger after they had seen Eskeles, his uncle had with his usual clumsy violence tried to hint that someone had seen him there.

'I am no small child, that you could take me in with such so-called white lies. No one could have told you that I was seen there, seeing that I was never there except with you.'

Allegro molto e con brio

Schlesinger hadn't stolen him but he might as well have, for all the decency and affection he was getting from the boy now. The boy was on holiday. How come he was not visiting all the time? What was he doing, in Vienna, during this period when he had no studies?

Early in October Karl had returned to Vienna after a weekend with his uncle, saying he had to catch up with his studies. There had been the usual scene followed by the usual letter: it is cold, the winds are like hurricanes, it's not safe for me to be at Baden with my catarrh . . . I hope you never have to be ashamed of your callous behaviour towards me. I hope the reasons you gave for your return to Vienna are true. . . . I-am-good-and-kind. Are-you? . . . Towering rage: my anxiety for you, seeing-that-dangers-can-so-easily-threaten-you. Don't make me anxious. O just think of my sufferings! . . . How much have I already endured?! . . . Remember that I am stuck here and may fall ill . . . Karl read these points out to himself, nodding his head back and forth to an under-the-breath singsong chant.

Karl staved him off with a quick letter – just in time, for B had been planning to come to Vienna the next day. 'Only obey me, and love and inner harmony coupled with human happiness will be our portion; and you will unite an intensely spiritual life to your external existence; it is better, however, that precedence be given to the *former* over the latter.' Yes yes yes. Like some Old Testament prophet, unshaven of cheek or chin, climbing his mountains, book in hand. If only the old boy would stick to his compositions and not keep wanting to see him all the time!

The bloke was so easily won round. One letter. 'I embrace and kiss you a thousand times, not as my *prodigal, but as my newly-born, son.*'

What's this! 'I have written to Schlemmer!' The interfering..! 'I have written to Schlemmer. Don't be annoyed with me.'

Beethoven had written to Schlemmer before Karl's letter, voicing his suspicions that Karl was enjoying himself at night in bad company. 'I request you to pay attention to this and not to let Karl leave your house at night under any pretext whatever, unless you have received something in writing from me through Karl.'

A week later, Karl received a letter in which Beethoven shot from discussing arrangements for his departure from Baden into an abrupt explosion.

'It is my wish that *your selfish behaviour to me shall* cease once and for all. *It does me as little good as it sets you on the right and most honourable path.* Well, go on, persist in your behaviour, but you will regret it. This does not mean that perhaps I may die all the sooner, although that may be what you want.' Look at it: pages of it. In the midst of all this, Beethoven had taken time out to add, at the foot of the first page, 'I spend every morning with the Muses – and on my walks they make me happy.'

Even B had apologised for this onslaught, exonerating himself: 'I was extremely hurt that on Sunday you came so late and left so early.'

Karl had been charmed by Marie Eskeles during the period when he had been meeting her frequently with Schlesinger, and since Schlesinger's departure he had turned his attentions towards a young serving-girl in the tavern by the billiard-hall who bore, facially, a marked resemblance to her. Her initial encouragement had proved a tease: she was engaged to an older, burly brute who played in the hall and who had taken him for a fair deal of money.

Confident of his ability to win, Karl had pawned his uncle's diamond pin from Smart. Instead of winning sufficient to pay his debts and to redeem his pledge, he had lost this money too.

Now here was Beethoven, back in Vienna, expecting to see him. Partly through dread of being discovered, partly in a desperate attempt to raise money to redeem the pledge, Karl was rushing to Johann, to his mother, to Niemetz and his mother, trying to cover his tracks, to hide, to steer the conversation towards the soft touch. Johann was out, his mother laughed at the very idea of her having anything like that sort of money, and he feared he had soiled his friendship with Niemetz when his mother cried at the sums he mentioned, bewailing this reminder of her own poverty. Still fearing to go to Schlemmer's, he returned to his mother's, from where he wrote to his uncle, explaining the circumstances of his visit, explaining that he did not want to be there, threatening suicide in his terror. Never had he felt more friendless. Never had the hope of Beethoven's forgiveness seemed to him more the sole ray of light.

> My precious son!
> Go no further – Come but to my arms, not a single harsh word shall you hear. O God, do not rush away in your misery. You will be received as lovingly as ever. What to consider, what to do in the future, these things we will talk over affectionately. On my word of honour no reproaches, since they would in no case do good now. Henceforth you may expect from me only the most loving care and help – Do but come – Come to the faithful heart of your father Beethoven
> Come home immediately upon receiving this.

> Even for the immortal gods a man
> Come as a suppliant must not be shunned, as I now
> Approach your stream and your knees after much suffering.

He added on the top margin of the letter, 'Only for God's sake come back home today. It might bring you who knows what danger. Hurry, hurry,' and, in French, on the outside, under Karl's address, 'If you don't come you will surely kill me. Read this letter and stay at home, come and kiss me, your father, who is really devoted to you. Be assured that all this will remain between us.'

He had arrived in Vienna on Saturday evening 'Like a shipwrecked mariner,' as he had written to Holz in a trembling hand. He occupied four rooms on the second floor, besides a kitchen and servants' quarters. He fretted about the distance between the *Schwarzspanierhaus* and Karl's.

Karl was crestfallen and compliant. The gambling debt had been repaid. His uncle had visions of him being cut up by the burly fellow. Johann it had been who had said, 'The boy has been brought up with the sons of aristocrats. Then it won't be fist-fights, it will be, "Whose pistols?"' Schlesinger had indeed presented Karl with a beautiful pair of pistols, beautifully cased, as a farewell gift.

Cock-doodle-do! In the morning's darkness the bird's crow lost a note so that it became, as Karl used to mimic to Niemetz, 'Shut up Per-cy!' In the last fortnight of his holidays, he spent what time he could with the family and with Niemetz. He had told Niemetz of the cat and the cock, though Niemetz had never been there with him. They laughed about the cock. *Per-cy-vil the cock-er-il*, they called him.

The family were on the look-out for a hen for Percy. They wanted some eggs. Karl laughed to Niemetz, 'There's him with his cock up round his ears, and me with mine, and there's *him*, looking for a hen for a cockerel!' Until the Polytechnic re-started, he was expected to sleep next door to B.

Beethoven had been terrified when he had got back to Vienna to find that Karl was not at Schlemmer's. 'I think he may have gone to his mother's.' And what was he doing round there? That penniless layabout, Niemetz, whom he had always known would be a danger: involved with K's mother. What did K hear and see? What was K himself involved in! Johanna had no morals: marrying CC because she was pregnant; gossip when he got Karl that she sold herself at masked balls; carrying her bastard through the final court cases! O, she had ignored Karl then, her own son, when she had had her lover!

What had terrified him then, as he had paced and fumed, was that Karl had gone to her *now*, had swung back to her side. This could only mean that he had forgiven her *because he himself knew more*. Was the boy then a man, in the grip of his own sexuality? O, if so, *how do I rear him now?*

. . . '"Son, son, look after your health, son." Or what? Or the plagues of Egypt will strike you down and you will get a-gnawing at your vitals.' Karl showed Niemetz Beethoven's letters, dating back to the summer: 'Take care of your health in this heat. Dear son, do keep your good health. Avoid everything that can enfeeble and impair your youthful strength. . . . Don't forget to bathe – keep well. Take care of yourself so that you do not *fall ill* – and only spend your money in the right way.'

'He thinks I'm spending money on *women*! What money! Chance would be a fine thing!'

'He works hard, God knows,' Holz had told him. 'He's not asking you to do anything he doesn't do himself.' Karl had grown irate when he had learned that B seemed to have talked to Johann and Holz. He had put it in writing: *This will remain between us!*

'He has money to buy himself a drink with friends,' Karl grumbled to Niemetz. 'I'm expected to work and have no relaxation.'

He found letters from the time of B's illness. 'Look at this! *This* is what he writes to me: "O I must learn to give up everything, and I will gladly do so to obtain this benefit, namely, to know that my very great sacrifices are going to bear good fruit." . . . And this – here – he calls me "a vulgar man"!

'I'm not allowed to be a soldier, not allowed to go into business. What's going to happen when I do finish this course? He wouldn't let me go with Schlesinger. He's going to want to keep me with him always.'

The first time he had seen his uncle after telling him that he wanted to be a soldier, Karl had told him about the execution of an Italian corporal. Beethoven's eye had gleamed with the joy of malice. 'There you are, lad: promotion all along the line!'

'He seems to equate the word "soldier" with "slave,"' he had told Niemetz then. 'If he goes on any more! He stands there, quoting at me:

Wide-thundering Zeus strips half the good of a man
Upon the day when he *becomes a slave*.'

Karl gave this with his uncle's leering face and prodding hand. Niemetz laughed.

In August, during the week when there had been a hanging, Karl had made the acquaintance of a French prisoner of war who had fought under Napoleon. Wounded severely, he had lain in a Hungarian hospital until now. Quite without money, he had come to Vienna, and from Vienna he wanted to go to Paris, where his parents lived. He had nothing but rags on his body and not a bean. Karl had been the first person he could understand, for he could not manage a word of German.

. . . To be seen walking hand in hand, even arm in arm, with a man whose appearance was so bizarre he had once been mistaken for a tramp himself! And this to the very door of the Polytechnic! What hope had he of pulling the birds! Why, everyone who saw him laughed: people who knew him, people he was meant to study with . . .

The old man was so ill-kempt he had once been arrested as a tramp: in 1821, after his jaundice, he had set off walking by the canal, in an old coat, without his hat, and by the end of the day he had found himself lost, in Vienna Neustadt, peering into windows to try to locate his whereabouts.

Niemetz laughed when he told him. 'What happened?'

'O, he kicked up a hell of a fuss. Kept shouting, "I'm Beethoven!" His jailers just laughed. "O, so you're Beethoven! You're nothing but a dirty old tramp." It wasn't long after he'd had jaundice. He must have looked a sight. "I tell you I am Beethoven! Fetch the Chief of Police! He is a friend of mine." After an hour or two of this they sent someone to disturb the Chief of Police at his dinner. "We've arrested this tramp and he'll give us no peace. He keeps saying he's Beethoven. Keeps saying *you'll* identify him!" So the Chief of Police gets up from his dinner, traipses to the jail, takes one look: "But that *is* Beethoven!" He treated B to dinner and sent him home in the civic coach!'

'Can you imagine: seeing him, like that, peering in through your windows! "Go away! Go on! Go away! What do you want? Get away! Clear off!" – Beethoven backing away like a dog!'

His friends said to him, 'You'll be a rich man one day.' What use is that! I want money *now*!

Holz had said to him, 'He's got a crusty kernel but he does only want the best for you, you know. . . . He didn't have to take you on and devote all this time and money to you, you know . . .'

'I know . . .'

'Your mother couldn't have educated you the way he's done.'

'I am grateful but he thinks I've got no rights! He never trusts me! I would be a *better* person if he'd let me have a little money of my own. He'd see that I would spend it wisely. Instead I spend half my time running after him, the rest of my time trying to budget, without a spare kreuzer for emergencies – he treats me like a child but I feel like an old man!'

He recalled how he had felt during Beethoven's revived illness that summer: at least B can do one thing masterfully. Johann isn't even a masterful apothecary! He was fiercely embarrassed when listening to music with his uncle: Johann shouted 'Bravo!' and 'Encore!' before the music had fairly ceased; swore black blue and pink he had never before heard a work he had just heard for the third time; turned beamingly and exclaimed to his neighbour, 'My brother wrote that!' his hands in their white gloves whose overlong tips curled at the ends applauding mightily. At such times Karl felt sheer compassion for B. He had more than once wondered: are these two men really brothers? A kinship of sorts between his father and Beethoven; nothing of either or of himself in Johann.

'. . . Piece of music? I thought it had always been there. Did someone write it? O, *Beethoven*!'

Niemetz thought he meant the *Heiliger Dankgesang* but Karl said the same to Holz of the *Cavatina*. Karl had heard Beethoven, thinking himself alone, play this to himself in part on the piano.

Karl said to Niemetz in agitation, 'The bastard just gets better and better. He writes one thing, you think, he'll never top that; then he writes something else that makes everything that's gone before seem crap . . .'

Holz had told him, 'He'll never abandon you, you know . . .'

'Oh, I know that,' Karl said depressedly. 'He writes that to me in every letter.' In the midst of his abuse and complaints, exhortations to him to do better, even when he declared his wish to be free of him 'and that pseudo brother and his family who have been foisted upon me,' Beethoven always wrote that he would continue to support him, just as he had his father and even his mother.

. . . First he'd gone helping her, now it was all back to the old tack, bawling, 'Keep away from her!' . . . At the time when J herself was in such dire straits that B had been helping her, she still had enough maternal care to send him an ointment for his chilblained feet. He himself had been calling her a whore at that time . . .

. . . 'But he thinks everyone's intriguing against him!' Karl expostulated to Niemetz.

'So? He's very successful. People probably are doing what they can to pull him down. Lots of composers must be his rivals. There must be a lot of jealousy.'

Karl laughed. 'He doesn't make any money! That's what *he's* always saying!'

'More to it than money.'

Karl laughed harshly. 'You always side with him! He doesn't even *like* you!'

'I just try to be realistic. I like his music. So do you. I heard him play that time at Baden. I've never heard anything like it.'

'He always says he can't do anything else!'

'Well he probably can't. But it's still more than most people can do. So people pull him down. It's normal. If you and I were in a room, people wouldn't talk about us – they'd think we might hear them. *He* can be in a room and people can say anything.'

'He's a great composer. I know he's a great composer. But he's always talking as though I think him a fool. "Just because your uncle's never been to university . . ."'

. . . 'Well how can you dislike the music of B? It's like disliking the flowers of the fields. It is that natural. It is as though they'd always been there – waiting to be written by him, as though he simply picks them up, complete.

'I can't compete against that. No one else can compete against it. But you can't expect me to be happy about it.'

Later he said, 'I mean *he* tried to steer me into music. He's never done that with anybody else. He's had pupils – they've gone to him. He came to me, and took on the job of teaching me – I am B's only self-selected pupil.'

Later still he shouted at N, 'As a king's son you become a king! I am *not a king*!'

Niemetz diffused the situation. 'Well Mozart's son is an arrogant little sod. You've told me yourself. Talentless and arro . . .'

Karl burst out laughing. 'O I love you, Niemetz! You are so good for me!'

'O yes, you were a failure before you were eighteen.'

. . . 'I'm a "vulgar man" but I'm still good enough to represent *him* when it comes to business with Schlesinger – but I'm not *to be trusted* to have even a *florin* of my own!' he burst out at Holz.

It was obvious what was happening, thought Holz. The man was afraid of losing the boy. He could see a lonely old age closing in on him.

Karl had grumbled to him one day, 'All this "Come to my arms." He doesn't want me to be his son – I think he wants me to be his god-damned daughter.'

Holz knew what he meant.

. . . 'It runs in the blood,' Beethoven had told Holz. 'The boy himself was conceived out of wedlock . . .'

... All those meals of oysters and champagne, before he had slept with Janitschek's wife, with Peters' – a regular thing, those meals with Bernard and Peters, during the 1820 court cases – Karl had learnt of it, idly reading B's old CBs.

'I've seen him with women. Not just whores. Saw him walking arm in arm with a woman last year in Baden.'

Sometimes he dreamed that he was screwing Unger: Unger with her turned up nose, Unger with her *décolletage*, Unger with her singer's tits: Unger whom his uncle had had and he had not.

'He's an old man. And he's had jaundice. He must be all yellow. Ugh!

... 'I'm not supposed to have a girlfriend. I'm not supposed to grow up at all! He seems to want to keep me a little kiddie!' He indicated a foot off the ground. N laughed.

'Remember when you were his age ...' Holz said to Beethoven.

'When I was his age I was rearing his bloody father!'

He thought of his child and felt like crying. My son will know no happiness, no youth. He thought of his child and sex and knew despair. Looking at his own life, there were times when he could not do it for himself, times when he had been desperate, when a woman was a necessity. How would the boy survive? O what a terrible thing to do: to give life to someone who would never know joy.

All he could do was brush this to one side, the time was not yet, not yet. The boy was still a child.

For perhaps the first time, he saw his nephew's needs realistically until fear, suspicion, dread again enclosed the man and the boy felt himself to be imprisoned yet again by his uncle's mammoth love.

Anyway what good did sexuality ever do a man? Antonie had once said it was the source of his music and that was all it was good for ... transcribing itself into music, becoming the impetus for a work of art.

Housekeeper troubles – the old housekeeper not hearing, herself growing deaf, the new one not able to understand his voice. To listen to him was unnerving. He could not follow the pitch of his own voice. It was not like hearing a human being but some weird instrument played by a man with no training. So *he* was expected to do it. Karl said angrily, storming out, not bothering to write down for his uncle, 'O for the love of God! I haven't got *time*!'

... Work work work, and running errands for *you* ... No-good *son* ... *I did it all for my father* .. ! He was nearly in tears through anger. ... No life of your own, Karl. No life for *you*!

... Wonder what happened to Shakespeare's son? ... Shakespeare's son *died*! Lucky old *Shakespeare's* son!

... 'His coat's too thick. He wants to be in the shade.'

'He'd still fight even in his skeleton.'

Later when they sat on the grass with their books, Niemetz helping Karl to write up his notes, the cat came and rubbed itself against them repeatedly, paddling over their books and shoving their pencils as they wrote so that they could not read what they had written.

'You're very sociable today, aren't you?'

Karl said, 'He's a bloody nuisance.'

'Well he can't hear, you see. Everything must be tactile.'

'If you put Caspar and Ludwig alone in a room, neither of them would know the other was there. What's more, you could call both of them any names you liked – they wouldn't hear you.'

'That's cruel.'

'Well he makes you cruel. I don't know why you defend him so. *He* hasn't a good word to say about *you*.'

'He does write great music.'

Karl said in exasperation, 'Everybody seems to think that gives him the right to behave like a pig! He can be a pig to other people! I've had enough of his being a pig to me!'

Niemetz said after a silence, 'What are you going to do about it? . . . What can you do?'

'I'll pick that bloody cat up by the tail for a start!' The cat was still amongst their papers. Karl leapt up and dived for it; the cat sprang up and shot away.

'I liked that cat. You shouldn't have done that.'

'Everybody likes Ludwig's company. You want to try having him as your guardian!' He sat down close to tears, thumping the grass. 'I wish *my father* hadn't *died*!'

Karl gazed after the cat in despair, then exploded. 'Everything about him! I mean he even spells my name with a K! Right from the beginning I told him it was spelt C, like my father. My mother told him . . . even Johann spells it with a C! He will always spell it K! He doesn't seem to want me ever to have belonged to my father! He won't even let me have his *name*!'

. . . 'Don't let that cat into my study! It might look a mess to you – I know where everything is. Don't go into my study! Keep my study door closed!'

Karl had laughed, surprised.

'Don't laugh at me you little bastard! That pays your schooling – and buys your food, your frippery and, for all I know, your women. Bastard!'

' . . . He took me to show me my new half sister. Ludovica was less than a week old. My mother was flabbergasted. She stood there – I think she was in shock. I think she thought he'd come to steal her other baby. I stood in the doorway. I wouldn't go in. There was mother, dumbfounded, me in the doorway, and Beethoven holding this baby: he literally had the child in his arms. He claimed he had picked her up to show her to me. Well *I* didn't want to see her! . . . He didn't put her down. He just stood there, holding this baby. I mean that kid is nothing to do with him! She's called Beethoven – only because she hasn't got another name! No one knows what that kid's name should be!'

'Ludwig and your mother! O come off it!'

'I didn't say that! I know it's not his. It was just so unusual – him holding this baby. And he held her for ever such a long time . . .'

'Perhaps he was just feeling broody!'

They laughed.

'He's funny. He's not like other people.'

'Well he's deaf. And then there's his music . . .'

'No. He's funny. He's not like a person. He's different. Other people don't see him as a person.'

'He's a sort of hero. People make pilgrimages to him – because of his music . . .'

Karl shook his head, angry with his friend for not understanding. 'It's as though he's never learnt to be a person . . .'

'You don't learn to be a person!'

Karl felt cross. 'He's different. He's odd. Do you know sometimes he pretends to be my father – I mean he really thinks he *is* my father!'

. . . 'God help any kid of yours!'

From his facial expression B deduced what Karl had said; he lurched at him; the boy fled from the room.

. . . '*You* are German! *You* are Beethoven – your great-grandfather was *Kapellmeister* at the electoral court at Bonn!'

Karl wanted to laugh then noticed that his uncle spoke in the utmost seriousness; his eyes were blazing.

Beethoven, if he dared to admit to himself, thought Holz, was afraid of Karl. Karl himself these days was usually muted with him. The companions Holz reported to Beethoven as having seen with Karl were boisterous. Full of energy, always bounding about, hurling themselves around. Once Beethoven yelled at him, 'I wish that you were married and off my hands! Go to your whores, get yourself into trouble, get yourself married! Do what you like only don't come to me for money – I wash my hands of you!'

Once Beethoven thought that he saw a love-bite on Karl's neck, high up, half-hidden by the collar. He tore the boy's necktie down. Karl ripped his uncle's hand away. 'You stupid old fool! I've been playing the fiddle!' He snatched the fiddle from the wall and stuck it under his chin. '*Playing the fiddle*! Like *you* wanted! That's what *you* wanted! Isn't it!'

Karl flung the fiddle at his uncle. Beethoven stormed after him with it. Karl turned to him, 'All right, kill me with it!'

'Have you any idea how much this cost! Have you any idea how hard I had to work to get that! Have you any idea how hard I've worked for *everything* you've had!'

. . . 'That dreadful 4th floor, O God, *without a wife* . . .' Feeling ill, stopping on the second landing, heart pounding, not knowing how he could make it to the top.

I used to hold you in my arms. I held you when you were a baby. You used to be my son. – You are my son.

When he did make a noise, Caspar roared like a tiger. Karl also noticed that, rather than run, he hopped: on both back legs: he sprang: not like an animal at all. Whatever he had done to you, he would come back. Caspar had no fear of beast or man.

He was a very athletic cat. He did not climb trees like other animals but instead leapt half way up the trunk and then ran full pelt to his chosen branch.

. . . 'Don't let that cat into my study!' and for a time there was observed the habit of closing all doors. Caspar had followed him to the *Schwarzspan-ierhaus*. On occasions the cat did seem to appear where it could not possibly be: Karl was sure he had closed the door behind him but there was the cat, parading before him in the hall. 'Caspar!' he called involuntarily, and, perhaps by chance, the mute blue-eyed deaf cat turned to him and miaowed. Karl was shaken, almost unnerved: the cat seemed some sort of *doppelgänger*, weird mythical composite of father and uncle.

N would not believe the cat had miaowed until he did it once when he too was visiting the family: the cat stood by the window asking for milk, opened its mouth and emitted a sound: a decent miaow, like that of any other cat. Karl turned to his friend triumphant; he was still also scared. 'He's never done that before.'

'I think the cat is not totally deaf.'

'It *was* deaf.'

'That cat gives me the willies.'

The cat sat, sphynx-like.

The last time they had seen the cat, in colder weather, the cat had seemed subdued. Karl had thought then, it's getting old.

Today, after seeming old and desultory and confirming him in his opinion, as though aware of its audience the cat had sprung to life, leaping an elder tree after a grey cat but shooting up a different branch. It swung itself round and flew onto the branch bearing its quarry.

'That cat's like a squirrel!'

'Yes, it is. It's the tail.'

Later the cat would not return but continued playing even when food was laid.

From his vantage point up a tree, seeing Karl, the deaf cat leapt down and bounded over a hedge at Karl's greeting. Strolling between Karl and Niemetz, the cat nuzzled their legs, letting itself be stroked. Niemetz bent down but Karl squatted, letting the cat rub against his bottom.

'Isn't its coat long? It's like a sheep's coat. Poor thing. No wonder it's confused: it doesn't know if it's a sheep or a cat or a squirrel. No wonder he flies: look at the width of that tail.' The thickness of tail and coat constantly astonished Karl.

Abruptly the cat, without warning, leapt at Karl's arm, scratching him deeply with both its front paws, drawing blood from his hand and, more painfully, his arm. Gripping tightly his arm where the pain was excruciating, expecting to see blood through his sleeve, Karl called after the retreating cat, 'You little devil!' The cat trotted arrogantly back through the hedge and to its food.

'Look at him. The damn beast's disdainful.' Never had he seen a more arrogant backside.

'Why is it always me that he scratches,' Karl complained to N when they were alone. 'A deaf cat called Caspar – always me, never you. That damned cat has never once scratched you,' he said, showing N his wound.

'No wonder he was grinning,' N said, seeing the deep punctures in Karl's arm.

'Even his bloody backside was grinning,' Karl said, dabbing at the wound.

'You'd better bandage that, to be safe,' the middle-aged woman had said. Washing the wound now, Karl said to Niemetz, 'If you told my uncle to bandage a wound he'd take offence. "Telling me what to do!"'

Niemetz laughed. 'Yes!'

Holz said to Beethoven, 'He's very like you.'

Beethoven exclaimed, 'He's not like me at all! When I was his age, instead of *getting an education* I was supporting my father – and *his* father! *I* never had a chance to get educated, let alone have a rich guardian whose purse I could filch to spend his hard-earned money on *gambling* and *frippery* and *women!*'

'The boy's nineteen now. You must remember what you were like at his age . . .'

Beethoven stormed to his desk and began rifling through piles of manuscripts from his years in Bonn. He turned to Holz with a blazing red face of fury, the vein of wrath throbbing in his temple. 'When I was his age I was *creating* – *this* and *this* and *this!*'

'. . . We can't all be Beethoven . . .'

'*He is* Beethoven! . . . I could be a bloody *great musician* if I'd had the money spent on my education that *he's* had spent on *his.*' He saw Holz's face. He stormed angrily, 'Greater, greater!'

. . . 'Don't be a Viennese, son! Don't be a Viennese!'

'I am Viennese..!'

'You are a *Rhinelander!* Your great grandfather was *Kapellmeister* at the *Electoral Court* at *Bonn!*' Karl wanted to laugh but Beethoven spoke in passion. 'Writing to me of killing yourself! Killing yourself is a sign of weakness! If *I* can live out my life without killing myself, *you can.*'

'If you go on like this I shall kill myself.'

. . . 'I want to live a normal life! And I could, the whole thing would be all right, if only he'd let me have some money. Not a lot. Just enough. He won't let me have a kreuzer . . . sends me on errands . . . I have to account for *everything*! He makes me appear some shrivelled old miser! . . . People make a mistake in their change, an honest mistake, I can't let them get away with it. I have to point it out, if they disagree I have to shout and bawl – he won't ever think they could make a mistake, he'd think *I'd* stolen it, always it comes back to *me*!

'I was with him once when he was going to a prostitute. He stood at the edge of the street and told me to go off to the tavern. He was very embarrassed. I knew where he was going. "Son, son, look after your health, son!" He thinks I'm going to get the clap from dirty old bastards like him!'

'I could go in first. I'd have to creep in, looking round.' Niemetz made to peer up the staircase in a brothel, chanting in a nasal voice: '"Ludwig. Ludwig. Aya there, Ludwig?"'

Karl burst out laughing and Niemetz joined in.

'You wouldn't keep a dog in the conditions in which he keeps me,' Karl said when he had sobered.

'You'll just have to wait till you know he's in his study. Then we'll go. "Ludwig, Ludwig, aya there, Ludwig?"'

Karl said, 'It is filthy. I want to live a normal life. He's driving me into the sort of life that he hates – and *I* hate. Who wants to go to those sort of places where he's been and old men like him have been before?'

'Never mind. You'll be back soon, at Schlemmer's.'

'When I was living with him after he took me out of Giannatasio's, before he sent me to Fröhlich, he always got up earlier than I did and he thought I should get up then. Well I know it was summer, but five o' clock! This was at Mödling. I was about eleven or twelve. He'd sacked the housekeeper when he found out she was bringing me sweeties from Mama. So there we were. In Mödling. No servants. And he always only had coffee first thing. I liked breakfast in the morning – not much, but something: just the odd roll or, if the wind were in the right direction and it didn't make the stove smoke, toast. O! You don't know what a ceremony there used to be about that bloody toast! He'd kicked the servant out so he made it himself: made me this toast. He brought it to me, all burnt on one side and raw on the other, and I was expected to be ever so grateful.'

Niemetz was laughing.

'It was always presented as a *treat*. *Toast*! I was always expected to swoon with gratitude and the damn stuff was always inedible. I was always expected to eat the damn stuff. I'd kept him from work, you see. I'd made him late. One day I didn't eat it – I mean I couldn't, it was dreadful – and there was such a bloody palaver, it went on all day. He wasn't angry. He was *hurt*. "You didn't eat your toast." Just like a bloody old woman. Worse. I mean, that old woman he's got now wouldn't kick up half such a fuss just because you didn't eat *burnt toast*! . . . I don't know why he took me on. He didn't want a kid. Why didn't he get married! I think he was lonely, he wanted someone with him, but . . . even when he was being nice to me it was as though this was . . . stolen time . . . I was *in the way* . . . this was at the expense of *something else*. His work. Half the time you'll hear him talk as though he lives like a monk and he should have done, he should have done. . . . He *pretended* to be *my father*! I mean really pretended . . . told people he was. Holz had him write and say he wasn't. Thank God. Holz knew I was going mad. Why did he do it? *Pretended* to be my father. . . . He wouldn't have wanted me any more if I *had* been his own kid.'

Everyone else saw them as an old man and a young man; but Beethoven saw himself as a grown man walking with a boy. Streicher had said to his wife, 'He won't let go of that boy. Calls him his "son" but won't let him grow into manhood.'

His wife replied, 'He's never felt he owned him. That's why. To let go properly you first have to feel that something properly *belongs*.'

. . . 'What do *you* think? Not Joe Bloggs! Not the man sitting next to you! *You*! You've got a God-given brain and a God-given conscience. Use these, or you might as well not be alive – you might as well never have existed.' They had been to a piano recital at the Streichers' where Karl had been asked his opinion of the music. Not having really been listening, he had asked his uncle, 'What did you think?' 'If you're going to be like someone else you might as well *not be*! The only voice worth having is your own individual voice!'

'Why he thinks everyone else has to be weak I don't know.'

'Perhaps it makes him feel stronger . . .'

'He thinks other people have no brains. He thinks he's the only one in the world who can do anything – and I sometimes think he thinks he's the only one who suffers.'

'He does convey things – that everybody else feels . . .'

Karl was left feeling dissatisfied by this conversation.

One day B had said to him in the middle of one of their rows, 'I wish I'd had a beautiful daughter instead of you. Daughters love their fathers more.'

Once in the early days B had embraced him: 'We're not uncle and nephew, are we, we're father and son.'

Karl recalled the day that B had won him: on his knees, hugging him, so that the short man was near-level with his own head; a welter of passion and kisses which to him had meant glimpses of the restless pockmarked face, the bushy head. No sooner had he done kneeling, kissing, than he had yanked him forcefully down beside him to pray, flinging his arm about his back, tearful red-rimmed eyes turned heavenward, the voice breaking with gratitude and love.

'I hate this "I've done my duty." As though good things are done to get you well in with God. I'd rather they weren't done at all. I'd rather bad things were done – there's something wholehearted about being bad when you want to be bad.' Karl was standing beneath a large old apple tree. There was a plentiful supply of fruit at his feet. He kicked it around desultorily then began to play foot-billiards.

... 'Am I not master in my own house!'

'You're not my father! You're my uncle!'

'Ungracious little toad!'

Karl kicked an apple the length of the garden. 'Just because he's a frustrated, randy old bastard he thinks he can stop me!'

... At his mother's, sitting on the edge of his sister's bed, with no girl and no money, bleating out his woes with a laugh to N. Johanna had come in to haul N off with her, leaving him in charge of his little sister.

He had picked up the apples and started hurling them.

... 'She called the bastard after him!'

He had thought that Holz would strike him. 'Don't talk about your mother like that – and don't talk about your uncle like that! You don't deserve his love!'

'I don't want his love! I don't want anybody's love – I want to be left alone!'

Meno mosso e moderato

'What's it like, composing?'

'Very like being in love.'

Stroking it, singing love-songs to it, embracing the ever-bulging manuscript.

His first notions for this pre-dated even the BACH-related opening of Galitzin's second, dating back to the time when he had considered this theme for the finale of Galitzin's first. It always seemed so much, when you were sketching; always so little, once you took up the book to start the score. In search of a counter-subject for the fugue's main theme, he had even tried combining it with the joy-theme from the *Choral*.

A few weeks ago, he had seen a neighbour on the day before she had given birth to a ten and a half pound boy. Her husband had exchanged pleasantries with him; she had stood to one side, saying nothing. He knew how she felt.

He felt sullen. He sulked. He pounded his piano.

And then he did what he had known he would do. He took a walk along his usual path, to the *Helenenthal*, and, at the spot where he had known he would, prayed. Briefly. For that. Unable to get close to God. Gazing across the sunless scene, watching the waterfall from the height of the mountain.

And that night, late, when he had already settled to sleep, he started to write and it started to come to him.

The next day he resumed where he had left off. That was it. He was composing.

Not composing, I'm like a fish out of water. Silly old sods, think that other is *me* – I'm *not alive* the rest of the time!

The terror goes. The impossible becomes possible. What was daunting is being done. But it also loses its mystery, its bigness.

Some days it flowed at him so easily that he could not believe it, he made no effort at all, he picked up the quill and it wrote itself, fully worked out, in final draft.

It never happened but that he stood amazed at his own facility. Brilliant. Great work. *Nothing to do with me.* I made no effort. I did not lift a finger. I picked up the quill, that's all. My brain did not bat an eyelid.

He remembered yelling at Toni once of the murderousness of writing a symphony, but this was the other side of it. It had happened, like that, in the past, with a symphony.

He always knew, just before it happened, just as it started, and then he picked up the quill and without stop or effort several pages were filled.

He felt good afterwards but not euphoric. More euphoria from a walk in the country. He did not even feel amazed any more, though, as he walked out later, he would not have exchanged his own life for any man's.

Exploding to her of the acolytes who seemed to expect him to tart up their works: ' . . . so-called composers should be shot at dawn! One every day, taken out. The world wouldn't miss 'em. Me? I was shot at dawn a long time ago!'

Art of creating musical skeletons he had called fugue to Schotts in his Tobias biography. You look death in the face every time you start a new work. And you also hold it at bay. Each time he began, he wondered if he would complete it.

'Do you really want to know what it is like to be in composition? It is like living in blancmange. Take that, you scoundrel! That, that!' He had been duelling. She had been laughing. That was why big works were the best: you got in so deep, it closed over your head: a coat of protection from God Himself; were Paradise like this he would not mind.

'Sometimes when you're working on one you can look at it and . . . simultaneously mourn and wonder that this which you are now so close to will at some future time seem . . . as unreal to you as to anyone else, as distant as if you had never written it.'

She had worried then lest his desire for the child be a fancy as transitory. . . . Pulling his ears, 'You can't take them back and re-write them, you know!'

. . . 'You say that I want to re-write people the way I correct my compositions. I have no wish to re-write you.'

He distantly thought that he could smell burning. He went to his study and looked at it. Closing the door, he thought to himself, it's like being pregnant – there isn't a moment when you aren't having that baby!

Like all the greatest works of art it was coming upon him before he knew of it; the art takes the man, it is not the man who makes the art: the art comes upon the man and takes him by the scruff of the soul and gives him no peace until he has fulfilled it.

'To make a fugue requires no art,' he had told Holz. 'I made dozens of them in my student days. But the fancy also wishes to express itself, and in the present day another true poetic element must infuse the form that has been handed down.'

... 'At first it's very funny. It can still be coming to you quickly but it's crap and you know it's crap. You live in a sort of high artistic delusion – you stand back and watch yourself living in it, but the part that is in it is so in it it carries you on to the next stage. You go high and you keep yourself buoyed up – or it keeps you up. Then you sink like a stone – my God, you feel *that* small! You get very depressed. Then something comes out of this depression – you react to it, you weep, then you write. Mind you, that's not to say it is good – you can still be writing like a soft fart.'

Well that was how he'd described it to Toni, when she had been carrying their child.

... Art! My refuge! My rock! My all!

... 'Even if I am alone, I am never lonely.'

... Leaving his work for the night, stroking it as one would one's child's face, reciting to it, 'Good night, sweet Prince, Parting is such sweet sorrow, But I must kippy-wip Until tomorrow.'

... 'For, thank God, Beethoven can compose – though I admit that is all he is able to do in this world.'

... It scares the shit out of me sometimes, but I seem to be able to do it.

... They say the more you put into life, the more you get out of it, but that has only ever been true for me with composition.

Allegro molto e con brio

Karl had returned to the Polytechnic, visiting his uncle at mid-day. There was trouble now about his crammer. Why did he still have to pay? 'I will try to be able to get rid of him as soon as possible. At the moment, however, it is still necessary.'

Karl was now back at Schlemmer's. Reisser, of all people, now wanted him moved away from there, though B had just paid three months' rent in advance. Schlemmer's wife was involved in helping B to find a house-keeper. Reisser himself was causing B worry: he had had the Mass for several months, allegedly with a view to having it copied that B's friends might organize a concert, yet every time Holz went to pick it up he was kept waiting in the anteroom like a servant and always told that 'it will be tomorrow.'

Beethoven warned Holz not to tell Reisser that the boy played billiards.

Schlemmer himself wrote for Beethoven, 'I can assure you that as yet he has never stayed away overnight. Also I must tell you that your nephew is at home daily in the evening, and that he goes out early only if it is time for school. But if he were going to play, then it would have to be instead of school. Otherwise he is at home and he can't play. Since he's been here he has been changing his ways favourably. He said today at lunch that his tutor is not really satisfied, he is negligent in his studies.'

Karl told his uncle, 'The lessons are not difficult for me; also I could not have taken up any *earlier* what I am taking up with *him* because we take up only those studies which are being given in college. From my lessons with him I save several hours in which I would have had to work by myself.'

He had already told his uncle how his time was spent. 'My class hours are all distributed. My tutor comes early, from 7.30 to 8.30. Then lectures from 9-12. Afternoon, lectures from 3-5. I have an hour from 5-6. In the evenings I do my assignments. It is always just like today.'

'How do I know you're at college when you say you are?'

'I would be glad if you would inform yourself,' Karl told his uncle acerbicly. 'Each day the professors are bound to know when I leave since the names are read out. In addition, Herr Reisser sees me daily.'

On November 15th the middle-aged woman found Karl, in the morning, when he should have been at the Polytechnic, crying into Caspar's fur. She took him to show him Percy's new hen: a dull brown chicken called Jezebel.

The cat leapt between the trees like a squirrel. In the air he took the breath: as high in the trees and at ease as any bird.

'My daughter once saw him lying full-length on the table. He'd got into the house. Gave her such a fright! She said, "Mum, I thought it was a *person!*"'

Karl had learned that his mother had originally granted B half of her pension in return for the usufruct of money left on her house. *This* house. The money was his: an inheritance from some grandfather or cousin. He had learned of it when listening to B and Holz whilst taking dictation of a letter from B to the taxman.

> . . . I am not only defraying the entire cost of my nephew's education, but am even supporting his mother.

'Give two concerts that lose money and the tax man sits up and takes notice!'

> It is not a matter of indifference to me to be treated in such a way. And most certainly no other government would do this, for I enjoy the respect of the highest ranks in all Europe.

. . . 'You never wait to let me show love to you . . .'

'You never do show me love! You forget my name-day, my birthday, not once, *every year*!'

I never do show love to you! What about you! – September: my birthday. November the 4th: my name-day. And today: the tenth anniversary of my father's death!

Time had stopped, he was working so hard. Instead of flying, time had stopped. He seemed to have been writing this for eternity. He could not remember when it had last been easy, when he had last enjoyed it. It woke him up during the night. He had a headache, catarrh, ear-ache, and his belly felt dreadful. He could have sat and howled like a baby. Once, unable to stop though almost faint from hunger, he did sit and cry, even as he worked. He was exhausted. He thought it was killing him.

He thought always of death, expected to die, did not think that he would survive to produce this.

He recalled that he had felt like this before: when he had heard Johanna talking with some woman of how having children dulled their hair, rotted their teeth. He had felt then that composition was sometimes like that. Sometimes it is as though it drains your life-blood.

He felt bled to the bone, feared madness, at times forgot someone's familiar Christian name. He feared for his sanity. He lived in dread of dying before he had finished this work that was killing him.

'When you're really working you're too busy working to get up and pour yourself a drink – that is what work *is*!' he recalled saying to Goethe.

Physically too tired to write it down. You think you're going to die of mental frustration. You feel as though you'll have a stroke. And, as he wiped the phlegm from his mouth and the sticky liquid from his eyes, and bent down to get his pencil and pad, he remembered saying to A, 'I want to sleep, but when the Golden Eagle shits you have to wipe the bird-muck off your head.'

The next morning he entered his study feeling quite calm. The next instant he was pounding the piano fit to break it, howling in fury, bitter grief. He had to put his arms round something – a pillar, the stove-pipe, the leg of his desk. He was on the floor, sobbing against his piano.

He had had to get up and sit and write. O God can I have *no* experience, *ever*, that is not converted into *this*!

I can go through that. I can live through grief. I can take my grief like any normal man. But when You take the fruit of my grief and turn that as a source of grief upon me – God, what do You think I am?

... Bloody notes, looking up at him, crying out, 'Find me my home!' The simple austerity cried to be left, the new unbidden work to be fitted, and art itself demanded the maximum. Thicken it ... power it ... show the bastards your art.

Lock on with me, You Bastard. Let's see what we can make of *each other*. *Leibquartett* he had called this one.

No vision of it. When you were in it. Yet trying to cling on to its integrity. He remembered talking about this to A. ' ... The *itness* of it ...'

'O, you mean its quiddity!'

'Quiddity! Quiddity! I'll give you its quiddity! I'll give you *my* quiddity in a minute!'

'O! Yes please!'

Drinking with Holz, he was muttering to himself from the *Choral*, ruminatively repeating, 'What custom impudently separated.'

Someone had told him that Holz was in love. Apparently he was thinking of marrying this one. 'What're you doing out with me every night when you've got her? O I see! Can't take no more of it.' Beethoven laughed at him sympathetically. 'O you poor man! I know! You're at the stage where you're so much in love that it's painful!' Beethoven clapped Holz on the shoulder. 'Aye, lad, I know how it is: the time when you're calling everyone "darling," even the dog! You wait. You'll see how it is – when you're a young man it's so intense you pray for it to ease. When it does ease you start to wonder what's matter with you. I used to fall in love every five years. When I was a young man. ... Aye, that's right, I did. Every five years.' He began listing them, as much to himself as to Holz. 'There was her, whatshername, when I was 25. Giulietta when I was 30. Josephine at 35 – aye, aye! ... Therese when I was 40! I proposed to her. Her and the first one. That is, I made a formal declaration – asked father, asked mother. The others, I just said "Will you?" and they said "No!"

'All Countesses. Penniless countesses, looking for counts with a bob or two. Or at least their parents were. Someone to replenish the family fortunes. Looking in the wrong place for that, with old LvB! You marry her, lad, if she's the right one for you. You'll know if she is. You won't be able not to marry her. Won't be spending time swilling beer with me!

'It happens to everyone, my dear fellow! Everyone! Even the little monk in his cell! I said to her once, at Karlsbad, half-laughing, half-angry with her – I was composing: "Just think of me as a little monk in a cell!" She said to me then, coyly, "But I want to *marry* the little monk!" Now my Toni is a lady. My Toni is even an Edle von. More class in her little finger than those other bitches had in the whole of their carcasses. So much love in that woman. So much bloody giving love. ... I ruined her life ...'

'What happened?'

'She was married! She had children ... I thought when I was fifty he would die and she would come to me. I don't know why. Believed it implicitly. – Instead he has grown younger as I've grown older. He's five years older than I am but *he's younger*!

'She loved string quartets more than any woman I've ever known. Isn't it funny – I'd forgotten that until recently! Round there, every day, playing the piano to her, when she was ill – O that was all right but what she wanted was string quartets! Bugger the bloody piano! Yet our son, apparently, loves the piano ...'

Holz spurted beer across the table. 'Jesus Christ! You've got a *son*?'

'Does no one understand me when I speak plain German! I have a son. His name is Karl. His name is Karl Josef. Josef, the patron saint of adulter ... of cuckolds. *Basta!*'

Beethoven took Holz home and showed him the pictures: the miniature A had given him in June 1812, perhaps when she was already pregnant;

the sketch of her done by Stieler in 1819, posed as the Virgin Mary, with Karl Josef as the infant Christ in her lap and Georg, behind, as the Baptist.

'Warm, beautiful, intelligent, cultured, rich. They say you don't get everything in a woman, but she has everything. She is.'

Holz laughed incredulously.

'O yes she is.'

'Everything but famous!'

'Well I'm famous!'

They laughed.

'I've been telling people for years I've got a son, his name is Karl, and not a soul has ever believed me.

'No one knows how often in these last twelve years I haven't wanted to go to her, give her another one.' He downed his glass and poured another. 'She just saw the whole world from my angle. What more do you want in a wife? Very beautiful, very intelligent, and the kindest heart I've ever known. I hurt her and hurt her and she went on loving me. If you're one part as happy with your wife as I was with her, you'll do well.' He re-filled Holz' glass. 'Get yourself married, Holz. Have your children. Stick with her and stick with them and never stop thanking God for your good fortune. Nothing like seeing a child grow up, from infancy to manhood.'

Saying farewell, he called after Holz, 'Don't forget, Holz – I'm to be godfather to your first son!'

The next day Holz said to him, 'Did you tell me you had a wife and son or did I dream it?'

'You dreamt it,' Beethoven said. 'Don't forget to talk to Karl for me.'

'He should mind his own business!' Karl said when Holz tried to talk to him.

'He is involved, you know. If you get a woman pregnant *he* has to pay for it.'

'*He* paid for my mother when she was pregnant!'

'No he didn't. He only tried to help her out with her pension. Hofbauer paid for that.'

Karl laughed. 'More fool him!'

'He just wants you to be careful. He wants to see you grown up and married and with a family.'

'If I wanted to get married now he'd say I was too young!'

'You are too young. You're still a student. A man has to make his own life before he can ask a woman to share it.'

'Does he say that or do you?'

'He doesn't want you to make some of the mistakes that he's made.'

'What mistakes has he made?'

'He doesn't want you to be alone.'

'He didn't want my father to make mistakes but *he* married and *he* had me!'

Holz said to Beethoven again, 'Did you tell me you really were a father?'

'Aye well. That's for me to know and you to find out.'

He dreamed that he was playing the piano while Toni sat with Karl on her knee, whispering to the boy to listen to his father as she stroked his silk-like hair back from his face.

Allegro

... Franz in Franzensbad, pointing at Fanny: 'It's not only her that you're taking from me: you're taking her mother from *her*.'

Meno mosso e moderato

Christmas 1817: The gat-toothed Polish woman holding her toddler grandson in her arms, white snow upon her frizzed black hair as he had struggled with the frozen lock. The key turned. 'That's fixed the bastard!' She exclaiming with delight. Spontaneously hugging, both laughing, the warmth of this solid stout woman against him, the child she still held bobbing close to his face while in her embrace she slapped his back, 'You good man! O you good man!'

Allegro molto e con brio

You could tell when his music was going well. An aura of peace round the lips. A faraway look in his eye. He looked pregnant.

'It's always like this: he leans on me for two-thirds of the year, then, come the autumn, he falls in love with his work.'

He had but to think of his work for the wrinkles to clear from his brow.

Pulling his spectacles onto his ears, B had been heard to say, with more good cheer than bitterness, 'These just about serve to hold my spectacles on my face.'

'*He* ... demands freedom in *everything*, demands for himself − do you know when I was at Giannatasio's he wouldn't teach me the piano ... take me every night ... it was "too constraining" − he said he was constrained by the *Archduke*! The *Archduke's* never here! He wants freedom − for him − always − freedom in *everything* − freedom − all the time − for *him*!' Karl told his friend. 'Aye: freedom's all right so long as it's Ludwig van Beethoven's freedom!'

N was grinning at him. 'You sounded just like him then: *Aye!*'

All the griefs of life fall away and you become that complete being, man woman and God rolled into one: man the artist.

I have no wife, no love, my child is ill, that one deceives me; no home no money no prospect no love − and I am the luckiest man God ever made, the happiest man to walk upon God's earth.

So that is what it means to be alive, so that is what I have lived all my life for.

The unreality of knowing at the time that the present was one's happiest time. Like all other knowledge now, it was laced with love.

He saw his brain become more than his own brain was; whilst inside this, whilst working, stood back and saw himself being blessed by God.

Veni creator spiritus in the midst of all this he had had the notion of writing.

It was not unknown for him to call God 'The greatest composer above.'

He had now but one love of his life, and it was not Toni and it was not Karl and it was not his own son. When he went to his study and locked himself in with his work, which by now meant his God, he became himself. Nothing else mattered. This little old frail man fell away. He thought once, it is not even what God has given me. It *is* the God in me.

Whatsoever ye do, do it heartily, as to the Lord, and not unto men.

Chapter 12

Mid-December

The manuscript was giving off its new-baby aura; people turned to look as he passed them in the street, as though expecting to see a new white-shawled baby within the man's black arms, not a music manuscript against his dark coat.

He was still too close: as he left it with the copyist he felt bereft. He did not know what he had done, he was overwhelmed by it and blind to it. For several days he had had diarrhoea; he physically could not eat: his throat closed, he could not swallow. Overawed, in terror and ecstasy.

That is the finish because that has to be the finish: if I do not finish this now, I die.

But he loved that one. There was something in it: him in it, God in it, destiny in it, depth breadth and longevity. That one will go on for as long as the world lasts. If they remember me for nothing else they'll remember me for that. That and the Mass.

He walked in a sort of unreal dream, at once dazed yet fully alive. In love with it, fearful, tremulous, and yet, despite those fires, profoundly calm.

It was as he had once told Antonie: getting to know this thing he had made. 'You know you talked of . . . having a baby, and getting to know the child you've had . . .' There was more of God than him in this, this one he never would know; yet he knew pride that God had chosen him to pierce with this dense majesty; humility before the might of God.

'. . . And when you've finished, two things always strike: it is less than it seemed, and it always is: as its conception.' There was a density to this one, this was all density and destiny; he could spot himself popping up here and there, especially in that first main fugue, but he had objectified it perfectly: this naked profound subjectivity had been transmogrified and stood as art. He could stand it, others could stand it, there was decency here and yet a nakedness, nakedness that would touch suffering naked-ness. *Touch!* – it would reach out, *yank* – that sense of objection, ferocity – but it was a ferocity of the living and it would claim response in the living: as hot as life, forged in hot steel, held in the cold indifference of art.

. . . There were things in this that he did not know, things in this that scared him, yet he loved these for all his fears, his love leapt, his love became yet more fierce.

At moments he knew terror: there are things here that *I should not have written*. No one should have written them. Yet I have written them and there they stay.

I have written them? I? I? O where did *you* come from, my little sweeting, my naked darling that I held in my arms? He wanted to take the manuscript and rub his cheek back and forth against it; fling his arms wide, his soul gaping, fling his arms wide and hurl it into the world. To me . . . from me . . . From God . . . to man – O the *circle of love!*

Throughout all this, life had gone on. Linke had given his benefit concert, with Galitzin's second. He had offered Peters a quartet or his money. Peters had asked for the money and had been repaid. To get money himself, he had even briefly thought of dedicating the *Choral* to the Czarina. Now he'd heard the Czar had died. He'd begun to be alarmed about Galitzin. He had written to him in late July sending him two overtures, Opus 124, dedicated to him, and Opus 115. Since then he had heard nothing. Halm had played a trio of his, in E-flat, and he'd finally been elected a member of the *Gesellschaft*.

Just as he had finished the fugue, Frau Schlemmer had given birth to twin boys.

At Baden he had caught sight from his window of the woman's husband, two days after he had stopped to talk to him, his wife sullen, to one side. The man's step was jaunty, his jacket was hooked by one finger over his shoulder as he strode home in his shirt-sleeves in the hot sun. You only had to look at him to know that his child was born and that it was a boy.

He had been terrified of writing this and, now that it was here, he felt numb. His exultation was brow-beaten relief, he expectantly watched its slow rise to the surface.

Days passed. It did not rise. It remained as repressed as his prayer had been; yet, as his whole soul had been behind that brief soulless prayer, so his whole being dwelt within this suppressed, boneless exultation: a slow orgasm.

He was this. This one thing. The author of the *Große Fuge*. Already sketching a new quartet, which began with a fugue, *that* was his link to life, *that* brief distant prayer his link to God.

He had walked back to the same spot the next day, thanking God, almost equally distantly. That day a deep golden evening sun had shone.

All the times I got down on my knees to You, sobbing my ring up, howling, supplicating, keening, my soul in torment. You let me suffer on. *That* tiny little seed of a prayer You answered. You even guided me to that prayer, that speck of a prayer, at that time and in that place. O, You'd written that for me before I was born.

His pain hung down like rags from this slow, unburning exultation; shocked as by grief: close, recent, bereavement.

He had to go back to the *Helenenthal*, to the same spot, on the same mountain, to consecrate this work to God.

He strode down from his tryst like a fit, healthy man, his feet pounding out the theme of his fugue. He felt the fugue throbbing through his body. Through every pulse. Through his head. Through his heart. . . . *Beauty is not the aim. The arrow in its flight must curve* . . . The strangeness to him of this thing still foreign yet wholly the product of his uncurtailed love: the spirituality only a fugue can attain whilst yet the music of the earth, wholly the music of the earth, in which the same listener could hear would he but put his ear to its shell the moans and last gasps of the dying; the sound of conception; the cries of the fury and exultation of birth.

You think you *set out* to get that? You don't *set out* to get *that* at all: you sit down to write, it wells from within, it has been waiting, pressing you *to be written* yet you did not know it *before* it was written nor did you give any of these names to it: *birth, death, conception, spiritual*: the very idea is laughable.

He realized that this was what Toni had meant when she had said, 'I have never known spirituality and sensuality so meshed.'

He was at once feeling all the things he had said to Toni: you don't reach out to get it: if you *reach out to get it* you've no right to be *doing* it . . . *getting to know the baby you've had*. Never had he felt this more clearly: you don't know what it is you are going to produce. He had once said to her, laughing, 'It's as much a shock to me as it is to anybody else!'

They were hardly parted. His spirit was still wet with it and it wet with his spirit. O my beautiful strapping offspring! You are bigger and greater and stronger and wiser than I shall ever be! O but there was a fury in that music. Sometimes you only find consolation in fury.

And your power alarms me, your power engulfs and swallows me.

Flesh to his flesh. Flesh about him. 55 years ago today, he had been born.

A young woman of not yet twenty, her dark hair flowing. And she turned his bereavement orgasm into flesh and blood and semen.

Chapter 13

21st March-April, 1826

'Cattle! Asses' heads!' he stormed in the tavern to Holz after the performance. The 2nd and 4th movements only applauded. 'Why these delicacies! Why not the *Fuge*! *The one they should have encored was the Fuge!*'

He hurried from the tavern, detesting Holz for trying to meet his eye and perhaps to dare show sympathy. He hurled into his room, locked the door, and stood silently in the farthest corner, his hand to the wall, with tears down his face, detesting being seen by God.

Some time later he got out the autograph of his *Große* and as he saw it he began sobbing and sank to his sofa with it clasped to his lap, keening.

He got a glass of water and sat gulping it, he lit his pipe and smoked and drank water, still with the autograph beside him, breaking into a voiceless scream.

He took it to bed and lay with it on the bed beside him, still smoking, drinking water. He put out the candle and lay down. He put his hand upon it and sobbed helplessly.

Holz had run after him when he had stormed off. When he had locked himself in Holz had had the servant keep watch. The next day he sought out Karl and sent him to him.

Karl wrote on the slate, 'They liked your *scherzos.*' Beethoven without looking at Karl took his notebook and pencil and left the room, not slamming the door. For the rest of the day he was to be seen going about his rooms in silence, notepad and pencil in one hand, a cup of coffee in the other, avoiding all eye contact, leaning to write on any available surface, standing stock still or dropping to sit where he wrote.

No one no one! Not even God!

He had locked the manuscript away.

. . . I gave You my soul and You sneered at me!

Why did You make me!

He wanted to be alone in a field. He wanted to be away from everybody.

About the eyes he looked grief-stricken, he had the appearance of one bereft. Karl came upon him once asleep on the floor, his notepad beside him, as though weeping had made him heavy-lidded and forced him to sleep.

The maid returned and began cleaning his rooms. Karl stayed in the room where she was cleaning.

Beethoven avoided all contact. He hated all nature, he hated everything that drew breath.

He went for a walk.

He walked fast. His teeth were chattering as he set off. By the time he was half-way home, he was sweating. He felt a fraud. He felt deluded. He felt ashamed. He felt that his life had been a total failure. *Everything I do including music is badly done and is stupid.* In the tavern when Holz had told him he had felt, *forgive me my trespasses.* He felt that no trespass had ever been forgiven him. When he had started stalking away, struck as though by a physical blow, he had felt, God, look into my innermost heart! That was *my best* . . . the most sincere, the most in *God.* The foundations of his world had crumbled. *If I am wrong in that then God, O my God, I am wrong in everything!* If that were wrong then everything that he had ever done was wrong, everything that he had ever stood for, his whole life had been in vain.

He returned relieved to find that Karl was not there. He was as he had been after Caspar Carl's death, in a state in which he could not envisage joy.

He could not escape that sense of doom that is like physical pain. He bruised his shin tripping over the pile of his own compositions which had been left by his piano. He swore in angry sotto-voice, 'Ah, you bloody lot, I don't know why I bloody wrote you, you've never brought me any pleasure.'

He scalded his hand as freshly-made coffee spilt over the top of his cup. He could have turned to God and howled, *O You Bastard!*

Come on. Come on. Come on. Wasn't I weak enough for You? Hadn't I suffered enough for You? What happened – did I get too happy for You? *You* gave me that happiness, You Bastard. What sort of Father does that to His child? – Ignored my child completely – at least *I* never did a deed as bad as *that.* To his astonishment tears were hot on his face, in anger and contempt he dragged them off. *I* don't want to cry before *You!*

You turn and make a mockery of all my work – of all my hopes, all my good feelings. All those hours of living through torments to hold him, to hold her . . .

What a price to pay for one free whore. One free woman, after all these years! *Have You not exacted enough!* He had not even set out not to pay, felt bad about deceiving her. A private house, in Baden. Had she then not been a prostitute after all? She had just sort of drifted away, into another room. No sign of her when he had left. Perhaps she had expected him to just leave the money. It had been his *own* fucking birthday!

He had not even set out not to pay: had determined to write verses for the girl. He had been writing these when Molt from England had visited. He had written Molt a canon: *Freu' dich des Lebens:* Karl Josef's favourite song before the burning.

Loving Father! Kick-you-in-the-goolies-Father! Loving Father my arse!

O I know Your ways! You Bastard! All You ever give me is this! The only joy You ever give me is this – give me this so I can be sneered at!

His chest ached from grief.

Leaving his flat the next morning, he almost tripped over a parcel of eggs. He knew who had left them: an acquaintance of Karl. The eggs left by this man were always delicious and new-laid.

Beethoven wept afresh as he took up the eggs and closed the door. A parcel of food outside his door was a direct message to him from God: *Yes, your treatment at others' hands has been unjust.* In the past it had been treatment at God's own hands: God had made his son ill, taunting him to live by daily sending to him the gat-toothed woman bearing black bread. He was clutching the eggs now, just as he had in those days clutched the conical loaf. Keening, unable to stop crying, day after day. The message then had been *I may not help but I know you are there.*

This was not so bad. This day God had sent him a message. *Yes, you were wronged.*

Beethoven unwrapped the eggs, grinning. Being wronged by men is nothing to a man who has been wronged by God.

He cried more that day. His nose was so swollen it pained him to wear his glasses. O what a beautiful big red nose you've got, fella. Big red nose and eyes like piss-'oles in snow. He laughed as he recalled his father's expression, way back, from childhood. *Eyes like piss-'oles in snow.* His father had tried to stop him composing. He raised his eyes to his Heavenly Father. You don't try to stop me doing that, do You? Everything else You try to stop but that, eh, that is permitted. Won't let 'em like it, mark You. Bastard. He felt quite calm, his shaking fist breaking into a wave as he laughed to God.

He caught sight of the eggs and began singing,

Yummy yummy yummy yummy
Just the stuff to fill my tummy.

So that I can get *energy*, so that I can *compose*! Eh, Fella!

It was not easy getting back to work after such a blow. He felt like a fraud. All his confidence had gone. No one wants it. He felt bitter: his work had built up such a good head of steam before. . . . Give of your best and your best is rejected . . . his best love . . .

To look at the pages of sketches filled him with distaste. *What're you going to make out of these that you couldn't make with that one?* He still felt that the *Fuge* was the best work he had ever done. Others did not think so.

He struggled to work for a day. The misery that he felt was like bereavement.

O God, give me back *my art*! If you don't give me back *my art* I shall *kill someone*!

The next day a friendly letter had him in tears. God I don't want to cry any more! He felt as though he had been kicked in the face. He was almost blind in his right eye.

That afternoon, shooing a wasp out of his window, as he put out his hand to get the catch his finger caught on a large brittle thorn. He pulled his hand away, the thorn still embedded.

'I'll chop you down! I'll chop you down to the bloody ground! And that's only you – it's nothing to what I'll do to the rose!' Karl, approached where he sat at his desk in the next room, laughed as his uncle thwacked him amiably across the head.

They had all been shit-scared before they had even seen it. Holz, when Rampl had arrived with the manuscript, 'A fugue always occurs to me first like a building which is worked out symmetrically according to the rules of architecture; I admire it, but it never charms me.' Said he had heard no fugues of Sebastian Bach played well. And O, when he did see it: the circumspection! 'I think that here the nature of art and the artistry of nature is taken to its limit.'

That was nothing compared to the horror of the others. Falstaff: 'I'd still like to be able to look over my part a little at home before we rehearse . . .' Wanting to give it at an *evening* concert, with *Adelaide*, 'sung prettily,' to soften the blow, and the *Archduke* Trio, because, O, they all knew that, they would listen to *that*. He had seen it, writ large, all over their faces: What the hell are we going to do about *this*? What the hell did he have to go and compose *this one* for! What the hell could have prompted him! Christ, what a nuisance! Trying to prepare him for failure before they had fairly seen it: one look, and they were off, trying to deflect their horror and animosity with talk of the subscribers taking it ill if they had to pay yet again, and how people wouldn't be prepared to fork out yet another 10 florins every time. Every time he came up with crap like this. That's what they'd meant.

Gott ist eine feste Burg my eye. O yes, they all knew better than he did. One of the *Verein* directors had asserted of one of his works played by the *Gesellschaft* that the tempo should be much slower, and B himself didn't know it! Society of the *Friends* of Music! The bastards had overlooked him for a decade whilst making members of all and sundry. Now they had got round to offering him a diploma, fourteen others had been elected at the same time! Holz had told him that in the *Hamburger Zeitung* Spontini was said to be the greatest composer of all time! Go through life giving them bouquets and they sock you in the mouth!

His friends had planned to put on a concert of the *Missa Solemnis* and the *Choral*, but that had come to nothing. He had been ill then anyway. One of the Fröhlich girls suggested for the alto part had turned out to be the sister of Katharina, Grillparzer's fancy-woman. 'Eternal bride' he called her. Holz had joked to him on the planned day, 'Today is Beethoven's concert; are we going together?'

He had heard that old Unger had got herself married, though Johann had said that it wasn't true. Prince Lobkowitz too, pupil of Peters and son of his late patron, was said to be engaged. He had written the *Lobkowitz Cantata* for the young Prince in 1823. Old Lobkowitz had been one of the signatories of his annuity agreement. The family still paid. Holz had told him when he had gone to get his half-yearly annuity payment from Kinsky that the clerk had said that it would be a greater pleasure for him to undertake something for Beethoven than if Minister Metternich had given him a gracious commission in the name of the Kaiser himself!

The involvement of which Holz had told him when he had been writing the *Fuge* had come to nought. 'Women here are the devil; the day before yesterday I heard tales of one woman for whom I'd have put my hand in the fire.'

Holz himself had started fishing. First there had been that business of the sketchbooks. During his illness, he had thought of giving Holz various papers in case he popped off. Holz had suddenly written, 'If you leave nothing but your sketchbooks there will be no such dispute. They are hieroglyphics where no man will be intelligent. They're the secrets of Isis and Osiris!' Then, when he had been giving him bits of background for any future biography, Holz had joked of selling his secrets. 'I go in there with my face full of secrets and I whisper in his ear: Should I make you happy? "What is it, then?" Something from B. "In God's name! Where did you get it!" Patience! I must represent you as an art-dealer. There's no speech without ducats!' Telling him that the new quartet was finally ready to be rehearsed in his rooms, Holz had written, 'Wednesday at 7 in the evening will the Beethoven *Leibquartett* with drums and pipes in the heights of the Black Spain march off and manoeuvre!' And, when they had been talking about Mozart's *Requiem* and of Constanze selling extracts from his works after Breitkopf and Härtel had already begun to bring out a complete edition, Holz had written with glee, 'The wife of Mozart and the wife of Beethoven!'

He had written to Holz, 'Last night I dreamt that your parents were begetting you and I saw in my dream how much sweat it cost them to bring to light such an amazing piece of work. I congratulate you on your *existence* − how, why?! and so forth, the riddles solve themselves.'

Holz had once expressed his opinion of religion. 'There is no other religion than to do right. And be no egoist! Normally men are only good from fear.' He worked with that clown Castelli, author of salacious anecdotes known as *Castelli's bears*. Beethoven had once written one for Castelli. Castelli had wanted to publish it. . . . If I'm not to be known for my *Fuge* I might as well be known for my *Castelli's bears*.

You are where God wants you to be. He had been where God wanted him to be with that one. They had booed him.

'Only the praise of one who has known praise can give pleasure,' he had written beneath a sketch of his current quartet. They had even been talking of asking a hundred for this one. With the death of the Czar share values had tumbled; Schlesinger's agent had not had the 80 ducats to hand for Galitzin's third; again in danger of selling a share to meet his commitments, he had sold his quartet with fugue to Artaria. This was not the firm from whom he had borrowed money but Mathias Artaria, son of the Mannheim music publisher, Domenico II. 'Herr Mathias the First,' Holz had named him.

The man had seen him then, when he had already agreed to buy the quartet: what was he getting sniffy about the fugue now for? As if he hadn't known it contained a bloody great fugue! 'I hear you're writing six fugues,' the man had said, offering to down a bottle of champagne to him and, when he had gasped, 'Spare me the labour!' had said, 'I hope *Mathias* won't be forgotten with the fugues!'

They had got on so well he had finally scuppered Steiner, telling Schotts in the future to write through Artaria instead. Artaria even lived in a house bought from Prince Razumovsky . . . the grounds of the Palace hard by the Birkenstock House. 'His daughter in Frankfurt I know well,' Artaria had written. In his embarrassment Beethoven had held onto the book to sketch his new quartet. *If Franz died they would all move back to Vienna and he would marry Toni and live in the Birkenstock House.* Artaria had bought the Erdberg House from Prince Razumovsky in 1821, on the Danube, at the foot of Razumovsky's Palace gardens. That same year he had been a guest at a party in Frankfurt. Bettina had been there, but Toni had been with Karl Josef in Paris, visiting Gall.

Artaria had been to London four times. 'If you go to London I'll go with you.' Holz had even suggested Karlsbad for a summer stay!

. . . 'He says that he first yesterday understood the *adagio* properly,' Holz had told him of Falstaff, 'and he'll hardly be able to play it for pleasure.' O, they all loved the *Cavatina*. They had been all over him then, in January, Holz making comparison between his and Mozart's instrumental music, to Mozart's detriment. 'That is what is always missing in Mozart. Especially in his instrumental music. A definite character in a piece of instrumental music, I mean a parallel representation of any frame of mind – in his work, not in yours. I always ask myself if I hear anything, what is the meaning of it? Your pieces have throughout a certain exclusive character. I make such a distinction between Mozart's and your instrumental compositions: to one of your pieces a poet could only write one work; to Mozart's he could write 3 or 4 parallel works.' . . . Asking if the quartet could play part of the new one, the one he had only begun a month before. . . . 'Your genius is like a kaleidoscope, you could look at it 1000 times and 1000 times you see something new without it wearing out.' O, Holz had said that. Not of the *Fuge*.

The secret of life is approbation. That alone is the source of joy. He remembered the laudatory letters he had got from Peters when he had first offered him the Mass, the disapprobation that had followed.

It was *right*: as right as that fiddle solo in the *Sanctus*. . . . Crying in the first movement before the fight comes back, crashing into the tears in its anger and opposition. And then he stuck his tongue out at the Viennese: or rather, gave them a little sausage or a Viennese pastry. He'd done the same with the fourth movement, after the repression of the third: the high, black wall of repression: bouncing upon grief, the most painful state of all.

Yes, he'd given them their little dance, and how they'd loved it! Those Viennese! It was a wonder they hadn't got up and danced to, let alone applauded, his German dance! He'd originally meant that for that earlier quartet anyway.

And then his love story, *his* love story, that little boy . . .

And the fugue of it all. God, he had been wanting to write that fugue for *years* . . . had had it in him . . . the high black wall of repression, all those years, up against his eyes.

He had written his *Fuge*. And they had hated that.

. . . 'We always rehearse only your quartets. The Haydn and Mozart go better without rehearsal.'

After that day's work he felt himself sliding back into himself. Climbing into bed that night he thought, no, I'm not a great man. But sometimes my work is touched with a state of grace.

It had been easier, writing this. He had almost resented the thrust of creativity upon him. He had begun this almost resentfully. He had wanted to rest and the bugger kept coming at him. In the street, walking with Holz, having to stop to write. 'Something has again occurred to me.' Too busy even to accompany Karl and Holz to a New Year ball. This new quartet had a fugal opening.

'Now we'll have new sources of cash opening up,' Karl had said, 'Artaria and Galitzin.' Holz had told him that same January day of the Decembrist Revolution. 'Yesterday news came that among the military who swore an oath to Constantine a terrible revolution has arisen on account of his resignation.' He had had no reply from Galitzin to his letter of late July, knew not whose side Galitzin might be on, was he dead or alive? He'd told Karl that he thought the man a *weak Miserablatzin*.

One week later, he had had a letter, blaming his failure to write on illness and a journey into the depths of Russia. He had read in the *Leipzig Musical Gazette* that the new quartet in A had been performed in Vienna, imploring that it be posted to him. 'I am going to have 75 ducats sent to M. Stieglitz to be sent on to you through M. Fries: 50 for the quartet and 25 for the overture which is splendid and which I thank you very much for dedicating to me.'

Holz had said he should reply in the same terms: '"I'm going to . . ." but nothing comes of it.'

Beethoven had sent the quartet in A in February. Artaria had wanted a letter to the censor about dedicating Galitzin's third to Galitzin. . . . To have to write to the *censor* even about dedicating a new quartet to the

Prince who has commissioned it . . . to have to show the censor the *title* of a *string quartet*! Holz had told him, 'The police cost the most here. There isn't a table in the worst alehouse that doesn't have its spy sitting there.'

He worried now about having sent the quartet before getting the money. Johann had advised him to write to Galitzin himself and to write all important letters himself if he didn't want anyone knowing about them. He had offered to help. 'Tell him you've sent the quartet, you're worried in case letters have gone astray . . .'

Johann had again invited him to spend the summer at his country house. Therese's immorality was getting worse. *Fettlümmerl* had even once met her lover at Count Lichnowsky's, to where she and Amalie and Johann had been invited, although Johann hadn't gone!

His other sister-in-law too was a source of trouble. The boy, he thought, could not have been borrowing from Johanna since she was herself in debt, coming to him to act as guarantor for 200 fl C.M. in return for making over to him her full pension. 'And then what will she live on?' Holz had told him, 'She should go to your brother.' Schindler had laughed, 'Your brother should help, since in any case he's got such a sympathetic soul!'

Holz had remarked, 'Johanna still has too kindly a fate as her reward. What does Karl say?' 'I don't need Karl to tell me right from wrong.' Holz had urged him to stop helping her. 'You might as well be married to such a hussy if you're going to carry on like this.' Holz had told him the house where she lived was swarming with others of her ilk. 'You are doing enough for her son. She stays in bed till half past eleven and says she is indisposed.' Later Holz had told him that 'now she's a procuress. Falstaff saw her with a lady of pleasure going round in the street.' He seemed concerned for Karl. 'The so-called clumsy or awkward years are still not behind him.' He said that Ludovica looked quite like him. Johanna herself had apparently grown very fat. In April Holz told him Johanna was saying she hadn't heard from Karl 'for such a long time.'

In February, when he had been ill, when the weather had been so bad that Karl could not visit him frequently, Beethoven had suggested that Karl move back to live with him again. The boy had replied, 'You go ahead and do what you think best. I believe simply that the distance would cause a great loss of time, instead of my being, as I am now, a few minutes from home and able to study. In the summer we will not feel the distance so much. But it is the *last year*, and then we need never be separated any more.'

When he'd heard that Schlemmer had been keeping things from him, 'things that he doesn't trust himself to say to you,' he'd decided: that's it. That boy's coming to live with me. Distance from college or no distance from college. He had set about getting an extra room in the *Schwarzspanierhaus*. Holz had been laughing: 'Beethoven as Jupiter throwing the bolt!'

'Why are you laughing! I don't think it's damned funny! One chance!

To bring up that boy! What has he done that's worse than what I already know!'

Holz had said at New Year: 'I have spoken with Reisser. He says Karl is behaving himself the way you would expect of a reasonable person.' Karl had wanted to go to a pre-Lenten ball; when it came to seeing him, it was always, 'There is now a great deal to do, and it is frightful to give up Sundays.' . . . Money for tickets; money for janitors; the boy had taken to smoking *cigarros*, for *that one* a pipe wasn't good enough! . . . Artaria, when they had talked of going to England: 'Smoking and billiard playing is as odious in England as bigamy among the brave Viennese.'

When he had been ill the boy had neglected him. Gout, pains in the back, pains in the bowels, diet and rest prescribed, eye-troubles on top of these. Karl reluctant to come even to do letters! He had had Johann talk to him.

At the start of March Johann had said, 'Today I spoke with him earnestly about why he had been to see you so little. His answer was roughly as follows. He would very much like to be with you but he fears the frequent rows and reproaches for his mistakes of the past, also the frequent rows with the servants. But please don't reproach him with this, otherwise he would no longer be candid with me. From here, however, I think that you alone can draw him to you completely.'

'Did he say the bad weather prevented him?'

'Every day I walk six hours in the country. Karl has time and is fit, he can walk for a long time. From Schlemmer's to here is half an hour's walk.

. . . 'In 4 months Karl will be finished with everything, then you must urge him to go immediately into a local or foreign business-house, otherwise he will become a lout and will let himself live off you for as long as you live; that way he'd just idle away his time. – What did he do in the whole of the year 1824? – go for walks!'

'Have you given him any money?'

'I haven't given him a great deal.'

Johann had advised, 'In the last instance, give the guardianship to Dr Bach. You are as little able as I to be always running after him.'

After that Johann had come back with platitudes: 'Every day Karl goes straight from home to the college and back again.'

In the dark! How can I bring him up if I'm in the dark! How can I do what's right when I *don't know*! Blocked ears, relying on others to tell him, and: buttering-up, softening, fabrication! To act at all, a man needs to have hard *facts*!

Johann had talked to Reisser about Karl's supervision. 'He said that he was quite satisfied with him – in any case it'll be over by August.'

Karl himself when confronted had been snooty. 'I told you I only go to Klaps if some exceptional event happens where there is much to be done. But naturally this has happened less often in recent times, because I was ever more easily in the position of helping myself. It didn't happen in the evenings, it happened, as you have already learned, after 2 in the afternoon. I have never said that I go to him every Sunday. This also specifically depends on the difficulty of the work that I have to do. That I apply my time well, incidentally, the crammer can testify, to whom, I believe, I have never given any cause for dissatisfaction. On this point he will also have had only good to report of me in the discussion which, as I hear, he had with Holz.'

That snotty-nosed kid thought that he knew it all. Rows with house-keepers! He was still in the hands of Frau Schnaps, who Holz said was dying. He had had two sisters working as housekeeper and housemaid. He had given both sisters 14 days' notice two days after the failure of the *Fuge*.

Those two had replaced Housekeeper Lindner. Holz had pointed out one day when they were dining that the silver serving-spoon being used was not Beethoven's own. Laying the table himself for Housekeeper Lindner, Beethoven had discovered that another of his spoons was missing. He had charged his housekeeper; she had retaliated, accusing him of stealing her own spoons; he had written to Holz, 'God forbid that we should be reduced to stealing *spoons* in our venerable old age!' The housekeeper had been sacked; only now did he wonder if Karl had sold the silver, this time drawing lucky and replacing one of the spoons.

Holz said that Blahetka, the pianist's father, was entirely in favour of the *Fuge*. Johann told him, 'Of your last quartet, the whole city is full. Everyone who approves is delighted by it and says that the last movement has to be heard more often for it to be understood; the others want it not to appear because it was too hard to understand.' Artaria had come to him for a piano, four-hand, transcription of the *Fuge*. He had put the young pianist Halm onto this, too busy himself with his new quartet. Seven movements, no break ... the fourth a long variation movement ... the sixth, relic of his research dating from talk of a cantata for the consecration of Vienna's new Synagogue, drawn from an old Hebrew devotional theme.

Galitzin's first had now been published by Schotts. He had dedicated the *Choral* to the Prussian King. He himself had now had recourse to the censor, complaining of the 'barbarously worded' titles of opus 114 and 116, brought out by Steiner. He replied immediately to Schlesinger's letter of April 13th, willing to restore the rupture over Galitzin's third, offering him the new quartet. Karl wrote to his dictation, adding his own wish that Schlesinger 'pay us a visit very soon.'

Johann had urged him, 'Write an opera.' Others urged him to set *Melusine*. He still had the 10th symphony to write for England, perhaps too the BACH-overture, notions for both of which had occurred to him when he had still been busy with the *Fuge*. Kuffner, rejecting Bernard's text as 'lacking the character of an oratorio,' had presented him with an outline for an oratorio on *The Elements*, concerning Man and Nature. Now he had come up with the idea of *Saul*. Rellstab, he thought, had first suggested this last year, on learning of his love of Handel. Kuffner was to produce a revised text, emphasizing the triumph of man's nobler impulses over untamed desire.

Now there was talk of a Requiem Mass urged by, of all people, Abbé Stadler. Gottfried Weber had published in *Cäcilia* an article casting doubt on Mozart's authorship of certain obviously genuine passages of his *Requiem*. Stadler had immediately defended Mozart in a monograph, a copy of which he had sent to Beethoven. Beethoven had taken up the attack against Weber and now this man, Stadler, who fiercely opposed his *Razumovskys*, who left the room before his overture, who admitted having missed Galitzin's third, was so relieved to have him as an ally in support of his beloved Mozart that here he was offering to help him!

At the turn of the year the news had got around, 'When the Kaiser was in Prague, a Requiem by Vitásek was played and the Kaiser was very pleased. Vitásek dedicated a Mass to the Kaiser and the Kaiser said that Vitásek was not to be forgotten.' Holz had exploded, 'His Majesty's made a Bohemian *Vice-Hofkapellmeister!*'

Holz was telling him now, 'If Stadler tells you to write a Mass it is certain that something will be done for it. He knows better than anyone which way the wind blows. He has Dietrichstein and Eybler in his pocket. You'll be well looked after if Stadler favours it.'

He had once fallen to his knees before this man at Steiner's: 'Reverend Sir, give me your blessing!' The man of God, quite unabashed, had placed his hands on his bowed head: 'If does no good 'twill do no harm.'

Chapter 14

Summer

Holz had quoted to him in April a favourite saying of Toni's which he must have repeated himself: 'Old love does not rust.' He had shot up a mile when he had read it. '"Stay single!" says Papageno!' Holz had winked, putting a finger to his lips.

In May Breuning told him, 'Ferdinand Ries has a disease of the lips which has already lasted a year and which threatens to become cancerous, and this has alienated his wife from him and is causing her to turn to others.'

Let this be a lesson to you, he had thought, not to be jealous of others. Holz himself seemed to have had more luck, since by June he was getting his feet under the table of his fancy-piece's family at their summer residence in Ober-Döbling.

Halm had delivered his four-hand arrangement of the *Fuge* at the end of April. Beethoven disliked it, determined to undertake the task himself. Holz had declared of Halm in December, 'If technical aptitude were more developed in him, I should know no one better to play your piano works. He plays with head and heart, but his fingers slip sometimes off the right keys.' In March, when Halm had been rehearsing the piano part of the *Archduke* Trio for Falstaff's concert, his wife had expressed the ardent wish to own a lock of Beethoven's hair. He had boasted, 'I fobbed her off with goat's hair!' Beethoven had cut off a lock and sent it through Holz. 'My wife thanks you very much as a compatriot for the treasured lock of hair, and if we're not troublesome we'll call on you together,' Halm had said when he had been transcribing the *Fuge*. 'I find it all easy, only the first section is very hard . . . I will apply all my strength.' Holz had said then, 'When I saw him to talk about the *Fuge* he didn't greet me and looked down his nose.' By mid-May Holz was reporting, 'He's still boasting that he made such a good job of it. He still has no understanding of the *Fuge*.' Halm had been paid 40 fl. for his botched job by Artaria. By the middle of June Holz was writing, 'Halm has noticed that you're not content and he doesn't venture to come here.'

Courier Lipscher, who had taken the third quartet to Galitzin and was supposed to have returned with the money, had written in early May from Petersburg. Holz told Beethoven, 'He went to the home of the Prince, who excused himself, said he had no time; he would see him another day. Lipscher went 5 or 6 times but was never received; all sorts of excuses were given. A note for 5 fl. given to the servant helped him finally to get through to the Prince again. Galitzin was embarrassed again, fumbled through his scores, and finally said that Lipscher might come to him before leaving for Vienna, to get the money. The fellow believes it's nothing but a Russian trick! But he adds that he's not to be put off so easily; he thinks he will be back in 4-5 weeks. And it's certain now that Galitzin received the second.' By June they were in contact with Graf von Lebzeltern, a diplomat in Petersburg, hoping to exert pressure through diplomatic channels. By late June Holz was telling him, 'The courier Lipscher has written: "7 times I went to see the knave, the last time he had left for the coronation in Moscow – a Russian trick!" Several couriers have told me that there has been little action from the embassy – they don't want to have a quarrel with this man.'

He had offered the new quartet to Schlesinger, who hadn't replied. Through Holz he had offered the quartet to Artaria, though he had since wondered if Artaria had received all his messages since Holz had apparently been annoyed by something he'd read about himself in a conversation book. Schotts however had agreed to take it for 80 ducats, to be paid in two equal instalments.

Schotts had accused him of having sold Galitzin's first, which they had just published, to Schlesinger. Karl had told him last year that Schlesinger was buying the rights to that from Schotts. 'They are afraid that, if they don't give it to him, he will pirate it.' Schlesinger wanted them all, for his complete edition. He had written to old Schlesinger in Berlin when the son in Paris hadn't answered. Now it seemed that the Paris office had been destroyed by fire. Schotts were paying him through Francks' banking-house: Fries, to whom he had dedicated the 7th, had gone to the wall in April.

It was one of those times in his life when he stood in great artistic trauma, the creation was so much more than he and came unenforcedly and quickly, its wrongs promptly, easily, righting themselves: as when he had written at Karlsbad.

Abruptly, vividly, he remembered what A had said about his music and religion. His sick body then had quivered with it. God to man and man to God. And yet he was inside it; he was whole. As close to God as he had been at Karlsbad. This part of his life was separate from all others; in this he was a whole man and more than himself. The effort contained no sense of effort. He felt sure of this before it was given. He was relaxed.

He kept coming to in it, coming to himself in it, or rather coming to it around him: like opening one's eyes in a carriage to the sight of a distant horizon of trees in a golden sunset.

It was a calm passion, a fire that glowed rather than flared; what struck him each time about this was the calmness. He lived in it rather than its living in him: and thus brought to life the child which he never contained.

Like every massive work of art, this had a special aura about it – but this one was warmer, relaxing, after the *Fuge*: where that one still scared him, this one for a day or so made him feel proud. He could not believe that he had made that, he knew he had made this, the thought made him want to fling out both arms and embrace his nearest neighbours, whomsoever fell to his embrace, man woman or child.

Over 600 pages of notes for this one! He marked the movements: 1, 2, 3, 4, 5, 6, 6.

... All those troubles with that ending, before he had hit on it ... and that 6th movement: for the troubled, for those in grief. Like having the hand of God stroking your head ...

He had thought of adding one more movement ...

Karl urged his uncle to make summer plans. Some watchmaker had taken out a 5-year patent for the discovery of mechanical wheeled shoes 'with which one would be able to negotiate even the most traffic-bound streets without great effort and faster than with skates on ice.' Holz had been joking in February, 'We don't need a carriage any more to get to Baden: there are *speedy shoes!*'

Schindler was back on the scene, trying to get his uncle interested in some libretto by Kanne. Schindler resented Holz, Holz detested Schindler, both snubbed Johann; all three were united only in the glee with which they told tales to his uncle about him.

Karl had told his uncle, 'Johann always came to us to eat his fill, then he didn't have to buy anything for lunch, and he always had an appetite like a wolf.' At the time of the quartet rehearsals, Holz had deliberately stood Johann up: 'I gave him a rendezvous at a place where I didn't care to venture; perhaps he's sitting there still.'

They had looked further into exchanging B's bank-shares for lottery tickets. Holz and Johann had explained things fully; the logistics of this B still could not understand.

Karl it had been who in May had urged Beethoven to make peace with Holz. Beethoven seemed to blame Holz for the fact that Artaria had failed to bid for the new quartet, although he himself had only mentioned this in a postscript to the publisher; Artaria had thought the matter was not pressing. 'In the business with Artaria, Holz still took trouble; who knows why Artaria didn't answer at once? In other cases he also took pains to do your bidding. An invitation to him would give him the height of satisfaction; it may turn out for the best if we are together; it would also permit no idle talk with the servants.'

... Constant troubles with servants ... Frau S spying for him, exaggerating the lapses of Housekeeper Lindner; B wanting to beat her until Holz had warned that he could get into trouble with the police.

... 'The old bag is a rogue who should no longer stay with you. Recently she didn't want to admit the housekeeper. She turned her away with the words, "This is no service for you. The master and Holz equally turn you down."

'The old woman is a beast, Holz says. She will supplant everyone, and in the end she will be just about alone.'

The old bat was on her last legs anyhow. When not with B she seemed to spend half her time at St Mark's Hospital. 'People say that hospital should be turned into a barracks! The old dears who are there now would be allowed to die off, and then the barracks could be made out of it.'

He'd been round there one lunchtime when there had been no clean plates to eat off. One housekeeper had turned up with her slavering brood. 'Those children are very rude. The woman says to the small girl, leave the glass alone! The child gives the answer: no, don't leave the glass alone!' Then there had been the one with pretensions: Frau Elisabeth Passy, wife of a silk merchant. In 1817 he had gone bankrupt; he had got some sort of official position and his wife had gone into service. Johann had told B, 'You wrote a song in her album. This woman has fallen into poverty; speaks and writes French and Italian and is one of the best cooks in Vienna. Wolfmayer knows her very well.' She had seen his portrait by Deker in the lithographic institute; said Beethoven's quartets were her favourites. 'I asked the old wench how she liked her; she said she thought that she would not want to work and would almost allow herself to be served.' Karl had spoken French and Italian with her and told B that her French pronunciation was no better than her German spelling.

Frau Passy had been all over him. 'I'll care for you as though I were your own child ... My dear sir, *you* should not be left alone!' She hadn't wanted to sleep round there. She had lasted but a few days.

After that it had been the old woman, and another old woman who had had to care for a mother who was an even older woman. Karl had called her a *Canaille*. So pressed for a housekeeper had they been, Karl had even been urging his uncle to take Frau Schnaps!

And all the time it was: account for every kreuzer! He spent all his mornings in the college and all his lunch-hours doing addition! 'The old woman didn't deceive you; only now victuals are cheaper.' Explaining to B that certain things were cheaper in summer! 'It would have been my own preference so as to avoid all suspicion on your side if we could buy everything together, only it can't always be done in a hurry.'

He had wanted Holz back to deal with this lot! ... Holz back with his feet under the table, bragging about some mistake he had found in Schotts' edition of Galitzin's first ...

... 'Travel would be best; a short change of air, on the way to England,' he had been urging him at the turn of the year. 'You don't need to be a lord. Living there wouldn't cost you a kreuzer.' The old man had remained absorbed in his work, even standing up the Archduke in January. The Archduke was back in Vienna now; Beethoven was doing his best not to have to see him. 'Can I still get my pension if I go to England?'

Beethoven had learnt two words of English: *my dear*. Holz had taught

him how to pronounce it. Karl had told Niemetz, 'The next two words'll
be "How much?"' Niemetz had laughed. 'Regency rake!'

Now it was all talk of Ischl, a salt-bath 32 miles away, for his
rheumatism. Beethoven was already looking for larger rooms. Karl knew
growing fear that, when he left college, he would have to leave Schlemmer's and return to live with him. Karl told his friend in great distress, 'He
wants me living with him. After last autumn, I couldn't bear to live with
him again.' The thought of spending another winter with his uncle in that
flat reeking of *Opodeldok* . . . B had begun noting in his CB the deaths of
other composers, younger men: *Weber died in his 40th year.*

   . . . So *now*, at Schlemmer's, spied on and curtailed, was to be the acme
of his freedom! Those two silly interfering bastards, *Beste* and Holz, had
even planned to set a sleuth-hound on him! As if he hadn't grown up in
Vienna, where under Metternich every flannel-foot had his own sleuth!
He had once even joked about it to Niemetz, that time when their
servant's bastard had been born: 'Just think, somewhere in this city
there's this woman gazing fondly down at her new-born: "What is he
going to be when he grows up?" He's going to be Metternich's *flannel-foot!*'

His own mother was again a bone of contention. In April Beethoven
had lashed at him, 'Mercenary little sod, aren't you? No, don't go to your
mother when she's poor, don't go to your *mother* when she's got *nothing to
give you!*'

Breuning had asked, 'Has Karl no fortune at all from his father?'

Yes. He had had 2,000 fl. invested in his father's house for which his
mother had given B half her pension in return for the usufruct, and now *he*
had given her full pension back to her! He had wanted to yell at his uncle:
It's my money you're giving away – giving back to her! Why shouldn't I
have some of my own money? *My* money, from *my father!*

Holz had been telling B that if he could sort out her debts now, he need
have no future contact with her. Despite having pledged the whole of this
year's pension to B, she had been asking for Karl's half of the pension, as
before, to use as some sort of surety. Holz had written, 'Supposing she now
were also to have the chitty from Karl, wouldn't the trouble be still worse?
I certainly think so. There are so many usurers who simply lend money on
such mortgages at inhuman rates of interest, she'd find herself in an even
greater mountain of debt.'

Johann had declared that for as long as he'd known Johanna she had
been in debt. The bell-founder, Hofbauer, had told Johann that he had
paid her debts and that she had cost him 30,000 fl.

B seemed to have asked Holz why Johanna had not married Hofbauer.
'If she marries she loses the pension.'

In June, when Karl had briefly mentioned something about his
mother's finances, Beethoven had hit the roof.

'So you've been seeing her!'

'It's only to speak about the pension.'

In his usual manner B had let it drop, until suddenly, when he had been joking about Johann 'living in the country on 24 kreuzer a day!' B had started in again. He had upbraided his uncle, 'I am not a child.'

At their next meeting, telling him that he had a great deal to do because it would soon be the exams, Beethoven had come down on him again, 'Yes, you've no time for me now, it's all your mother!'

The suddenness of his outburst had shaken Karl. He had been joking again about Johann's meanness: 'Your brother would have liked to see the menagerie but it was too expensive for him ... He got hold of an old carriage somewhere which he has so restored that it almost looks like new ... He's still got the apothecary ... These empty earthenware pots we must send to the brother ...'

Several days later, he had written for his uncle, 'I hardly wanted to tell you the following, but it's important so that you can get to know his spirit. The last time Johann was here, he began as soon as he spoke with me to refer to the mother; he said it really saddens me that she is in such poor circumstances, my brother should give her something!!'

He had told his uncle, 'If we go to his place, we might have to go out to eat all the time so as to assuage our hunger!'

The examinations were looming. In mid-June Karl had asked his uncle, 'In case I should not go into a counting-house, could I take other subjects: physics, chemistry?'

'Yes, Johann was right about you: you will go on living off me *for ever*! What is it with you? Don't you want to go out into the world? O, I see: you haven't studied; you think you're going to fail in the coming exams.' Now the boy was saying that he regularly met his schoolfellows in the evening so that they could go through their homework together; that he must cut short his visits at lunch-time since 'the crammer will come from 2-3 because he is busy in the mornings. That suits me.'

There had been a vile row one Sunday at the end of June. Holz had been there, ill with rheumatic fever, so embarrassed that he'd had to leave, although he had used his illness as his excuse. Holz had been questioned by B, in front of him, as though he had not been there, in the third person: 'Well is he going to fail? Hasn't he studied?' Holz had restricted himself to, 'He has only begun to study properly lately.'

The receipt for the 80 florins rent which had been paid in May had gone missing. Karl was certain that he had given it to his uncle and that it would turn up. Beethoven suspected that the boy had purloined the money for nefarious purposes. Karl told his uncle, 'You know the times when I'm at home. You know what I'm doing all the time in detail. If I go to my fellow-pupils it is not so that they might join me in cribbing but rather that we study jointly. I've already told you the reason many times over.'

Beethoven was shouting that Johann had complained, 'Karl's not doing much to help his mother!' Karl wrote whilst he was being howled

at, 'Your brother is a wretched fellow who might afford more easily than I
. . . To be able to complain about me can therefore be no authority . . . My
innocence I can prove if it comes to the point. But I hardly thought that
this conversation could have got to this stage.'

There had even been the hare-brained scheme of putting on a concert
to help Johanna. 'I don't think that a concert publicized under the
announcement, "For the benefit of a distressed widow," would find more
approval than if you announced it for your own benefit.'

His uncle had asked him how he did spend money. 'When I go out for a
walk and have a drink and the like. I don't have any other expenses.'
Beethoven had visited him at Schlemmer's, cross-questioning him about
the rent receipt, berating him for insolence.

'You consider it insolence if, after you have upbraided me for hours
undeservedly, this time at least I can't switch from a feeling of bitter pain
into jocularity. I am not as frivolous as you think. I can assure you that,
since the scene on Sunday in the presence of that fellow, I have been so
depressed that people in the house have noticed it. The receipt for the 80
florins which were paid in May I now positively know, after a search, that
I already gave you, as I said on Sunday; it must and no doubt will be
found.'

'It's insolence the way you sit there, head in your books, when I'm
talking to you!'

'If I continue to work while you are here it is not in a spirit of insolence
but because I believe that you will not be offended if I do not permit your
presence to keep me from my labours, which are now really piling up, all
the more since we see each other *here*. You are mistaken, too, when you
think that I wait for your coming to become *industrious*. You also seem to
accept as *my views* what I repeat to you as the opionions of *others*, such as
the twaddle of Frau Passy. . . . I hope that what I have said will serve to
convince you of my real views and feelings, and put an end to the strain
which of late has existed between us, though not on my side by any
means.'

Karl had pawned his watch, telling his uncle it needed repair and
gambling the money given to him for this purpose. His luck had been in;
he had had a watch to show the old fool when he had started getting
suspicious about it.

Some of Beethoven's friends were saying that they had seen Karl
gambling dishonestly with shady characters in disreputable coffee-houses.
Beethoven had taken to walking Karl back to the Polytechnic after lunch,
arm-in-arm. He enquired about him every day from Reisser. 'He tells me
you have to book him in and out every day. Your job – to see you do it!
You are his *co-guardian!*'

Beethoven was now receiving regular reports from Schlemmer, some of
which he noted in his CB. 'One night in the Prater. Two nights did not
sleep at home.'

Karl had begun trying to flee the constraints of Beethoven and Holz.

. . . 'Having to put up with my brother coming to me, "The nephew is gambling again." His words to me were, "He's no more successful at that than his mother has been at hawking herself in the street."'

Karl's debts were getting worse. He was out gambling most nights trying to recoup his losses, but lost more. He stole some of Beethoven's books and sold them.

'Now he's talking about not going into a counting-house!' Beethoven had exploded to Holz on that fateful Sunday. 'Well what do you want to do if you're not going into a counting-house?' Beethoven accosted Karl with blazing eyes.

'You know what I want to be.'

'What's that?'

'Soldier.'

'You are not going to be a dirty little soldier boy! . . . O I see, that's it, free women, you just think soldiers have free women – that's it, eh, eh, isn't it, that's it! You'll end up diseased, you'll be no good to yourself, no good to anyone. Who's put this into your head? Your mother? O no, I see, her paramour, your young schoolfriend, that young friend of yours, Niemetz . . .'

Karl looked at him in disgust. Beethoven salivated when he got this worked up: like a drunkard, like a mad dog. Always now Karl stood his ground, the turmoil tight, controlled within him: gazing steadfastly at his uncle in icy hatred, pure contempt.

'Don't you stand and look at me like that, you little devil! Answer me when I talk to you! Write something down!'

The boy's gaze said: what can I say? You're deaf.

'I might be deaf. I'm still your guardian. You're still under my control. I might be old and ill, infirm. Wasn't that a victory, eh? They said I couldn't have control of you: law forbids it, he's infirm. Infirm or not, I got control. I control *you*, so don't think *you* can be a soldier! Over my dead body! You young whippersnapper, you pipsqueak . . . !'

The *you, you* had been accompanied by pokes to the chest.

Holz came in as Karl clutched his uncle by the lapel, one hand reaching for his throat.

Karl fled the room ablaze with fury. O yes, he wanted to be a soldier: do his own bullying! Clap his own people in irons!

. . . Not like old Constantine! Alexander had died in the Crimea, miles from anywhere. Constantine had been in Poland. Alexander had left sealed papers in Moscow; only when these were opened did people realize what was happening. Constantine had not wanted to be Czar, but this had not been revealed to the troops in Petersburg. The troops, having heard that Constantine had been locked in a dungeon, had rallied to the cry, 'Long live Constantine and Constitution!' believing *Constitution* to be

Constantine's wife. And now 5 of the Decembrists sentenced to death had been hanged . . .

. . . 'If only because you have at any rate obeyed me, all is forgiven,' Beethoven had written after one of their earlier rows. 'Do not take any step which would make *you* unhappy and put an early end to *my* life. – I did not get to sleep until 3 o'clock, for I was coughing the whole night . . .'

In fine weather especially, when he had the window open, Karl could hear Beethoven coming from the sound of his hawking and spitting in the street. He realized B could not hear this. He hated feeling compassion for the man.

The postscript had read, 'We shall be alone, for I am not letting Holz come, the more so as I should not like anything of what happened yesterday to leak out. Do come – don't let my poor heart *bleed any longer*.'

What about my poor heart, Karl thought. What about my poor life.

. . . When he did give him a present, it was usually a book, inscribed with such elevating promptings as 'to encourage the emulation of the highest human virtues.' He's always trying to make me *better* – better than he is, even, better than *he* could ever be – he even admits that! *Emulate my virtues but not my faults.*

. . . The terrible vulnerability about him, and the defensiveness that could not bring itself to let itself be punctured, even by love. It shone off him so that even men as well as women noticed; his anger at this and his long-standing total deafness had made him a recluse. If only there were not that about the man that cried out to be consoled and that found itself inconsolable. Standing with one hand to his neck, about to throttle him, the man's weakness had startled him: *my God, he is a little goat!*

. . . Coming upon B at work. The bespectacled face that peered out from the shoulder-length grey hair, hunched over the once-massive shoulders, wore a look that bespoke all the pain of the suspicion caused by his deafness, yet at the same time paradoxically an open pleading that could best be defined as trust – trust somewhat wary of having its faith misplaced . . . yes, that was it, a sort of aggressive trust. The rheumatic, colourless eyes peering over the glasses made him think of Caspar, but, whereas the cat's blue eyes resembled those of a man blind with glaucoma, his uncle's upward glance was questioning, piercing, eager for any sign of response in his listener's face. Frau Streicher had exclaimed during B's eye infection, 'That poor man – he can't hear and he can't see!'

He hated having people near him when he was working. He could grow irritable as hell at the sight of movement of another person anywhere in his rooms. He hated to come out of work and see someone there, or be aware whilst working of their presence: his thought-processes missed a beat. At other times he hated having people in the house when he was in the middle of work. 'I am still *in it*! Just because you do not see me with a quill in my hand doesn't mean to say *I'm not working*!'

. . . 'Dear God, control my tongue or I'll say something I'll regret!' Karl had heard him once explode. 'O if only I were not deaf – I should live alone, with no son and no servants!'

When the first reviews had appeared of the quartet *Fuge*, Karl had had to mollify and lavish praise upon him.

'There is so much evidence that people treasure and admire your work. This should have set you free long since of any particular anxiety. . . . But I do know that these minor composers are dreadfully angry that such a thing has not occurred to them. . . . It is already quite well understood. It was thus for other great men, for example with the great Cortez, one of the greatest men who have lived or will live. He still had his enemies too, even on account of the fact that he was a great man. . . . Even that must increase your fame. Everyone is amazed not simply that you write so but that you write so despite such misfortune. I believe that even that contributes a lot to the originality which rules in all your work.'

He had gone on to praise B's lack of derivation. Beethoven had angrily grieved over this review:

> The first, third and fifth movements are solemn, sombre, mystical, sometimes bizarre, abrupt, capricious; the second and fourth are full of playfulness, cheerfulness and fun; in these the great composer who, particularly in his most recent works, seldom knew how to find a measured goal, has expressed himself with unwonted brevity and conclusiveness. A storm of applause greeted both movements and encores were demanded.
>
> But the sense of the fugal finale escaped your reviewer entirely: it was incomprehensible, Chinese. If the musicians struggle with vast difficulties in the regions of the South and the North Poles, if each one plays a different figure, irregularly crossing over under an immense number of dissonances; if the players, each mistrusting himself, have an incomplete grasp of the whole, then there exists a Babylonian confusion; then you have a concert which at all events would be a source of delight only to the Moroccans who are here for the Italian opera: and their only pleasure would lie in the arrangement of the instruments in bare fifths and the universal tuning up in all the keys.
>
> Perhaps so much might not have been attempted in the one composition had the master been able to hear his own work. But still, we would not presume to deny its worth precipitously. Perhaps the time may yet come when that which at first sight appears clouded and muddled will be recognized as clear and delightfully formed.

. . . The *sense of objection* in that first fugue, the *power* . . . Towards the end: they're wiping the floor with it, they're *trying* – if you don't wipe the floor with this, it'll wipe the floor with you. This is a *fight!*

Another string quartet by Beethoven, this time with the accompaniment of 4 voices, the *Elegischer Gesang* written twelve years earlier for the third anniversary of the death in childbirth of his friend Pasqualati's wife at the age of twenty-four, had been published in July by Haslinger. A quiet, gentle, moving piece, overlaid with the solemnity of church music.

Gently you lived,
Gently achieved your end.

Here am I doing all this despite my infirmities and there are you, a vulgar man, who, on his second chosen course, cannot even pass an exam.

Beethoven was overheard in the street muttering out loud, 'Now *here's* the prodigal son!' As Karl had gripped his lapel and he had struggled to pull him off, he had been vividly surprised by how big the boy had grown: he had expected to find in his grasp a child's limbs, yet the arms that he gripped were thicker than a woman's. He had felt the muscles tense as the boy's grip tightened upon his coat. The next thing he knew, the boy had lifted him off the ground. The strained face into which he stared was shouting with venom, its neck tendons bulging and eyes fierce with hatred. The suppressed no behind the yes, the yes behind the no, screaming out its truth more forcefully than the spoken word.

Already I have suffered much and endured many toils on the waves and in war. . . . Brutus was a hater of tyranny and had a brave and beloved wife who was worthy of him. He also of course killed the man who by reputation was his 'father'. . . . 'At this time he had not fully decided on war or peace, but on one thing he was determined: not to be a slave.'

In the sun, eating cherries, he recalled hanging these over A's ears.

Lying on his back in the sun, the thought had come to him, I was a bastard to her. I didn't want to stay away. I thought I was doing right.

He could not now bring himself properly to think of Karl, though sometimes the thought came to him unbidden.

Instead he took each crumb of comfort they offered him as gospel truth and responded to it on that level, refusing to read beneath the surface. He knew he did this and saw his weakness but felt incapable of acting otherwise, even as he denounced himself.

. . . I did not want ever to hurt her. What you wanted and what you did are, as ever, two different things. It was always like that. Always. Except in music. He turned onto his belly, took up his pad and wrote.

He had already begun sketching the new quartet for Schlesinger before he had finished that in 7 movements for Schotts. The postlude that he had planned to follow that seventh movement he would turn into the slow movement of this one.

Zmeskall had once said to him, 'There are people who have lives like yours and don't have the music. Be grateful.' He had wanted to reply, I know that.

Sometimes he saw what Zmeskall meant, sometimes rebelled strongly: that *is not so*!

Sometimes he was stabbed to the heart by the realization that he did have a sick son, aged about 12 now, who knew nothing of his own burning love during those first few years and whom he had never seen.

Karl had sought Niemetz after the fight with his uncle, having seen little of him in the preceding months. Niemetz had said, 'Why don't you come and see me any more at your mother's?'

'If I go round there again I shall end up screwing my own little sister!' Karl exploded now to Niemetz, 'Free women, free women, why should I want to join the army to get free women, he's always telling me Vienna's full of loose women! "Have you got a girlfriend? Have you been impure?" Dirty old bastard. He wants to mind his own business. And all the time it's, "Oh, my morals are too high for you, my life-style is too *pure* for Master Karl!" If he tells me once more his way of life is too pure for me God help me I'll strangle him, I shall take his head and thrust it between his fucking piano-strings . . .'

Niemetz laughed.

Karl stayed the night with Niemetz at his friend's home, talking about the fight.

'No doubt this'll get reported as well to the old fool. "He wasn't at his home last night!"'

'What would you have done? If Holz had not arrived. Would you really have killed him?'

Even as his heated complaints of B were blurted out to Niemetz, Karl suffered guilt at the recollection of what his uncle had done for him; the doors that would now be closed had he had no education, doors which he, with his youth and strength, had felt that he could stride through with one bound, success certain. . . . B in expansive mood, speaking of how he often wrote in the dark: 'O, more than once I've written on the pillow!' . . . That *tiny* man he had held by the neck: shameful to have an adversary so fragile! Could he but disentangle the *tyrant* of genius, with the tyrant's pride, from the poor little goat who wrote through the night, his glasses sliding down his nose. 'I suppose these just about serve to hang my spectacles on.' *All for you, boy*! It wasn't, of course. Beethoven composed for Beethoven. Beethoven could no more live without composition were he the sole man on earth than he could live without air and water. But sacrifices had been made for him, struggles had been fought. Had he lived with his mother, he would not have met men like Schlesinger and Falstaff, whose friendship he valued. His mother could not have afforded to give him an education. He baulked at the thought of living with Johann: all of his other uncle's faults without the justification of the music. *If only my father had not died*!

Karl found himself telling Niemetz of the first summer he had been with B, when they had encountered the deaf cat who looked like Caspar. 'The cat is deaf,' Karl had said to him through his ear-trumpet. B had solemnly removed the ear-trumpet and placed it beside the cat's ear.

'I'm a man; I have my feelings.'

Niemetz agreed. 'The poor bastard's deaf . . .'

Karl's thoughts were elsewhere. He had heard his uncle once in the night, from the next room, crying; in the dark he had thought he had made out, '*Karl*, Karl!'

Niemetz had asked, 'Do you really want to be a soldier?' 'After living with him it would be like freedom!' Breuning when they met was sympathetic. 'I think you do need to get away from him. For both your sakes.'

Breuning had had Beethoven storming to him, 'The boy wants to be a soldier! Hardest blow of my life. My son. Me! *A soldier*! Wants to go round killing people. As if I didn't see enough of my friends killed and wounded in the last lot. He just wants to play pool and pursue women. That's all *he* thinks being a soldier is.'

Karl too recalled Beethoven's saying, 'If you'd seen as many upheavals and wars in your lifetime, laddie, you'd not be so eager to rush off to war.'

'He's trying to live my life for me.'

'Yes, I know he . . .'

'Not only this, it's in all ways . . .' Karl found relief in talking to Breuning. 'He'll say I'm no good if I fail these exams but he won't let me do what I want to do, where I *know* I could do well . . .'

Holz was almost convinced that what he had thought he had heard Beethoven tell him, when they had been drunk, at the time he had been writing the *Fuge*, had been the truth. By allowing the boy no money, no life outside of his own and no freedom, Beethoven was, Holz saw, building a rod for his own back – but his inability fully to separate Karl the nephew from Karl Josef, to see him as a man and not a boy, his conviction that Karl had the advantages of health, intelligence, looks, and he must use them, above all his conviction that he must seek his propitiation by bringing Karl up to be a good man to make up for his failure to fulfil any part of his duty to Karl Josef, appeared to Holz, himself now seriously in love for the first time, to be what lay behind this obsessive possession. Beethoven would not discuss it with him and he was certain that Karl did not know.

Karl had had his hand about Beethoven's neck when he'd arrived. Holz had pulled him off. 'He's an old man! You'll kill him!' Many men were shocked when they saw Beethoven for the first time. *This* the embodiment of all that music . . . that veritable furnace of reported fury? In the flesh he looked quite small; since his illnesses, had seemed even more to be shrinking. The famous head, so big in pictures, itself seemed shrunken, the features far less imposing. Seeing Karl at the man's throat, Holz had felt minded of the first time he had met the composer: standing with an ordinary-looking, small old man, perhaps too close to death for comfort, whom he himself was dwarfing.

'How dare you lay hands on him!' Holz said to Karl despite himself when they next met. 'He's not only the greatest composer you'll ever know, he's also the greatest man!'

'Why is he a great man? I know he's a great composer . . . Why is he a great man?'

Holz floundered, still forceful, ' . . . Your mother! It's not only you . . . That man's looked after her! He doesn't bear grudges!'

Holz tried to calm down. 'He deserves better of you. He works his balls off for you.'

Karl laughed, surprised. Holz laughed too. 'It's what he said to me: "I work my balls off for him!"'

'He enjoys it.'

'"Every gulden I earn is for my Karl's education."'

'I'm not his Karl . . .'

'"I'm getting all the hardships of bringing up Karl and none of the joys!"'

'What joys does he expect?'

'He wants you to love him.'

'His love is exclusive – he wants me to love him and no one else! Love him, be grateful to him – everyone's always so busy telling me to be these things I don't know how I do feel about him! If you'd all leave me alone I might at least *like him*. . . . There's no *fun* with him, there's no levity, everything is so *intense*. I'm *nineteen*! I can't live like that! "I don't want to have expended all this effort to have put an ordinary man into the world!" Well how does he think *I* feel – he had high hopes of me, now he thinks I'm rotten.'

'Listen, boy, he dotes on you. Do you really not love him?'

'I have to. Don't I! Whether *I* want to or not. *I* have *to*!'

The family resemblance was striking. Karl in a Beethovenian rage, made more feverish, more ferocious by control. Holz thought, good God, you even look like him.

'. . . Love me! I don't think he's ever *seen* me! To love someone you have to see them! – He doesn't love me, he's in love with the idea of me. I wish he had married. I wish he had had his own child. Poor bastard – what miseries *that* would have gone through!'

Karl sat at his books that night but could not work. During the winter months of ice and snow, he himself had got earache. It had been agony; he had been scared; Schlemmer had helped him, having his wife prepare his own special diet, giving him a book to read on the subject. Karl had seen Beethoven at the time of the *Fuge's* failure make up the fire and kneel staring into it, his gargoyle face beautified by grief.

When he had first moved in with Beethoven, Johann had urged them to beat the chambermaid.

'Your brother said it would certainly help if you beat her a little.

'–Anyway nothing else helps.

'—Nothing will happen to us, for she will not defend herself strongly against the two of us.

'—I am not afraid for myself.

'—You are just as punishable as a criminal.

'—If only no one comes to help her.'

Beethoven had written frigidly to Karl asking him to attend to write letters. Holz walked in to hear Beethoven exclaim, 'Now the kid's talking of topping himself!'

'I wish we were in England. I'd run away to sea. I'd kill myself.'

Karl drew a finger across his throat.

'Kill yourself! Kill yourself! What do you mean, you'd kill yourself! Silly young brat! Reading too much Goethe! Won't study, can't do his exams, so *he* says he'll kill himself!'

'Exams!' Karl exclaimed, laughing. 'That's all he can think of – all it could be! Exams! *You* -' turning on Holz, 'are as bad as he is, spying on me, having me followed, setting a *flannel-foot*! No life of your own Karl! O no! *You* mustn't live! Stop me at every turn, watch me, spy on me, and all *he* can think of is *exams*!'

Beethoven was muttering to himself over his sketchbook, 'Prodigal son, prodigal son. Anyway I don't need you. I have another son. She's right: where there's life, there's hope.'

Reisser's condemnation of Beethoven's too-frequent enquiries had made matters worse. Beethoven linked the boy's arm as though he were his bride; only Karl could sense the violence with which he held him. 'Well what am I to do if you say you will top yourself?' Karl always detested being seen with B: the spitting; the laughable dress, B's coat pulled down one side by the sketchbook, the other by the conversation book; the uncombed hair on end, cheeks and chin a black stubble, from which proceeded the voice that roared should B want to do no more than order a pound of cherries; the miming and gestures of others should B meet a friend. He imagined some of the sordid mimickings, kept from him, that had gone on during his boyhood when that filthy Peters had been there. . . . Writing to the *Magistrat*, 'Herr Peters is a fine man.' He had been made co-guardian! Just because he let you screw his wife!

Holz was right about the women of Vienna. Devils. Avaricious, mercenary sluts. Mercenary and mendacious. Karl became fearful. If he couldn't attract love and loyalty now, when he was, people told him, not without good looks, and personable, what hope had *he*, when he grew to be B's age?

He hated approaching the Polytechnic, where his fellow-students might see B holding him like this. Karl tried to free his arm. 'No you don't.' Beethoven gripped him tighter.

Street-boys jeered as they passed. One boy yelled out, 'Who's your girlfriend?'

Karl wrenched free of his uncle's grip and fled.

The streets of the inner city were so narrow that, despite the flat stones laid along the sides for walkers, pedestrians must often leap out of the way of converging carriages. Coachmen roared of their approach. Unable to hear, Beethoven would be cursed, dragged to safety by passersby, or, at times, feel the carriage whisk by close enough to skim his hair.

Beethoven had fallen when Karl had thrown him off. Returning through the city centre in desolate grief he was again knocked to the ground, his stick spun out of his hand by a carriage.

People were gathering round him, thinking he had been killed.

Karl strode back towards the *Alservorstadt*, trembling with passion. He would get into trouble for that too. He had already been told off for not wanting to walk with B. 'You'll hurt his feelings.' Gerhard, Breuning's twelve-year-old son, would go smarming round, 'O, I love walking with Uncle Ludwig!'

Karl stood before his father's house.

Percy's coat glistened as he pecked behind the hedge. The white hen had got egg-bound and died, but the dull brown hen, Jezebel, had proved to be a good layer. The middle-aged woman had gone into hospital, though the man, who had now got a source of supply from his cousin, still delivered eggs from time to time.

A black cat screamed and sped past him, its fur all pulled: torn locks stuck out at either side. Caspar had trotted up to Karl. Karl watched the cat rolling upon the cobbles, banging its head. Clumps of black fur blew all over the garden, stuck to the hedges, across the grass. Karl stroked the wild, unpredictable white lion, gazing across his old garden with tears in his eyes.

Chapter 15

Early August

'The story in brief,' wrote Schlemmer, 'since you have heard it already from Herr Holz: I learned today that your nephew intended to shoot himself before next Sunday. As to the cause, I learned only this much: that it was on account of his debts, but not completely; only in part was he admitting that they were the consequences of former sins.

'I looked to see if there were signs of preparations. I found in his chest a loaded pistol, together with bullets and powder. I'm telling you this so that you may act as his father. The pistol is in my keeping.'

'The boy must be found!' Beethoven cried.

'Be lenient with him or he will despair.'

Holz questioned Schlemmer regarding the rent.

'I have been paid completely – up to July, but not yet for August.'

Holz left for the Polytechnic to find Karl. He returned to report to Beethoven at Schlemmer's, 'He will not stay here. I could not detain him; he said he would return to Schlemmer's, but he wanted to get his papers from a friend. Meanwhile I talked with Reisser. I said that I couldn't wait more than a quarter of an hour.'

'You had him with you then you let him go!'

'He would have run away from you just the same. I think that if he's made up his mind to harm himself, no one can stop him.'

Beethoven's first reaction had been, 'What's going to happen about his exams!' Holz had written for him then, in exasperation, 'He certainly will not take the exams.' Now he replied to Schlemmer's enquiries, 'He has till September 3rd to make up his examination.'

Holz sat on the floor at Schlemmer's, searching through Karl's papers. He found the residue of Schlemmer's board – a mere 30 kreuzer. 'Karl said to me, "What good will it do you if you detain me? If I don't escape today, I will another time."'

Schlemmer wrote for Beethoven, 'I will unload the gun. My wife has the second pistol.'

Beethoven wrote in fear, 'He will drown himself.'

Schlemmer showed him the gun: charged with powder and ball to above the middle.

Karl went to a pawnbroker and pawned his watch. He bought two new pistols, powder and balls. He caught the coach to Baden where he spent that night, a Saturday, writing a letter to his uncle which he enclosed in one to Niemetz.

On Sunday the 6th he took his pistols and climbed up to the ruins of *Rauhenstein* by the *Helenenthal* valley. Turning, he saw the stream, the rocks, the waterfall, the tall trees in the valley. One of the large smoothed rocks over which the stream tumbled looked like a seal.

He picked up his first pistol, checking to see that the ball and powder had stayed intact. . . . *Constantine and Constitution!* And what was his rallying cry to be? Probably Carl and Caspar.

He pulled the trigger. Nothing happened. He lowered the pistol to have a look and as he did so the bullet splattered the ground by his foot.

He had nearly shot his foot off!

You stupid prat!

He remembered: *first pressure!*

You didn't even need to have it to your head to get to first pressure; all that mattered was that you put it to your head without jolting it when you had . . .

A teamster came across him upon the rock where he had fallen, blood flowing from his head.

Karl was carried to his mother's lodgings in central Vienna. He was lying on his sister's bed when Beethoven arrived with Holz.

Karl wrote, 'It is done. Now, only a surgeon who can hold his tongue. Smetana, if he is here.'

The trembling man sat down beside him. 'Don't plague me with reproaches and lamentations,' Karl wrote, 'it is done. Everything can be sorted out later.'

Beethoven looked around him. His eye fell on Johanna. 'Why haven't you got him a doctor!'

'She's sent for a doctor, but he is not at home. Holz will soon bring another.'

Karl turned away in exhaustion, crying out at the movement of his head.

Beethoven asked Johanna, 'When did it happen?'

Johanna wrote, 'He has just come. The teamster carried him down from a rock in Baden and has just driven out to you. . . . I beg of you to tell the surgeon not to make a report or they will take him away from here at once, and we fear the worst. There is a bullet in his head on the left side.'

Beethoven wrote swiftly to Smetana, 'A great misfortune has happened, which Karl has accidentally inflicted upon himself. I hope that he can still be saved, especially by you if you come quickly. Karl has a *bullet* in his head; how, you shall learn – But quick, for God's sake, quick!'

Smetana had performed Karl's hernia operation almost a decade ago. Holz took up the note to Smetana, but before he could leave the surgeon summoned by Johanna had arrived. Holz left anyway, returning with the message that Dögl was a capable practitioner and Smetana would not come unless Dögl requested a consultation. The doctor wanted the room cleared. Beethoven returned alone to the *Schwarzspanierhaus*. Holz remained to hear Johanna's pleadings that the incident be not reported to the police.

'The police have to know. If we try to hide this we'll all be in trouble.'

Holz took it upon himself to report the incident.

He advised Beethoven that, if he recovered, Karl would be subjected to a severe reprimand and thereafter police surveillance.

Beethoven wanted to return. Holz stopped him. 'Blast that doctor! Who does he think he is, forbidding me!'

Holz told him that it had been Karl who had said, '"If only he would not show himself again!" and "If only he would quit his reproaches!"' Karl had threatened to tear the bandages from his skull should another word be said to him about his uncle.

. . . A at Karlsbad, Franzensbad . . . at Prague, telling him, '*Ludwig, I'm having your baby.*' All her love and warmth for him then . . . in Vienna . . . and since, in 1816, when she had thought he was suicidal, her cheering letter the day he had first won custody of Karl. The shirt she had made. He had worn it in court; standing up proudly to give the firm handshake, resolved to his task: *I shall be a good father to Karl.* . . . The letter with the shirt, 'Karl is a beautiful baby' . . . thanking him for Karl. Her grief, his grief, in 1817. He had been like a dying animal, on its belly, crawling on the floor, sobbing under the table, barely able to lift himself to walk into that church to pray to that God who paid no heed, '*Grant help to my son!*' The desperate prayer, through Christ, through Mary, through Toni, as he bent crippled before the icon, praying through a Christ in whom he could not believe before an icon in whom he did not believe, the Virgin with the child in her arms, uttering his most urgent pleas according to the words on the stand before his blinded eyes, adding as intercessor Toni, that his prayer be made valid by her belief. The incessant tears and pain and weakness, all outside of his control, the incessant God, His existence more real to him than his own. The God who watched and made no move. He had made a move: had sent the woman with black bread, day after day, to keep him alive: black bread which, with his belly, he could not eat. One human contact daily. The gat-toothed woman holding out the conical loaf in her oustretched hands.

Cuddling it, like a baby, under the table, keening with it. The bread he had often left by the church for the poor. . . . Gave me bread that I must go out to the church, to pray again to God. Who made no move. Save to send me, the next day, more black bread. 'My son is baker. Is free. Take, take.' She had been Polish. Tool of the living God.

. . . 1819, writing to Sailer for him, trying to get that . . . kid! into Sailer's. Trying to help him *educate* the boy, when his mother had gone to court and had taken away his guardianship. Trying to help him, when she herself had been suffering.

. . . The suffering of 1820 . . . doctor after doctor . . . 1821, going to Gall, to Paris with the boy. The boy undergoing all that treatment, when all *he'd* done was write piano sonatas for them. '*Will you permit Gall to burn his loins?*' ... Piano sonatas ... Op 109, for Maxe. Op 110 and 111 for her. Bungling publishers! She hadn't even *got* those! ... 1823, the *Diabelli*, he had finally got *that* to her – when the boy had had all that treatment and none of it had worked.

... And all the time, the parallel scenario, when he had been made non-guardian and then perhaps co-guardian, in 1819, and then when Johanna and *Nussböck* had been *his* guardian: nothing for me here ... go to Frankfurt ... marry a servant ... start pumping kids. All those years, his desire to be with her, 1816, be with her, give her a daughter. Ha! 1816: that lust, that pining, that longing, that urge! Ha! – Like being a monk! No one had any *idea* of those years! *No one!* Just because I'm not with her, do you think that means that I don't want to go, that I don't, for every second, think of, being with her, *every second*! Her love *for me*, my love *for her*, all of it, all that warmth from her *to me*, relinquished, I could have had, all my ... great, over-flowing, *good* love, fruitful, *for her*. All of that, relinquished, never-stopping, relinquished. Given up for *that kid* who now *repays me* by going out and trying to *top himself*!

They have no idea! Of any of it! *He* hasn't! Just because Karl turned out the way he did, do you think that *stopped it*? Stopped my love, my need, my greed, to be with her, to give her more, to give my love to *him*?

... I gave my love to him instead and, O God, the boy's tried to kill himself!

He raised his tear-stained face to heaven, thumping the table that he knelt beside. 'That was my *propitiation*!' I tried to *make good*! You know! *You* know! I tried to bring him up instead, not to go there and break up that family, not to hurt those other children ... not to *break vows*!

I thought You sent him, to need me, I thought You meant me to be *his* father! You did! You did it! Why have You done this to me now? *Why?* ...

You haven't just hurt me, You've done this to her and them and *all of them*, Toni and Karl and all those children, Franz ... You stand there and mock us ... try to do right ... follow Your way, give up our own inclinations, put others first, follow Your path, not ours. Thy will be done, Thy will, not ours, try to comply, You turn, sneer at us, yes, like You are doing now, look at You, sneer at us, as though we're rag dolls, gutless puppets. We're men! Trying to live by Your Word! I tried to do right, what I thought You wanted, I didn't take the Primrose Path, God knows, *You* know, how much I wanted! '*Ha!*' He cried out, as he had once cried out in thought to Johanna, 'Why have You stopped *my propitiation*!'

He rose from the floor. Now there is no point in any of it. Now.

... Why did he do it? Who led him to do it? Who's behind this, that's led to so much pain for *so many*? His blazing eyes sought for the cause. Niemetz? Johanna? Niemetz, one of his friends? *Johanna*! O I'll lay the blame for this, I'll lay the blame! I am not guilty here! I am *not guilty*!

I pulled out every one of the stops I could ever think of, I did everything

I could to make this right, I have given up . . . *everything* . . . all along the line . . . *always*. I have not done wrong here! At *every step*, I put *truth* and *justice* first here, gave up my own will, time after time. I lived against my own desires, all the time here, for *years*. *All the time*. I put God's will first. I did not slack or linger. I did *not* break.

. . . If this is God's will too, then here's another heavy burden: find out the cause. I've still that boy to save.

He felt invigorated and yet old, the flame of his energetic desire at this moment to go out and sort this out and get to the bottom of it and still bring the boy home safe and sound not hiding from him his own infirm and aged self, that self who thought it had fought its battles and by now was nearing the end of the road, wanting no more than its pipe and its slippers and its music, watching the boy he thought he had almost got there taking over his own development any time now.

O! He'd thought he had done it, nearly done it!

This is how Franz felt in 1812. This is how you made *that* man feel then.

He raised himself out of the chair by his desk where he'd been sitting. Franz pulled himself up then and I must now.

He wanted to write to the man he had offended.

He slumped afresh as he saw himself through Karl's eyes. . . . 'The world would treat you like a god in England.' . . . '*Get him out of here!*'

He looked at his desk, his gaze falling upon music. The eyes of the world: the great hero. Not a musician alive, or probably before, or even in the future, who wouldn't like to string my guts out across this table in envy. And how does . . . Never mind that, Beethoven. How does God see me? And what must I do for him? What to do now for the boy?

. . . *I allowed that treatment on him and what good did* that *do?*

Poor Toni. Poor Toni. He wept for Toni's grief.

A younger man can suffer more easily, can go to women, can drink, can even pray more easily. He has hope. He may not even have suffered before: this may all be new to him.

But an old man has a ruined gut and a swollen belly, a weak, aged, face, he can't even trust his sex: can't trust his desire for sex not to let him down, or the girls not to giggle and mock behind his back that he should even approach them. An older man can drink but this aged belly plays up the sooner, upsets his liver, might even trigger a jaundice or a nose-bleed. An older man can pray but he knows God's dark side.

The only light side You've let me see of You for a long time has been in *my music*!

Never mind that. Never mind that. Man must go on. All that matters is man's relationship to God. O! If that only meant *music*! It means man's relationship to man, and getting out there, and fighting, and trying not to let them down. God forgive me, Toni.

He recalled crying out to Countess Erdödy, 'My love *hurts* people!'

Get up. Go on. Go on. Out into the world, old man. Save that boy. Only, God help me, I don't know what to do.

The day after the shooting Karl was removed from his mother's and taken to hospital. Beethoven stood on the Ferdinand Bridge, gazing the length of the river. Grief like a physical pain weighed down his chest. He recalled Karl some years ago, he had been but 16, relating to him the story of some actor's suicide ... trying to get out of some contract with Palffy ... curtailing his contract, killing himself from shame. The boy had written then, 'Suicide is not such a frequent occurrence here as in Paris, where they play *faro* in the Palais Royale and, having gambled and lost everything, they only have to go up a flight of stairs where there is a man with pistols which they can hire with their last coppers.' To his disgust he recalled that the boy had said some painter had decorated and sold boxes depicting the man in the act of pulling the trigger.

Seeing Holz searching through K's papers had made K appear suddenly like a dead man ... this is what one does with the effects of the dead.

... The *Helenenthal*, his own favourite spot, where he had stood and thought of Karl Josef, where, writing the *Fuge*, he had gone to pray ...

Karl's action had made him want to rush to Frankfurt. *You cannot escape. You ignored your own son when he was ill, you left all the grief to be borne by his mother: now this son is ill, and all the grief is yours.*

It was dark now. He found a path down to the river. He had no fear of footpads. His own life had ended.

That walk by the canal after his jaundice in 1821. He had gone out without his hat or stick, lacking a purpose, dwelling on Karl Josef; wandering all day along the banks of a canal until by nightfall, lost, peering through windows for orientation, the people into whose houses he gazed had taken fright and called the police and he had been arrested as a tramp.

... Things die, people die ... you sometimes think you could live without any of them.

He had retraced his steps and saw again water glinting over the balustrade. ... This bridge on which he had stood when along had come CC with Karl and Johanna, shuddering in their lack of winter clothes. He had bundled them all into a carriage, agreed to sell works to Steiner, made CC his agent, 'Of course I must help you! It's only money! Of course!'

... Seeing Ludovica for the first time since she was a babe in arms. ... The infant's flickering hand reaching out to him, and in an instant he had been transported to when his son had been thus.

Except that he had never seen his son thus. He had never seen his son at all.

He had envisaged himself with a wife and children who would love him, pelt to him and cuddle him, the minute he walked through the door.

You give me a wife and make her belong to another man. You give me a son and make him mad. You give me a child and let him kill himself.

He recalled Countess Erdödy and Gustav's death and Mimi's attempted suicide.

A man passed following a boy with a lantern and he set off behind them, still engrossed in thought. . . . Karl had had one set of pistols and when he had fled Holz he had *bought another pair*! . . . Toni on the grass at Karlsbad, laughing at *The Passion of Young Werther* – 'The thing is, he decides to do it and then he *sleeps on it* and then he wakes up and decides he still wants to *go ahead with it* – it just doesn't happen like that!'

He remembered when he had dreamed of going to his son's wedding, of someday maybe holding his own grandchild.

. . . Holz had said of Karl in April when talking of his future, 'He has so many talents.' . . . Falstaff had won his friendship . . . Schlesinger too . . . Holz suggesting that he ask K's opinion of Kuffner's oratorio text: 'He has sound views . . .'

And the one went out from me, and I said, Surely he is torn in pieces; and I saw him not since;

And if ye take this also from me, and mischief befall him, ye shall bring down my grey hairs with sorrow to the grave.

Holz reported to him from the hospital, 'Four of the most skillful doctors come four times daily. He is getting unfailing care. As yet there is no fever, but if it should come then there would be a dangerous crisis. The *Magistrat* as a criminal court is now concerned with this.'

Karl lay in hospital. He had wanted to die. He had not wanted to go through all his. Now he was just as before, but with a bullet in his head.

The whole paraphernalia of Metternich's Vienna now weighed down on him. The authorities wanted to know the cause. Where once he had had his uncle shouting, 'How? Why?' now he had questions from the police. The threat of religious instruction hung over him, since his attempt to kill himself had been a crime against both church and state.

He was kept confined alone in dingy quarters, airless and windowless and almost dark, lest he try to escape, lest he should contaminate others. The scuttling of vermin disturbed his night.

'It's still a question of if he will recover,' Holz told Beethoven. 'Any head-wound endangers life. It could take a few days before it is known if the brain was damaged, in which case he is lost.'

'Why does he say he did it?'

'Weariness of life! If he should die, then according to the law he must be buried at the *Rabenstein*.'

Walking the next day Beethoven saw a mother comforting her young son, carrying him in the crook of her arm after he had fallen over, her hand wiping the tears from his pink face.

. . . 'I just hate travelling when I'm pregnant . . . I was sick all the way here in the carriage.' If I hadn't left her to go to Teplitz, if I'd stayed with her – *been a man*! Scurrying away to avoid the issue! *That's* why my boy is as he is ... my son.

The woman put down her now soothed child and Beethoven saw that the boy was crippled. The boy set off, hobbling on his club foot, at quite a pace.

He felt embarrassed by his old love, his towering love for his son which would not die, his old dream, recurring, of being with the boy, then an infant, now a child; of being in a room with them, saying to all of them, even to her, 'Let me be alone with him.' And then of holding his child, enfolding him. Whatever the boy was like. *My son.* And the feeling: that all the square edges of his life would evaporate, the pain that he knew every day would fall away, replaced by this rightness, this *oneness. I made him. He is of me.* The suffocating love that he had felt for that boy, was still feeling, the burden that weighed upon him, every day, the ache behind every moment, that only the composition of music ever relieved.

He had hurried home and was at his desk. Suddenly he was in tears. My own flesh and blood. My great composer. He was wiping his face with his hands. I don't know why I want that for him anyway. I've got enough troubles of my own, doing this.

He periodically kept thinking that it could not be so; the horror would not sink in; it was as though all that he had to do was lift out part of his own brain and place it into the boy to make him whole. – He *can't even walk*! O my God, forgive me. O God I have sinned! Forgive me! O my God, *forgive me*! Punish me but let him be all right – let him get better – spare him *for Antonie*.

He had grown impatient at not getting constant perfection immediately from his nephew: you have all this – that boy has nothing! You must use *all your abilities* to the utmost; *you* must realize what you've got; you must fulfil yourself as he cannot – and be bloody grateful; be bloody grateful to God for *everything* – you have got *everything*!

He had tried to tell Karl about this. 'Some boys haven't got what you've got. Some boys haven't got your brains. You must use *all your abilities* to the *utmost* ...'

He recalled sobbing once to Zmeskall, 'I envisaged him as a younger Karl ...'

Grief at a death brings back every other grief. Toni had said that in Karlsbad. In his mind's eye he saw Toni and his son passing. The boy was walking straight and tall.

The dreams had returned, those dreams which had been placated for a while by Stieler's picture: if Stieler had drawn *him* so pretty, clutching tight the *Missa*, how much must he have glamorized the boy?

They hadn't neglected him; *he* had neglected him: it was as though the boy had been born and left to fend for himself and had grown up not like a boy but an animal.

O God, be on my side now. I can't live without You. I can't even die without You.

The letter to Beethoven enclosed in that to Niemetz had been unearthed by the police and was now passed on to him. Holz was with him when he opened it, and read it with him.

Holz urged Beethoven to let his ward go for a soldier. 'Here you see ingratitude as clear as the sun; why do you want further to restrain him? Once with the military, he will be under the strictest discipline, and if you want to do anything more for him you need only make him a small allowance monthly. A soldier at once. Do you still doubt? This is a marvellous document.'

Karl had arrived at his mother's with black face, scorched hair, blood in his hair and down his face and neck. Holz had had Johanna's terror and anger to deal with, when Beethoven had left. Now Beethoven had learnt that Karl had called him to Niemetz 'the old fool.' Beethoven had almost died during his illness last year. That must have scared him, made him look back over his life, feel keenly his losses, made him the more determined to cling to Karl for fear of loneliness – even of dying alone: a fear so fierce that it drove him to build his bridges with such vehemence that in building them he burnt them.

Holz said to Karl in hospital, 'Well, lad! You've broken the all-time record in your name-day present to him this year! What're you trying to do? Kill him? O he's tougher than you are, he'll out-last *you!*'

Beethoven walked in the street with his head bowed. . . . 'Didn't ask to be taken to him; that boy asked that teamster to carry him to *her* . . .' He could see how he would go down in history, the headlines emblazoned all over the world's press, perpetuated by the fame of his music, *fame, infamy –* like this, for *ever* . . . L v B – own son a retarded crippled bastard; adopted son killed himself . . . Reality or dream: 'Don't start in on me! The boy's shot himself!' The child Ludovica crying at her feet. 'My son's lying there with a bullet in his skull!' He could hear them now, their recriminations: '. . . spends so long with his art and his immortal soul he's forgotten that flesh and blood boy.'

Frau Breuning met him on the *Glacis*. 'Do you know what has happened? My Karl has shot himself!'

'O no! Is he dead?'

'No, it was a glancing shot, he's still living, there's hope he can be saved – but the disgrace that he has brought upon me! And I did love him so!'

She walked back home with him.

'What made the boy do it? Why? *Why?*' He felt spiky-edged with grief. 'God will never forgive me for that. Not if I've ruined two men's lives!'

Frau Breuning fretted for him. She feared for his sanity. She sent Gerhard to him to invite him to take all his meals with them. She told her husband, 'He mustn't be left alone. He looked dreadful. He was walking with his head down, like this. I didn't recognize him at first. When he saw it was me he couldn't stop talking. I couldn't make out some of the things he said – sometimes he was shouting out and sometimes he was muttering to himself. But O, he looked dreadful! He looked about seventy! You'd have thought that he was that boy's father and that Karl really had killed himself.'

Beethoven paid his first visit to the hospital. Dr Seng, assistant in the surgical ward, was astonished when the small man in a grey coat whom he had taken to be a simple borgeois turned out to be Beethoven, talking to him about his nephew. 'I didn't really want to visit him; he doesn't deserve it; he has caused me too much anxiety. I've done everything for that boy, reared him, paid for his education, and this is the way that he repays me! Puts a bullet in his skull! Ungrateful young swine! Absolutely spoiled!'

Karl had been moved to a 3-florin ward. He complained that the people were common. He refused to be interrogated by Beethoven as to the cause of his deed. He told his uncle that he wanted to be a soldier.

'You could have done the exams, you say. Why didn't you? You could have become a musician. Your father thought of doing that. You've been taught by me. You could have been a composer.'

Karl laughed.

'What's funny about being a composer!' Beethoven was angry, believing that the boy mocked him. 'Not enough money for Master Karl!'

Karl said to Holz, 'You tell him.'

Holz said, 'I can't. He won't see it.'

'"Composed by Beethoven? O, *Karl* van Beethoven!"' Karl gave a bitter laugh of self-mockery.

'What are two talking about! How dare you laugh at me!'

Chapter 16

August-September
The 7-movement quartet had been despatched to Frank on August the
14th. It had been rehearsed several times at Artaria's at the beginning of
August. 'Artaria was enraptured, and this fugue at its third hearing he
found totally intelligible.'

Beethoven roared. 'There can't be that much in it, if he's tumbled it
already! So much for that one and posterity!'

Schotts had asked him for a 'totally new quartet.' Resenting their
implication that he would offer them second-rate goods, he had told them
he had cobbled this together 'out of bits and pieces filched from here and
there.' Schotts had taken him at his word! He had had to tell the silly
buggers it was 'really brand new!'

. . . That slow variation movement, aspiring towards the simple source
rather than decoration of its theme . . . the tenderness of the Hebrew 6th,
compassion from the very hand of God Himself.

O, everyone loved this one. All the dissonance of the previous quartet
had gone, to give place to a perfect blending of compassion and of peace.
The New Testament after the Old. The rage of the *Fuge* had liberated
tranquillity.

There was more trouble over the four-hand piano version. Beethoven
had now prepared his own; Artaria was upset at being asked to pay anew
for a work he had given Halm 40 florins for. In the margin beside the last
17 measures, Beethoven had written:

1) Fine consisting of 2 Clementi books of exercises for the piano and 3
   selected reproductions of the portrait of L v B.
2) A penalty for this and that as well as for other things.
3) The manuscript of this piano arrangement must either be paid for or be
   returned to the composer.

Holz attempted to placate them both.

Asking twelve ducats for his work, Beethoven sent Holz the piece, with
a canon:

There is the work! Dig up the
Gold! Dig! Dig!
One, two, three, four, five, six, sev'n, eight, nine, ten, 'lev'n, twelve,
                              one, two, three, four, five, six,

sev'n, eight, nine, ten, 'lev'n, twelve, one, two, three, four, five, six,
sev'n, eight, nine, ten, 'lev'n, twelve,
twelve ducats, ducats, ducats, ducats, ducats!

Instead of paying, Artaria had asked for Halm's manuscript. Beethoven agreed to exchange this for his own but refused to part with his for no fee and objected that in no wise could Artaria's payment to Halm be laid to his charge as a debt. On September 5th, Artaria paid Beethoven his 12 gold ducats.

Artaria had already engraved Galitzin's third but instead of publishing it he was hanging on to see if Holz could persuade Beethoven to substitute a new finale for the hated *Fuge*.

'The man refuses to answer me when I offer him my next quartet, demurs when I ask him to pay for my piano arrangement, and now has the nerve to come crawling to me *through you* to ask if I'll ditch the best thing I've ever done and replace it with some *catchy tune*! For which he offers to *pay me again*! I *shit* on him!'

Breaking from composing the following day, Beethoven went leaping across the room, punching the air with his clenched fist. *Substitute finale*! He would give those bastards *substitute finale*!

Since Karl's suicide attempt, Beethoven's friends had offered him their support. Schuppanzigh had invited Beethoven to dine: 'Wolfmayer will bring the drinks.' Johann offered to have him at Gneixendorf. Beethoven replied, 'I will not come. Your brother?????!!!! Ludwig.'

The first balloon flight in Vienna of Madame Garnerin had been announced for August 28th. She was to let herself down to earth from the giddy heights by means of a parachute, a display never yet seen in Vienna. The date was also Gerhard's thirteenth birthday, and Breuning invited Beethoven to join their festivities where they were able to watch this display from their window, overlooking the Prater. Beethoven brought with him a copy of Stieler's portrait which had been engraved by Artaria, wanting Breuning to send it to their old friend Wegeler, in Coblenz. The party decided that, in comparison with other portraits, Stieler had seen him whole.

Beethoven was presenting Gerhard with a copy of Clementi's *Klavier-schule*. Frau Breuning hoped that he might occasionally be able to give her son lessons. She herself had never heard Beethoven play; her husband in his kindness forebore to ask him. 'It might cause him distress to be asked to play what he himself cannot hear.' He had played late into the night, so she had heard, for Stephan and his first wife when they had been engaged. He had dedicated the piano arrangement of his fiddle concerto to Julie. She had died so suddenly, so young. Stephan had been devastated and Beethoven had been unable to do anything, passing his friend in concern to Gleichenstein's care.

He often invited Frau Breuning for coffee but she usually refused. 'He's got such dirty habits,' she complained to her husband, seeing Beethoven striding through their rooms, lost in thought, spitting onto their mirror which he had taken to be an open window.

'And yet he's very popular, you know,' her husband told her, 'especially with women.'

She had gathered that he had courted Julie for a while. He had also not been above paying court to her. 'O, he always was very gallant towards women.' He had once met her in the street and accompanied her to the bath-house. To her shame she had felt averse to being seen out with him: his animated gestures, loud voice and indifference to others surprised people in the street. Several people stopped and stared at him, taking him for a madman, particularly when he laughed, a sound peculiarly loud and ringing.

The water being warm, she had stayed in the bath-house for three-quarters of an hour, to be astonished upon leaving to find Beethoven still waiting to escort her home. As he took her arm, enfolding it within his own, she realized that he got a frisson from being seen out in the street with any reasonable-looking woman. *People will think she is mine.* It had caused trouble at the time of Marie Bigot. He often told her of his longing for domestic joy and his keen regret that he had never married.

Breuning encouraged Beethoven to give Karl his freedom. 'But you left home when you were 16. You left home for good before you were 22 . . .'

'Every time that I left home, one of my parents died!'

He wrote in his conversation book: *On the death of the dead Beethoven.* Holz had urged him to look through these books and remove sensitive details about his work, lest they be demanded by the police in their search for evidence of Karl's state of mind.

The first book he picked up was from mid-May, when the boy had been dining with him daily. 'Lay down the guardianship,' he had written, 'it can't go on like this.' . . . Karl doing his correspondence . . . Karl advising him against Kanne: 'For *you*, that is not the book.' He had suggested Kind, who wrote the libretto for Weber's *Freischütz*, advising that he select a Greek subject.

He wrote in his current book: 'Mental aberration and insanity; the heat too – afflicted with headaches since childhood.'

The boy had stolen other things from him beside the books. Holz knew about the spoons. Now that the boy was under police arrest in hospital, Beethoven knew terror lest any of this should come out. To whom else did Karl owe money? Had he gambling debts? Was that why he did it? Was he in danger of being called to account for himself anyway? *If he carries on like this with some of his aristocratic friends, it won't be fist-fights, it will be 'whose pistols?'*

Karl at first had had two ward nurses in charge of his care; Beethoven was being presented with hospital bills. Writing to Holz of Karl's desire to join the army, Beethoven had told him, 'I am worn out; and happiness will not be my portion again for a very long time. The terrible expenses which I now have to meet and shall have to meet in future are bound to worry me; all my hopes have vanished, all my hopes of having near me someone who would resemble me at least in my better qualities!'

Beethoven resented what he saw as the *Magistrats* infringement upon his rights as Karl's guardian; Holz tried to make clear to him that the *Magistrat* was here concerned in its capacity as a criminal court. Breuning and Bach were both urging Beethoven to relinquish the guardianship. Bach thought that Karl should be placed in a commercial house, somewhere other than Vienna. Breuning sided with the boy's own expressed wish to join the military. 'A military life will be the best discipline for one who cannot endure freedom, and it will teach him how to live on little.' Beethoven thought of approaching General Ertmann, the husband of his 'Dorothea-Cäcilia', for whom he had played when her own son had died and to whom he had dedicated opus 101.

Reisser had resigned the guardianship. 'Pistols now, is it! The comic hero!' he had exploded in laughter to Holz before the attempt. Holz told Beethoven that it would be the *Magistrats* duty to find a replacement and that he could then decide what more he wanted to do for the boy.

Holz urged, 'Resign the guardianship; this will make an impression upon him.' Holz was stirred by thoughts of the boy's ingratitude. He reminded Beethoven of the sacrifices he had already made. 'Had your good nature not so often got the better of your firmness, you would have driven him out long ago.'

'The boy hates me.' He was recalling the letter that Karl had sent him through Niemetz.

'He said it was not hatred of you which he felt, but something entirely different.'

Beethoven offered the guardianship to Holz, but Holz had just become engaged and did not want the responsibility. The guardianship was taken up by Breuning, whom Karl himself would happily have chosen.

Beethoven wrote to Breuning, 'Regarding Karl, three points I think should be borne in mind. Firstly, he must not be treated like a convict, for such treatment would not produce the result we want but the opposite – secondly, if he is to be promoted to the higher ranks, he must not live too frugally and shabbily – thirdly, he would find it hard to face too great restrictions on eating and drinking – But I do not wish to forestall you.'

Beethoven had planned to send Karl to a military academy as a cadet but Breuning persuaded his acquaintance Lieutenant-Fieldmarshal Stutterheim to take Karl into his regiment, stationed at Iglau in Moravia.

Beethoven sent Karl affectionate letters, to Holz' annoyance; he thought it necessary to see him, to see if he approved of the arrangements being made with von Stutterheim.

Karl's case had been placed in the hands of Referent Czapka of the *Magistrat*, who brought Beethoven Stutterheim's advice as to the allowance he should make Karl: no more than 12 florins in silver a month, the most that the richest cadet in the service received.

At ease now regarding Karl's physical state, Beethoven was kept anxious by the inquiry, which was so protracted as to lead him to dread that something terrible might be disclosed. Beethoven wanted to go himself to the Minister of Police, dreading the ordeal of the examination. Holz told him, 'The court will not annoy you – the mother and Karl at the most.'

His mother had spent a great deal of time at his bedside when Karl had first been in hospital. Holz had told Beethoven of being at the hospital when he met Johanna at her son's bedside. 'If you have anything on your mind,' she had enjoined, 'tell your uncle now. This is the time: he is weak, and now he will do anything you want.' Karl had replied sullenly, 'I know nothing.'

'How,' Holz had said to Beethoven, 'can anyone find out a single trace, if he persists in remaining silent?'

Holz had complained to Beethoven of the lack of mercy in Johanna for denouncing his conduct as her son's guardian.

Hoping to be able to keep Karl in Vienna, Beethoven had suggested that Johanna might be sent away, to Pressburg or to Pesth. 'I wanted only to accomplish his good,' he wrote in a conversation book. 'If he is abandoned now, something might happen.'

September the 24th was Gerhard's name-day and Breuning invited Beethoven to join them for a small family party. This time Beethoven took along to show them his gold medal from Louis XV111. In the afternoon they walked to the *Schönbrunn*. Walking in the Palace garden, Beethoven pointed in disgust to the alleys of trees grossly trimmed against nature so as to accord with the French style. 'Nothing but artifice, shaped like hooped petticoats! I only feel the benefit of nature when I am out somewhere where nature is free!' A soldier strode past. Beethoven commented loudly, 'A *slave*, who has sold his freedom for five kreuzer a day!'

Karl was due to leave hospital. Beethoven had written to Czapka urging that Karl be allowed to leave the hospital only with himself and Holz. 'It is out of the question to allow him to be much in the company of his mother, that extremely depraved person. My anxieties and my request are warranted by her most evil, wicked and spiteful character; her enticement of Karl for the purpose of getting money out of me; the probability that she has spent sums of money with him, and too that she was intimate with Karl's dissolute companion; the sensation that she has been causing with her daughter, *whose father is still being traced*; and, what is more, the likelihood that in his mother's home he would make the acquaintance of women who are anything but virtuous. Even the habit of being in the company of such a person cannot possibly lead a young man along the path of virtue.'

Karl strongly objected to restraints being placed upon their meeting. 'I do not want to hear anything derogatory to her; it is not for me to be her judge. If I were to spend the little time I shall be here with her, it would be only a small return for all that she has suffered on my account. In no event shall I treat her with greater coldness than has been the case heretofore, whatever may be said on the subject.' His mother made no objection to his choice of a military career. 'All the less, therefore, can I deny her wish to be with me during these days, since I probably won't be here again for some time. Obviously this does not prevent you and me from seeing each other as often as you wish.'

The man's stupidity exasperated him; as though he had no wish but to return permanently to his mother. Now this absurdity was being repeated by the examining *Magistrat*. The silly sod thought it 'only natural' that 'the boy' would want to be with his mother. Want to be with my mother! I haven't wanted to be with my mother for years! Not since I was a kiddie. What! Mama and Niemetz having it off in the big bed, me with little sister on my tod in the next room, the sounds coming through the wall – Big deal!

He did not need any of them now: father, mother, uncle. He had got his own way. *Karl* van Beethoven: *soldier*! Forgetting first pressure . . !

He had tried again with the second pistol to lift the barrel to the centre of his forehead, but the thing had been so heavy and so overloaded with powder, like his first set, and he had found it so awkward to maintain first pressure whilst he manoeuvred the cumbrous weight, that his wrist had knotted as he had tried to aim for his mid-temple and the shot had gone off to his left, giving him a flesh-wound.

Ever since he had been carried, bleeding and passing out, into his mother's, people had been asking him the reason for his act. A Redemptorist priest had been assigned to administer religious instruction. Holz had held forth the hope to Beethoven that this man would unearth the cause. 'These Liguorians are like leeches,' Holz wrote.

Fear of the examinations had been dismissed aggressively by Karl. 'It would have been easy enough for me to prepare myself to pass,' he had told Holz. 'Once I decided to kill myself it seemed futile to keep up to date with my revision.'

'He said that he was tired of life,' Holz reported to Beethoven, 'because he found in it something different from what you could fairly and wisely approve.'

Karl had told the examining *Magistrat* that his reason for shooting himself had been 'because my uncle tormented me too much.'

'What do you mean, torments you? Did he beat you? Was he brutal to you?'

' . . . I grew worse because my uncle wanted me to be better.'

'Well surely you can hardly think it wrong that your uncle wanted you to improve yourself?'

Breuning appeared before the *Magistrat*, where he spoke with Czapka and Karl, who had been brought by the police.

Breuning reported to Beethoven, 'Karl will not see you. At the *Magistrats* I assumed the guardianship, upon which Karl was placed at my disposition.'

'What do you mean, won't see me! Bring him here!'

'I fear that, if he is here, you will talk to him too much, which would cause fresh disturbance.'

'How can talking to the boy cause disturbance!'

'Because he told the police that it was too great torment by you that led him to the step.'

Beethoven was horrified. He had thought that Karl was coming back to him. Now it appeared that Breuning had sole authority, Karl refused to see him, Breuning went along with this; the boy was to be whisked off into the army before he could so much as clap eyes on him.

'Who's paying! Who's paying! Are *you* paying? If I'm paying I've got the right to see him! What is this! My own friend, take my son from me!'

Breuning calmed him down. 'Then let him be brought here by Holz; then on Friday I will take him to Lieutenant-Fieldmarshal Stutterheim, in 5 days he will be equipped, and in a week he will go.'

Beethoven thought that Karl should be returned to the hospital.

'It's very doubtful whether the hospital would take him back again.'

'But what if he runs away?'

'If he ran away from here, he could equally run away on his journey to the regiment.'

'He'll run to see his mother!'

Breuning sighed. 'Referent Czapka himself said that Karl will not speak with his mother.'

Breuning had envisaged Karl's leaving the hospital and being presented to von Stutterheim, taking the oath of service, and leaving for Iglau immediately. However, Karl himself pointed out that his hair had not yet fully grown over his scar. Breuning could not see how he could keep Beethoven from seeing and pestering Karl, nor Karl if he did so from taking flight.

After his investigation before the *Magistrat* Karl had told Breuning, 'I told you: I'm always wrong.'

'No, you're not wrong. You do need to get away. I never was in favour of his having the guardianship. He loves you but his love is overpowering. I also think that you are too dependent upon him, for all you want your freedom: he is always there to fall back on, with an open purse.'

'I want to earn my living! "Mother," he says, "mother!" I don't want to be with my mother! I'm a grown man! . . . He seems to think I'll forget him completely, that he *won't exist for me*, just as he tried to make *mother* not exist for me, if I'm not under his eyes, if I'm out of his sight – but I don't see how a man can't be out in the world and still have love for his mother and his uncle!'

'Tried telling him that?'

Karl hooted. '*You* try telling! He doesn't see me as *my age*! I'm his *little boy*!'

'Well haven't you sometimes behaved like his little boy? Gambling debts – he has to pay those.'

Karl stared at him open-mouthed.

'No, I'm not against you. It's all getting sorted out. But you're going away, into the army. Don't gamble more than you can afford to lose. I'm your guardian – I can't afford to bail you out – I've got a family to feed. Do you see? You're not a nonentity. What you do affects other people.

'You've got a clean slate: your wound's healed, your debt's paid. And don't let there be a next time, because the next time you will know how to load a gun and the next time you won't be here for me to talk to like a Dutch uncle.'

Beethoven wrote again to Czapka, stating that Karl should be allowed to stay with him for the few days until he left Vienna. 'His statements are to be ascribed to the outbursts of anger caused by the impression made on him by my reprimands when he was thinking of taking his life. But even after that time he behaved affectionately towards me. Rest assured that even in its fall humanity is always sacred to me. An admonition from you would have a good effect. Moreover it would do no harm to let him realize that during his stay with me he is being watched unseen.'

Johann again invited Beethoven and Karl to visit his estate at Gneixendorf. The authorities were pressing for Karl to leave Vienna. Beethoven had no choice but to accept his brother's offer.

Beethoven was hanging on in Vienna until the bound presentation copy of the *Choral* was ready to be despatched to the King of Prussia. Johann wanted to leave swiftly, he had urgent business interests, and Karl too urged his uncle to go. He had spent one night in a police cell before being given the priest's certificate stating that he had received religious instruction, which he had to have before he could be discharged, and he was not eager to see the inside of another jail cell.

Karl spent a day with his uncle bringing his correspondence up to date, including a request to Schotts to 'hasten the necessary preliminaries connected with the publication of my collected works.'

Before the end of the month, uncles and nephew had arrived in Gneixendorf.

Chapter 17

October-November
Gneixendorf

Gneixendorf was a tiny village on a high plateau of the Danube valley a few miles from Krems. Its one street was narrow, rough and dirty, with low huts for houses. Johann's estate, Wasserhof, lay outside the village, reached by a wagon trail along the edge of a ravine. There were fields and vineyards, but few trees. The estate ran to 400 acres, most of it leased out to tenant farmers, and two fine large houses. From Beethoven's rooms on the east side lay a view of the Danube valley to the distant Styrian mountains. 'The name resembles a breaking axle,' he wrote to Haslinger. 'The air is healthy. As to everything else, one must cross oneself and say Momento Mori.'

They had arrived at Johann's estate in the afternoon of the 29th. Johann had walked through the fields with his brother, giving him a chance to take a look at the property, on which he had but two more years to pay. The next day they walked in the morning to the hill to see the vineyards, and in the afternoon to Imlach, where Karl pointed out to his uncle the cloister where Margarethe, wife of Ottokar, had died: 'The scene occurs in Grillparzer's piece.'

It was strange to Johann to have his brother here, after his many refusals and his unbending abuse towards Therese. Beethoven's letter to him, 'I will not come! Your brother??????!!!!' had co-incided with the publication of the *Choral* by Schotts. 'He calls me "My brother, brackets on, pseudo, brackets off,"' he had complained to Therese then. Therese had laughed. He began laughing, too. '*Alle Menschen (ohne Johann) werden Brüder!*' he sang.

'He always said if he'd been Beethoven the composer he'd have been swimming in millions,' Beethoven recalled Holz' saying of Johann as he strode with his sketchbook around the estate. Holz' future wife was from a large family, one of 8 daughters and 3 sons. In September he had gone off with his beloved to Baden; Beethoven had pulled his leg about the good influence of women wholly melting his icy surface so that he no longer resembled 'a dried fish'; calling him 'Mr Enamoured'; joking about things being '*pregnant with consequences*'. Writing to ask him to see to the binding of the Symphony for the King of Prussia, he had closed his letter, 'Mr Enamoured, I bow my knee before the almighty power of *love*.' Beneath his signature he had added the sign of the cross and 'Momento Mori.'

During his stay here at Gneixendorf, Beethoven had written to himself, *Freu' dich des Lebens*.

He was writing his quartet and it was coming easily. *Therefore I say unto you, What things soever you desire, when ye pray, believe that ye receive them, and ye shall have them.*

As long ago as autumn 1824 he had been joking to Haslinger over handing the score of opus 116 to Dietrichstein for some Court festivity, 'Give it up, my good fellow, *es muss sein . . .*' Since then he had used this catch-phrase when one of the two sisters who had become his housekeeper to the other's maid had come to him for money; to Dembscher when he had refused to let him have Galitzin's third for performance until he had paid 50 florins for Falstaff's subscription series. Dembscher had grimaced, '*Muss es sein?*' He had roared at the man's presumption: nicks my quartet, now nicks my joke *for free!* '*Es muss sein!*' Someone had apparently tipped off Frau Schnaps: one Saturday morning she had appeared beside his desk, swinging her basket to let him know she wanted money to go to market. '*Muss es sein!*' he had cried resignedly and the old bitch had come back at him with, '*Ja, es muss sein! Heraus mit dem Beutel!*' 'Out with the money! You saucy cow!' He had got up and chased her round the room, the 70-year old laughing like a schoolgirl. He had got the last laugh: he had turned it into a canon. Po-faced, the canon had now turned *itself* into the driving force behind the last movement of his new quartet. *Der schwer gefasste Entschluss*: the resolution taken with difficulty. *Muss es sein? Ja, es muss sein!* But there was no difficulty here: it was like being on the *Helenenthal*, casting up his brief, half-formed prayer, so brief as to be dismissive, but it was answered, O yes; like the *Fuge*. The damn thing had even had the stroke of genius to come up with that *pizzicato* near the end – all four players plucking away, then second, viola and bass with the leader singing away fit to beat the band.

O, it was gay! Where had *that* come from? *Freu' dich des Lebens* indeed! The whole thing was a smashing quartet: . . . first movement arrived *as though the audience had walked in and found the music already playing*; second movement that haring *scherzo* which ought to bring tears of delight to the eyes of those who really loved music and the sausage-eating Viennese; that *lento*, the closest he had ever got to it, God help me, I almost touched it there; and then a cheerful wave, as though it really were all right, as though everything now really were resolved.

As though Mark 11:24 were the answer after all. The Old, the New, and now the Pearly Gates! He laughed to himself as he wrote to Haslinger, who had taken over Steiner's firm, addressing him in music as 'First of all Tobiases!' and asking if he could arrange to collect the fee from Schlesinger in gold. He made a joke on a popular song: 'for it is *not* the same thing whether we have some money or have none!' another about Holz: 'If you happen to meet Holz, put the peg in a different hole. It is horribly afflicted with amorous inebriation; it has become almost inflamed with it; someone wrote in jest that Holz is the son of the late Papageno!'

There was no copyist to be found in the whole of Gneixendorf and he found that he must needs spend the whole of the second half of October turgidly copying out the quartet he had had so much fun writing. When in the first half of the month he had written to Schotts enclosing the metronome marks for the *Choral* and reminding them of his collected works, he had told them that the district 'reminds me of the Rhine country which I so ardently desire to revisit. For I left it long ago when I was young.' But now his mood had changed. In his deaf isolation he kept himself apart from others when he accompanied his brother to meet friends or business colleagues, so that a surgeon's wife whose husband revered his compositions, seeing him sitting in isolation on a bench behind the stove, took him for Johann's servant; and an official's clerk with a passion for his music, irritated by his long standing motionless in the doorway, took him for an imbecile.

He felt keenly his isolation in this treeless setting: a deaf man in strange surroundings, among uncongenial company. He spoke hardly ever to Therese and seldom to his brother. He wrote in his little book, 'Breuning should *not* have let *me* come.' At first the cook had made his bed and tidied his room, but, seeing him at his desk, gesticulating, beating time with his feet, muttering and singing, the woman had burst into a laugh and Beethoven had driven her from the room. Instead Michael Krenn, son of one of the vineyard workers, was given a florin by Beethoven and became his servant. When Beethoven lost his pocket sketchbook, Krenn it was who found it. In the evening Beethoven had Krenn sit with him and write down what had been said about him at dinner. Therese sacked Krenn once for losing the money given to him to buy wine and fish; on learning of this Beethoven in great agitation reimbursed the 5 florins and thereafter had his meals brought to his rooms.

In Vienna his ways were known; likewise in the nearby spas where he returned year after year to spend his summers. Here his deafness and his actions when he was lost in thought, composing, gave rise to offence or fear or ridicule. He rarely returned greetings. His wild gesticulations and untuneful singing led his brother's peasants to regard him as a madman. One young peasant, driving a pair of scarcely-broken oxen from the tile-kiln to the manor-house, called out to the shouting, waving man, 'A little quieter!' Beethoven was unaware of the situation; the oxen took fright and ran down a steep hill; only with great difficulty did the young peasant stop them and return them to the road. To his horror he saw that Beethoven had turned and was again frightening his beasts. He called out again; again Beethoven heard nothing; this time the oxen rushed towards the house. They were brought to a stop by another peasant; when the driver caught up and asked who that fool was scaring his oxen he burst out, 'A fine brother, that one!'

After an incident like this he felt no more a man but a creature. Miserably he felt that now he was not even accorded the status of a human being. He recalled the time in his youth when he had come upon a peasant snoring in a barn and turning to his fellows said, 'I wish I were as stupid as that man.'

You can't like me and not like my music. That is where my being is. Reject my music and you reject me completely. Sometimes he wrote out of anger, out of sheer insupportable hatred, as the only way to stop himself from killing someone. And sometimes he wrote out of such deep love and such profound gentleness that he himself as he wrote was overtaken, suffused by it, he saw it break around him, saw in his very music even as it left his quill the man stroking the woman's hair and all similar affiliated moments of tenderness; even as he wrote, still writing, tears streaming down his face. 'It's *words*! That's not music, that is *words*!' someone, perhaps Wolfmayer, had exclaimed during the *Heiliger Dankgesang*, tears streaming down his face.

And *this* is glory, *this* is why I am *alive*! – bowled over by it even as it's coming off the quill!

As ever joy merged with thanksgiving, God's creature even as being raised to God.

The best ones are always *straight* . . . they're on the paper before they're through the head . . . the artist is as astonished and then as gleeful as anybody else.

He did a little dance as he poured water over his hair. The muse was upon him again and he had on his last note worn out his last quill, and his pencil, also to hand, was blunt. He called out urgently to Karl, who had begun to laugh in astonishment, 'Shut up! Hurry up! Run, it's urgent! Run run run!' He was still laughing, though it was terribly urgent: this time it really felt like a bodily function. 'Quick! Quick!' He felt he would soon be losing it. He made a snatch for the pen. 'Come on!'

Karl found something approaching city life in nearby Krems, to which he willingly undertook errands on foot for both his uncles, for there he found soldiers stationed in the village, a theatre, and a billiard-hall. Therese told Beethoven once when Karl was absent, 'Don't be alarmed. He will certainly be home by one. It seems he has some of your rash blood. I have not found him angry. It is you that he loves, to the point of veneration.'

. . . The wages for lower-ranking officers just about matched those of a factory worker – only twice what he paid his kitchen-maid! The government punished certain criminals and unruly students with enforced military service, the poor mutilated themselves to be exempted, the rich paid bribes – and here was the boy *volunteering*! The army had long been the preserve of the younger sons of Austrian aristocrats . . . Yet soldiers were often treated as social outcasts, suspected of theft, brawling and rape

... The rank and file were addressed 'Er', like common servants, subjected to corporal punishment, flogging, and running the gauntlet . . .

Packing his pistols with powder, in a moment of panic Karl had wondered whether his uncle possessed any guns. He had once thought of buying a book on the art of shooting for the huntsman. . . . Never given up trying to get his hands on a country estate like Gneixendorf. In a moment of euphoric mania he envisaged B with a gun. The only thing *he* could ever put a bullet through was his own foot . . .

Therese came upon them once, the old man in his dressing-gown, the young in his shirt-sleeves, playing a four-hand march at the piano.

At the end of October Johann took the newly-copied quartet to Vienna. There he met Linke and learned that he was anxious to have the new finale to Galitzin's third for a concert.

'You could easily have made two quartets from the B-flat quartet,' Holz had said. 'When one thinks so highly of art as you do, it cannot be any other way; but it would be more money for you, and the publisher would have to pay the costs.'

The *Fuge* crashed down onto the *Cavatina*, smashing it and all that had gone before. That was the *purpose* of the *Fuge*! Take the *Fuge* from the quartet and there is no quartet! The *Fuge* can live without the rest but the rest cannot live without the *Fuge*.

. . . Trying to get round him by talk of paying twice, softening him up, as though Artaria had *done him a favour* by taking his piano arrangement rather than Halm's. Artaria had done him no favour! Artaria had only paid once for each work he'd got!

When he had watched Falstaff's quartet in rehearsal he had told them, 'Take that sound out of your feet and put it into your fiddles. Then you'll play it.' Someone had said it was 'too powerful.' 'Too powerful! *Too* powerful! It is not possible for art to be *too powerful*! Art is fighting *the devil and all his angels*!'

He could feel the years closing in about him. Shat on, his work shat on, all those months of creating the work, when it had seemed that he gave of his best . . . This work out of the gravest depths of creativity, his base as an artist, his godhead.

Deluded. Deluded in the depth of his conviction.

The fault all his, the inadequacy his; he the one who should crawl off into a ditch and die.

He had thought so often over the years, I would have sold my immortal soul for that. As the memory revived he thought again fiercely, and if I were Faust and *that* were offered to me now, God knows that in all truth I should sell my immortal soul for *that*. Yes, you are wicked, and God does know, and you pay for it all the same, even though you are not Faust and the offer was not made.

He'd never been more fully himself in his life than when writing that. Maybe as happy with Toni. Maybe with Toni. As happy.

. . . Every time thereafter when she had wanted money Frau Schnaps had chanted to him, '*Es muss sein!*' and, if he were in a good mood, he would respond. It was the sort of silly, tedious yet pleasurable repetition he had expected to have in his marriage with A – every night she had said to him, 'I suppose you want a bedtime drink?' 'Yes please, Antonie!' and after a while she had taken it over, nodding her head as though in time to music, saying the whole thing in a send-up, nasal voice: '"I suppose you want a bedtime drink?" "Yes please, An-ton-ie!"'

He had sometimes reached the point of thinking, art is where the unloved go. Now he remedied this: art is for the unloving. No, it's not true I've never loved, but it's probably true that I have never shown love.

It's nearly over. My suffering is nearly done. I'm too old to pray for the alleviation of anyone else's suffering – even hers. Even his. Too old. Too tired. I don't live any more.

Of late he had thought, God, what a lot of time I wasted. It doesn't matter whether they're illegitimate or not – all that matters is whether they're healthy.

My life has been a waste of time. I have made neither woman nor child happy. I might have given a bit of joy, sometimes, with my music.

. . . Music of the fucking furious angels. You didn't know that there were furious angels? O, they're fucking furious. They're wild!

He wanted to be on the floor, playing with Karl Josef, telling him about the fucking furious angels.

You want an ice and a little sausage? I'll give you ice and a little sausage. I'll give you a *happy ending!*

Sing, O Muse, of how it feels to be kick-ed in the teeth. *There is the work. Dig up the gold.* He held up his middle finger and wiggled it. 'Bastards! Reject *my Große Fuge!*' *Eins zwei drei vier fünf sechs sieben acht.* Recalling the 5-part canon he had sent Holz with the 4-hand version, the thought had suddenly come to him: set *this* as the last movement! The *substitute* they wanted! In this way *I still keep the Fuge!* And all music-lovers will hear it and fall about laughing. *Eins zwei drei vier fünf Goldenen Dukaten.* Fall about laughing! In the concert-hall! They won't be able to play it! I'll kill it! By writing it! He had visions of them all, rolling in the aisles, audiences clutching their sides, players falling off their seats. . . . O, and he could use his old joke about notes and needs, *noten und nöten* . . . vielen noten . . . vielen nöten . . . *Eins zwei drei vier eins zwei drei vier eins zwei drei vier fünf Goldenen Dukaten geben Sie mir in das Hand*, with 'goldenen Dukaten' and 'vielen noten' 'noten-nöten' running throughout, amongst, between and behind the numbers. Something anyway along those lines.

Since his recent spate of illnesses his belly had grown big again. He had long since abandoned that bloody truss. As his angry thoughts careered at him he was bandaging his belly. Much more of this and I'll look like a woman at term.

What was it they were giving him for that piano arrangement? Twelve

for that, was it? Fifteen for this? *Eins zwei drei vier fünf sechs sieb'n acht . . .*
goldenen Dukaten . . . Gebt sie mir in meinen Hand . . . Falling ducats . . . ducat
upon ducat . . . just about pay for Karl's new uniform. He hitched his
pants over his bandages, sat down and proceeded to set.

All right, you fucking prats. You like my *scherzos*? I'll give you a fucking
scherzo. He picked up his pen and wrote viciously, in blind hatred: he
wanted to *hurt them*. In the middle of the bastard rondo-sonata movement
he had the weirdest experience: he saw himself lock-on and freewheel. Let
it stand, mate. Let it stand.

Music for Moroccans, eh? There, there, my wild Phaeacians, sing and
dance – never let it be said that *Beethoven* could not write *music for
Phaeacians*!

He could just hear them squealing: 'Reversion to classicism.' – That's
about as classical as one ball! And for how many years are you going to
play *that*? You prats. Take it to your bosom. Like the Septet – *ha*!

And do you understand, you cloth-eared Viennese, absorbed in your
love of pleasure and *Gemütlichkeit*, that *Cavatina* and *Große* are opposite
sides of *the same coin* and *this* is *one* part of *one* side of that coin – which I had
already given *you* in abundance – in *perfection*; and do you understand . . .
O, you don't understand anything outside your ices and little *sausages*!

One two three four five six seven eight nine ten eleven twelve thirteen
fourteen fifteen gold ducats – *Fuck off*, you *miscarriage of art*. He wished his
bloody belly would go down. Even so he went back to it . . . bit of an alto
clef so as they'll notice the difference. Spell it out for 'em, Beethoven. A
nice heavy *bass* for the *Phaeacians*. *That* will delight my *Viennese friends*.

A nice *bouncy finale* for the *Phaeacians*! Heavy on the 'cello – they like
that! – no 'cello in the treble clef for this!

Stamp away, lads!

Stamp away!

I could have written that at *20*, standing *on my cock*.

He was eager to get on with other works, the quintet, the tenth
symphony, an oratorio and, if he could get one of the *idiot* poets to come
up with a *text*, an *opera*. If his health would let him. I look like a 12-pints-a-
day man . . .

He had started work on the quintet. Show the fuckers how to do *that*
now. – No one *since Mozart*. Call themselves composers! Ignorant bastards.
No more write a string quintet than fly to the moon.

There's your *Dukatenscheißer*. *That's* what you get for killing your *golden
goose*!

He closed the door, calling out to it over his shoulder, 'Goodnight,
sweet frog!'

O, you had to specify gold ducats: Schlesinger had paid him for the last
quartet in *paper*, then had the nerve to bellyache about the length.
'Circumcised ducats, circumcised quartet,' he had remarked. *Huh*! *Castrated ducats, castrated quartet*!

On the 22nd he sent the thing to Haslinger, who delivered it to Artaria in return for fifteen ducats on the 25th. After squaring minor debts Haslinger made over the remainder to Therese's brother, the baker Obermayer. Therese was going to Vienna and Beethoven accepted her offer to collect the stump of his 15 ducats, most of which by now seemed to belong to Johann anyway.

Johann had led him to believe that he could stay here for nothing. Then, when the climate seemed to have alleviated his eye-trouble, there had been talk of his staying permanently. 'If you want to live with us, you can have everything for 40 fl. C.M. a month, that makes 500 fl. for a whole year. . . . You will only need half your pension.' Now it was, 'I will charge nothing for the first fortnight; I would do more were I not so hard-pressed with taxes.'

Karl told him, 'Regarding expenses, wood is so cheap that it is inconceivable that the brother should be at any considerable costs, for you can heat for a long time with one cord and he is already overpaid.'

It was too cold now for his uncle to take long walks: in cold weather he grew ill and his feet were beginning to swell. His other uncle was occupied on his estate and his aunt was in Vienna. When he could get away to Krems, Karl had freedom: no Holz, no *Mr. Shitting*; no one who knew him, to spy on him, to report back to B. This time he had been lucky at the tables; he had also caught the eye of the village girls. This dark, handsome, young Metropolitan stranger had come among them, with his mysterious romantic background – could it be true that he had shot himself? Had he fought a duel? Could it have been for love? These were the rumours spreading amongst the wenches, and Karl reaped his rewards.

Breuning had written to Johann and now Johann wrote to his brother:

My dear Brother:
I cannot possibly remain silent concerning the future fate of Karl. He is abandoning all activity and, grown accustomed to this life, the *longer* he lives as at present, the more difficult will it be to bring him back to work. At his departure *Breuning* gave him a fortnight in which to recuperate, and it is now two months. You see from Breuning's letter that it is his decided wish that Karl *shall hasten* to his calling; the longer he is here the more unfortunate will it be *for him*, for the harder will it be for him to get to work, and it may be that we shall suffer harm.

It is an infinite pity that this talented young man so wastes his time; and on whom if not *both of us* will the blame be laid? For he is still too young to direct his own course; for which reason it is your duty, if you do not wish to be reproached by yourself and others hereafter, to put him to work at his profession as soon as possible. Once he is occupied it will be easy to do much for him now and in the future; but under present conditions nothing can be done.

I see from his actions that he would like to remain with us, but if he did so it would be all over with his future, and therefore *this is impossible*. The longer we hesitate the more difficult will it be for him to go away; I therefore adjure you: make up your mind, do not permit yourself to be dissuaded by Karl. I think it ought to be *by next Monday*, for in no event can you wait for me, inasmuch as I cannot get away from here without *money*, and it will be a long time before I collect enough to enable me to go to Vienna.

Karl himself when confronted wrote, 'I cannot argue against it since we have been here longer than was planned, but *Breuning* himself said that I cannot go to the Field-Marshal until I am able to appear without any visible sign left of what happened to me, because he wants to overlook the whole affair. This is almost accomplished now except for a little bit which really won't take much more time; therefore I think that we should stay until next week at least. If I had pomade then it would be unnecessary. Besides, the longer we remain here, the longer we can remain together, since once we are in Vienna I shall have to leave right away.'

A quarrel ensued between the two brothers, with Beethoven urging Johann to make a will in favour of Karl, cutting out Therese. Johann responded by writing in pencil on the back of the letter, 'Let us leave this until the day you go.' Beethoven was not satisfied; he wanted this resolved. Johann thought it not right to leave her unprovided for, pointing out that she would, by the time he died, in all probability be 'an old woman. She has her share and will get no more.'

'What is the matter?' Beethoven asked Karl. 'What are you hanging your head for now? Isn't the truest devotion even with its shortcomings enough? The idea of going from here continues to pain you and I have also taken this into consideration.'

'Did you see me speak a word? Hardly – for I was not disposed at all to speak, everything that you say about me needs no refutation. So I beg of you once and for all to leave me alone. If you want to go, good. If not, good again. But I beg of you once more not to torment me as you are doing; you might regret it, for I can endure much, but too much I cannot endure. You treated your brother in the same way today without cause. You must remember that other people are also human beings. These everlastingly unjust reproaches! Why do you make such a disturbance? Will you let me go out a bit today? I need recreation. I'll come again later. I only want to go to my room. I am not going out, I only want to be alone for a little while.'

They left Gneixendorf on the 1st of December. Cold and growing colder as they travelled, Beethoven was acutely aware of being alone with Karl. He became aware that he was not well. He realized that Karl was about to leave him, that he would be left alone.

That night they broke the journey and in the raw, damp, frosty conditions found only an unheated room without winter shutters. Near midnight Beethoven became chilled, with a hacking cough and cutting-pains in his sides. His throat was on fire; Karl brought water, icy to the touch.

He tossed, sleepless. He became feverish. In his fever he called out, 'Antonie! Antonie!'

Karl heard him and said nothing.

Chapter 18

On his return to Vienna Beethoven wrote to Holz but then mislaid the letter. He wrote again on the 5th, telling him that he was indisposed and confined to bed; asking him to visit; enclosing a canon: *We all err, but each in a different way.*

Braunhofer had been sent for but said it was too far. Staudenheim had also failed to visit. On receiving Beethoven's letter, Holz called in Dr Wawruch, a Professor at the General Hospital and doctor to his fiancée's father, Bogner.

The doctor found Beethoven gravely afflicted with inflammation of the lungs. His face glowed, he spat blood, with each breath he seemed close to choking, wracked by the painful stitch in his side.

'How come I was not sent for until the third day? This man has pneumonia.'

Beethoven fought for his life. The fifth day found him sitting in bed, propped up by pillows, telling his doctor of his fearful journey from Gneixendorf, when he had been lifted out of his sickbed in that God-forsaken village inn to continue his journey in a rack-cart: 'That most wretched vehicle of the devil, a milk-wagon!'

He replied to a year-old letter from his childhood friend, Wegeler, the doctor to whom he had so bitterly related the symptoms of his deafness two and a half decades before. Wegeler had married Breuning's sister, Eleonore; she too had written. It had been in the house of her widowed mother that he had spent some of the happiest times of his young manhood. Frau Breuning had become a second mother to him, after his own mother had died. Wegeler and Eleonore had written about their youth in Bonn, about their friends, about their children: the daughter 'not very musical,' who nevertheless played his sonatas; the son who was musical, now training to be a doctor in Berlin. In his weakened state, re-reading these letters brought tears to his eyes. He recalled his youth in Bonn; the time when Wegeler and the Breunings had whitewashed his room while he was away to give him a pleasant surprise; he told them he still hoped 'to create a few great works and then like an old child to finish my earthly course somewhere among kind people.'

Wegeler had urged him to refute the Encyclopaedia entry which gave him as the love-child of the late King of Prussia. The present King of Prussia was supposed to be sending him a ring – a beautiful diamond, in return for his dedication of the *Choral*. When the ring arrived it turned out to be a cheap-looking rose-coloured stone, valued at but a few hundred paper florins.

The choleric attack this prompted seemed certain to end Beethoven's life. Insult *me* but don't insult *my art*! He was vowing to return the 'costume jewellery' to the Prussian ambassador.

He had been able to get out of bed, walk about, read and write. Wawruch, an amateur 'cellist and ardent admirer of Beethoven's music, had been congratulating himself that his patient had weathered pneumonia; on the morning visit of the 8th day, the doctor found him greatly disturbed. Beethoven was jaundiced all over his body; a frightful attack of diarrhoea and vomiting had threatened to kill him the previous night. A violent rage, a deep grief over ingratitude suffered and undeserved mortification, had, he now learned, caused this dramatic reversal. Trembling and shivering, Beethoven bent double from the pain in his liver and intestines. The doctor pulled down the blanket to find that Beethoven's feet, hitherto only moderately swollen, were now tremendously inflated.

His friends tried to calm his violent anger. Holz told him, 'Master, keep the ring: it is from a king.' Beethoven rose up in the bed declaring, '*I too am a king*!' Karl told him, 'You need nothing from any king. You have more than they. They know it and you know it.'

Breuning had called on Beethoven soon after their return, intent upon getting Karl into the army. Breuning had told Karl, 'He's very ill, you know.' 'Is he?'

Karl had told his uncle. 'You are mistaken if you think that I have become undecided. On the contrary, I rejoice that the matter is being resolved so closely according to my own desires, and I shall never regret my decision.'

Karl had visited Stutterheim, who had confirmed his previous promise to take him into his regiment. 'He was very nice after all and said that before my departure I should come to see him again. I shall be here 5 or 6 days longer.' Beethoven himself wanted to accompany him; instead Breuning helped him make the arrangements for his departure. Karl was busy now getting his kit and tipping the tailor. He had been to a beerhouse where he had seen Holz. Karl told his uncle, 'Holz drinks heavily.'

'What's the matter with you?' Holz had said to Karl on finding that no doctor had been called in. 'Do you want him dead?' *Do you suffer from haemorrhoids? Have you a headache? When was the last bowel movement? Take a deep breath. Since when has the abdomen become so swollen? Frequent urine? Without difficulty? The feet were not swollen? Never any bleeding seen from the rectum?* For Karl, writing down Wawruch's questions at the first consultation, the excitement that hung round that sick-room was incredible. Something was going to happen. Something hung in the air. At first he had thought that he too was coming down with a chill, like his uncle. His intestines seemed chilled, he too was suffering from diarrhoea. Then the whole thing became physical in a different way, his lust seemed insatiable, he did not know how he would manage to bear himself if the maid should appear or if anyone female should visit. He felt stricken, he did not think that this was right, yet he felt powerless against this just as his uncle might yet prove powerless against his fight.

Karl took the oath on the 12th. Breuning told Beethoven, 'Now he only needs to buy whatever one can best get here, then he can travel, since everything else will be done in Iglau. Here he only has to buy a *szako* and a sabre.'

Breuning himself became ill. Arrangements for Karl's departure were delayed.

Karl had shared many a consultation with Dr Wawruch, buying a bedpan and urine-flask at his instruction, telling Beethoven that the urine must be measured. Karl had suddenly found himself in the position of next-of-kin: having discussions with the doctor away from B's presence, being told, 'It is very grave.'

. . . 'He told me he has a strong constitution . . .'

'He always says that. He's going back years. It used to be, once. . . . He was ill a lot, earlier this year, last year. He still thinks that he can take these knocks. He had jaundice five years ago, that took it out of him . . .'

The doctor pricked up his ears at the word 'jaundice.'

Karl told Beethoven that he could eat rice-soup and fruit, rebuked him for drinking water at night, said that Thekla, the maid, should be near him at night, to make warm cloths for him when he was awake; sat with him while he had an enema. 'You must hold your breath, or it will run out. Take a breath. Do not hold your breath, draw it in. Hold it in hard, but longer. Now hold on, then the enema will work.'

Falstaff had played Galitzin's third with the new finale. Beethoven was told how delighted with it everyone was. Beethoven threw back his head and roared. They had told him they found it *Köstlich*. Aye, no doubt you're looking for 'hidden depths' – like looking for something subtle in a fig!

The *Große Fuge* was being dedicated to the Archduke. That blind rage, fury at impotence, at the transparency of all panaceas, the desolate absence of all understanding. Shitting and vomiting himself to death, he was beginning to understand it himself now.

Lying here, ill, with no energy. So many plans, so many plans. He would have liked to have been setting Kuffner's *Saul*. He had Karl look out his old conversation book to remind himself what the man had said.

'Allegorical people leave me cold, and, as for personified ideas: mere wax figures in clothes. Also, everything always and eternally turns about a single point, that the Christians and heathens want to make converts, and so all pure human interest falls away. . . . God said: let there be light! Now might one gladly pray: let night fall. It became light and now can it no more become entire night. Amen.'

He had still not got sorted out an edition of his collected works. 'We cannot at this time make a decision, since we are occupied with other obligations,' Schotts had said. Old Schlesinger however had written, 'It would give me very great pleasure to bring out your complete works.' Artaria had said something along the same lines last summer. Schotts had written to him bellyaching about the pirating of Galitzin's first in Paris. Beethoven had replied on the 9th, laying the blame on Schlesinger, adding that it was always hard to find absolute proofs. 'Old Schlesinger of Berlin was here during the summer and he too wanted the Viennese publisher Mathias Artaria to give him one of my quartets.' Schlesinger had told him that Galitzin's second had been given successfully in Berlin. When he had been in bed for two weeks, Beethoven wrote to Schotts with Rudolph's coat of arms for the Mass, telling them of the success of the performance of the *Choral* in Berlin and asking for songs and bagatelles to be sent to Wegeler.

In the middle of the month he got the real *Saul* – Stumpff of London had sent him all of Handel's works! *Handel*! 'Handel is the greatest composer who has ever lived. I would uncover my head and kneel at his tomb.' Before he was 20, he had written an organ *Preludium* on a theme of Handel and, at twenty-five, the piano and 'cello variations on a theme of *Judas Maccabaeus*: *See, the Conquering Hero Comes*. He had told Potter, a visitor from England in 1817, that he had hitherto considered Mozart the greatest of all composers, but since he had become more familiar with Handel that place he now gave to him. ... Blethering on about Mozart 'immortalizing' the *Messiah*. 'It would have lived without it.' Mozart had been commissioned to adapt four of Handel's works by Swieten. He had reduced 5 voices to 4 – *two sopranos*, tenor and bass. *Rejoice Greatly* he had given to the tenor instead of the soprano. The art of playing high trumpet having fallen into disuse in Mozart's time, Mozart had given the part to the horn, whilst of course setting German words, so that the poor bloody Huns had ended up with singers belting out 'the trombone shall sound!' to the accompaniment of French horn! And here it was, here it was, in all its original splendour, 'And the trumpet shall sound!' and they sang it to *trumpets*! O how wonderful it was!

'I have long wanted these! I can learn much from him!' He fingered the books with great reverence.

He had thought recently, well, mate, you won't be a Seb. Bach, founding a dynasty. You'll just have to settle for being like Handel, with your deafness in place of his blindness. He recalled the panic of previous years, when he had feared he would be deaf and blind.

Every Englishman he met he had urged to jog the memory of the Prince Regent, to whom he had sent a copy of his *Battle* Symphony a decade ago. To Stumpff for some reason this unpaid debt had become 'a tortoise of £600.'

Bugger the Prince Regent. Bugger Friedrich Wilhelm. Now *this* was a gift fit for a king!

Schindler was back on the scene. Johann had arrived from Gneixendorf on the 10th and gave his advice to the doctor on food suitable for an invalid. Beethoven's dropsy had developed; Wawruch found the segregation of urine becoming less, the liver showing the indication of hard nodules, the development of jaundice. The nights were a torment, the enormous volume of water threatening to stop his heart and lungs, leaving him choking.

Beethoven was advised of the urgent necessity that he be tapped. 'If the fluid reaches the heart, then all is lost.'

Staudenheim had been called in for this consultation. The two doctors stood, waiting for his decision. Beethoven was thinking of the 14 burnings to the loins suffered by Karl Josef. He had been finalizing piano sonatas for A at the time ...

During the preparations for the operation, which was to take place on the 20th, a servant, Thekla, was found to be dishonest and was dismissed. The day before the operation, a Dr Jenger paid a visit with two letters from the Pachler-Koschaks who had meant to invite him to their summer estate outside of Graz. Frau Pachler-Koschak he had met during that dreadful summer of 1817, when he had first learnt about Karl Josef's illness. Dr Jenger found Beethoven in great pain, unshaven for three weeks, everything about him in the room lying pell-mell.

Dr Seibert, principal surgeon at Wawruch's hospital, had been called in to perform the operation. As he lay on his back looking up Beethoven saw the faces of Johann, Schindler and Karl. . . . Can't show myself up, the boy is here, the thought ran through his mind, to be followed by the thoughts of Karl's undergoing his operation for hernia, the pain he had inflicted upon himself by the shooting, as the doctor made the incision into his abdomen and introduced the tube. Seeing the water spurting out Beethoven cried, 'Doctor, you remind me of Moses striking the rock with his staff!'

'Thank God it is happily over!' Wawruch wrote. 'If you feel ill you must tell me.' Beethoven declared he felt much better. 'Did the incision give you any pain?' Beethoven made a dismissive movement of the lips. 'From today the sun will continue to ascend higher.' Beethoven said in English, 'God save you.' 'God save you!' said the doctor. 'Can I have coffee?' 'Lukewarm almond milk.' Beethoven grimaced. 'Do you not now feel pain?' 'Feel bloody thirsty.' 'Continue to lie quietly on your side.'

The doctor measured off the water. 'Five measures and a half. I hope that you will sleep more quietly tonight. You bore yourself like a knight.'

The doctor noted that the liquid amounted to 25 pounds but the afterflow was at least five times as much.

Carelessness in removing the bandage at night led to the setting in of a violent inflammation. There were fears that the wound would become gangrenous.

Stutterheim's adjutant had taken Karl to the barracks for his examination by the regimental doctor. He had taken the certificate to Stutterheim, who was giving him a letter for his commanding officer.

'A uniform is ready,' Karl told his uncle. 'On Saturday I will get everything; but tomorrow there's a great deal to do. The brother must buy the necessaries with me. It's the festive season. After the holidays, I have to be with the regiment at Iglau.' Among other things, a watch had to be bought: the one Karl had appeared not elegant enough.

'I must ask you for some money, since I had to promise a gift to the tailor.'

Finally Johann wrote, 'Now you need not buy anything more, for he has everything.'

Karl was planning to travel by stagecoach because the mailcoach cost 38 florins more. 'The stagecoach costs perhaps 12 fl. and that involves a two-day journey.'

The excitement still gripped Karl: as though the weak old man, even now, would rise up from his sick-bed and stop him.

Karl wrote a new year's greeting for his uncle: 'I wish you a happy new year, and it grieves me that I should have been compelled already on the first night to give you cause for displeasure. It might easily have been avoided, however, had you but given the order to have my meal taken to my room.'

The following day, Karl left for Iglau.

> Vienna, Wednesday, January 3, 1827
>
> Before my death I declare that Karl van Beethoven, my beloved nephew, is the sole heir to all my property, including, chiefly, seven bank shares and whatever cash may be available – Should the laws prescribe alterations pertaining to this bequest, then try to turn them so far as possible to my nephew's *advantage* – I appoint you *his trustee* and ask you together with his guardian, Hofrat von Breuning, to be a father to him – May God preserve you – A thousand thanks for the love and friendship you have shown me.

Beethoven sent this letter, intended for Bach, to Stephan for his opinion. Von Breuning wrote:

> I am still too weak to write much to you, but I think that the following few words from a candid heart should be said. Since through Gerhard you have told me that I should read the letter to Dr Bach, I have done so and return it to you for the time being with the following observations. That you name Karl as heir in the event, hopefully far distant, that we all leave this life, is appropriate considering your way of thinking and what you have already done for him. But Karl has

shown himself up until now to be very reckless, and one doesn't know
how his character will shape itself at present; thus I would be of the
opinion that for his own good and for the security of his future you limit
his power to dispose of capital either during his whole life or at least for
a few years more until he has become 24 years old, the age of his
majority. In any case he would have enough yearly income at hand
and the limitation would protect him from the consequences of reckless
actions before he reaches maturity. Speak of this with Hr. Dr. Bach,
whom I should think it would be best for you to have visit you. He will
arrange everything in the simplest way; I should be glad to be able to
talk with you or with Dr Bach about my observations, for I fear that a
mere time limitation will not keep Karl from contracting debts which
he will have to pay subsequently from his whole inheritance.

The *Rotes Haus* where the Breunings lived stood at right angles to the
Schwarzspanierhaus. Gerhard ran back and forth with these messages, or
with plates of soup made by his mother. *Ariel* Beethoven called the boy,
because of his fleetness of foot in carrying out these errands, or *Hosenknopf*,
trouser-button, because of his attachment to his father. Here was a boy of
almost exactly Karl Josef's age, a lively, amiable 13 year old who revered
him and to whom no errand was ever a duty but always a lively joy.
'Ariel,' the ageing man called, and the boy was up and running almost
before the message had left his lips.

He had lived for years in fear of losing Karl, of the boy's death, and now
he was en route to become a soldier. But God has been good, he has sent
me a boy, the same age as my Karl, who loves me . . .

Karl had hated being in the street with him, he said street urchins
taunted them, imitating his singing and stomping out the melodies that
occurred to him as he walked; the state of his clothes, his hat with a hole in
it where it had been jammed back onto the peg after each excursion;
particularly the way that some of his circle, too lazy to write, tried to
mime their thoughts. – All this Karl had objected to, Karl, the boy I
brought up as my son for all these years. They had argued. He had been
very hurt. Karl had refused to be seen out with him. But Gerhard loved
accompanying him, was proud of being seen walking with him, trotted
beside him, happy, clinging to his every word, and *held his hand* – just as
he'd always imagined a son would be.

Now he visited him often, was there even when the operations took
place, giving him the strength to be brave for the boy's sake. Gerhard said
he wished he were a doctor, so that he could help him.

'May I hold your hand? Just something to grip onto so I don't cry out
and scare you all.'

A fine, agile boy, six months younger . . . six months younger instead of
six years older . . . August 1813 to Karl Josef's March . . .

'Has your belly become smaller? You are supposed to perspire more . . .

How was your enema? Have you already read Walter Scott?' He offered to bring him Schiller, the world history by Schröck, travel descriptions.

Karl was told that a second operation had taken place on January 8th, without complications. The water was clearer and the outflow greater than the first time. Ten measures had been drawn off.

Beethoven had written to Karl through Schindler and on the 13th Karl replied, telling his uncle that his captain was very cultivated, that he shared a nice room with the sergeant-major, 'a very fine young man.' There was no such thing as an officers' mess; in the evenings they dined out of barracks. 'For reasons of economy I have already changed my eating place several times.' He had an orderly who got 1 fl. C.M. per month 'aside from the outlays for white lead and chalk for cleaning uniforms. Washing comes to several gulden too, if one wants it clean.' He asked for extra money since he had expected to be paid from the day of his enrolment, but the enrolment list was still in Vienna. A First Lieutenant had requested the flute part from the first piano concerto. 'He loves music and especially your works.'

Karl had addressed him as 'My dear Father' and signed himself 'Your loving son, Carl.' The postscript read, 'You must not think that the little privations to which I am subjected make my lot distasteful to me. On the contrary, rest assured that I am happy in this life and only regret being so far from you.'

Beethoven was growing impatient with his doctor. When Wawruch's name was announced Beethoven would turn his face to the wall: 'O, the ass!' He was encouraged to have faith in his practitioner, though Karl had expressed his distrust and both Johann and Schindler thought that Wawruch should consult Beethoven's earlier doctors to find out more of his medical history.

Beethoven wanted to see Malfatti. He sent a message through Schindler, who brought the reply, 'Tell Beethoven that he, as a master of harmony, knows well that I also must live in harmony with my colleagues.'

Mendacious Malfatti, the Kaiser's doctor, all smooth-talking bedside-manner and smarming to the women of the court. He'd say you weren't dying as you drew your last breath. Malfatti was no different from these other leeches. Malfatti knew well why he wanted to see him.

Malfatti had been his friend as well as his doctor for some years, together with his partner, Bertolini. Bertolini had dined with him when the overture to *Fidelio* had come to him. Malfatti's niece, Therese, he had proposed to in 1810. His friend, Gleichenstein, had married Anna, Therese's sister. He had even written a loyal toast for Bertolini to have sung at a name-day party for Malfatti that must have cost a bloody fortune. Bertolini he had broken with in 1816, when the man had had the nerve to bring to him a Major-General Kyd from England commissioning a symphony *for which he had laid down the rules*! The quarrel with Malfatti had taken place in 1817: Monday, April 14th, 1817, when he had fled to his doctor after learning the first dreadful news.

Further appeals were made to Malfatti. Finally Schindler brought the news that he could get Malfatti there by stealth, under the guise of a consultation with Wawruch. 'The insult he says he suffered still wrankles . . .'

Bugger all that. Beethoven had told Schindler, 'I must see Malfatti alone.'

Malfatti arrived. He took up the chalk and wrote on the slate, 'How is your son?'

In the silence that followed he pondered lest his question had hurt Beethoven, as he recalled their last meeting of almost a decade ago. The frame had shrunk, the once brawny arms like sticks, the cheeks sunken, the broad nose narrow and hooked.

'She might have heard I'm ill. She might want to see me. Write to her. Tell her I'm all right. She'll take it from you: you're my doctor.'

'You don't want to see her?'

'Another thing. There are some papers. Letters from her. If anything does happen, send them to her. I was supposed to burn them.' He wrote down the address as he spoke. 'Some of them I burnt . . .'

Malfatti wrote down again, 'How is your child?'

'I don't know.'

'Would you like me to find out?'

'O yes. Please find out.'

Malfatti went to Beethoven's desk. Beethoven instructed him how to unlock the secret drawer. Malfatti brought the contents to Beethoven. The sick man went through his papers. 'These . . . this one and this one . . . Letters from her . . . Letters about him. Please see that these get back to her.'

The miniature he returned to the pile with his bank-share certificates and other letters, to be returned to the drawer. Malfatti caught sight of the other miniature: another beauty. The 'planned offence' of which he had spoken to Schindler had involved his own niece: Beethoven hurling it at him as he had stormed through the door: 'Thank God we didn't let him into *our* family, thank God that child didn't come out of *her* belly!' Returning the possessions to be kept, Malfatti found himself thinking, you've been loved by some pretty stunning women . . .

Beethoven was holding Stieler's drawing. 'My son.'

'He looks like his mother.'

'Yes.'

'What about this?'

'Could you keep that . . . but bring it to show me – when there's just you and me? I'll see more of it this way than if it's stuck in that drawer.'

The doctor took the sketch and put it with the other papers he had been given. 'They are both beautiful.'

While Malfatti examined him, Beethoven realized Malfatti was hinting at asking him whether he wanted to leave anything to his Karl. Beethoven shook his head. He had always made it a condition of his having Karl that Karl would be provided for. *I'll see he's provided for in my will.*

Beethoven had wanted Malfatti to replace Wawruch and see him daily. Malfatti said that he was too busy.

'If you're not my doctor you're not bound by confidentiality!' Beethoven said in panic.

Malfatti agreed to work in consultation with Wawruch.

Malfatti prescribed frozen punch in place of Wawruch's medications. Beethoven noticed an immediate improvement. He wrote to Schindler, 'Miracles! Miracles! Miracles! The highly-learned gentlemen are both defeated! Only through Malfatti's skill shall I be saved!'

His mind raced off in all directions: the quintet, the oratorio, the 10th.

'The doctor says you're not supposed to work,' Schindler said when he asked for his sketchbook.

'Listen, pal, the man hasn't been *born* who can stop Beethoven composing when he wants to!'

The punch was flamed and heated with fruit-juice before freezing. Beethoven was restricted to one glass a day and forbidden to take it in liquid form but, rather, as an ice. Beethoven however felt so restored by the effect of the cold punch upon his infirm organs that he strove to double or treble his prescription, convinced now that he was saved.

Beethoven felt so greatly restored that he dictated to Schindler a detailed letter to Schotts of essential corrections to the *Choral* and the first Galitzin.

On the 25th Schindler had told Beethoven that the mother of Fräulein Schechner the singer had told him of two remedies which had helped her father when he had been suffering from dropsy. One was juniper berry tea, the other a vapour bath concocted from a head of cabbage, 2 handfuls of caraway seeds and 3 handfuls of hayseed. This latter treatment, said to have been prescribed by the physician of the late King of Bavaria, was recognized by Malfatti who prescribed it for Beethoven, the aim being to encourage him to sweat.

'Malfatti says that this must be tried now since the internal medicine is not having the desired effect. It is nothing but hayseed in two piles placed on warm jugs; however the first bath is to last no longer than half an hour.'

Jugs of hot water were placed in a bath-tub onto which Beethoven was lowered, all of his body save the head being covered by a sheet. Instead of perspiring, his body drew in the vapour.

He was tapped for the third time on February 2nd.

Schindler wrote, 'I am just wondering whether Malfatti won't want to check up today on the condition of your liver and belly. Naturally Seibert wants to see you again today. The water is going through the liver. The well-being of the liver is the key to the whole sickness.'

Wawruch strove to prevent Beethoven returning to the punch. He had slept all through the first night on Malfatti's treatment and had begun to sweat profusely. He had been lively and felt refreshed for a few days. But colic and diarrhoea had resulted from the chill of the iced punch on his intestines; after his self-prescribed increase in the treatment he suffered a rush of blood to the head. He grew soporific, the snore of intoxication mistaken by some for the death-rattle. At times he grew hoarse and even speechless; when he did talk, he rambled. His violence increased.

He sat in the bed in fury when he had visitors. 'This is no way for a man to be. Folk come to see you, they want entertaining. Bit of grub. Smoke and a natter. In a tavern, pint at your elbow.' He ate the grapes that they had brought him, spitting the pips with venom onto the bed, onto the floor.

'I'd give anything now to be able to walk round the glacis, come back and work on that symphony.'

He wrote the same thing to Zmeskall, adding, characteristically, Zmeskall thought, 'Yet there is no evil which has not something good in it as well.' Zmeskall had tried to change rooms to be near him. He was very concerned lest Beethoven should feel the need to talk of Karl Josef. Unaware of the arrangements made with Malfatti, Zmeskall did not know whether he ought to write to Toni. She had written to him once, in 1815, before Caspar Carl's death, when Beethoven had written her a letter she thought hinting at suicide. She had written begging him to watch over Beethoven and befriend him. He cursed his crippled state which barred him from close intercourse with Beethoven.

At times his concern rose to anger: You! You think nobody cares for you; you think you make no impression on any life! You've got the whole of Vienna and half Frankfurt besotted about you – everyone is concerned!

'Wolfmayer likes you very much,' Gerhard told Beethoven. 'When he went away he said, with tears in his eyes, "O, the great man, the pity of it!"'

Beethoven had heard from Wegeler again, who apparently had not heard from him. He made arrangements for the letter and picture he'd thought Breuning had sent to be forwarded through Schotts, then later through another courier. Meanwhile he asked Schotts for fine Rhine wine, the prospect of which, Malfatti thought, might encourage him.

He had written to Stumpff on the 8th, thanking him for the Handel, asking if further help could be made available to him from England. Schindler and Breuning thought that this was wrong. 'Apply again to Galitzin: that man owes you 125 ducats.'

Beethoven grew frantic about the cost of his own treatment, outstanding bills for Karl's uniform. They were urging him to sell a bank-share. Breuning tried to tell him, 'The boy's out in the world. He's earning his living. You've done your duty as a father.' . . . Not to have got so far, to see it whittled to nothing at this stage! *I'll see he's provided for in my will.*

Beethoven wrote begging letters to Smart and Moscheles, reminding them of the handsome offer made by the Philharmonic Society a few years ago to organise a concert for his benefit and asking them to fulfil this without delay since he was too ill now to make a living by composing.

He was still up to talking international politics with Falstaff and Linke; he had made a point of wanting to read Canning's speech of December 12th in full; though when Gleichenstein visited with his wife and son he failed to recognize Countess Anna, Therese Malfatti's sister.

Diabelli had given him a print of Haydn's birthplace. He showed it to Gerhard. 'Look, I got this today! See this little house, and in it so great a man was born!'

He was sick of this. He stank. The room stank. They said they could not let in fresh air, he mustn't get cold. . . . So used to being clean, every day, clean underwear, whatever the outer. Now he lay at the mercy of others, to clean him, to bring him his bedpan, to give him an enema. Can't sleep, can't eat, can't shit, can't even pee!

February drew towards its close. On the 27th he was tapped for the fourth time. This time the fluid drained from his body flowed half-way across the floor to the middle of the room.

The bedding was saturated. The doctor suggested that an oil-cloth be brought and spread across the couch.

Schindler wrote, 'The maid will put a wooden vessel under the bed so that the water cannot run over the room. No more straw in the house to fill the other mattress. The straw is all fouled. This evening the other will be filled and you can have it then.'

Gerhard had tried to cheer him. 'I heard today that the bugs wake you every moment. Sleep is good for you. I'll get something for the bugs. When you see one, catch it with a needle, you'll soon get rid of them.'

Breuning adjured, 'You must cheer up, poor spirits stop you from getting better.'

Someone had written, of the disgusting fluid the poor maid was still on her hands and knees trying to clear, 'This should be bottled and given to other composers!'

Beethoven turned to the wall, finally overcome by his state of illness, neglect and lack of love.

When Karl had left, leaving him on his sickbed, the thought had crossed his mind, 'I should have stayed with the other.' He had said it aloud, but nobody present, Schindler, Johann, had had a notion what he meant. They had not even cared. They cared for him, bodily. As for his inner soul, he was alone in the world.

Standing before him in the fields that one warm day in Karlsbad: slim with small boobs but lovely, no *Fettlümmerl* for him! legs that were everything his own weren't: long, shapely, smooth; her still-flat belly containing his child.

No, I don't need anything from any king: but I need my queen, the love of a woman, my beautiful Toni. O God, even if she were old and ugly: the *essence* of Toni, Toni's love *for me*.

He wanted to be reached out to and touched. A tight frozen ball of loneliness. O you silly old man. You've been on your own all your life.

He thought of all the times in his life when he had willed death to him, by God's or by his own hand; recalled the odd instance of old people's lingering who must know and feel themselves to be a burden when they knew as well as their children that their time had come; recalled the shock of the death of a child. Now it was as though a rock-face had shifted, he stood at the further side of the divide.

The business of dying. He had found that now, here, a man does not easily accept his own death. Yet strangely there was, yet, none of the panic that had filled him when he had so yearned for death in 1813, 1817 . . .

He wanted to laugh, I'd have liked to have died writing music or making love. No, not the latter, how unfair to the woman.

. . . Toni, his grief, his fear of seeing her, wondering how she had changed, a matron now. 'Antonia was the greatest of all the Roman matrons, noted throughout the Empire for her virtue and her beauty.' 'Was she?' 'Yes. You're better.' He still recalled her as he had known her; it was her sight of him that terrified him and he felt that some of his friends were urging him to it, Zmeskall he knew wanted . . . Holz . . . perhaps even Malfatti; he dreaded their taking the step behind his back when he was too incapable to act . . .

He wanted no more visitors. He was terrified by the prospect of a visit by a woman. . . . 'Demoiselle Schechner,' almost forcing her way to his bedside to tell him of her great admiration for his music, of her successes . . . 'Is she young? Pretty?' he had said in great agitation. He had cried out that he did not want to see her. She had been already in the room, making her way to his bed. It was not her.

He grew terrified at the thought of her walking through that door.

'Don't let a woman come in!' he begged of Schindler, clutching his arm. 'Don't let a woman!'

I've given her nothing . . . why should *she* come to see me? . . . Don't want *her* to *see me like this*!

They would not announce a woman. They would announce a woman with a child . . .

He wished that he had married her, got Franz to divorce her and married her – Karl – bastard – I would have owned him – then there would have been nothing to find out. I would have been *with her*. I could have spent my life *with her*.

2 of his great-grandfather's 4 children had died . . . 2 of his grand-

father's children had also died; his own mother had lost half of her sons and all of her daughters. Grandfather Ludwig had died on Christmas Eve. Grandfather Ludwig had been trained to play the organ from the age of 13. He had been recalling his grandfather's death from a stroke when he had written to Bach about his will just as he was beginning those last 5 quartets . . . had to see Bach about his will . . . *He* hadn't died of a stroke. He was dying now, of something or other . . . Time when he had told Bach to pay Franz 600 florins from Schotts. Had that been paid?

. . . Getting notification that the *Cäcilia-Verein* of Frankfurt wanted to subscribe to his Mass. He had wanted to run to Zmeskall and say, 'Toni still loves me!' It had made him want to cry in gratitude for her love. O Toni, one letter from you! He had felt vividly alive, bursting with creative energy, eager to write everything in the world for her, as though it were already written, pluck it from the skies, the way he had felt the night she had told him, 'Ludwig, I'm having your baby.'

You're so good to me, you're so good for me, you love me . . . without hurting anyone! Who else in the world would know how to do that!

I didn't deserve her love, and yet I got it. Got it and kept it, after all I did to her. He was beginning to think that, in this life, you got love but always from those you did not expect to love you, whilst those whom you loved and you thought you deserved . . . Josephine's love he thought he had deserved, his intentions towards her always honourable . . . Karl's love he knew he'd earnt, he believed he had bent over backwards, moved heaven and earth for that boy . . . and yet I got more love from Maxe. All the love I get comes from that family . . . Little Maxe, who threw water over me!

. . . Dedicating the *Diabelli* to Toni, scarcely daring to touch the paper lest he mark it, trying to work out a classical dedication:

To you who are the best wife and mother
From the unworthiest musician.

. . . Walking across carriage-busy roads, indifferent whether he lived or died, preferring to die, he did not want to live. O, you won't die now! You never do die when you want to this much, Beethoven!

He was terrified of anything bad happening to his child, terrified of his being left alone, ever in his life, abandoned, lonely.

Wawruch sat by him, promising an amelioration of his suffering with the coming spring.

'If there were a physician who could help me now,' he looked at the doctor and said in English, 'his name shall be called Wonderful!'

No Schlesinger quintets. No 10th symphony. He had had notions for the 10th when writing the *Große*, when he had had thoughts of going to London . . .

No requiem for Wolfmayer, Mass for the Kaiser. 'A B C D – Abbé cédoit,' Karl had written of Stadler. No letters from Karl, not even the translation of a letter to Smart into English. 'The carnival at Iglau must be preventing him.' 'Holz never comes to see me. Karl won't write. The only one ever around is Mr *Shitting*!'

Schindler claimed to have had an accident. The brokenness of Beethoven's letter of sympathy, full of non-sequiturs which he recognized as the names of directors of the London Philharmonic, led Schindler to return to the bedside, ashamed.

'I always carry a notebook on me, and, should a thought occur to me, I jot it down at once. I even get up in the night when something occurs to me, otherwise I might forget it.' The boy, his son's age, had held his hand in the street, proud to be with him.

Gerhard often found him sleeping. He sat down quietly, turning the pages of the conversation book. Once he had come across the entry, 'Your quartet which Falstaff played yesterday did not please.' When Beethoven awoke the boy showed this to him.

'It will please them someday.'

The boy hung on the man's every word as Beethoven declared that he wrote as he thought best, undeterred by the judgement of contemporaries. 'I know that I am an artist.'

. . . The artist is one who cries, *Don't hate me*! – but if you do I shall be strong enough to take it, for I know I am right.

Vita brevis, ars longa – God help me if it's the other way around!

He closed his eyes and saw himself. . . . I don't understand it either . . . I probably understand it less than anyone else does. He realized that this was what A had been trying to reach when she had asked him so often about composing. It had never even occurred to him before: the Terrible Mystery that is art.

O how strange it is . . . No, I see it less than anyone else does.

How strange to be other. How strange to spend the whole of a life without that. What did people do, what were people . . . fancy having a whole life to live through without being possessed by *that*. Incredible.

It had rather surprised him on his deathbed to realize that he had lived out his time after all and had not taken his own life.

The greatest pleasure I have had in life has been when I have lived like a monk and have been composing. Pure unalloyed – *decent* – without guilt – probably even without faith – there is no *forcing* – you just are. You pay dear for your art but you'd pay dearer without it. *They cannot take away from me my place in the history of music.*

I shall never fuck a woman again. All those fucks related to composition. Fucks at the start. Fucks at the end. Often not so many in the middle. Fucking his hand, fucking himself: fucking the thing into existence. No one had any idea how sheerly *physical* creating music was. . . . Fucking the backside off the music. No women ever for conception fucks. . . . What about writing the 8th inside her!

Part of the 8th. It happened sometimes. No whole idea was ever conceived inside a woman . . .

. . . Conception fucks. Bereavement fucks. 'Composing is sexual with you . . .' Antonie, *Antonie*!

. . . Such a wide, open letter for an 'L' to tip onto its back and enter . . .

No, I shall never have a woman again. No more *Namenlose Freude* for you, mate!

And what was the last piece of music he had composed – the last, it seemed, that Beethoven ever would compose? Why, why, he supposed, his canon to Holz! *We all err, but each in a different way.* He had written the same thing to Frau Streicher, in 1817. 1817, when Karl Josef's illness . . .

And what had been the last? The last full movement? Judas got 30. I did it for half that. The *great flight* from the *great fugue*! He had nearly died the night they first performed that.

'O, I shouldn't have done it! O! O! O, *the wages of sin is death*!' He was laughing, wiping the tears of laughter from his eyes.

Later that day he found himself throwing Sir Walter Scott at the wall: 'The man writes for money only!'

If you have played the *Cavatina* right, there is no way you can follow it with *that*. He had thought they would have understood that, yet here they were, prancing around like a dog's bollocks over that rondo.

The first principle of art: when something is as right as that, you do not touch it. When it's right and you've put it into the world, *even the artist* has not the right to touch it.

Each in its own way. Art demands of us that we shall not stand still. It certainly does not expect of us that we shall go *backwards*.

He should write the boy one piece of music . . . give it to Malfatti . . .

'Perhaps you'll write a piece for me someday . . .'

'You stupid bitch! Everything that I do is for you now!'

Karl had told him a year ago that Malfatti was a brother-in-law of the new Czar. He meant Constantine, not Nicolas. 'They have two sisters for wives.'

A pile of letters . . . his thank-you letter from Maxe for Opus 109, Toni's letter after Opus 120 . . . her letter of 1816, when she had thanked him for Karl. He almost wanted Malfatti to read the letters: he wanted someone to know that someone at some time had loved him.

He dreaded Toni's walking through that door as she had done at Prague. 'You've given me Karl and deprived me of you and deprived me of our other healthy children.' He could not envisage her coming in love, heard only her voice begrudging.

He told himself that he still remembered the weight of her round breast cupped in his hand, the soft skin of her waist, her thighs: no woman ever had softer skin; her skin was as soft as that of a child . . .

. . . Tawny, swarthy, *The Spaniard*, broad-shouldered, 'the unlicked bear,' ugly but strong. Who was this small stick-like figure lying on a bed in the *Schwarzspanierhaus*? Embarrassment enough that Malfatti, who had known him when he was fit, upstanding, broad of shoulder, firm of foot, should meet with this: a bony scarecrow, its huge belly quivering with water.

Thinking Malfatti had written, or that A had read the news in the papers, he grew daily more anxious at the thought of a visit. He lived in terror of opening his eyes and seeing in his doorway the mentally-retarded boy that he had brought into the world.

He said to Breuning, 'You are lucky. You have a lovely son.'

Breuning wrote on his slate, 'You have won my boy's heart.'

'You're the best of them all,' Gerhard said. 'All the others are scoundrels.'

Gerhard leapt onto the bed, embracing him.

He held the boy to him with unrecognized skeletal arms. 'I love you, Karl! I love you, I love you, I love you!' Gerhard's face was pressed close to his chest. He tried to hold the boy tighter. 'O my son, I really love you, I really want you! Why, you're not crippled at all, you're wonderful!'

Karl had acknowledged the receipt of money, returned the translation, and on the 4th of March wrote:

My dear Father,

I have just received the books you sent me and thank you very much for them.

You will have got the translation of the letter to Smart; I don't doubt that it will have favourable results.

Just today a cadet, who has been in Vienna on a furlough, returned to his battalion; and he reports having heard that you had been saved by a frozen punch and are feeling well. I hope that this last is true no matter what the means may have been.

There is little new about myself to tell; the service goes its usual way with the difference only that the weather is much milder, so the watches are easier.

Write to me very soon about the state of your health; also give my hearty greetings to Hofrat Breuning. I kiss you.

Your loving son Charl.

P.S. Please stamp your letters because I have to pay a lot of postage here for which I hardly have enough from my account.

The day that this arrived, Beethoven sent another begging letter to Smart.

He felt somewhat revived two days later. What was the date now? March the 8th. Why, my little baby, you're *14*!

The Old Adam was in him. He wanted to do something rebellious. When Hummel was announced with his pupil, Beethoven made them wait until he had had the maid and Schindler help him pull on his long boots, drawn his dressing-gown about his fat middle, and sat down to greet them at his window-seat.

Hummel, his old competitor, pianist and *Kapellmeister*, who as a child had taken lessons from Mozart. He had succeeded Haydn as *Kapellmeister* to Prince Esterhazy before living as a virtuoso in Vienna. He had left in 1816 to become *Kapellmeister* at Stuttgart and, since 1820, at Weimar. His pupil was a 15 year old called Hiller, who sat taking notes, to Beethoven's amusement: this isn't Weimar and this ain't *Goethe*!

The two men embraced with the warmth of old rivals who know each other's worth. To Beethoven's delight he found himself conducting business: one of Hummel's concertos had been pirated before it had been brought out by the lawful publisher. Hummel sought his signature on a petition to the Frankfurt *Bundesversammlung* seeking to outlaw the pirating of musical works.

'Yes, yes!' Beethoven agreed enthusiastically. 'This is vital for my own collected works!'

While Hummel sat at Beethoven's desk drafting the petition, Beethoven talked to the boy, telling him about Karl. 'Not much older than you. Just gone for a soldier. Had to leave Vienna. Authorities wouldn't let him stay. Lot of nonsense, over just a trifle. They hang the little thieves but let the big ones go!'

He asked about Hiller's own musical studies. 'Art must be propagated ceaselessly.' When told of the exclusive interest in Vienna for Italian opera, Beethoven declared, 'They say: *vox populi, vox Dei*. I have never believed it.'

Hummel brought him the petition to sign. 'Frankfurt, eh,' he cried. 'Frankfurt! Frankfurt! Frankfurt, on the 8th of March!'

When Hiller visited again with Hummel five days later they found him in a very different state. Beethoven had discovered the loss of his ring that morning. His fingers had grown so thin it had fallen off.

Johann said he had it. In fact the ring was lost. 'It must have fallen out in the straw,' Johann said to Schindler.

He wanted his ring from Johann. Johann made to fetch the bastard diamond from the King of Prussia. 'Don't give him that, for God's sake – he'll go mad!' Johann reluctantly pulled off his own wedding-ring and Beethoven lay fondling and kissing the ring which Therese had placed on Johann's hand.

Hummel and Hiller found Beethoven in bed, groaning in pain, bemoaning that he had never married. 'You are a lucky man: you have a wife who takes care of you, who is in love with you.' He sighed heavily, bemoaning his bachelor state. He gripped Hummel's arm, begging him to bring his wife to see him.

When they had calmed him he showed them the picture of Haydn's birthplace and asked Hummel to play at a concert for Schindler at which he himself had once planned to co-operate. 'He is a good man who has gone to a great deal of trouble on my account. Now I should like you to do me the favour of playing. We must always help poor artists.'

Johann took back his ring as soon as he could, fearful lest Beethoven spot the difference. 'What was his like?' Schindler asked. 'This one's not a patch on it,' Johann said, down on his hands and knees, seeking his brother's ring. 'Ten times the amount of gold in that.'

Beethoven cried out from the bed above him, 'Where's my son Karl? Where's Karl? My son Karl? Where is he?' He was patting the bed, trying to locate the boy's hand. Schindler said to Johann, 'He means Gerhard. He was calling him Karl earlier.'

Beethoven, after his own puncturings, recalling the fourteen burnings endured by his son, had suddenly grown agitated, flaying himself about the bed, crying out, 'Karl! Karl! O God, I love you! O, O, O my son!' haunted by the pain of his child. *What kind of a father have I been?* I loved that child. . . . Love . . .

I wanted to feel my child move in you, Toni! O God, I've never ever held my child.

Beethoven was by now allowed all the punch he wanted.

He was sending requests for wine to Pasqualati and Schotts; Malfatti himself had given him several bottles of *Gumpoldskirchner* and broken a bottle of champagne with him.

Pasqualati was in touch daily, sending select plates of stewed fruit and game, asking the doctor's views on wine, sending champagne. Beethoven responded when he could, once even writing in ink, in shaky hand. Pasqualati had been his landlord when he had been with Toni.

He wrote to Moscheles on the 14th, 'Truly my lot is a very hard one! However, I am resigned to accept whatever Fate may bring; and I only continue to pray that God in His divine wisdom may so order events that as long as I have to endure this living death I may be protected from want. This would give me sufficient strength to bear my lot, however hard and terrible it may prove to be, with a feeling of submission to the will of the Almighty.'

Before his first letters to Moscheles and Smart had reached London, Stumpff, who had already heard of Beethoven's condition from Streicher, had gone to them himself requesting that a meeting of the Philharmonic Society's directors be held to look into this matter. This meeting had taken place on the 28th of February when the 18 men present, many of them Beethoven's friends, passed a resolution that £100 be sent to Beethoven.

On March the 15th Rau of the banking house of Eskeles called upon Beethoven to tell him the good news. Rau wanted to hold on to half; Beethoven replied that he considered this money sent from heaven and that he needed it all. 'May God reward them all a thousandfold!' he cried several times.

The news of the love in which he was held by the English had him swelled with pride – literally, it seemed, for during the night the wound from his last operation abruptly burst, bringing swift relief as the accumulated water gushed out.

A grandfather chair was bought for him to sit in for half an hour a day while his bed was aired and turned. 'Just in time!' Schindler cried. 'But 340 paper florins left in the cashbox! Now we can have something better than bits of beef and vegetables!'

Schindler dined with Beethoven every day. Beethoven's favourite fish dishes were now prepared, but after a spoonful he pushed the bowl away.

Hüttenbrenner was in Vienna and arrived at Beethoven's lodgings with Schubert. Schindler thought Beethoven too weak to cope with two visitors and asked Beethoven whom he wished to see first.

'Let Schubert come first.'

Schindler had shown Beethoven Schubert's songs during the crisis in his illness between the third and fourth operations. Beethoven had grown enthusiastic. ' . . . Had I known of these, I would have set them . . . surely the divine spark lives in Schubert!'

Schubert had delivered a set of his 4-hand variations to Beethoven in 1822, but Beethoven had been out. He had left them with a servant. He had learnt since that Beethoven had been delighted with them and had played them often with Karl.

Beethoven now embraced him warmly: Schubert, who, instead of raging as he had done at the advent in Vienna of Rossini, had taken the piss by writing two 'Overtures in the Italian Style' – when, God help us, he had been no more than 20.

'By God! Look at this! *An der Musik*! By God, I'd have set this had I known of it! But no, no, you've done a fine job!' – a composition of beauty and integrity, the music aptly reflecting its theme.

How come they'd hardly met before? Schubert always attended Falstaff's concerts: he'd thanked Holz for the pleasure they had given him. 'He talked very mystically, always,' Holz had said of Schubert; that had put him off. But here was a man, even smaller than he was, with round face, round glasses like his own; a man who set songs fit for the angels. Someone in Schubert's circle had once laughed, 'God had this big piece of clay. He looked at it and thought, what shall I do with that? Give 'em one composer? Too big. Make two. He broke it in half, a bit unevenly. So we've got Beethoven and Schubert!'

Schubert was writing of Falstaff's subscription series. Beethoven said, 'You heard my *Große*?'

 . . . A year ago almost to the day. The first mighty fugue was tremendous, the 'cellist lifting off his bow in a whipping motion, slamming it down, so that what he was seeing was the rape of the 'cello. His musical confidence, assurance, his mastery – in all senses – of his instrument: exhilarating, as was the whole musical sound: an incredible sound, it almost goes beyond music, pushes music to its boundaries, almost it stops being music, it stays this side but takes you out there, every time you catch yourself thinking it: it takes you to the edge but then brilliantly doesn't, does not push you over, all the time it remains as music, yet your heart is in your mouth in disbelief at this fearful, incredible, this brilliant *sound* . . . surrounding you . . . you are lost inside it.

O! No one has ever written one like that and no one ever will write one like that. That is it, that is music, and that is the whole, the end of music, no more music can be written in the world after that for that is all: he has finished it: he has written music to the edge of the world and stood it at the brink and there left it toppling, not toppling, swaying, but you fear it might topple, and music and listener stand there swaying, wondering with each instant whether they might topple . . .

O this O this you can never top this O take me out of here I am not a composer any more.

He has killed it! That bastard has killed it! Taken music out to the edge of the earth so that no more music can be written!

He had not got up and fled, he had stayed, to hear it descend into that first *meno mosso e moderato*, the first time played much better than the second, at Dembscher's too sweetly, but by Schuppanzigh . . . harsh beauty: beauty through harshness, *harsh, harsh*, O aim not for beauty . . . yes aim for beauty but not in a straight line, *curve* to it, this music is not the arrow, play this as the bow . . .

And then the incredible trills, the thrills the trills trilling to all eternity, such force, such power, and pure Beethoven, no other man God has ever made could have done it, and no man He will make, had Beethoven not done this then this would have stayed undone for ever . . .

. . . Merry this time, after the frenzy . . . the jolly tune earlier, he had forgotten that – in the middle of a fucking *Fuge*, for the love of *God*! – and then the ending: the fist slammed down on the table.

Beethoven had become for him in that thrilling incredible 15, 17 minutes what Bach's 48 had been hitherto: you say *Bach's 48*, you say *music*. Not now! Not now! For him now, for Franz Schubert, you say *music* and you say *Große Fuge*.

Schubert wrote, 'I wish I had written that.'

Listening to it again, even after having had sight of the score, he still did not believe that any man had written it: *did you ever hear a man fight so*!

Any man could die happy having written that.

'Made me write another movement. *Gemütlichkeit. Gemütlichkeit.* They didn't even like the first, third and fifth movements!'

That man has taken an art-form and he has killed it, Schubert had thought. No man can ever write a string quartet again. But now he was being shown a new quartet by Beethoven: his last, in F, four movements. 'No, no one has played this yet.'

All the pain is in the piano sonatas, Schubert thought. The pain *and the relief from pain* is in the string quartets. Overcome by the slow movement, he was almost passing out, as he was to come close to fainting at opus 131 a year later when taken to hear it by Holz. He combines pain and beauty . . . to such a heartbreaking extent . . .

I set songs. *He* puts the words *into the music*!

Schubert almost fled from Beethoven, crying as he pelted down the stairs, 'The man is hardly writing music. It is damn nearly words.'

'I'm glad you've brought your wife,' Schindler greeted Hummel on his next visit, on the 20th. 'He keeps saying he wants to see someone beautiful. All his visitors have been men.'

Frau Hummel was Röckel's sister. Beethoven had known her since before her marriage in 1813. Röckel had been his Florestan in the 1806 revival. She was still good-looking. He thought she must be Toni's age.

'What can I do to make you comfortable?'

'The first thing that you can do is to give me a cuddle.'

It was hard for him always to sit up in bed, yet she embraced him and he pulled her to him, seeing Hummel above her. 'Aye, aye, if I had the strength I would take her – you'd lose your wife!'

Hummel held him by the shoulder. 'You're all right! – Nothing wrong with you! . . .'

Aware that he was dying, he yet spoke of grandiose schemes: all the things that he would do for London. 'I'll compose a grand overture for them, aye, and a grand symphony! And when I've done that, I'll visit you, Frau Hummel!'

His eyes, still lively on their last visit, were now drooped and closing. His visitors no longer wrote anything for him.

He still insisted on a kiss from Frau Hummel before she left. She bent and kissed the dying man on the forehead.

Beethoven said, 'On the mouth.'

When she had kissed him he was laughing, 'Knew that I hadn't had my last kiss!' He motioned her to bend towards him again and whispered, 'I shall hear in heaven.'

Frau Hummel was crying when she had left him. 'He's so *little*! He doesn't look like a full-grown man, he looks like a child.'

Hummel slipped something into her hand.

'What's that?'

'It's his quill. I took it when he'd signed the petition. So he didn't get even that kiss for free. Cheer up: you've got the last quill he ever used.'

Beethoven signed a declaration that his 7-movement quartet belonged to Schotts. He had asked them to dedicate this to Wolfmayer, then realized that he had given no gift to Stutterheim. He had written again to Schotts requesting that their quartet be dedicated to the Lieutenant Field-Marshal. The last quartet he gave to Wolfmayer.

He wrote again to Galitzin's bankers, requesting the 125 ducats said to have been deposited by Galitzin before his departure for Persia.

Hüttenbrenner visited again with Schubert, this time with Teltscher, who wanted to make a sketch of Beethoven. They stood in the doorway, waiting to be admitted. Beethoven fixed them with an immovable gaze, making incomprehensible signs with his hand. Schubert, moved beyond endurance, led his companions from the room.

Abruptly he sat bolt upright in bed and yelled with the force of the devil, 'They liked my *scherzos*! They *liked my scherzos*!' He raised himself up and with all his strength thumped the wall.

Karl had called the *Schwarzspanierhaus* 'a place where noisy cripples come to die.' Confined to a room, to a bed, to a chair, for four months gazing at the same four walls. Unable to go out, see sights, breathe country air, to walk: to see the trees change with the seasons, walking at will, on your own hind legs. I've had a bellyful of it!

I've had it for four months. He's got it for a lifetime. Karl, Karl, a lifetime of this – but without the music, without the memories.

He writhed on his deathbed. O, now I understand you, my son!

It was March 23rd. There were papers to be signed: the transfer of the guardianship to Breuning, the signing of the will. Beethoven lay in a half-stupor. Breuning, Schindler and Johann raised him and pushed pillows under him for support. The documents were placed before him one at a time and an inked pen put into his hand. He signed laboriously, his fist shaking, one time forgetting the 'h', another an 'e'.

Breuning had drafted a new will allowing Karl only the income of the estate, fearful lest Karl should dissipate the capital or keep his mother in dissolute ways. The sick man argued against any change. When he at last acceded, he copied the whole in his own hand, not content to sign theirs.

When they saw the will they knew why. He had changed their 'legitimate' to 'natural'. The will read: 'My nephew Karl shall be my sole legatee, but the capital of my estate shall fall to his natural or testamentary heirs.'

He threw his pen down with a flourish. 'There! I'll write no more!'

Breuning read with concern. 'There will be controversy.'

He urged Beethoven to sign his draft.

'I've written it. I've signed it.'

'But you've put "natural" not "legitimate" . . .'

'It's the same thing.'

Wawruch had studied as a theologian, and Beethoven had had Johann and Schindler dropping him hints. Inside himself Beethoven was angry. They were so diffident, wary, so po-faced. If you've got something you want to say to me, say it! Terrified of asking *him*, as though *he* were going to rise from his deathbed throwing punches and abusing them for their temerity in making the suggestion. Sin, sin, what is a sin? Sin is when you don't get up in the night for your music. His three doctors were departing, heads huddled together after a long consultation. He raised his head, calling after them, '*Plaudite, amici, comoedia finita est!*'

When the Hummels visited he was exhausted. He could not speak.

Sweat stood out on his brow. Frau Hummel took out her own fine handkerchief and mopped his forehead. He gazed at her gratefully with broken eyes.

When she had gone he gazed at the door, fearful of her appearing with Karl even as he mourned her non-appearance. I don't deserve love from any woman. *I am begging for help.* He groaned in self-hatred. O God forgive me – punish *me*! Don't take it out on her, on him. In my last hours on earth, God make me suffer agony *if it will take the pain from her and him.* Immediately he filled with burning love for them both and regret to the point of such agony that he thought, my prayer is being answered.

... *and Josef shall put his hand upon thine eyes.*

O God, don't let Toni die while he's alive. Please please please grant a long life to Toni! Don't let him be *put away, locked up*! Keep him with you! O Toni, Toni, *love him*!

That night he was up to his old tricks, spitting grape-pips on the bed, only now he was too weak to eat grapes, he spat the whole lot on his bedding.

... spitting grape-pips on the bed, stupid Schindler trying to restrain him. He wished it had been a daughter. He wished she had been here now to mother him. – Unfair to her! – Bring him comfort on his deathbed. He was violently angry but impotent, inside he raged but he had no outlet, no strength. His thin wan hand tossed the grape-pips onto the floor, his mouth pursed. The expression on his face was one of extreme anger.

Schindler saw first the lips: he looked like a man locked in extreme concentration. He had seen his own father look so when absorbed in work. Then he saw there was something implacably livid, enervatedly livid ... livid bitterness; he knew not whether at life's disappointments or at dying.

Once Beethoven yelled, full voice, full force, '*Bastard!*' – O God, to be able to write that quintet! Who will write it now? No one. No one. Bastard!

To have no one but Schindler at one's deathbed. Schindler and God! *Ha!* He thought of her, he did not want to weep, was anyway too angry. He spat out another whole grape and tossed it away; later noticed and lay gazing at it with a subdued relish that for an instant could be called gleeful.

Schindler adjusted his pillows behind him. 'You're a vicious bastard, aren't you? Vicious bastard.' Beethoven's broken eye met his; Schindler wanted to cry.

The priest was called the next morning. 'Get them out of here,' Beethoven cried. 'I'm not confessing to the public gallery!'

Toni had crossed him once as the priest now crossed him. The certainty of the genuflecting Catholic. He had longed for that all his life. He had told the priest, 'I'm not a Catholic.' 'You want someone of another faith?'

He wanted to laugh. Faith! What a weak word! Wanted to laugh: I *know* God. I know that my Redeemer liveth. But my Redeemer is God. Not Christ. God.

'I believe in God the Father Almighty.'

Schindler, Breuning, and others present returned to the room to witness Beethoven receive extreme unction.

At one o'clock that day the special consignment of wine and wine-with-herbs shipped via Frankfurt arrived from Schotts. Seeing Schindler unwrapping the bottles, Beethoven muttered, 'Pity, pity – too late!' He spoke no more in consciousness. A little of the wine was administered to him in spoonfuls from time to time while he could still swallow it. As evening approached he lost consciousness and the death-struggle began.

Schindler sat with a glass at his elbow, writing to Moscheles. Rudesheimer Berg, vintage 1806, eh? Not bad. He needed this, it was no easy letter, with Beethoven lying *in delirio*, he having to excuse himself from the fact that Beethoven had drawn the whole £100 at once. He had still seemed to think that they would give a benefit concert for him, from which they would deduct their £100. Not that it mattered now. He was comatose.

No sooner had he thought this than Beethoven was crying out. Schindler thought that he cried, 'Anton, Anton!' Schindler went to him.

Schindler had spilt wine on his letter, startled by the voice. He started again:

> My dear Moscheles, when you read these lines, our friend will no longer be among the living. His dissolution advances with giant strides, and we all have but the single wish that we may see him soon relieved of his terrible sufferings. Nothing else remains for us to do. For the past eight days he has been lying like one well-nigh dead, save frequent moments when he gathers his last energies to ask about something or for something. His condition is terrible and exactly like that (as we have recently read) of the Duke of York. He is continually plunged in dull brooding, hangs his head on his breast, and stares for hours at a time at one spot. He seldom recognizes those whom he knows best save when he is told who is standing before him. In short, it is horrifying to see all this, and it is a condition which can last only a few days more, for since yesterday all his bodily functions have ceased. So, if it be God's will, he, and we with him, will soon be relieved.

They had expected to find him dead the next morning, but he lived through that daylight and the next. He lay completely unconscious, breathing so stertorously that the rattle could be heard from the ante-room. Many visitors called. None was admitted. Schindler had to manhandle some of them.

When Hüttenbrenner was admitted at 3 o'clock on the 26th he found in the room Breuning with his son, his own friend, Teltscher, and the woman he had mistaken for Therese, in reality the maid. Teltscher was sketching the dying genius. Breuning soon found this offensive, spoke out, and Teltscher left. Soon after this Breuning himself left, with his son and Schindler. Hüttenbrenner found himself alone with the dying man.

Breuning and Schindler made their way to the small village of Währing to select a grave beside the spot where Breuning had buried his first wife. A heavy storm hampered their return. The horses were rearing at the violent thunder and one of them threatened to bolt. The snow had turned to hail and they could not see. The coachman pulled up his carriage at the side of the road.

Hüttenbrenner, a wealthy young man from Graz who had come to Vienna in 1815 to study with Salieri and had formed a deep friendship with Schubert, was gratified but surprised that Beethoven's closer friends had left them alone at this auspicious hour. Beethoven's first words to him, when he had interrupted the composer at work with two copyists to show him his own work, had been, 'I am not worthy that you should visit me.'

Hail lashed the building. Lightning shot across the blackened sky. Thunder shook the house, deadening the death-rattle. The leafless trees roared in the wind. The window-catch banged. The rose that had once pricked Beethoven rattled against the window.

An awesome peal of thunder made Hüttenbrenner start. Lightning lit up the bedchamber. Beethoven opened his eyes. The arm of the dying man shot up. The eyes glared in defiance. The thunder died. The arm fell. Hüttenbrenner closed Beethoven's eyes.

Chapter 19

Breuning and Schindler had waded through the snow to Beethoven's bedchamber to be greeted by the words, 'It is finished!'

Gerhard had wanted to cut off a lock of Beethoven's hair but had been told by his father to wait until others had paid their respects. When Gerhard finally entered the room for this purpose he found that all of Beethoven's hair had already been cut off.

Breuning now grew fearful lest any of Beethoven's possessions had been interfered with. Beethoven's cashbox was untouched; inside it, the whole £100 from London lay intact. Over half of this sum was entrusted to Breuning, as Karl's guardian, for payment of the funeral and other expenses. He also found it incumbent upon him, when drafting an obituary notice, to write, for the sake of the English, who must be as horrified and as angry as he was: 'While possessing lofty musical genius, a great and cultured mind and rare depth of soul, Beethoven was from boyhood perfectly helpless in all economic and financial matters.'

An autopsy was performed the day after the death by Dr Joseph Wagner in Wawruch's presence. The corpse was found to be very emaciated, especially in the limbs, dotted with black spots, the distended abdomen containing four quarts of greyish-brown fluid. While the facial nerves were of unusual thickness, the auditory nerves were shrivelled, the arteries dilated to more than the size of a crow quill. The left auditory nerve arose by three very thin greyish striae, the right by one clear white stria. The convolutions of the brain, full of water and remarkably white, were much deeper, wider, and more numerous than usual. The calvarium itself was half an inch thick. The liver by contrast was half its normal size, leathery and greenish-blue, beset with knots the size of beans, all its vessels being very narrowed and bloodless. The spleen was twice its normal size.

The two men settled to look again at the ears. Even the large external ear was irregularly formed. Wagner said to Wawruch, 'Didn't Mozart have an irregularity to the outer ear?'

Breuning gave permission for Joseph Danhauser, a young painter then in Vienna, to make a cast of Beethoven's face, but this was not done until the day after the autopsy, during which the temporal bones had been sawn and removed.

Breuning, Schindler and Johann had meanwhile conducted a search for the bank-shares. This lasted the whole morning of the 27th, Johann growing more and more irritable as Schindler laughed, '*He* spent half his time at his brother's deathbed trying to find out where these were!' 'It's a pity I didn't find out! One of us would have known where to look!' At lunch-time Johann cried, 'This is a sham! Someone's found them already!' Breuning, who held himself responsible as Karl's guardian for the integrity of the estate, blazed at him, 'Are you accusing me of theft?' 'Not you, no . . .' 'Well it has to be me or Schindler you are accusing, there's no one else here!' 'Other people have been in . . .' 'Yes, and I hold myself responsible for that, too. This room has never been left unguarded and I resent your implications!' With this Breuning left.

He returned after lunch, accompanied by Holz. Holz had visited but infrequently in the last three months, detesting both Johann and Schindler who were frequently at Beethoven's bedside. He had even let Beethoven go on believing the impression he had got from somewhere that he had just married, though in fact his wedding did not take place until May. Now that Beethoven was dead, he had spent a disturbed night worried that he perhaps should have done more for the man who had trusted him so far as to make him responsible for his biography. Now that it was upon him, he was worried too about this bloody biography. Was he supposed to write it himself? He had spent a night like Beethoven, armed with pad and pencils about him on the bed, planning to write what he could remember, though the words would not flow. Where the hell did he start? He hadn't *known* him long enough. He hadn't been around to be involved with the great successes: that first concert in May when they'd played the *Choral*, when he had been cheered to the rafters, the crowd shouting, '*Vivat!*' the police commissioner shouting for order. All he could remember of the last premiere of a Beethoven work in which he had been involved was having to report to the composer the audience's reaction to that accursed *Fuge*: inspired, astonished or questioning, failing to find fault with it only because of their awe for Beethoven. . . . And then having to ask him in September to come up with that substitute for Artaria instead. Holz had thought then of taking his fiancée to see him, but he had no time for other people's financées. He wanted his own triumph, he wanted it *with that* – Holz had sensed that the rejection of this piece was far worse to Beethoven than that of any other would have been.

There had been some pretty sticky times with Artaria of which Beethoven had known nothing. Holz had let slip the thought – he did not now know what he had himself meant – that it was 'mathematically perfect.' The publisher had hit the roof.

'I'm not publishing mathematics, I'm publishing *music*! – It isn't mathematically perfect, it's mathematically all wrong! Mathematics! Mathematics! I'm not paying 80 gold ducats for mathematics! Nobody's ever paid 80 gold ducats for a string quartet! Mathematics! Mathematics! The man can live like a king for a year on 80 ducats! . . . This firm is not a charitable organization! I can't publish a quartet that won't sell!'

'He's right about you! – You are in danger of killing the goose that lays your golden eggs.'

'Well what do you think of it! Surely you don't like it? He must have had things like that said to him before!'

Beethoven had spat on the ground at his feet when he had first asked him for that new finale. Then they had gone out and got so drunk Beethoven had even forgotten which string quartet he was working on. 'Yes, that's right, I'm hung over, go back to bed, don't write any string quartets today, good-bye C Sharp Major – Major? – Minor – God, I am drunk, I don't know what key my pissing quartet's in!' He had pulled a face. 'Holz, Holz, let's go and get drunk.' With that he was writing. 'Holz, Holz, let's go and get drunk,' he repeated absently. He was singing to himself the *Große Fuge*. He suddenly heard himself, stopped, burst out laughing. 'What! That! I must be drunk – you've got to be drunk to sing a four-part fugue! What did it sound like? Horrible?' Holz laughed. 'Yes. Well. You don't like it. Best thing I've ever written!' He waved his quill at him. 'That and the Mass. Substitute bloody finale. Substitute . . .' He was writing again, so fiercely that he tore a hole in the paper. '*Shit*! Shit! Piss fuck*ing* shit!'

'Beethoven, keep your voice down!'

'Why? The lad's not here, is he? I'll tell you something – he's not my son. Piss off for the love of God and let me *work*!'

He had already finished the C-sharp minor by that time. They had played it through several times for Artaria. Artaria had said delightedly that he understood the fugue of the new one after three hearings. 'Huh! As if any fugue should reveal itself so soon! A shameless hussy of a fugue! *My* memory's not going to last very long if my fugue can be understood *after three hearings*!'

. . . 'Aren't you going to write any more for the piano?'

'It is and remains an inadequate instrument. In the future I shall write in the manner of my grand-master Handel annually only an oratorio or a concerto for some string or wind instrument, provided I have completed my 10th symphony and my requiem.'

That paragraph was the only thing he had got down.

Breuning brought Holz into the bedchamber to look for the seven bankshares. Holz went at once to the writing desk, pressed a protruding nail, and a secret drawer flew open. Inside were revealed the seven bankshares, two miniatures, and a letter in pencil in Beethoven's hand. Holz had not seen the letter before, though he recognized one of the miniatures as that which Beethoven had shown him. He began looking for the picture of the woman with the children, that biblical picture, posed as the Baptist and the Christ-child.

Johann had hold of Toni's miniature. 'I know this one! Seen it before. Had it out on his desk at my place in Linz when he was writing his 8th!'

'Who is she?' Breuning asked.

Johann shook his head. 'Don't know. Never saw her in life. Never met her . . .'

Schindler felt excited, Holz and Breuning intrusive, as though Beethoven were still alive, lying on that bed over there.

'My angel, my all, my very self . . .' Schindler was reading the letter. 'This is a love-letter! Which one of them did he send this to?'

'Never sent it by the looks of things,' Johann said.

Schindler exclaimed, 'Or sent it and got it back!'

'What's the date on that letter?' Johann asked Schindler.

'There's three dates! . . . There's no year . . .'

'Perhaps he wrote it to her before he came to see me! Tried to stop me marrying Therese! . . . *And* he had a ring on – you know,' he blurted excitedly to Schindler. '*Told* you it was a bloody fine ring!'

Breuning tried to catch his eye to shut him up in front of Schindler. Holz too, now confirmed in his theories, knowing that it had not been a drunken dream, wanted to get Johann alone. Johann had a right to know; probably Breuning too, as Karl's guardian. He was damned if he could see why Schindler, splitting his seams with joy, should have vicarious pleasure out of this tragedy.

Breuning said, 'Leave these. They're part of the estate.'

'They're hardly for Karl!' Schindler objected.

'Leave that letter,' Breuning told Schindler. 'I shall take these and ask among his friends.'

Breuning left, taking the two miniatures. Holz followed him.

'Breuning, I know something about this. I don't know who she was, but he showed me another picture, and letters – different letters . . .'

Johann had followed Holz and Breuning. 'Are you in on this?' Johann accosted Holz.

'I don't know who she is. We can't talk in the street . . . What year did you marry?' he glared at Johann.

'Who, me?'

'Yes. What year?'

'1812.'

'Breuning, may I take these? I will ask around . . .'

'Why you?' Johann asked accusingly.

'Because I didn't do enough when he was alive, all right!'

Holz walked away bearing the miniatures of the two women who had told Beethoven they loved him: Giulietta Guicciardi at the turn of the century and, in 1812, Toni.

Zmeskall had dreamed of himself insisting on being taken to Beethoven's bedside where, on hearing of the death, he had fiercely wanted to be. In his dream he sat by the bed, two thoughts running in canon through his mind: *You had been through too much . . . You gave.* He had an impression of other people around him, seen through a fog. He wanted to scream out to everyone else, *O but you don't know, you don't know*! He took hold of the cold hand, his face streaming with tears. *Goodnight, friend.*

When Holz called on him Zmeskall's first question was, 'Who was with him when he died?'

'I don't know . . .'

'Has he had any visitors from Frankfurt?'

Holz showed him the miniature Beethoven had shown him. 'Is she from Frankfurt?'

It was a relief for them both to talk. Zmeskall agreed to be visited by Breuning.

The infirm man sat wrapped up in rugs in a chair when Breuning arrived with Holz. He agreed with Holz that there had been more letters: 'One from him, telling him of the birth. One from her, before they knew of the illness, thanking him for Karl . . .'

'There was so much sympathy that could have been his that he chose to live without.'

Breuning was shattered. 'He should have told me. Why didn't he know he could tell me! Instead he has to go to you and Holz − nothing against you − but we were boys together, we spent a lot, a lot of time together in Bonn. My sister was the first girl he fancied. He should have told me! The mad old bastard. He should have known I'd understand.'

'He didn't tell me until some years later − about the illness. He will go through things on his own . . .'

Holz said, 'Apparently he never saw him . . .'

'He never saw him? O, that is wrong.'

'He didn't want to start it up again. With the woman.'

'The boy could have come here! What is she like?'

'He came running in here three, four years ago, "Antonie still loves me, she still loves me!" She'd got the Frankfurt *Cäcilia Verein* to buy his Mass . . .'

'Will she be at the funeral?'

'There won't be time for her to get here,' Holz said.

'I felt very bad when he was dying. I wanted to go to him . . .'

'Yes, of course. In case he wanted to talk.'

'I thought he might want to say something about the boy. In his will. I didn't know Holz knew. Did he say..?'

'Nothing. He left it all to Karl.'

'Nephew Karl?'

'Yes. He specified nephew. And the capital to his "Natural or testamentary heirs."'

'*Natural?*'

'Yes. We told him he couldn't say that. "It's the same thing," he said. "It's the same thing."'

'So if Karl dies leaving a bastard . . .'

'All Beethoven's money goes to Karl's bastard. Oh yes. It's the last thing he wrote. People will just say, "He was dying." But if you'd been there. He knew what he was doing. He made an issue of it. He threw the quill down. "I shall write no more." And he wouldn't. We wanted to write it out again, as we'd originally put it, just get him to sign it. He was adamant. "You can write it out again but I shall not sign it." Schindler was horrified of course.'

'Does Schindler know?'

'Schindler knows nothing.'

'Keep it that way. He would never have told Schindler. When Karl was born he said to me, "He's going to be a little nobleman and ride horses and I wanted him to be a composer." When he adopted his nephew, he thought *he* would be a pianist at least if not a composer . . .'

Holz laughed, 'I'll say he did!'

'. . . Schindler comes along, "O Master, I'm studying your Sonata in F, I'm working on the one in C . . ." He had adopted Karl before they found out about his son.'

'What was she like?'

'Many men pursued her. She was just naturally attractive to men. I don't just mean she was beautiful, although she was. There was a flirtatiousness about her, inborn, nothing vulgar – she never was aware of it, she never dreamt that she was doing wrong. She wasn't: she was always loyal. I shouldn't think that woman's ever so much as kissed a man in her life, apart from her husband and Beethoven. But she had warmth as well . . . she'd never scorn you. I only met her once . . . twice. I've never forgotten her. Lovely woman.' He had never forgotten the terrible gaffe he had made with her when talking about Beethoven's sexuality and that she, instead of taking offence, had seemed concerned only for Beethoven's well-being.

'Do you know one of the things that hurt him most? Malfatti said once the trouble with the child might have happened at the time of birth. O, it was only one of a list of things, one of several things Malfatti said. Beethoven latched onto his asking if he'd had VD, but that wasn't it, that wasn't what worried him. He could not rid himself of the idea that if he hadn't left her, if he had been there at the time of the birth, the child would have been all right. No one knows what it is. No one knows why it happened. She's had that boy to the best doctors, she's consulted specialists all over Europe. He couldn't blame her. He had to latch onto it being some fault of his – not nature – some sin of omission.'

Holz said eventually, 'He's been telling people for years he's got a son called Karl. No one believed him.'

'Did he say that?'

'Yes. He laughed.'

Breuning asked, 'But what about the will?'

'The child was adopted by the woman's husband. He's never seen the boy.'

'Is he still alive?'

'As far as I know he's alive. In Frankfurt.'

'He wants to leave the boy nothing!'

'No one is supposed to know.'

Zmeskall looked ill. He spoke tiredly. 'She wanted to live with him. He gave her up because of her other children.'

Holz asked, 'What was she like?'

'Worthy of him.'

'Shouldn't we write? Otherwise she'll just read it in the papers . . .'

Breuning said, 'Johann ought to be told. He's the adult next-of-kin. Perhaps he'll want to write . . .'

'The boy was born March the 8th, 1813. Give him his due, he's always remembered . . .'

Breuning exclaimed, 'That poor man! Why didn't he tell me!'

'I think perhaps because you were censorious about his having Karl . . .'

'I wouldn't have been censorious if I'd known! O for God's sake! O the bloody stupid man!'

'He was afraid of being shunned. And he didn't want her to be shunned of course. It was for her . . . he could have taken anything for himself. You know he had this vision of himself as *Kapellmeister*? Everybody else hero-worshipped him but he for some reason seemed to think he had failed because he had not been granted a *Kapellmeister* post like his grandfather. That was the only reason, for himself. He would have loved to have been known as a man who had a wife and child. It hurt him greatly that he couldn't be seen as a man who had won the love of a woman. – *That's* why he left the letter! And of course, when he got Karl, he had to instil moral virtues into the boy. I know you thought he was too strict with the boy. Everyone thought he was too strict. That was why. He couldn't bear to see the boy repeat his own mistakes. And I sometimes think, on occasions, he confused the two . . . saw the nineteen year old boy as a thirteen year old child . . .'

'He never *saw* the boy?'

'He used to say he would stop off at Frankfurt on his way to England.'

When Breuning and Holz had left Zmeskall they realized that they still did not know her name.

Reluctantly they asked Schindler. 'Yes, he has friends in Frankfurt. He called them his "best friends in the world." They lent him money without interest . . .'

'Some of it hasn't been repaid . . .'

'Is that true?' Holz asked Breuning when they were again alone.

'I said it to put Schindler off the scent. Too many people know already.'

'What are we going to do about the pictures?'

Schindler had thought the younger one might be Giulietta, whom he had seen and who, like the miniature, was still very beautiful. Schindler thought that the letter was to her, grew irritated and puzzled when Johann had said, 'Was that in 1812?'

'What are we going to do? We must keep it secret.'

Zmeskall had said, 'Pick someone outside Vienna. Say it's Erdödy.'

'Did Schindler know Erdödy?'

'I don't think so.'

Breuning thought that the best thing to do was to write to Frankfurt and offer it back to her. Holz said, 'You can't do that because of Schindler. He's seen it.'

'We must tell Johann.'

Holz said, 'He loved children. I used to tell him he could be godfather to my first son. You've seen him with Gerhard.'

'Gerhard misses him. God, I feel dreadful about this.'

'I didn't know about that letter. If he hadn't left that I wouldn't have said anything.'

'We have to keep it from Schindler ...'

Holz laughed, 'He could never have stood being a *Kapellmeister* anyway. You have to be a *Kapellmeister* to someone!'

He saw that Breuning was deeply upset and continued, 'They have money. He is well looked after. He thought that he'd done the best he could, in the circumstances, for his son. Perhaps he did. He tried to make it up with the nephew. That was another reason for his strictness.'

Breuning was deeply shocked. 'It is fearful.'

'The nephew didn't kill himself. He's in the army. Perhaps he'll make a good life. Beethoven did the best for him, by his lights. Now you know the reason for the wording of the will ...'

'I'd better apply to buy them from the estate.'

'What? O, the pictures ...'

When Johann had found Toni's miniature he had exclaimed, 'I know her!' Now Breuning said to him, 'Do you know her? She is the mother of your nephew. Karl. He has a son. He has a nephew. They're both called Karl. His son is fourteen years old. He's six months older than Gerhard.'

'Why that two-faced old git! After the way he went on about me and Therese! ... And Amalie! "Are you her father? You're not her father!" Told me I'd no right to marry Therese. "She must be free for the father to marry her!" ... And that ring of his! He wasn't married?'

'No, she was someone else's wife.'

'That two-faced toad!'

'Go and see Zmeskall. Zmeskall knew her. Keep quiet for the boy's sake – well for everyone's sake, not least your other nephew.'

'Yes, yes.'

Zmeskall, on his sickbed, had been studying the score of the fifth. He had burst out laughing, 'And Beethoven wondered why Karl wanted to be a soldier!' His mood had slumped by the time Johann arrived.

'. . . I gave him a chance to tell me, once! When he was round at Linz, forcing me into marrying Therese. "Am I to be an uncle? A man has a right to know if he's going to be an uncle." "Am I to be an uncle?" We'd been scrapping! Ended up slapping each other on the back!'

Zmeskall felt ill, irritable that this had been placed on him: why didn't Breuning tell you himself! 'What did Breuning say?' He could hear Johann rabbiting on, pressing him. Sometimes he felt as deaf as Beethoven. He was concerned that his health hold up, to get him through the funeral; the events of today had brought vividly alive to him the visits of Beethoven to these rooms: in 1810, when he had been courting Therese Malfatti, coming round here to borrow his shaving-mirror; his grief when he knew that he had been turned down; 1813, when he had stood over by that wall, trying to bring himself to tell him about Karl Josef, he himself ill with a cold in this bed. . . . 1818 or 1819, he could not now remember when it had been, telling him 'My son is an imbecile!'

'Pour yourself a drink and get me one.'

Johann's first thought was for the will. As Johann sat down with his drink, Zmeskall said, 'The boy is retarded. Partially crippled and retarded. I don't think they'll want money. Breuning should have told you this.'

. . . Beethoven had come running round bearing Stieler's sketch. 'Like that! Karl looks like that!' They had rarely met since the start of his own illness, eight years ago. At their last meeting Beethoven had said to him subduedly, 'My boy has a lovely home. My boy has everything that money can buy.'

Zmeskall had told Holz, 'She has a beautiful art collection. I believe she had many of her father's works transported there. Half the eminent men on the Continent visit. Goethe met the boy at an early age.'

He recalled Beethoven's adding, 'At first is one thing. Later is another.' Zmeskall had assumed he had meant that any step to reclaim the boy should have been taken early; with the passage of years it had become too late.

'Wouldn't she marry him?'

'She would. He wouldn't. He felt he had done wrong. She had four children. He left before the child was born. He never saw him.'

'What was she like?'

'She is a lovely woman. You know who she was? Edle von Birkenstock.'

'He got his Countess after all.'

'He got his Countess.'

Johann remembered walking once with Beethoven past the Birkenstock House and Beethoven's telling him he had friends who had lived there.

'He let me walk her home once. We talked about Beethoven and Genesis.'

'Genius?'

'Genesis.' Zmeskall could still remember her, leaning over Beethoven as he lay, cold-filled, in bed, crossing him in one swift, exhilarating gesture, and that he, apparently in all sincerity, took it. That was after he had kissed her goodbye, his hand to her head. That was after she had warmed soup for him. Zmeskall had told him off for that: 'That woman has never heated a bowl of soup in her life! You treat her like a fucking servant!' In the street, talking of Beethoven's loyalty. 'I could be, as well. If you had a sister.'

He told Johann, 'She was good. A really good woman. She was good as well as beautiful. She wanted to have a girl for him.'

'Was she pregnant then!'

'She wanted to be.' He had thought she had been: 'Nature is blossoming!' 'She talked a bit about her own father. "If you are a man in this world, and if you want power, don't have a wife and don't have a son. Have a daughter." I told her he had some good friends, we'd look after her and the baby . . .

'He was born in 1813. Beethoven found out he was ill three or four years later.' His own concern was for Beethoven's papers. 'Did he give you anything to send back to Frankfurt?'

They were both worried. Johann set off again to look for the letters Beethoven had had from Frankfurt. Zmeskall had said, 'I don't think he burnt them.'

'Is he still alive?'

'O yes. As far as I know.'

. . . She is the mother of his child . . . He remembered taunting Ludwig about her at the time of his own marriage. I'll have to write to her, see if she has got the letters . . . He wondered whether he should go to Frankfurt, see her, see his nephew.

He had said to Breuning, 'What sort of a slut was she?'

'Not a slut at all. An ardent Catholic . . .'

'So *that's* why he consented to see the priest! So someone could tell her, "He called the priest in!"'

'Will you do it? A word from you to her . . .'

The night before his brother's funeral, Johann sat drafting a short piece to Antonie detailing his brother's last days. A man called Moritz Treneck von Tonder made contact with him. He said he had communicated with her regularly about Beethoven until a few years ago. He agreed to see that the letter reached her. He knew nothing of recent mailings to Frankfurt.

Holz meanwhile was helping Breuning to sort through Beethoven's books. 'We should make sure that there are no letters in these. I found this as a page-mark, but it's only a list of expenditure.'

Whilst Breuning was flicking through the pages of Beethoven's other volumes of Shakespeare, Holz was reading the passages marked by him in *Othello*: 'Put out the light' heavily underscored; three vicious question-marks beside 'I had rather to adopt a child than get it.'

Breuning had found more papers at the back of a closet. 'Here is a letter!' Breuning cried triumphantly. He held up Beethoven's 1802 *Heiligenstadt Testament*.

Of the 44 volumes and sets of books left at the time of the *Nachlass* auction that November, five were seized by the censor as prohibited writings: Seume's *Foot Journey to Syracuse*, Kotzebue's *On The Nobility*, W.E. Müller's *Paris at its Zenith*, Fessler's *Views on Religion and Ecclesiasticism* and *The Apocrypha*.

Schindler broke into the officially sealed flat. Beethoven on his deathbed had told him that he could take something as a momento. He took the conversation books. He took the Immortal Beloved letter. He took two desk sketch-books and about a dozen pocket sketch-books. He took the score of the second *Razumovsky*. He took the manuscript of the 9th symphony, in return for saving Beethoven from Therese's poker.

Fanny Giannatasio was one of those who had hoped to attend Beethoven's funeral, but the square outside the *Schwarzspanierhaus* was so full when she arrived, she could do no more than join the crowds thronging the streets. This, she felt, was not fair. She had loved him. She had chosen him for her own before he had ever appeared at her father's institute in 1816, where Karl was to live as a boarder. Her sister had married her own deaf fiancé in 1819; long before then, Beethoven had spurned her. It had all been her father's fault: he had spoken of her love to Beethoven, with a laugh, just before Karl had had his operation for hernia; and Beethoven had taken this to mean Nanni: 'Why, she can't stand me, she has her butterfly!' After that he had stopped using her as his intermediary in conversations with the family and had started talking to Nanni. He had started calling her 'Madame Abbess,' because of her big heavy bunch of keys. 'Nanni's fiancé treats her as a source of joy,' she had confided in her diary, 'whilst Beethoven sees *me* as a housekeeper!'

She had called to pay her last respects, but this had been at the time when the body was undergoing the autopsy. She had introduced herself to Schindler as one who had known Beethoven and Karl, regretting that she had not visited the great man on his deathbed, but Schindler had told her not to regret this, Beethoven he said had grown alarmed at the prospect of visits by a woman.

> So I shall be ob-nox-i-ous
> And I shall get a flea
> I'll
> Feed it on the court-i-ers
> And never upon me!

Fanny had walked down the stairs with the thought of Beethoven's flea song ringing in her ears. After a dissertation on Kingly and Kaiserly power, Beethoven had suddenly sat himself at the piano and at the top of his voice sung these words to his setting of Goethe's *Floh*. He had pounded out the last notes relentlessly, exclaiming in exultation, '*That's* the way to kill him!'

Fanny had seen him, when Karl had been clambering all over him, suddenly clasp the boy to him. 'Do you love your father? Eh? Hah!'

How he had loved Karl! What a shame that Karl was not here now – in the army, Schindler had said.

Breuning had had to call in military assistance from the Alser Barracks to control the crowd. In front of the *Schwarzspanierhaus*, the courtyard was full to overflowing. Even the schools had been closed.

The dead man had been placed in a polished oak coffin which rested on ball-shaped gilded supports. Beethoven's head, adorned with a wreath of white roses, rested on a white silk pillow. The folded hands clasped a wax cross and a large lily. The bier stood in the room in which he died, his head facing the room in which he had composed. Eight burning candles stood either side of the coffin; on a table at the foot stood a crucifix and holy water, together with ears of corn.

Around noon on Thursday the 29th the invited guests around the bier found themselves being handed each a rose bouquet with white silk stitches. These were to be fastened around the left sleeve. Approaching three o'clock, poems by Castelli and Seidl were handed out as keepsakes. The singers of the Italian opera were gathered in the packed courtyard, which Breuning had even had cleaned that morning.

'They lost Mozart,' a visiting singer from another town had laughed, 'they're making damn sure they're not going to lose Beethoven!'

'He would have hated all this,' one of Beethoven's friends whispered to another by the bier.

'Perhaps he would have hated it. I can't help feeling that perhaps he's laughing.'

'So long as he can still compose. Searching in his pockets: "Where's my pencil? Where's my sketch-pad?"'

At three o'clock the coffin was closed and carried down and placed in the court. The pall, ordered by Schindler from the 2nd Civil Regiment, was spread over the coffin; the cross was adorned with a wreath, and the Holy book and civic crown set up. Wreaths also stood around the coffin. Nine priests from the *Schottenstifte* blessed the dead. The singers intoned a funeral chorale from B. Anselm Weber's *Wilhelm Tell*.

The crowd were still stormily demanding entrance outside the locked courtyard gates, but now these gates had to be opened to allow the procession to proceed towards the church. The crowd amounted to some ten or twenty thousand; such was the press of people that the procession could not even form. Even the priests were jostled; Johann and Schindler had to fight to retain their places behind the coffin.

The eight singers lifted the coffin onto their shoulders. From the coffin itself hung down broad white silk bands. The ends of the pall were taken by eight *Kapellmeisters*: Gänsbacher, Gyrowetz, Weigl, Würfel on the left,

Eybler, Hummel, Kreutzer, Seyfried on the right. They carried torches wrapped in crepe. On either side of the coffin walked the torchbearers, several dozen in number: writers such as Grillparzer, Castelli, Bernard; the piano-makers, Konrad Graf and Streicher; the publishers Haslinger and Steiner; musicians like Böhm, Karl Czerny, and Falstaff's quartet; the singer David; Schubert; and Wolfmayer. Bouquets of lilies adorned their shoulders; each torch was decorated with flowers.

The procession started to move, beginning with the bearers of crosses decorated with flowers. Members of welfare institutions followed. Behind them came four trombonists and a choir. Beethoven's three equali for four trombones, written for *Kapellmeister* Glöggl at Linz in 1812 as music for All-Souls' Day, had been arranged for voices by Seyfried and were now performed as the *Miserere* and the *Amplius lava me*.

The parish crucifer was followed by the nine priests from the *Schotten-stifte*, who led the coffin. The cross-carriers, priests, corporation and director of ceremonies wore rose bouquets. Behind the coffin, after friends, nobles, dignitaries and the boisterous crowd, came the beautiful ceremonial carriage pulled by four horses, which had been ordered from the *Kirchenmeister* of St Stephen's Cathedral.

People were fainting in the throng, and carried across to the hospital only with great difficulty. The procession took one and a half hours to cover 500 yards. When it turned into the *Alsergasse*, a brass brand played the *Marcia funebre* from Beethoven's opus 26. When they finally arrived at the Trinity Church of the Minorities, the church was already filled to capacity. The soldiers did not want to admit anyone after the coffin had been carried in, and even Johann had to shoulder his way through the crowd to attend his own brother's funeral.

The inside of the church shone with candle-light. Wolfmayer had had candles lit at all altars, wall brackets and chandeliers at his own expense. The corpse received the blessing before the high altar. The sixteen-voice male choir sang the hymn *Libera me, Domine, de morte aeterna* by Seyfried.

After the religious service the coffin was placed in the ceremonial carriage. Some of the crowd had been dispersed by the soldiers; thousands remained to close in on the procession which passed first along the hospital street. As it crossed the *Alserbach*, passed by the almshouse and the brick-kiln, and entered Währing, the crowd was swelled by an escort of 200 equipages.

At the village church the procession was met by two priests. Candles were burning on three altars as the coffin was carried into the church to be blessed. Singers from the parish sang the *Miserere* and the *Libera*. The bearers again took up the bier. Before the coffin went the priests, the sacristan, and the acolyte with the censer. Village school children joined the large crowd that still remained, together with the local poor. To the sound of bells, the procession made its way between the brook and the gently falling slope towards the fields of the parish cemetery.

The bearers put down the coffin before the gates. The tragedian, Heinrich Anschütz, stepped forward to deliver Grillparzer's funeral oration.

Two days before Beethoven's death, Schindler had gone to Grillparzer and asked him to prepare a funeral oration. Grillparzer had been the more shattered since he had scarcely known the man was ill, but the following day he had set to work. There was, it seemed, to be no opera produced between them; he had scarcely seen Beethoven of late since the business of writing down his side of a conversation was distasteful to him.

When Schindler returned to tell him that Beethoven was dead, Grillparzer was shocked by the flood of emotion within him. Tears sprang to his eyes. He realized that he had loved Beethoven. He could not finish the funeral oration in the lofty rhetoric in which it had been begun.

'. . . He was an artist – and who shall arise to stand beside him?' intoned Anschütz.

Standing outside the cemetery that held his own first wife's grave, Breuning gripped his son's hand. Following near the back of the procession, he had feared for Gerhard's safety at times. . . . 'He had a son.' He had seen the excitement of hope fill Johann's features, as it must have his own when Zmeskall had told him: the limitless world of musical possibilities. 'The boy is retarded.' The bitterness Beethoven must have felt he found unbearable to contemplate.

'. . . He who comes after him will not continue him; he must begin anew, for he who went before left off only where art leaves off.'

Breuning gripped his son's hand harder, trying to quell the tears that rose to his eyes. . . . He knew better than any that what you have got to do is to use your pain. Draw on your experience to make better life and better art.

'. . . He was an artist, but a man as well. A man in every sense – in the highest. Because he withdrew from the world, they called him a manhater, and, because he held aloof from sentimentality, unfeeling. Ah, one who knows himself hard of heart does not shrink! The finest points are those most easily blunted, bent or broken. An excess of sensitiveness avoids a show of feeling! He fled the world because, in the whole range of his loving nature, he found no weapon to oppose it. He withdrew from mankind after he had given them his all and received nothing in return. He dwelt alone, because he found no second self. But to the end his heart beat warm for all men, in fatherly affection for his kindred, for the world his all and his heart's blood.

'Thus he was, thus he died, thus he will live to the end of time.

'You, however, who have followed after us hitherward, let not your hearts be troubled! You have not lost him, you have won him. No living man enters the halls of the immortals. Not until the body has perished do their portals unclose. He whom you mourn stands from now onward among the great of all ages, inviolate forever. Return homeward, therefore, in sorrow, yet resigned! And should you ever in times to come feel the overpowering might of his creations like an onrushing storm, when your mounting ecstasy overflows in the midst of a generation yet unborn, then remember this hour, and think: We were there when they buried him, and when he died, we wept.'

A poem by Schlechta was distributed. The coffin was carried into the cemetery. The priests consecrated the tomb and blessed the corpse for the last time. As twilight fell the coffin was lowered into the earth. Haslinger had brought three laurel wreaths. Hummel placed these upon the grave. Earth was thrown upon the grave. The torches were extinguished.

News of the death did not reach the Rhineland until after the funeral. Schotts had been writing a business-letter to him at the time.

A man at Franz' office drew a newspaper entry to his attention. 'That composer Beethoven has died. Didn't he owe you money?'

Franz sat at his desk feeling devastated. He had not expected to feel this. He would have put money on feeling liberated if he ever heard that Beethoven had died: free, a new man, out of danger. Instead he felt as though he had gone with him.

His knees were shaking as he sought out his wife. 'Antonie, I've got some bad news. It's about Beethoven. He had been ill for some time . . .'

He had wanted to say to her, come to me to grieve. He was my friend too. Anyone but him I'd have killed all those years ago. Instead she had sped upstairs. He hurried after her, scared of what Karl might do. The boy was big, he now often scratched and bruised her.

He found her on her knees, by Karl, clutching him, rocking him in her arms. Tears fell down her face onto the boy's head. 'He's seen you now! O! He's seen you now!'

Chapter 20

Thirty years later

Breuning had died two months after Beethoven. Johanna's distant relative, Hotschevar, had become Karl's guardian. At the age of twenty-four, Karl had come into the interest on his uncle's money. Therese had died soon after Beethoven; her daughter Amalie a few years later, leaving a husband and a four-month old son; Johann himself in 1848: Karl had inherited 42,000 florins from Johann.

He had enjoyed the army, which he had left in 1832 as a Second Lieutenant to marry and settle in the country. For two years he had run a farm; for two more years he had worked as a frontier commissioner. He had returned to Vienna. Since inheriting from Johann, he had lived as a man of leisure.

He saw nothing of his mother nowadays. She lived in a suburb of Vienna, holding Saturday parties at which young men were invited to attend, for a fee. His half-sister, he had heard, had been one of the girls employed as flesh-pots, though she must have grown too old for that now.

At Beethoven's death he had shocked himself by the depth of his inner grief. A light had gone out in many lives. The centre of the circle had gone. During his uncle's lifetime, he had never thought it true that he was a great man outside his music. He still did not know why he was: violent, aggressive, overpowering. Yet many had mourned his loss as a man. Perhaps it was that he never dissembled. It was true that he never spurned anyone in need.

'What you must never do is to pass judgement.' No one but God knows all the facts. Never condemn.

He had been allowed to retain the £100 from London, being a minor, though *The Times* of that city had run a piece stating that this sum would be returned and expressing surprise that Beethoven, being in possession of £1,000, should have sought help from foreigners. They had at least published Beethoven's thanks to the London Philharmonic Society and his gratitude to the whole English nation; commenting further on the endless stream of carriages at his funeral that rather more attention to him on the part of their occupants while he was alive would have been more to the purpose.

He had hurried to Vienna on hearing of Beethoven's death but had arrived too late for the funeral. Beethoven had left just over 10,000 florins C.M., just over 9,000 after legal, medical and funeral expenses. At the

Nachlass auction of his works, the autograph score of the *Missa Solemnis* had gone for 7 florins C.M. The Septet fetched 18.

He still had some of Beethoven's papers: the *Stammbuch*, a *Tagebuch* which Beethoven had kept from 1812 to 1818. After the publication of a dreadful biography of Beethoven by someone called Schlosser in Prague, Hotschevar had temporarily made over these papers to Artaria & Co, where Anton Gräffer, who had worked on the *Nachlass* catalogue, was helping with the new biography planned by Karl Holz. Zmeskall, the Bonn publisher Simrock, Beethoven's ex-doctor Bertolini, his attorney, Bach, and others, had contributed documents and memoirs, but nothing had come of this despite Holz' attempt to revive it in 1842, after Schindler's biography. For some reason the *Heiligenstadt Testament* had been returned to his mother, not himself. She had sold it.

From the *Tagebuch* he had read with surprise of Beethoven's guilt over Johanna, his concern for her debts, and his attempts to sort out a contract equitable to both mother and ward even while listing civil clauses designed to keep her from the guardianship.

There were works from Hindu literature, texts presumably considered for setting: extracts from fate tragedies, *The Odyssey*, *The Iliad*, and several Herder poems which seemed to have been written at the time of his own father's death. There was much of secrecy, of guilt.

... A verse partly translated into Italian ending with 'I alone am wretched and unhappy.' There were entries that might relate to a brothel and lists of letters to Frankfurt. One that included, 'Without tears, fathers cannot instil virtue into their children,' and one of grief for Caspar Carl. The Schiller quotes included the Monks Hospitallers in *Tell* and 'He who would reap tears must sow love.'

... Ear-trumpets, acoustics, consultations with doctors, talk of suicide. There were entries on endurance, resignation, opposition, paeans to art and cries to God. There were records of debts to 'F.A.B.', there were proverbs. References to some cheating servant. There were references to some 1813 concert, the pronunciation of *Eleison* in Greek, trochaics and dactyls, and an entry that he had revised *Fidelio*.

... 'You don't *choose* to write them. They come and pick you. Oiy. You. Silly old fart. It's me. I'm 'ere.'

Memories of him composing, glasses sliding down his nose, dead to all else in the world as he strove to keep up with his hurrying muse. ... Correcting with his carpenter's pencil, that big, butch thing clamped firmly in his hand, scrawling across the paper as he corrected, deleted or made additions. Strange that, though he had so often been ill, the memories Karl retained were those of strength.

Sometimes he had asked him for his opinion – shall I do this, shall I do that? Soon Karl had learned that he was but a sounding-board: the decision was taking place in B's own mind. ... Standing before Schlesinger and Schuppanzigh, banging his chest, '*I* decide what *Beethoven* writes!'

He had never had the slightest desire to be a composer. He had not at the time realized how much his following in his footsteps meant to B – indeed, that this probably had been the chief desire which had propelled B to take him on. . . . After he had tried to commit suicide: 'Composed by Beethoven? O, *Karl* van Beethoven!'

Galitzin had written in the November before Beethoven's death, acknowledging receipt of the '2 new masterpieces' but speaking of great financial losses and several bankruptcies. He had however promised to remit the sum of 125 ducats before his departure for Persia 'in a few days . . . Please let me keep on hearing from you, it means a lot to me.'

Two enquiries to Galitzin's Viennese bankers from B on his deathbed had produced no result. Two years after B's death, Hotschevar had called upon the Imperial Chancellery to ask the Embassy at St Petersburg to collect the outstanding debt of 125 ducats still owed by Galitzin to B's estate: 50 ducats each for the last two quartets which he had commissioned and the 25 he had offered for the overture B had dedicated to him.

Galitzin had demanded an explanation. After repeated application from Karl himself, Galitzin had paid 50 ducats in two instalments, the latter received in November 1832. Karl had badgered him for the outstanding 75 ducats. Galitzin had promised to pay in 1835, not as a payment due but rather as a memorial to the man '*que m'est chère*,' but even then the money was not paid.

'No man has ever done more to make another immortal,' Karl had complained to his wife of Galitzin's behaviour, 'and now he won't pay up! My uncle damn nearly died writing the second of those three. Galitzin was all over him: B could do no wrong. He *gave* him permission to publish them! He said this music was so great it must be played! Now he's trying to say B treated him shabbily! No one would ever have heard of this old creep if B hadn't written those three quartets!'

By this time Schindler had stuck his oar in, alleging that B had received no payment at all for the quartets. Galitzin was by now saying that he would sooner not have had the Mass.

'He loved that Mass!' Karl told his wife. 'Said, "It's better than Mozart!" Goes down in history as the man who first puts on B's *Missa Solemnis* and now he says he'd rather not have had it!'

In 1852 Galitzin had sent Karl a long, rambling letter. 'He sounds drunk,' said Caroline, reading it over his shoulder.

'He's trying to say he never wanted the Mass: yet he agreed to subscribe for 50 ducats, he said it brought "inexpressible joy," he had it put on because he loved it! "Your genius is centuries before your time . . . Future generations will honour you and bless your memory . . ." He offered my uncle an open purse: told him to withdraw any amount he needed from his bankers in Petersburg.'

'Did he?'

'He did not! Galitzin paid him for the Mass, he paid him for the first quartet. He received the overture dedicated to him, and the last two quartets, dedicated to him, and he never paid a kreuzer beyond that first 100 ducats. He paid me 50 ducats more and told me that was for the third. He owes 25 for the overture, and 50 ducats for the second. My God, if I never do anything else for his memory, I'll sort this! What business is it of his how much my uncle left on his deathbed!'

Finally Galitzin had sent the outstanding 75 ducats in 1852, Karl acquiescing to Galitzin's request that this be receipted not as a debt but as a voluntary tribute to Beethoven.

Schindler had brought out his biography in 1840. Karl had read there for the first time the Immortal Beloved letter. He did not know who Giulietta Guicciardi had been. He had been told she had been the mother of four illegitimate children, each by a different man.

There was something in the *Tagebuch* about an 'A', and also a 'T', whose devotion 'deserves never to be forgotten' and something else about 'T': 'Leave it all to God, never to go there where one could do wrong out of weakness.'

There were things in this *Tagebuch* about his own upbringing: about getting 'a tutor in the house,' his hernia operation, and one entry: 'Regard K as your own child, disregard all idle gossip, all pettiness for the sake of this holy cause.'

Since becoming a father himself, he had understood: the fears that lay behind the ferocity, blatant bullying meant to convey the signs of love. He had been blessed with daughters. His son, born on the 8th of March 1839, he had baptised Ludwig.

Once, whilst listening to one of his uncle's compositions, he had wept to recall how his uncle had displayed him – his capacity for Greek riddles; he had hated it then; he saw it now as pride. Not even a late work he was listening to: the fiddle sonata, opus 30 no. 2, written before his birth. Though his emotion had been fierce and genuine, he found that he had slid back into the music and felt cheerful towards the end. You bloody bastard – how do you do it? He wished that he could talk to his uncle now; despite its strength, this feeling bore no pain.

He remembered vividly when B had first got him: standing, holding him, pulling his head tight to his own midriff, one hand tight to his head, 'O thank God, boy, thank God!'

... 'Come on. Eat up your food. You've got to be big and strong, otherwise you won't be able to make mice for your children.'

Karl had looked at him in terror, thinking that he had gone mad. He had taken off his jacket, took off his shirt, and shown the child how to make mice. Laughing, Karl joined in, flexing the muscles of his biceps, '*I* can do that!' 'Can you do that? You can't do that. Eat up your food, so that when you're grown up and married and you have a little girl, you can show her how you make mice.' '*I* don't want *girls!*' 'Every man wants a son but it's nice too to have a daughter. You want one of each.'

. . . 1817, pacing the room like a caged animal. Returning him to Giannatasio's school: 'Pray for me, boy.'

Ever since he had gone to live with him in 1818, his uncle had had him pray 'for a little boy called Karl.' When he had grown older his uncle had asked him if he still prayed for this. 'I'm not a little boy any more!' 'There are other boys in the world called Karl as well as you!'

He had heard that in his youth B had pursued only women of noble birth. As a young man Karl had thought it puzzling, odd, obscene that his shabby, sometimes filthy old uncle had been able to attract titled gentlewomen. As he had grown up he had learnt, apart from any merits his uncle might have had as a man, the pulling power of great art for many women. He had even himself been offered openings by good-looking women simply by virtue of being Beethoven's nephew. These were always the ones who wanted him to play the piano for them. These days he had the piano played for him, by his growing girls.

. . . That time when they'd been laughing over his Haslinger biography: 'Be my dear son, my only son, and imitate my virtues but not my faults. But, since a man must have faults, do not have worse faults than I . . .' That had been just before that outburst when he'd led him to think he'd been saying he *was* his father . . . Holz he had since learnt had made him write, 'I did not beget you.' At the time he had believed him: someone had told him that his father had been staying in his uncle's rooms at the *Theater-an-der-Wien* and that his mother had visited there; only since had he discovered that his father had not known his mother then.

'You're not my father!'

'I am a father!' Beethoven had said, trying to lunge past Holz at him. 'I am a father as bodily and truly as you are a filthy city skunk who spends my money on women of the streets and gambling! Not a father, you little skunk!' – making to hit him – 'By God I am!'

. . . The way he wrote in his CB whenever a child was born . . . their ex-serving-girl's baby in 1824; the birth of Piringer's son the following year.

. . . 'Anyway I don't need you. I have another son.' As he had grown older Karl had come to the conclusion that Beethoven did have a son. Without that none of it made any sense; with it, it all fell into place.

. . . Aged fourteen, in the street, yelling in his uncle's face after he had taken him to see his new-born half-sister: 'She's a whore!' Fleeing to his uncle's lodgings, writing on his uncle's slate, '*Whore!*'

'Women have needs. They need to have babies. God makes them like this. Don't hate women.'

He even knew the boy's name. Karl van Beethoven. Karl with a K. Whereas he, to himself, to his mother, to Johann, to everyone save his uncle, had always been Carl with a C.

'Don't go to any woman before you're ready to give her a child! Boy, are you listening to me?' He had been fearfully embarrassed, thinking his uncle was about to tell him the facts of life. In fact he had said – he couldn't remember it now but it had been something like, 'It's worth waiting for. Don't spoil it, lad.'

He had learnt in the army what he had done wrong. With his layman's ignorance, he had stuffed up the barrels of his pistols with lead and powder to over half of their length, believing that thus he could not fail to make a good job of it. A professional soldier would have realized that the length of the barrel was needed to give the bullet a true aim. He had rendered the guns almost inoperable, certainly too heavy to lift and fire at the temple. His layman's ignorance had saved him.

Beethoven himself had borne more of a look of his mother; there was even, somewhere in the family vaults, a picture of her which, the cap and hair covered, was exactly B without the pock-marks. The older Carl had grown, the more he had come to resemble a cross between his uncle Johann and his unknown cousin.

One thing he could put his hand on his heart and say. He had never done a thing to disrupt the music. Towards the music he had always shown the reverence that B himself had shown.

Balls. B didn't *reverence* the music, he *revelled* in it. But he did put it first. The godhead in him. He could see that now. Well, he himself had never done a thing to shame or attack that godhead.

When the biographies had started appearing and he was attacked, his young daughters had tearfully wanted to defend him, but he had never said a word in his own defence. He had said to B once, 'Everything is depicted in your music.' B had written a canon, on the same page as a sketch for the fugue from the *Gloria*:

Cacatum non est pictum.

O no. Shit is not depicted. But everything else is.

Chapter 21

Frankfurt, Summer 1868

She did not often come to this part of the garden these days but, pursuing a dog escaping from one of her great-grandchildren, she had encountered again the half-buried ice-house. It had always made her think of Maxe and the iced water she had poured over Ludwig.

She sat on the deep brick wall of the ice-house, gathering her breath in this cool part of the garden, beneath the high shading trees, fondling the puppy which had allowed itself to be captured and stroked.

Eighteen months after Ludwig's death, people had remarked on how revived and stronger Franz had seemed. She herself had not felt revived and strong but distraught. Karl had shown no improvement after his cure at Würzburg, his doctor had moved to Holland to start up a clinic, Gall had just died and she had been trying in vain to find another doctor, unable even to draw joy out of the presence of Maxe and her three dear children, the youngest just six weeks. Clemens had persuaded a Father from Dülmen who was taking the cure at Wiesbaden to spend some time with Karl and also to assuage her anguish. Karl had become wholly bestial and totally helpless; unable to walk, his life, all said, was sheer monotony. The child was by now confined to his room, his illness having so progressed that he drew no advantage from company, whilst his presence at table disturbed all the others and had driven all visitors from the house.

She had heard nothing from Malfatti during Ludwig's lifetime. She had learnt since that he had wanted to contact her. He had apparently sought to make contact with one of Karl's doctors. It seemed unlikely, she thought, that he had given Ludwig any news.

Maxe had developed some sort of typhoid and had been so ill that visiting relatives had not known her. Josepha had been attracted by a non-Catholic; that marriage prospect had faltered when Franz had insisted that any children of the marriage be brought up as Catholics. Within the month, she had received another proposal, but this time the man was an *Ultra*, like Clemens. Christian had introduced him as a second Savigny only more learned, more child-like, a devoted Catholic. Arnim had commended him to Bettina with the word: *Tartüff*. She herself had taken to her bed in the uncertainty.

Josepha had always been the one who had taken against Karl. 'He'll stop my chances! He'll stop me marrying! Look at *that!*' – pointing to her brother at table. 'How is anyone going to come to the house with *that!*' Toni had clipped her ear for referring thus to her brother.

Two years later, when she and Maxe had again both been ill, Maxe's husband, the lovely Blittersdorf, had refused to have dealings with Josepha's then-intended, the Ultra-Catholic, and Franz had refused Fanny to a Württemberg Major, son of a Minister.

The two girls had been so eager for marriage that they had been close to despair. They would have married anyone to get away from her. She had been in black humour, withholding all treats from these two who could not approach marriage in a Christian way.

Georg had invited several of his dissolute young friends to witness how he could go up to his father in company and tweak his nose. Franz had laughed it off. Georg told the whole of Frankfurt that his father was crazy or simple-minded, holding this up as evidence. Georg did nothing to help his father in the counting-house, living off his allowance of 3000 gulden a year and the money which she sometimes gave him, just as she had given money to Hugo as a girl and tried to shield him from her father's displeasure. Her father had eventually disowned her brother. Like Hugo, Georg reputedly kept several mistresses, like Hugo he was afflicted with vile disease. As long ago as 1821, she had been writing to her brother-in-law, the jurist Savigny, the father himself of a little boy called Carl whom her Karl had loved, bemoaning the lack of new children in the family, that Georg was then not allowed to have children, 'and I, you will think, am unable to any more!'

It was to Savigny she had turned in those dark days before Karl's treatment, sending details of the opinions offered by different doctors for perusal by his own doctor, thanking him for taking Sailer to her. 'He is nothing but the purest love and this time I found what I needed – consolation and love – to a deeper extent than during his first visit. He has really made his place in our hearts, father and friend, inspiring belief and hope in the whole family like no other person.'

Franz had seemed to grow jealous of her fondness for Savigny, just as Savigny's wife Gunda had earlier accused her of wanting to play Eve to Savigny's Adam – 'No, I am too ill to entertain any such healthy thoughts, too healthy to carry them out' – those earlier years, before she had met Ludwig, before she had had Karl.

Karl himself had always loved travelling by carriage. In those dark days of decision-making, when she had felt that she stood alone, with no help from Ludwig, she had agreed that she would set off with Christian at the start of his return journey and she had taken Karl: to Coblenz, to Cologne, to Düsseldorf and almost to Dühlmen. Then the weather had turned: they were in an open carriage, drawn by her own horses. She had returned with Karl, repenting her folly, arriving before Franz who had forgiven her 'as the lover is no rival for him.'

'The most beautiful thing is to turn grey in love and fidelity,' she had told Savigny. 'That we shall do.' But the winter of 1820-21 had been terrible for her: all the time hoping that Ludwig would visit, all the time left on her own to decide. Even Sailer had fallen ill. Winter sometimes brought an improvement in Karl's condition, but for two months she had been in a state of mental exhaustion and spring found her 'autumnally gloomy. . . . How can one have any desire or strength at all if one has to drink daily, hourly, from such a cup of bitter sorrow?'

Ludwig had agreed to visit. Simrock too had been expecting him in Bonn. Then he had fallen ill with jaundice. This too, like all else, she had had to endure alone.

All of her other children had finally married. She had long kept up a correspondence with Georg's wife. Georg had in the end produced six offspring. As early as 1837, Toni's own daughter, Fanny, had died.

How different it had all been before Karl's illness! As late as April 1816 she had been writing to her father's friend, Gerning: 'The mystery of the artist's consecration is beautiful, more beautiful still is the art of loving as nature teaches us, but the most beautiful of all is the art of reciprocal happiness.' Ludwig had then been writing *An die ferne Geliebte*.

She had never stopped loving him, during his lifetime. That year there had been much contact between them: he sending friends with letters of introduction: Neate, with that engraving of him, and young Simrock from Bonn. It had started up when he had sent that letter, just before his brother's death, late in 1815: 'For his life is very precious to him, though indeed I would gladly relinquish mine!' She had written in panic to Zmeskall. To Ludwig himself she had sent a long love-letter, thanking him for Karl.

The now-long, yellowing list recording the deaths of her friends had begun with:

Beethoven, 26 March, 1827.

It had been during Simrock's visit that they had first known something was wrong. *Epilepsy*. The shock of the first attack, the terror of waiting for another.

The puppy sprang down to pee and sniff but to her surprise he soon returned to her.

In some ways Stieler's portrait looked more like Ludwig's grandfather, whose picture Ludwig had kept in his rooms. 'He looks like you,' Toni had told him, 'around the eyes.' The cheekbones were wrong: too high for Ludwig, though almost exactly those of the *Kapellmeister*. . . . Standing with him beside this picture: 'L.v.B the *Kapellmeister*; L.v.B the non-*Kapellmeister*!' She had held his head and kissed him, 'O, I think you'll be remembered!'

She had said in 1816 of the copper engraving, 'It's got the sad, mistrustful, open, kind side of his personality. It lacks the ferocity. That's

presumably the way he likes to see himself. It's not wholly the way he is.'
She had talked as though the rest of her family had never seen Beethoven.

None of the pictures she had seen were any good. They captured the
pathos of his life; none of them conveyed the power, the ferocity – an
unlicked bear he said he was and that's what he was – none of them
conveyed his capacity to hurt.

He had been so fearful about this child's being deaf. There were many
afflictions within this child, but his hearing and, at the best times, his love
of music were faultless. Being with him, playing to him, as he rested his
head against her, she had often thought that the whole of Beethoven
seethed, locked in this child, and could not find its freedom. 'I really do
think he could do something with him – he could play to him to match his
change of moods – he's the only man in the world who can!'

She tried to see things from his point of view: the horror of walking into
a room to see your son for the first time in his life at the age of 8 or 9 when
that son was violent, disturbed, after nurturing such high hopes of him;
the difficulties with Franz and the other children; whether they after all
this time would not be shocked by the changes in each other; his illness; his
other Karl; his composition. It's not fair on him to deny him for all these
years and then call him in; Franz would not have invited him had the boy
been well. She recalled Ludwig and Dorothea Ertmann: he was too
shocked and hurt at first to give help when her child had died, until he
was begged. But he did go to her; he had not come to Karl. Sometimes she
could not stop herself thinking, you've done more for everybody else than
ever you've done for your own son.

Jealous of his seeing her, indeed! Already she had been getting old, and
wore her hair under a matronly bonnet of fine linen and lace. Towards
the end they had lost contact, after Franz had advanced Simrock's fee for
the Mass and Ludwig had not sold the Mass to Simrock but had gone in
for the subscription sale to sovereigns before selling elsewhere.

They had kept in touch in other ways. Ferdinand Kessler of Frankfurt,
whom Franz had introduced to Ludwig just before the first news of Karl
Josef's illness, had done the proof-reading of both the *Missa Solemnis* and
the *Choral* for Schotts in Mainz.

Maxe's one-movement piano trio had remained unpublished after his
death until Ries had arranged for its publication in 1830. He had seemed
surprised at their lack of initiative: how else was it to be published; he had
kept no copy: he had given the actual autograph to Maxe. Ries she had
sensed had got the impression that they did not know what to do now
about their relationship with him; or maybe it was that they had too
much trouble of their own. For the last fifteen years of his life, Karl had
been perpetually under the care of three attendants.

Schindler had been appalled by Wawruch's report of Beethoven as a
heavy drinker, which had been published in the *Wiener Zeitschrift* of 30th
April 1842. When the editor returned Schindler's protest without com-

ment, he had had it printed in the *Frankfurter Conversationsblatte* of 14th July.

Schindler himself had brought out his biography of Beethoven in 1840. He had produced some later revised versions. Giulietta Guicciardi the Immortal Beloved, indeed. She wondered how much Franz had paid him to write that. She had no doubt that Franz had bought him off. . . . Squatting beside that fire together, burning Ludwig's papers. She had stood in the doorway. 'There's a lot of smoke.' Bertolini, Malfatti's partner, had also she had heard burnt Beethoven's medical records. That's it, she had thought, alter history. You can't alter the fact of that boy in that upstairs room.

Ludwig could have followed his moods. Ludwig alone could have brought out what was locked in his child. For years she had cried desperately, 'At least he should *try!*' And now Ludwig was long dead and now here were his friends destroying his letters to her, her letters to him, tearing out some pages from his conversation books though more often they threw whole books onto the fire: all the books for 1821, some from the end of 1820 and well into 1822: that period when he had been considering all the options of the doctors, when he had been writing those piano sonatas for Karl, when Karl had been undergoing Gall's treatment.

Franz had died on the 28th of June, 1844, in his seventy-ninth year.

She had written to Christian of her sadness and loneliness after the death of Franz: 'Nevertheless I recognize the hand of Our Father in Heaven who has glorified good Franz before the outbreak of the progressive madness of our age.' Exemplary folly had reached its height, persecution and wickedness in all forms; the growing number of anti-Christian pamphlets and newspapers. 'All the more ardently do I seek salvation in the womb of Our Lady and sink my Catholic heart into the inexhaustible fount of grace and true salvation.'

. . . The arrival of Ludwig's letter of December 1821: *Your excellent, one-and-only glorious Toni.* 'Are you going to keep that one?' 'Why not? The man is praising my wife. You'll be all right there if I pop off.' Early in 1821 he had come to her, tapping a Viennese newspaper: 'Tidings about lover-boy in this.' Later that same year, when Maxe had received her sonata, she had heard that he had said, 'You can tell from the style that he wrote it for a woman. I'm just not sure my daughter is the woman he wrote it for.' Every work Ludwig had ever sent her was made out to her in full in her married name and in her maiden name. Franz had once remarked that he could never work out whether this was because her maiden name was aristocratic or because *he* had reason to take her back to her maiden name, or whether this were done merely to niggle him. . . . Franz of the 8th: 'Not a bad symphony for a man who must have been pretty pre-occupied at the time.'

At times, she thought, he prized her for her success with celebrated men. Once when Clemens had started attacking her, Franz had ticked them off on his fingers: 'You've got Beethoven, Goethe, Grimm, Bishop Sailer, and even, once, you yourself, Clemens, five men of international standing, all eulogising her. That wife of mine must be quite a woman.'

She remembered him when he had come to tell her of Ludwig's death, running upstairs after her, a man of 60. He had knelt with his arms about them both, gripping them to him. His own chest gave a quivering heave. Karl was fretfully half-weeping, perhaps in puzzlement. When they broke from each other Franz stared at the boy's face, absurdly like Ludwig's with its over-long thick hair. He took a lock in his hand and said, not unkindly, 'This child's hair needs cutting.'

... 'Don't go to Vienna, love. There's nothing to be gained now. You will have missed the funeral. Don't go. For Karl ...'

He had tried to tell her that perhaps Ludwig had wanted to keep her image of him intact, but she would not be appeased: that she had not known, that she had not gone.

She suddenly wanted to laugh. 'Our marriage wouldn't have lasted without him!'

'That may be true ...'

'All the tragedies of someone's life become so real when they die! ... He always said I should die first, he didn't want me to grieve ...'

Over the following months she had tried to console herself: *he is out of pain now* ...

'It's God's will. God's will, my love.'

... *God makes all children. Even bastards.*

... Press-cuttings and funeral notices from Trenck von Tonder, including the short account of his brother's last days from Johann. Tonder had written before the funeral, 'The sufferings of Beethoven in the course of his last year were really more than terrible, and made his death desirable. I saw him often, but his shattered appearance – a consequence of his pain – and his complete deafness always made me sad. Now he rests in God. He is at peace and everybody who saw him during the last period of his life and loved him was relieved to see him freed from the torture of such an existence. This man will live on into future centuries and from his unmatchable works great minds will gain knowledge and so Beethoven will live forever and bring joy to the world.'

Some weeks after the funeral Tonder had written, 'Beethoven suffered during the last period. His irregular lifestyle contributed to his fate, but he refused all advice. I myself talked to him about a year ago – and urgently – and warned him, but with his stubbornness it was no use. He could have lived on his income but he neglected everything and was betrayed and robbed by his servants. His own nephew (his heir) cost him dearly and caused him grief, on top of his deafness; and his misanthropical nature, which often made him seem rougher than he was on the inside, made him an orphan, so to speak, during the last span of his life.' She herself had made copies of the cuttings he had sent her, from French and German newspapers. Beethoven's brother had been taking steps to see about the erection of a monument.

. . . Dismal, almost suicidal herself, for the few weeks before his death. Just before his death she had been uplifted: full of energy and confidence and plans. She had prayed often for his immortal soul, rose often in tears – sometimes joyful: if he hasn't made it, none of us will. She had read over the funeral oration Tonder had sent her, and wept. No one has mourned for you as I mourn for you. She remembered the moment she had held Karl. . . . There'll be no more music from your father. Grieve for him! Grieve with me!

In her grief as she thought she must give in to this she knew she must not give in to it. He saved my life . . . not for me to die when he died. She rose from her knees. Not only for Karl. She tried to immerse herself in good works, aware as she did so of the stupidity, obviousness, futility of her actions. At times she knew relief, even moments of high spiritual ecstasy, but these seemed related not to good works but to her involvement with art, after good conversations during her art parties – or sometimes to nothing at all: as she turned a corner once, two years after his death, she was filled with such joy and such calm; God-given spiritual joy, the love of God which passeth all understanding, such *wholeness*, that she had thought she could not be still alive upon this suffering earth. Too calm to be called ecstasy, she was yet in a state of such completeness and rightness, so held by God, she felt that this was the moment of her life; and contemplated years later whether each life contained this moment: had *his*? Would *his*? Is this what we are all born for: *one moment* of knowing we are God's and knowing what that means. After this grief rose again, she found herself thinking: it is true that blessed are they that mourn, for they shall be comforted; but what no one tells you is that after you have been comforted you sink back into mourning. Her bitterness was vast. It dispelled with the years. At times she felt she must collapse. She still found herself thinking, out of the blue, not often but when so, fiercely, of that moment of spiritual contentment.

Seeing Karl for the first time in her arms: 'You've got your little genius.' Franz had been getting older as Karl got progressively worse. The remaining years of Karl's life were among the hardest of her own: only then did she realize the support that Franz had given her. She was 70 herself: too old to cope with a physically strong 37 year old man who had inherited his father's strong build.

On Saturday the 18th of May 1850 she had written to Christian, 'With a sad heart I must tell you that the child of my sorrows, my poor Karl, passed away at 4 o'clock this morning, having suffered short but violent pain. Certainly God took this innocent soul into heaven and will also strengthen my heart, shot through with pain as it is, so that I can eventually bear this hard trial, for He does not abandon those who put their trust in Him. But I suffer profoundly.'

She had been cast back four decades, to when she had met Ludwig, and all the hopes they had had for this child. This child was to have been the composer taught by Beethoven. ' ... Just someone with me, with my blood, because I think I can compose.'

'You don't know what you are, do you?'

'Yes, I do know, but it's too big: this can't be my life.'

What a poor life that child had had! What a terrible life!

She had tried to console herself then: *his life starts today*. He's with you now.

And once again I am left alone to bear the grief of this bitter life.

Two years later, she had been writing to Gunda Savigny 'that after so many loved ones had preceded him, it was God's wish that I had to lower my one remaining son into the cold burial-vault after sufferings beyond description!'

She had thought then that she would have to bear this bitter sorrow for but a short time, yet here she was, a decade and a half later, chasing puppies around gardens!

She recalled when she had thought, morality runs through Ludwig. . . . All the attempts to be moral, all the human failings, all the renunciations. Yet two years after Georg's death, she had been writing to Savigny, from Schlangenbad, 'All kinds of so-called spa amusements are being stealthily introduced here: fireworks, balloons, improvisations, Tyrolean yodellers, music on the Jew's harp, a concert of Beethoven's music is announced. Poor Schlangenbad, what is to become of you, O, don't lose your innocence!'

Often when she had looked at Karl she had thought of the 'ever ours.' He had never lived. He had never even kissed a woman. His condition had grown far worse when he had reached manhood: all the strong instincts of herself and his father, but with no outlet. He had died without giving anything or even accepting from anyone except her. Yet he had been a God-given soul. She had prayed for his life. She had known no need in her life like the need to bear Ludwig's child.

I know that he had to be born. I don't know the reason. That child, more than any of my others, much more than any of them, in a different way, much fiercer, had to be born.

Throwing a stick for the dog, she found herself laughing. People used to say he had a hard life. His life was a bowl of joys compared with his child's. There are children who are simple but loving, but his life towards the end was nothing but violence. She had always had the feeling that their little boy was not mentally retarded but intelligent; that he did not know how to reveal his intelligence; that a need for expression as great as his father's was locked up inside him.

The Maurin-Chevillard Quartet had opened their first tour of the Rhineland in Frankfurt on 7th December 1853 with Opus 130. Two years later, Rühl had performed the *Missa Solemnis*.

In 1856 Bettina had told Varnhagen that Beethoven had been in love with her and wanted to marry her. 'I had to lie to Varnhagen – he's the man Beethoven was supposed to meet the night you met him in Prague!' O, these silly cover-ups! Bettina had invented two letters from Ludwig to herself, Bettina, one from Teplitz at the time when he had been with her in Franzensbad. Toni had laughed at the thought of Ludwig's ever writing, 'Adieu, Adieu, most charming girl, your last letter lay on my heart for a whole night and refreshed me there. Musicians can take *every liberty*. Dear God, how I love you!' Bettina had been annoyed, 'It'll take the heat off you!' That had been too near the knuckle for Franz, who had seen to it that Schindler discredited it. 'Keep it out of our family!' ... Opening the door to let Schindler see Karl. 'My son.' 'How dare you use my child in this way!' she had stormed at Franz. 'It's not only we who are involved,' Franz had told her. 'We have children and grandchildren. I told you: this is for all our lifetimes.' 'I never agreed to any of it! How dare you use my child to shut that man's mouth!' Schindler had come out of the room laughing in shock, exclaiming later to her, 'It was like having Beethoven in one of his wildest rages storming at me!'

Franz, going through the *Konversationshefte* with Schindler, had come running through to her, holding a book which he slammed down before her. 'There you are. Does that satisfy you? He slept with his friends' *wives*!'

'Well what would you have him do in his position?'

'That's not what I'm telling you! I'm telling you – he didn't find *anyone else*!'

Alexander Wheelock Thayer had come over from America to research into Beethoven and, from what she could gather, disposed of the whole thing in two extremely ambiguous pages. He had told the whole story, factor by factor, but in such a way that no one was ever likely to interpret it – as truth-as-red-herring it was *par excellence*.

> Spending his whole life in a state of society in which the vow of celibacy was by no means a vow of chastity; in which the parentage of a cardinal's or archbishop's children was neither a secret nor a disgrace; in which the illegitimate offspring of princes and magnates were proud of their descent and formed upon it well-grounded hopes of advancement and success in life; in which the moderate gratification of the sexual was no more discountenanced than the satisfying of any other natural appetite – it is nonsense to suppose that, under such circumstances, Beethoven could have puritanic scruples on that point. Those who have had occasion and opportunity to ascertain the facts know that he had not, and are also aware that he did not always escape the common penalties of transgressing the laws of strict purity.

The result was that everyone now thought Ludwig had V.D! On the same page he had told how Ludwig had shunned a conductor who had lived openly with the wife of another man.

He had wanted to see her. She had felt too old. She had given her reminiscences, to Nohl, Reiffenstein, and Jahn. She had told Jahn, for heaven's sake, that he had come into her antechamber. Every day. What more did they want her to do – spell it out? Every time someone asked to see her about him she recalled Franz closing the door after their sight of Karl and his three attendants: 'My son.'

Bettina had died in 1859. Schindler had died. Franz had died, Karl had died. Maxe had died. Everyone who had known was now dead. The secret would go to the grave with her.

Maxe had died in September 1861: after two years of fighting and suffering, her physical and moral strength had broken. By this time she had become mentally and emotionally all too excited and volatile, 'hardly able to find tranquillity here on earth,' her mother had told Savigny. On her doctor's advice she had travelled to Brunnen in Switzerland where she had died after several days of violent vomiting caused by gallbladder rupture. Her three children had brought their mother's corpse home. 'I have now buried 5 of my 6 children. I only have Josephine now.'

She had heard Sailer say in a sermon in Winkel, 'Whomsoever God burdens with a cross, He puts His hand under it so that it does not press down too heavily.'

In a moment of tenderness which in part went against her better judgement, Maxe had said to her as she had sat holding her new grandchild, 'I understand better now, Mother.' Antonie had recognized her daughter's equivocation and accepted it. There was no part of this that was not equivocal for everyone involved.

Listening to Maxe play the last sonata Ludwig had sent, her mother had said, 'There is never a knowledge of joy in Beethoven without the knowledge that this is also temporary. Every happiness for him contains a striving.' Tears came to her eyes at this thought and she heard the music's advance into stillness as a coming together with her own feelings, as though it had been written for her, at this moment, to sooth this specific grief. By the last variation she was ready to share the music's gradual enlargement and its quiet end.

. . . Listening to Maxe play Opus 109: 'He's so intimate in his music, when you hear it played it's as though he's with you.'

. . . Maxe opening the music, 'Did he send this for Karl?'

'It doesn't say Karl on the front, does it? It says Maximiliane.'

'He sent it for you.'

'The music was sent to you. He loved all of us, Maxe. Don't you remember his teaching you, when you were young? You said you were going to marry him!'

'I'll write and tell him I shan't marry him!'

'As I recall, Maxe, he never asked you.'

'Ow you saucy Mummy!'

'Well really Maxe! "Oh no, we found Karl under the gooseberry bush!"'

'Why does he say he sees us as children! I'm not a child!'

'He could be shy of you, Maxe.'

'Why should *he* be shy of me!'

'You disapprove of him, Maxe. Don't you want to play what he's given you? There are not many people who get more than one dedication from him – apart from his patrons, I can't think of one.'

'Perhaps he sees us as his patrons.'

'Maybe.'

'Have you got a lock of his hair?'

Toni laughed. 'I once cut his hair. There were locks of it falling all over the floor. "You've got all the colours of the rainbow in your hair." He once said that to me.' She stroked her daughter's hair. 'The happiness of all of you children, and that of the boy he adopted – that, I suppose, outside of music, is what he hopes for in life.'

This sonata had arrived during the course of Karl's treatment with Gall.

'Play it for Karl. You know how he likes to be played to.'

'I shall write and tell him I'm learning to play it, and when I can play it I shall play it to Karl.'

'He'd like that.'

Her mother had told her she ought to send him a present. Her father had got her a new steel pen to send to him. Discussing what to send Ludwig had been one of their happiest family evenings. They had been joking, as a family. 'He never could sharpen his quills!'

'He'd like it. He'd use it. A nice one. In a case. Because look what he'd write with it.'

She remembered his saying, 'If you can't feel yourself flying somewhere in a work of art then it bain't art.' ... The unlicked bear, licking his compositions into shape ... licking them, shaping them. ... Franz after hearing *Figaro*: 'Mozart doesn't get inside; he stands outside and paints them. Beethoven gets inside.'

Maxe had been fortunate to be buried in the same year as her husband.

Toni sought pleasure in her eleven grandchildren and thirteen great-grandchildren, as many as possible of whom gathered in her house every Sunday, as today. 'They are all about me,' she had told Savigny at the turn of the decade. 'They knock at the door and at my heart.' Two years later, she had been writing, 'And I, a poor old woman, give audiences like a king, and, as it is with kings, nothing comes of it, and it is very tiring and without comfort.'

She had co-founded a women's society for the support of the destitute and jobless. She had devoted her later life to the support of missionary and social organizations, to the support of the arts, and to the Catholic Church. 'Frau Senator, the Mother of the Poor.'

The hardest thing in life, she had found, was passing judgement on sexual excess. Of course it was wrong to bring illegitimate children into the world, to break up marriages, to put into danger the wellbeing of existing children. Yet never had she recalled her year with Ludwig without her mind's hitting the thought, it had to be, it was *meant* to be . . .

Here she was, nearly ninety. Age is the weirdest thing. Sometimes she had to recall the fashions she had lived through to recall her own longevity. From tight constraints to freedom back to tight constraints. Absurd these days, these fashions, on a woman of her age.

. . . All the memories one has of people at different ages, as though those babies and children were different people, still alive somewhere, not these adults they have grown into . . .

One of her great-grandchildren had said of her, today at lunch, 'Nanni is good and wise.' Good and wise, am I? O no, I've made some grand mistakes. The longer she lived, the bigger the questions, the more blurred, distant and minute the answers, receding into a pin-prick of light.

A few years ago Beethoven's body had been exhumed. A photograph of the skull had been published, showing the cut from the post-mortem and bearing the scars of the sawn temporal bones. What did they think they were looking for? What did they think they would find? The answer doesn't lie there. Seeking the secret of genius in a tomb.

God makes all children. The devil doesn't make children. God makes all children, even bastards.

She recalled saying to him once, 'I once overheard a woman saying at one of your recitals, "Poor Beethoven, he does have a hard life," and I wanted to hit her − *you* don't have a hard life *at all*!'

'If I could have had anybody's life who has ever lived, it would have been Beethoven's.' She had felt that since soon after she had first known him, recalled telling Maxe of it in 1820. She had told *him* of it, in 1812. 'You're the only one who has ever seen that. All the others just harp on the misery.' 'I envy you your joy in composition. God has blessed you.'

The puppy jumped up and she tickled its tummy. 'Can you imagine what it must be like: to *be* writing the *Missa Solemnis*? Can you? Can you, eh?'

He had had her composing once, in Karlsbad. Passed her some Scottish songs. 'Just imagine you're writing a cadenza.' Adamant that she do it. When they had been together. He, she and Karl.

She recalled a story he had told her, one night in Karlsbad when they had been getting ready for bed. 'One of Brutus' distant ancestors in about 500 B.C. was a Consul of Rome. His son, an army commander, was under orders not to provoke a battle. And he did. And he won. And when he came home, he was tried and sentenced − for disobeying orders, even though he had won. As Consul, his father would have the job of ratifying sentence.'

'What was the sentence?'

'Death.'

She had claimed that she'd wanted her love tested and that it had been. When she had heard from Schindler that Ludwig had tried to kill himself, taking himself to starve in the grounds of Erdödy's estate at Jedlersee, she had grieved that she had not been there to comfort . . . the inextricable intricacies again arose before her, no more answer to that now than there had been then.

She had given his miniature away: the portrait of him on ivory which Stieler had painted especially for her. After Karl's death, she had given it away.

What more can be given a man than fame and praise and immortality. With or without the question-mark. He doesn't know how lucky he was. . . . Turning the corner, at the peak of spiritual joy: that time when a man knows his God. How lucky he was: he lived at that stage often. She often thought that he had been as lucky as his son had been . . . O never mind. She had heard one of her grandchildren or possibly one of her great-grandchildren announce, 'Nanni is old and wise and good.' 'Granny understands about things. She never blames, she never judges.'

Old and white-haired and tired and worn out. When will my time come? He had called her his Immortal Beloved and at times it seemed she damn near was.

Bored now, the puppy wriggled, ready for fun again. She put out her hand but it escaped her. She watched it bound away.

She too rose, smoothing her skirts, flexing her stiffened limbs. She walked away from the ice-house. Silly old woman. Get on with living life.

RAPTUS
List of Acknowledgements

p.13	CB4, 46, 38r-v	'Bester! You need . . . To bed!'
p.14	39v	'I do . . . still alive.'
	47, 14r	'She is . . . there.'
	5v	'At least . . . wine.'
	48, 12r	'The one . . . needs.'
	47, 7r	'Go . . . mouse.'
	48, 8v	'People . . . concert.'
	4r	'If . . . fantastic.'
p.15	28v	'Of course . . . silly reproach.'
p.16	cf.CB6, 65, 31r	'It's Unger . . . *Vomitative!*'''
	CB6, 66, 14r	'We want . . . concert.'
	CB5, 50, 15r	'Karl . . . infirm.'
	CB6, 66, 14v	'''I am . . . *brother!*'''
p.17	Frimmel *B.S.* II 117	'Christ . . . Jew.'
	CB6, 66, 5r	'Most beloved . . . Carl.'

Chapter 2

p.19	A.1288	' . . . I have . . . friendship.' (cf. p.8 & 21)
p.20	T-F 865	'I cannot . . . *government.*'
	A.1224	'Mr High-Flyer . . . fathomed.'
	T-F 866	'They deserve . . . so long.'
	A.1199	'that . . . schemer!'
		'that will . . . pistol shot.'
p.21	A.1231 n.4	'During . . . in you!'
	A.1198	'The weather . . . *lonely.*'
	T-F 867	'Be here . . . move.'
21-22	A.1288	'I have . . . *other people.*' (cf. p.19)
	A.1242	'If you want . . . vitium -'
	A.1157	'Your opinion . . . *bad soup!*'
	A.1195	'O very . . . coat!'
	CB3, 35, 38v-39r	'began . . . sleep.'
p.23	17r	'our . . . maid.'
	34, 3v	*Fatlump*
	CB4, 38, 20r-21r	'I have always shown . . . ground.'
	25v	'Base . . . fox-pelt!'
	A.1230	'that . . . object,'
	A. 1231	'that . . . fellow.'
	CB4, 38, 36r	'The main . . . Baden.'
p.24	A.1162, 1179	*Papageno*
	A.1180	*Samothracian Scoundrel*
	A.1183; 1250	Most . . . fellow!'
	A.1195	'O . . . coat!'
	A.1206	'Don't . . . with you,'
	A.1185	'When . . . necessary.'
	T-F 830	*Papageno*
	T-F 857	'an arch-scoundrel . . . earth.'
	T-F 858, n. 78	Schindler nick-names
	A.1282-3, 1279	'I despise . . . concert.'
p.25	CB6, 67, 2v	'This new . . . law?'
	68, 3r	'In the . . . understanding of music.'
	4r	'I am studying . . . quite the man!'
	5r	'Give . . . to do.'

Chapter 3

p.27	CB2, 17, 10r	'My husband . . . eyes.'
	T-F 796	'Everyone . . . fool.'
	A.1078	'Peace . . . your wife.'

p.28	A.1087	'As a tradesman . . . counsellor,'
	A.1133	'without asking me'
	CB3, 24, 16r	'I have given . . . today.'
	A.1127	'quite . . . him.'
	A.1182	'In all matters . . . *way*.'
	CB4, 47, 39v	'An opera . . . 5 or 6 times.'
	44r	'We have reason . . . more.'
28-9	48, 3r-v	'Your brother . . . can't be changed.'
p.29	7r-v	'It won't . . . crude.'
	CB3, n.649	*Fettlümmerl . . . triumphiert.*
p.30	S/M 384	'Land-owner'
	A.1256	'my . . . brother,'
p.31	MM 329, n.6	'You've . . . pants!'
	A.append.I, no.6	' . . . so many . . . aristocracy) . . .'
	CB2, 17, 14v	'Rossini . . . operas.'
	16r	'will . . . contentedly;'
	19r	'an English . . . melancholy.'
	A.1087	'Best . . . owner!'
		'my . . . son'
p.32	A.1086	'*What . . . I*!'
	A.1103	'Most . . . pharmacy!'
	MM 356 n.3	'quartets or quintets'
	A.1133	'My brother . . . O Frater!'
	A.148	'A spirit . . . against me!'
p.33	T-K III, p.69	'You ought . . . in your name.'
	CB2, 20, 9r-v	'A legal . . . radically.'
	CB3, 35, 5r-v	'You see . . . won't see her.'
	6r	'What . . . young man.'
33-4	12r	'The brother . . . death.'
p.34	CB4, 38, 40r	'There is . . . happiness.'
	39r	'said himself . . . hope.'
	A.1231	'You will not . . . strangle you.'

Chapter 4

p.35	CB6, 69, 8r-v	'Everyone . . . desecrated.'
	6r	'Umlauf . . . without you.'
	70, 28r	'The brother . . . *Redoutensalle.*'
p.36	27v	'Duport . . . theatre.'
		'He has . . . now.'
	71, 2v	'Everything . . . to it . . .'
	A.1233	'His evil . . . seriously.'
	CB2, 22, 3v	'The talk . . . garden.'
	A.1335	'Go . . . *gracious!*'
p.37	T-F 924	'I am . . . personal interest.'
	T-F 925	'The effect . . . can.'
p.38	A.1271	'His Majesty . . . feeling.'
	T-F 920	'Napoleon . . . differently.'
	T-F 884	'to inform . . . expectation.'
	A.1260	'a great . . . worthy of it.'
p.39	T-F 844	'Wonderful . . . end?'
p.40	T-F 917	'In that case . . . choice?'
	CB6, 72, 9v	
	Odyssey XVII, 322-3	'Wide thundering . . . slave.' (cf. p.133)
	Figaro march	'Non . . . bacco!'
p.41	CB4, 40, 30v-1r	'They get . . . arrested.'
	41, 5v & 6r	'But I . . . Father.'

p.41	CB4, 41, 6v-7r	'So it's uncertain . . . compensated?'
	44, 21r	'I find . . . "to adore."'
41-2	21v-22r	'who came . . . the dogs.'
p.42	41, 20r	'If I . . . circumstances.'
	Iliad IV, 349-55	'The wily . . . Trojans.'"
	445	' . . . increasing . . . men.'
	477-9	'He did not . . . Aias.'
	T-F 813	' . . . Unworthy of you.'
p.43	A.1299	'Within 6 weeks.'
p.45	A.1016	'one of . . . possessions.'
		'If there . . . Richard.'
	A.1086	'The Cardinal . . . fault.'
45-6	T-F 824	'Continue . . . mold.'
p.46	A.1248	'There . . . human race.'
	A.1175	'Things . . . *lèse-majesté.*'
	A.1163	'I know . . . *against me.*'
	A.1225	'Do not . . . again!'
p.47	A.955	'At court . . . endless!'
	T-F 457	'only one . . . art.'
	A.1215	'The only . . . world.'
p.48	A.1300	'on a stamped . . . patron.'
p.49	CB2, 20, 7r-v	'An experience . . . wrong choice.'
	A.1136	'For now . . . alone.'
p.50	CB6, 73, 6r	'Dear . . . child.'
	17r	'If . . . saved.'
	CB4, 44, 1v	'I remember . . . punishment.'
p.52	TDR IV, p.544	'an object . . . brothers.'
	A.1087	'shouldered . . . possible.'
	CB2, 20, 18v	'She and her . . . per month.'
	21r-v	'Although . . . good deed.'
p.53	T-F 481-2	**I am . . . existence** (slightly amended)

Chapter 5

p.54	**DSB** AB to Savigny 10th April, 1821 cf. p.63	His regular doctor . . . in the loins.
	Bettina/Arnim letters, p.325	In October . . . in Paris
p.55	A.1062	'excellent . . . mother' 'ever mindful . . . children.'
	T-F 780	'your excellent . . . glorious Toni.'
	Bettina/Arnim letters, p.354 20 March, 1822	14 times Gall had applied moxa . . . . . . angel of grief.
	A.1063	'Such a kind . . . fellow.'
	T-F 780 (A.1059)	'Do not question . . . be repaid.'
	T-F 780 (A.1064)	'Please be patient . . . unworthy man.'
p.56	CB4, 43, 7v	'They have been . . . in the world.'
p.62	A.874	'I would not . . . attack him.'
	Sol, *B Essays*, p.97	'How unjustly . . . majestic form.'

n.24: 'Cited Nohl, *Brevier*, pp.59-60, from Christoph Christian Sturm, *Betrachtungen über die Werke Gottes im Reiche der Natur* (Reutlingen, 1811); trans. as *Reflections on the Works of God in Nature and Providence* (Baltimore, 1822), p.290.'

| | **DSB** AB to Savigny 25 Oct 1820 | 'Help! Help! . . . his power.' |
| p.63 | **DSB** AB to Savigny 10 April, 1821 | 'How can . . . sorrow?' cf. p. 54 |

Chapter 6

Much of the background for this chapter is taken from *Achim und Bettina in ihren Briefen –
Briefwechsel Achim von Arnim und Bettina Brentano*, edited by Werner Vordtriede, with an
introduction by Rudolf Alexander Schröder/Insel Verlag Frankfurt am Main, 1961, 2
vols. Copyright by Suhrkamp Verlag Frankfurt am Main 1961.

p.64	Bettina/Arnim	watched his daughters at their work ...
	letters, pp.242-4	for his own parents.
	8 Nov 1820	
	ibid. p.224	first visit for a number of years
64-5	ibid. pp.242-4	'Only as old ... four year old.'
p.65	ibid. p.242	Toni ... had not changed.
p.64	**DSB** AB to Savigny	'Walter wants to burn him.'
	10 April, 1821	
p.66	Bettina/Arnim	... she had aged after 1822
	letters, p.398	
	23 Aug, 1823	
	ibid. p.325	... home alone, to be met by Bettina ...
	October, 1821	a party, at the house, laughter ringing ...
	ibid. p.467	... his son Georg ... 80,000 florins
	13 Aug, 1824	
	ibid. p.407	... Bettina had quibbled ... Savigny ...
	3 Sept. 1823	
p.67	T-F 780	*Your excellent ... glorious Toni.*
	Sol, *B Essays* p.168	'like a father ... father.' (adapted)

n.9: ' ... *Goethes Briefwechsel mit Antonie Brentano, 1814-1821* ed. Rudolf Jung
(Weimar, 1896) p.4.'

	A.1064	'fatherly happiness ... children'
	A.1152	'May the Lord ... *dear ones for you.*'
p.68	Sol, *B Essays* p.189	'She ... queen.'

n.100: 'H. von Schrötter-Firnhaber, "Antonie Brentano," *Alt-Frankfurt 3* (1930),
p.105.'

69-70	Bettina/Arnim	Karl Josef ... knowledgeable ...
	letters, pp.242-4	
	8 Nov, 1820	
p.70	Bettina/Arnim	his and Bettina's own son ...
	letters, p.242	ten months older.
	ibid. p.770-1	older brother, Anton ...
	8 Oct, 1828	simple-minded
p.71	Sol, *B. Essays*, 187	He would share the piano ... scratched face.

n.87: 'A. Niedermayer, *Frau Schöff: Johanna Antonie Brentano, ein Lebensbild*
(Frankfurt, 1869), p.12.'

	Bettina/Arnim	Maxe like him ...
	letters, pp.242-4	' ... spiritual reasons!'
p.72	ibid. p.477	'Your brother is sick ...
	31 Aug, 1824	... out of the house!'
	MacArdle 'Brentano'	"Were I the leading ... chorus."
	art. p.14	

(Quoted from Willi Reich, 'A Forgotten Beethoven Document', *M & L* vol.27
no.4, October 1946, p.249)

	ibid. pp.13-4	The once hearty ... Rhineland.
p.73	ibid. p.14	Went off to live ... for two years.
	Sol, *B. Essays* 187-8	He had dedicated ... of his work.
p.74	Bettina/Arnim	He had a tailor ...
	letters, p.477	... allegations to Franz about Georg.
	31 Aug, 1824	

p.74	ibid. p.895	Georg was plagued . . . disease
	cf. Sol. *B. Essays* pp.168-9	. . . bickered over her dowry.
	Author's own Birken- stock letter.	Their two families . . . several decades.
	GM Franz to Clemens 6 Oct 1812 (cf. 'One Son' art.)	He remembered writing . . . . . . eleven year old!
74-5	Bettina/Arnim letters pp.242-4	He had rebuilt . . . . . . backed onto the Rhine.
p.75	Sol, 'AB&B' *M&L*	She slept . . .
	lviii (1977) p.164	. . . often disturbed.
	ibid. p.164	No matter . . . the Father.

Chapter 7

p.76	CB6, 75, 3v	'She has known . . . now.'
	CB7, 77, 2v	'When I was . . . Schnaps.'
	78, 13v	'The Dean . . . soldiers.'
p.77	25r-v	'I leave . . . blarney between us.'
	A.1306	'is so talented . . . used to.'
	A.1321	'a lesson . . . day,'
	A.1322	'further . . . extent.'
	A.1325	'He is fond . . . arguments.'
	CB7, 79, 18r	'The Archduke . . . you.'
	A.1323	'really . . . businessmen.'
	CB7, 77, 13r	'But he has . . . basis of everything.'
	79, 6v	'He gets 1,800 . . . a year.'
p.78	CB3, 27, 20r	When wine . . . asleep
	CB7, 84, 34r	'Therese draws . . . would be saved.'
	85, 4v	'He told me . . . economy
	9v	At lunchtime . . . worse.'
p.79	Hamburger, 230	'The subject must attract . . .
	T-F 947	frivolous for me.' (amended)
	A.1324	'You have . . . *and me.*'
	A.1345	'He filches . . . can.'
	A.1349	'Steiner . . . *several things.*'
	A.1316	'Our Benjamin.'
p.80	A.1357	'Frank . . . publishers.'
	CB7, 80, 20v	'Haydn . . . famous as you.'
	A.1351	'But it seems . . . hoped.' (amended)
p.81	A.1350 n.3	'levers'
	CB7, 86, 2v	'stupid twaddle'
	3v	'foul accusations'
	3r	'Do you believe . . . tells you?'
	4r	'Just let him . . . to my face!'
	T-F 797	'The brother . . . fool.'
	CB7, 86, 2v	'The reason . . . well enough.'
	5r	'There are no . . . first instance.'
	85, 17r	'There were many . . . spare to hand.'
	86, 27r	'I told . . . derided me.'
	12v	'I must deny . . . difficult.'
	Köhler CB art. p154	'it had not . . . baking.'
p.82	CB7, 85, 16r	'Böhm . . . side.'
	16v-17r	'Doesn't . . . played.'
	Köhler CB art. p154	'In everything . . . four times.'
	CB7, 86, 26v	'He . . . conduct themselves.'
	A.1355	'People are saying . . . composed.' (altered)
	A.1368	'In regard . . . *this project.*'

p.82	A.1371	*Doctor* . . . Siechenfeld.'
	CB7, 82, 15r	'In England . . . green.'
	87, 16r	'No wine . . . seasoned.'
	16v	'Breakfast: . . . prescription.
	17v	'For you . . . can't eat anything.'
p.83	29r	'Work . . . night.'
	29v	'You are . . . better!'
	37r	'I give you . . . days.'
	39v	'that . . . apothecary.'
p.84	T-F 946; A.1371	'I spit up . . . nose.' (composite)
	CB7, 89, 7r	'I see . . . bleeding.'
p.85	84, 24r-v	'Two relatives . . . Saint Stephen's.'
	A.1110	*For Beethoven . . . world.* (altered)
85-6	A.1308	'Apollo . . . *complete.*
	Hamburger 225	It . . . music.'
p.86	A.1373	'a wicked old woman,'
	A.1375	'If only . . . spent.'
		'O where . . . heart!'
p.87	A.1377	'Am I to experience . . . vulgarities.'
p.88	A.1371	'Notes . . . need.'
	T-F p.888	'symphony in the ancient modes'
	Kirkendale, p.175	'remedy . . . body.'
	Creative World	

Chapter 8

p.89	A.1369	'Do you . . . a year!' (adapted)
	A.1379	Spoilt . . . father.
p.90	CB7, 89, 32r	'You're being . . . loud oafs.'
	A.1383	'Our heart . . . silence.'
	CB7, 89, 35r	'You get . . . lodging.'
	Proverbs, 28:7	Whoso . . . father.
p.91	CB7, 83, 39r	'It is . . . a Jew!'
	44r	'He's . . . himself.'
	Genesis, 28:17	*And he was afraid . . . heaven.*
	Luis de Camoens (new trans.)	Seven years . . . sought.
	Genesis, 29: 31	*And when . . . barren.*
	CB7, 84, 31v	'The Jews . . . our people!'
	CB3, 28, 25r	'You will . . . religion.
	25v-26r	You will arise . . . changeable.'
91-2	24v	I want . . . good.'
p.92	CB4, 46, 34r	'*Weber* . . . wishes.'
	48, 1r	'Weber . . . like.'''
	CB2, 22, 33v	'One . . . Beethoven.'
	CB4, 43, 43r	'Spend . . . embraces.' (re-arranged)
	Hamburger, 221	'My spirit . . . spirit?'
p.93	Exodus, 22: 22-4	the Lord's . . . child
	29	*the firstborn . . . me.*
p.94	T-F 781	*Ludwig Ludwig.*
p.95	CB5, 53,12r	'You ought . . . work harder.'
p.96	S-G/S p.47	'It seems . . . lost its way.'
	S/M p.232	'The devices . . . altar-piece . . .'
p.97	*Odyssey* VI, 180-4	May the gods . . . together . . .
	A.1386	'So if you . . . into the world.'
		'should . . . matured,'
		'You know . . . longer.'
97-8	A.1387	'His manners . . . health.'

p.98	A.1387	'Because ... my inferiors.'
	Hamburger, p.219	'That ... do with him.'
	A.1387	'I thought ... the money.'
	A.1324 n.2	'Everything ... stupid.'
	CB7, 89, 32r	'a contract in perpetuity.'
p.99	A.1387	'I wrote ... *without a wife* ...'

Chapter 9

p.100	A.1390	'My dear ... my heart,'
	A.1389	'Yesterday ... cooking.
	A.1390	I have talked ... *tolerably well*.'
	A.1391	'You are already ... quite differently.'
	A.1392	'Don't ... Ben.'
	A.1394	'I have already ... circumstances.'
p.101		'Things will ... faithful father.'
	CB7, 90, 37r-v	'You mustn't ... liquor!'
	T-F 934	'Whither ... lead us?'
	A.1404	*Santanas*
		'seething ... madness,'
	A.1392	*the old witch*
	A.1399	*the old goose*
	A.1404	'All week ... despise.'
		'To the devil ... always.'
	A.1401	'Remember ... money,' (paraphrase)
	A.1402	'We must ... too much.' (paraphrase)
	A.1396	'Come ... soon!'
101-2		'I am ... cares for you.'
p.102	A.1399	'lied ... again'
		'Surely ... *illis* ...'
	A.1400	'You are always ... fellow.'
	A.1401	'How depressed ... all these people!'
	A.1402	'Follow ... welfare.'
		'Success ... efforts.'
		'Be on ... with Thal.' (altered)
	A.1397	'Dear son ... strength.'
	CB8, 91, 6v	'Everything ... him.'
	A.1406	'the brazen ... witch.'
		'What ... are.'
	CB8, 91, 11r	'In winter ... anything.'
	A.1401	'What unfortunate ... Alas!'
	A.1397	*Pseudo-brother*
	A.1396	*Signor Fratello*
	A.1390	*Asinaccio*
	CB8, 91, 11v	'It goes ... Greeks.'
102-3	A.1408	'For I can't ... first claim.'
p.103	CB7, 84, 13r	'The best ... forth.'
	CB8, 91, 22r	'Have ... quartet?'
	A.1409	'Wood ... chip!'
	A.1424	'Why, ... noun!'
	T-F 943	'I am no ... alive.'
	CB8, 92, 22v	'Goethe ... text!'
	23r	'The Requiem ... hell!'
	28v	'He was ... evening.
	29r	He often ... art ...'
p.104	A.1410	'He usually ... *hard drinker*.'
		'I am ... fright.'
		'For God's ... same way.'

p.104	A.1411	' . . . a jest . . . publication.'
104-5	A.1345	Part 1 . . . societies.
p.105	A.1412 & n.2	*geleert . . . gelehrt,*
	A.1409	'It . . . disgraceful.'
		'It's better . . . monster,'
	A.1423	'Our age . . . than I . . .'
	A.1409	'Piringer . . . rape!'
	A.1414	'I shall compose . . . reformed.'
	CB8, 92, 39v	'Unto . . . born.'
	A.1415	'Most . . . mahogany!'
		'On the other . . . brain.'
	CB8, 92, 17v & n.202	'which most . . . year.'
p.106	A.1416	'Since yesterday . . . happiness.'
	A.1417	'Although . . . *from you* . . .'

Chapter 10

p.109	CB8, 93, 3v	'Last year . . . today,'
	4r	'We'll . . . Vöslauer!'
	5v	'He's hen-pecked!'
	8v	'Piringer . . . trousers.'
	4v-5r	'baked hare . . . Christ!'
	6v	'Steiner . . . wood!'
	7r	'Who . . . wife'
p.110	16r	*Kühl . . . lau.*
	21r	'Haydn . . . reached.'
	15v	'That is . . . resolution is . . .'
	T-F 920	'Why . . . dead?'
p.111	A.1394	'Because . . . previously,' (altered)
	CB8, 92, 27r	'I think . . . well.'
	94, 32v	'Tobias . . . this one.'
	A.1428	'Threaten . . . act,' (altered)
	CB8, 94, 33r-34r	'I was . . . practising long.'
	34r	'What . . . *Alservorstadt?*'
	34v	'for . . . endures.'
	35r	'He's . . . brother.'
p.112	Kerman, *Quartets,* p.119	'Do you think . . . muse is upon me!'
p.113	CB8, 94, 17v	'If you write . . . great works.'
	95, 2v	'I said . . . Beethoven writes . . .'
	T-F 833: Goethe	'*Der . . . und gut.*'
p.114	CB8, 96, 8v	'Frau . . . not bad!'
		'She's . . . bride,'
	94, 40v	'trilling . . . Naples.'
	96, 8v	'I've told . . . businessman.'
	12v	'Herr Smart . . . musicians.'
	13r	'To . . . Quartet!'
	14r	'Tobias, Tobias,'
	14r-v	'I hope . . . great lump.'
	T-F 963	'What shall I . . . full of genius.'
p.116	CB8, 96, 13r	'Two . . . other,'
	94, 1v	'We . . . name-day'
	21v	'a dumb ox.'
	97, 1r	'the . . . Tamino . . .'
	1v	'What . . . Englander!'
	2r	'You can't . . . springs back high.'
116-7	A.1430	'I too . . . between us.'

p.117	Odyssey II, 276-7	Few . . . fathers.
	CB8, 97, 8r	'Everyone . . . so much.'
	8v	'In October . . . with me.
	8v-9r	Fräulein . . . Eskeles'.'
p.118	T-F 965	'We will . . . can drink,'
	CB8, 97, 25r	'He said . . . help you . . .
	38r-v	You'll not . . . keep you.'
	37r	'We'll wait . . . England.'
	25r	'You can . . . than here,'
	10r	'Judas . . . rogue.'
	13r-v	'make . . . the quintets.'
	28v	'They are . . . pirate it.'
	36r	'These . . . capital.'
118-9	20v	'Don't . . . for Karl.'
p.119	29r	'I've never . . . liked so much.'
	47r-48r	'Do you . . . is sufficient.'
	(adapted)	
	CB8, 97, 46r	'As long . . . guardianship,'
	48r	'You . . . up.'
	48r-v	'For someone . . . London certainly.'
	49r	'A dealer . . . scholars!'
		'Now . . . do this!'
p.120	52v	'Who was . . . natural talent.'
	53r	'Cherubini . . . cannot.'
	57r	'Holz fiddles . . . cabbage!'
	94, 3r	'Woman . . . within.'
	97, 43r	'Is it true . . . Cibbini?'
		'You . . . bride.'
	A.1433	'I wish . . . bride.'

Chapter 11

Große Fuge

p.121	A.493	'spend . . . way.'
	MM 425	Recent . . . gained.
p.129	T-F 872	'Caspar . . . felt!'
	CB8, 97, 48v	'I am no . . . with you.'
129-30	A.1438	it is cold . . . may fall ill . . .
p.130	A.1439	'Only obey . . . the latter.'
		'I embrace . . . *son*.'
		'I have . . . with me.'
	A.1380	'I request . . . through Karl.'
	A.1440	'It is my . . . you want.'
		'I spend . . . happy.'
	A.1443	'I was . . . so early.'
p.131	T-F 955	My precious . . . receiving this.
	Odyssey V, 447-9	Even . . . suffering.
	T-F 955	'Only . . . between us.'
	A.1444	'Like a shipwrecked mariner,'
p.132	A.1397	'Take care . . . strength.
	A.1406	Don't . . . right way.'
	A.1375	"O I . . . good fruit."
	A.1386	"a . . . man"!
p.133	Odyssey XVII 322-3	Wide-thundering . . . *slave*.
	(cf. p.40)	
p.138	A.1387	'That dreadful . . . *wife* . . .'
p.144	A.1345	*Art . . . skeletons*

p.145	T-F 692	'To make . . . handed down.' (amended)
	A.1198	'Even . . . lonely.'
	A.1110	'For . . . world.'
	CB8, 98, 30v	'I will . . . necessary.'
145-6	34r	'I can assure . . . studies.'
p.146	34v	'The lessons . . . myself.'
	13v	'My class . . . just like today.'
	35r	'I would be . . . daily.'
	A.1455	. . . I am . . . mother.
		It is not . . . Europe.'
p.147	CB9, 106, 29v	*Leibquartet*
p.148	cf. p.4	'What . . . separated.'
p.151	A.1357	'The greatest . . . above.'
	Colossians 3:23	Whatsoever . . . men.

Chapter 12
Has no annotations.

Chapter 13

p.156	cf. **DSB** AB to	KJ's favourite song . . .
	Savigny, 10 April '21	(cf. p. 201.)
p.158	CB8, 100, 16r-v	'A fugue . . . me.'
	20v	'I think that . . . limit.'
	42r	'I'd . . . rehearse . . .'
	44v	'sung prettily,'
	T-F 971	*Gott . . . Burg*
	CB9, n.19	'Eternal bride'
	105, 32r	'Today . . . together?'
p.159	104, 15v	'Women here . . . the fire.'
	106, 6r	'If you . . . . Osiris!'
	7r	'I go . . . ducats!'
	29v	'Wednesday . . . manoeuvre!'
	34r	'The wife . . . Beethoven!'
	A.1518	'Last night . . . themselves.'
	CB9, 104, 30r-v	'There . . . fear.'
	CB8, 100, 27v	'Only . . . pleasure,'
p.160	102, 18v	'Herr . . . First,'
	21r	'I hear . . . the fugues!'
	26r	'His daughter . . . well,'
	22v	'If . . . with you.'
	21r	'He says . . . pleasure.'
	4r-v	'That is . . . parallel works.'
	101, 46r	'Your genius . . . wearing out.'
p.161	40r	'We always . . . rehearsal.'
	33v	'Now . . . Galitzin.'
	43v	'Yesterday . . . resignation.'
	A.1400	*weak Miserablatzin.*
	T-F 978	'I am going . . . to me.'
	CB9, 105, 8r	'"I'm going . . . of it.'
p.162	CB8, 101, 38r	'The police . . . sitting there.'

p.162	CB9, 105, 40v	'Tell him ... astray ...'
	CB8, 100, 29r	'She should ... brother.'
	30v	'Your brother ... soul!'
	18r	'Johanna ... Karl say?'
	101, 1v	'You might ... like this.'
	2r	'You ... her son.
	4r	She stays ... indisposed.'
	102, 15r-v	'now ... street.'
	15r	'The so-called ... behind him.'
	CB9, 108, 4r	'for ... time.'
	CB8, 103, 6r	'You go ... any more.'
	CB9, 105, 34r	'things ... to you,'
	36r	'Beethoven ... the bolt!'
p.163	CB8, 100, 29r	'I have ... person.'
	33r	'There is now ... Sundays.'
	102, 24r	'Smoking ... Viennese.'
	CB9, 105, 37v-38r	'Today ... completely.'
	39v	'Every day ... walk.
	41v	'In 4 ... go for walks!'
		'I haven't ... deal.'
	42r	'In the last ... after him.'
	53r	'Every day ... back again.'
	54r	'He said ... August.'
163-4	106, 20r-v	'I told ... had with Holz.'
p.164	A.1507	'God ... old age!'
	CB9, 107, 32v	'Of your last ... understand.'
	A.1479	'barbarously worded'
	A.1481	'pay us ... very soon.'
	CB9, 104, 24r	'lacking ... oratorio,'
p.165	CB8, 102, 2r-v	'When the Kaiser ... forgotten.'
	103, 31v	'His Majesty's ... *Hofkapellmeister!*'
	CB9, 107, 10r	'If Stadler ... favours it.'
	T-F 988	'Reverend ... no harm.'

Chapter 14

p.166	CB9, 108, 8r	'Old love ... Papageno.'
	110, 24v-25r	'Ferdinand ... others.'
	CB8, 98, 23v-24r	'If technical ... keys.'
	CB9, 108, 24v	'My wife ... together.'
	25v	'I find ... hard ...
	26r	I will apply ... strength.'
	19v	'When ... nose.'
	110, 17v	'He's still ... *Fuge.*'
	112, 7r	'Halm ... come here.'
166-7	110, 5v-6r	'He went ... the second.'
p.167	113, 11r-v	'The courier ... this man.'
	CB8, 97, 28v	'They are ... pirate it.'
p.168	CB8, n.809	'with which ... ice.'
	103, 10r-v	'We don't ... *speedy shoes!*'
	101, 42v	'Johann ... a wolf.'
	CB9, 104, 40v	'I gave ... still.'
	110, 33v-34r	'In the business ... servants.'
	105, 10v	'The old bag ... turn you down."'
p.169	13v	'The old woman ... alone.'
	CB8, 103, 29v-30r	'People say ... of it.'
	CB9, 110, 11v-12r	'Those children ... alone!'
	107, 66r-v	'You wrote ... very well.'

p.169	CB9, 112, 18r	'I asked ... be served.'
	113, 23v	'I'll care ... alone!'
	19v	'The old ... cheaper.'
	112, 4v	'It would ... hurry.'
	CB8, 100, 1v-2r	'Travel ... kreuzer.'
	CB9, 112, 24r, n.870	'Can ... England?'
p.170	113, 29v	*Weber ... 40th year.*
	110, 28v	'Has Karl ... father?'
	108, 14v	'Supposing ... debt.'
	39r	'If she ... pension.'
	112, 15v	'It's ... pension.'
p.171	16r	'living ... a day!'
		'I am ... child.'
	18r-19r	'Your brother ... the brother ...'
	113, 18r-v	'I hardly ... our hunger!'
	21v	'In case ... chemistry?'
	27r	'the crammer ... suits me.'
	40v	'He has ... lately.'
	43r	'You know ... times over.'
p.172	43v	'Your brother ... this stage.'
	7r	'I don't ... benefit.'
	3v-5v	'When I go ... by any means.'
	T-F 993	
	T-F 999	'One night ... at home.'
p.174	A.1489	'If only ... night.'
		'We shall ... *longer.*'
	MM.331	'to encourage ... virtues.'
	A.1423	*Emulate ... faults.*
p.175	CB9, 112, 2r	'There is so ... anxiety.'
	19v-20v	'... But I do ... all your work.'
	AmZ (XXVIII (1826)	
	310-11) 10th May	The first, third ... formed.
p.176	Prod'homme, Fanny	'Now ... prodigal son!'
	Giannatasio's	
	Memoires p.92	
	Odyssey V, 223-4	*Already ... war.*
	Plutarch, Brutus	'At this time ... slave.'
p.179	A.1386	'"I don't ... world!"'
179-80	CB3, 35, 14v	'Your brother ... help her.'
p.180	cf. p.176	'Prodigal son.'

Chapter 15

The published *Konversationshefte* cease just before nephew Karl's suicide attempt, the account of which is largely taken from T-F and TDR. Thayer's date of late July (T-F 996), however, is now known to be incorrect. The suicide attempt is now known to be one week later: Sunday 6th or, slightly less likely, Saturday 5th August (see *Schotts Briefe*, no.55, n.4.)

p.182	T-F 995-6	'The story in brief ... drown himself.'
p.183	T-F 997	'It is done. ... for God's sake, quick!'
p.184	T-F 998	'"If only ... reproaches!"'
p.187	CB2, 18, 23r-v	'Suicide ... last coppers.'
p.188	CB9, 108, 7r	'He has ... talents.'
	50r	'He has ... views.'
	Genesis, 44:28-9	*And the one ... to the grave.*
	T-F 998	'Four ... with this.'
	Nohl III 705	'It's still ... *Rabenstein.*'
p.190	T-F 1001	'Here ... document.'
	T-F 1000	'Do you know ... him so!'

Chapter 16

p.192	Sol. *B*, p.319	'Artaria . . . intelligible.'
	Unpub. CB Hft.115, 14r-v	
	T-F 983	'totally new quartet . . .
	A.1498	'really *brand new.*'
	MM 455	1) Fine . . . to the composer.
192-3	MM 461	There is the . . . (adapted)
	Misch, *B Studies* 138	ducats!
p.193	T-F 1000	'Wolfmayer . . . drinks.'
	T-F 1002	'I will . . . Ludwig.'
p.194	T-F 968	'And yet . . . with women.'
	Sol *B Essays* p.91	*On the death . . . Beethoven.*
	& p.75, n.54: 'Ludwig Nohl, *Eine stille Liebe zu Beethoven* (Leipzig, 1902) p.215.'	
	CB9, 110, 30r	'Lay down . . . like this.'
	46r	'For·. . . book.'
	T-F 999	'Mental . . . childhood.'
194-5	A.1521	'I am . . . qualities!'
p.195	T-F 1001	'A military life . . . little.'
	T-K III, 257	'Pistols . . . hero!'
	263	'Resign . . . long ago.'
	TDR V, 358 n.3	'He said . . . different.'
	A.1523	'Regarding . . . forestall you.'
p.196	T-K III, p.263	'The court . . . most.'
	260	'If you . . . remaining silent.'
	T-F 1003	'I wanted . . . happen.'
	Sonneck, 203	'Nothing . . . a day!'
	A.1502	'It is out . . . virtue.'
·p.197	T-F 1003-4	'I do not want . . . you wish.'
	T-F 999	'These . . . leeches.'
		'He said . . . approve.'
		'because my uncle . . . to be better.'
p.198	TDR V, 380	'Karl will not see . . . with his mother.'
p.199	A.1533	'His statements . . . unseen.'
	A.1531	'hasten . . . works.'

Chapter 17

p.200	A.1534	'The name . . . Mori.'
	T-F 1002	'I will . . . brother??????!!!!'
	CB9, 108, 7v	'He always . . . millions,'
	A.1521	'a dried fish'
	A.1525	'Mr Enamoured'
		'*pregnant with consequences*'
		'Mr Enamoured . . . *love.*'
		'Momento Mori.'
p.201	TDR V 384 n.2	*Freu*' . . . *Lebens.* (cf. p. 156.)
	Mark 11:24	*Therefore . . . have them.*
	A.1318	'Give . . . *sein* . . .'
	A.1536	'First . . . have none!'
201-2	Hamburger 250	'If . . . Papageno!'
p.202	A.1535	'reminds me . . . young.'
	TDR V, 383 n.2	'Breuning . . . come.'
	T-F 1008	'A little quieter!'
	T-F 1009	'A fine brother, that one!'
p.203	T-F 391	'I wish . . . that man.'
	T-F 1015	'Don't be . . . veneration.'

p.204	Sol. *B*. 324	'You could . . . costs.'
	Unpub. CB Hft 117, 12r	
p.206	T-F 1009 n.44	'Circumcised . . . quartet,'
p.207	T-F 1014	'If you want . . . already overpaid.'
207-8	T-F 1013-4	My dear Brother . . . Vienna.
p.208	T-F 1014	'I cannot . . . right away.'
		'Let us . . . no more.'
	T-F 1015	'What is . . . little while.'

Chapter 18

p.210	A.1541	*We all . . . different way.*
	T-F 1017	'How come . . . third day?'
	T-F 1016	'That most . . . milk-wagon!'
	T-F 1020	'not . . . musical,'
	A.1542	'to create . . . kind people.'
p.211	Sol. *B* pp. 288-9	'Master . . . *a king!*'
	T-F 1025-6	'You are . . . decision.'
		'He was . . . longer.'
	TDR V, 427 n.1	'Holz drinks heavily.'
	Cooper p.446	*Do you suffer . . . rectum?*
p.212	T-F 1023	'You must . . . will work.'
	CB9, 109, 5r-v	'Allegorical . . . falls away.
	11r-v	. . . God said . . . Amen.'
p.213	S/M 404	'We cannot . . . obligations,'
	Schotts Briefe	
	L.57, n.5	'It would . . . complete works.'
	A.1544	'Old Schlesinger . . . quartets.'
	T-F 871	'Handel . . . tomb.'
	T-F 920	'It would . . . without it.'
	T-F 1024	'I have . . . from him!'
	A.1314	'a tortoise . . . £600.'
p.214	T-F 1023	'Doctor . . . staff!'
	T-F 1023-4	'Thank God . . . a knight.'
p.215	T-F 1026	'A uniform is ready . . .
	TDR V, 428	. . . two-day journey.'
	T-K III, 278	'I wish . . . my room.'
	T-F 1026-7	Vienna, Wednesday . . . have shown me.
215-6	T-F 1027	I am still . . . whole inheritance.
216-7	T-F 1029	'Has . . . Scott?'
p.217	TDR V, 440	'a very fine . . . so far from you.'
	T-F 1031	'Tell Beethoven . . . colleagues.'
p.219	T-F 1032	'Miracles! . . . saved!'
	T-F 1033	'Malfatti . . . hour.'
219-20	T-F 1033-4	'I am just . . . sickness.'
p.220	A.1552	'Yet . . . well.'
	Hamburger 258	'Wolfmayer . . . pity of it!'''
p.221	T-F 1037	'Look . . . born!'
	Cooper 447 n.1	'The maid . . . then.'
		'I heard . . . rid of them.'
p.223	T-F 1038	'If . . . Wonderful!'
	CB9, 110, 16r	'A B C D . . .'
p.224	Sonneck 207	'I always . . . forget it.'
	T-F 1044	'Your quartet . . . someday.'
		'I know . . . artist.'
	S/M 445	*They . . . music.*
p.225	A.1541	*We all . . . way.*
	S/M 321	'The man . . . money only!'
	CB8,101, 33r	'They have . . . for wives.'

p.226	Hamburger 259	'You're . . . scoundrels.'
	T-F 1028	My dear . . . my account.
p.227	Hamburger 262	They hang . . . big ones go!'
	T-F 1046	'Art . . . believed it.'
		'You are . . . love with you.'
227-8		'He is . . . artists.'
p.228	A.1563	'Truly my lot . . . Almighty.'
	T-F 1042	'May God . . . thousandfold.'
p.229	T-F 1044	'Let . . . first.'
	T-F 1043	' . . . Had I known . . . Schubert!'
	CB9, 107, 73r	'He talked . . . always,'
p.232	A.1568	'My nephew . . . heirs.'
	T-F 1047	'There! . . . no more!'
	T-F 1048	'*Plaudite . . . est*!
p.233	*Genesis*, 46: 4	*. . . and Josef . . . thine eyes.*
p.234	Sonneck 219	My dear . . . relieved.
p.235	T-F 658	'I am not . . . visit me.'

Chapter 19

| p.236 | Cooper p.462 | 'While . . . matters.' |
| p.238 | T-F 984 | 'It is . . . requiem.' |

pp. 247-50: Details of B's funeral & Grillparzer's oration taken from:
    T-F 1053-55 & 1057-8; Sonneck 226-9; Hamburger 268

Chapter 20

p.252	T.11	'I . . . unhappy.'
	T.67	'Without . . . children.'
	T.111	'He . . . love.'
p.253	T-F 980	'2 . . . masterpieces'
		'in a few days . . . lot to me.'
	T-F 1100	'que . . . chère,'
	S/M 301	"inexpressible joy,"
	S/M 302	"Your genius . . . your memory . . ."
p.254	T.107	'deserves . . . forgotten'
	T.104	'Leave . . . weakness.'
	T.83	'a tutor . . . house,'
	T.80	'Regard K . . . holy cause.'
p.256	Winter, *B.Essays* (Harvard) p.245; London, British Library Add. Ms. 29997, fol. 10	*Cacatum non est pictum.*

Chapter 21

p.258	Unpublished letters AB to Savigny	
	DSB 10 April 1821	'and I . . . any more!'
	DSB 25 Oct 1820	'He is nothing . . . person.'
	DSB 21st June 1808	'No, . . . carry them out.'
	DSB 25 Oct 1820	'as the lover . . . for him.'
258-9		'The most . . . shall do.'
p.259	**DSB** 10 April 1821	'autumnally . . . sorrow?'
	Unpublished AB letter	
	GM 21 April 1816	'The mystery . . . happiness.'
	A.570	'For his . . . mine!'
	Sol *B Essays* 186	Beethoven . . . 1827.

n.79: 'Maria Andrea Goldmann, *Im Schatten des Kaiserdomes. Frauenbilder* (Limburg, 1938) p.100.'

p.261   Unpublished AB letter
           GM 29 Dec 1845   'Nevertheless ... our age.'
           T-F 780   *Your excellent ... Toni.*

p.262   Sol *B Essays* 185   'The sufferings ... such an existence.
           (Letter of 28.3.1827:
           original in Beethoven-
           Archiv, Bonn.)
           Unpublished contin-
           uation of above, kind-
           ly made known to me by
           Maynard Solomon.   This man will ... joy to the world.'
           Unpublished, as above 'Beethoven suffered ... last period.
           (Letter of 10 April (May) 1827:
           original in Beethoven-Archiv, Bonn.)
           Continuation of above,
           Sol *B Essays* 185   His irregular ... span of his life.'

p.263   Unpublished AB letter
           GM 18 May 1850   'With a sad ... profoundly.'

p.264   Unpublished AB letter
           DSB 22 March 1852   'that after ... description!'
           DSB 2 August 1854   'All kinds ... innocence!'
           (cf. Sol 'AB&B' *M&L*
           lviii (1977) p.165)

p.265   Anderson append B
           no. 2, p.1359   'Adieu ... love you!'
           T-F 244-5   Spending ... purity.

p.266   Unpublished AB letter
           DSB 30 Sept 1861   'hardly able ... earth,'
                             'I have ... Josephine now.'
                             'Whomsoever ... heavily.'

p.267   Sol 'AB&B' *M&L*   'They are all ... my heart.'
           lviii (1977) p.165   'And I ... comfort.'

Abbreviations & Acknowledgements

In the case of copyright material, the publishers below have granted permission to quote from the publications listed.

A. Emily Anderson, editor and translator, *The Letters of Beethoven* (Macmillan Press Ltd., London/1961, 3 vols). The number refers to the letter not page unless otherwise specified.

AmZ *Allgemeine musikalische Zeitung.*

Bettina/Arnim *Achim und Bettina in ihren Briefen – Briefwechsel Achim von Arnim und Bettina Brentano*, edited by Werner Vordtriede, with an introduction by Rudolf Alexander Schröder/Insel Verlag Frankfurt am Main, 1961, 2 vols. Copyright by Suhrkamp Verlag, Frankfurt am Main 1961.

B S'books Douglas Johnson, Alan Tyson & Robert Winter, *The Beethoven Sketchbooks* (Oxford/1985)

CB Karl-Heinz Köhler, Grita Herre, Dagmar Beck, et al., editors, *Ludwig van Beethovens Konversationshefte* (Deutscher Verlag für Musik, Leipzig/1968 continuing, 9 volumes to date). The number of the volume is followed by the *Heft* (*not* published page number) followed by the page number within the *Heft*.

Cooper Martin Cooper, *Beethoven: The Last Decade 1817-1827* (Oxford/1970); and Edward Larkin, Appendix A. By permission of Oxford University Press.

DSB This unpublished correspondence is quoted, with permission, from Deutsche Staatsbibliothek, Berlin. Transcription and translation by Gudrun and Dr R.T. Llewellyn. I am grateful to Maynard Solomon for bringing these letters to my attention.

Frimmel *B.S.* Theodor von Frimmel, *Beethoven-Studien* (Munich & Leipzig/1905-6), 2 vols.

GM This unpublished correspondence is quoted, with permission, from Freies Deutsches Hochstift (Goethe Museum) Frankfurt. Transcription and translation by Gudrun and Dr R.T. Llewellyn. I am grateful to Maynard Solomon for bringing these letters to my attention.

Hamburger Michael Hamburger, ed., trans. and intro., *Beethoven: Letters, Journals & Conversations* (©Thames & Hudson, London/1984).

Kerman, *Quartets* Joseph Kerman, *The Beethoven Quartets*, (Oxford/1978)

Kirkendale *Creative World* Warren Kirkendale, 'New Roads to Old Ideas in Beethoven's *Missa Solemnis*,' in *The Creative World of Beethoven*, ed. by Paul Henry Lang (Norton, New York/1971; copyright 1970 by G. Schirmer, Inc. First published by arrangement with *The Musical Quarterly*, in which the chapters originally appeared.)

Köhler CB art. Karl-Heinz Köhler, 'The Conversation Books: Aspects of a New Picture of Beethoven,' in *Beethoven, Performers & Critics: Detroit 1977,* edited by Robert Winter & B. Carr (Detroit/ 1980).

MacArdle 'Brentano' Donald W. MacArdle, 'The Brentano Family in its Relations with Beethoven,' *Music Review* xix (1958) pp.6-19.

Misch, *B Studies* Ludwig Misch, *Beethoven Studies* (University of Oklahoma Press/ 1953).

MM *New Beethoven Letters*, translated and annotated by Donald W. MacArdle & Ludwig Misch. Copyright © 1957 by the University of Oklahoma Press. The number refers to the letter not page unless otherwise specified.

Nohl Ludwig Nohl, *Beethovens Leben* (Leipzig/1867) 3 vols.

Prod'homme, Fanny J-G Prod'homme, *Beethoven Raconté par Ceux qui L'Ont Vu* (Paris/
Giannatasio's 1927).
Memoires

Schotts Briefe *Ludwig van Beethoven: Der Briefwechsel Mit Dem Verlag Schott* (Beethoven-Haus, Bonn – G Henle Verlag, München/1985).

S-G/S Joseph Schmidt-Görg & Hans Schmidt, eds., *Ludwig van Beethoven* (Beethoven-Archiv, Bonn – Deutsche Grammophon Gesellschaft mbH, Hamburg/1969).

S/M *Beethoven As I Knew Him* by Anton Felix Schindler, edited by Donald W. MacArdle, translated by Constance S Jolly. Faber & Faber Limited, London, 1966.

Sol 'AB&B' *M&L* Maynard Solomon, 'Antonie Brentano & Beethoven,' *Music & Letters* lviii (1977) pp.153-169. By permission of Oxford University Press.

Sol *B* *Beethoven* by Maynard Solomon. Copyright © 1977 by Schirmer Books.

Sol *B Essays* Maynard Solomon, *Beethoven Essays*. Harvard University Press, 1988.

Sonneck O.G. Sonneck, *Beethoven: Impressions of Contemporaries* (Dover 1967; by special arrangement with G Schirmer, Inc., New York).

T. Maynard Solomon, 'Beethoven's *Tagebuch* of 1812-1818' pp.193-288 in *Beethoven Studies 3*, edited by Alan Tyson. Cambridge University Press, 1982. A slightly-revised edition, without the German, appears in Solomon's *Beethoven Essays*. The number refers to the entry not page unless otherwise specified.

TDR A.W. Thayer, *Ludwig van Beethovens Leben*, ed. H. Deiters & H. Riemann, 5 vols. (Leipzig/1866-1917).

T-F Forbes, Elliot, revisor & editor; *Thayer's Life of Beethoven*. Copyright ©1970 by Princeton University Press, renewed 1992. Reprinted by permission of Princeton University Press.

T-K A.W. Thayer *The Life of Ludwig van Beethoven*, Eng. Trans. ed. Henry Edward Krehbiel, 3 vols. (New York/1921, reprinted London: Centaur/1960). Copyright assigned to Princeton University Press, 1949.

Winter *B Essays* Robert Winter, 'The Sources for Beethoven's *Missa Solemnis*,' in *Beethoven Essays: Studies in the Honor of Elliot Forbes*, edited by Lewis Lockwood & Phyllis Benjamin. Harvard University Press, 1984.